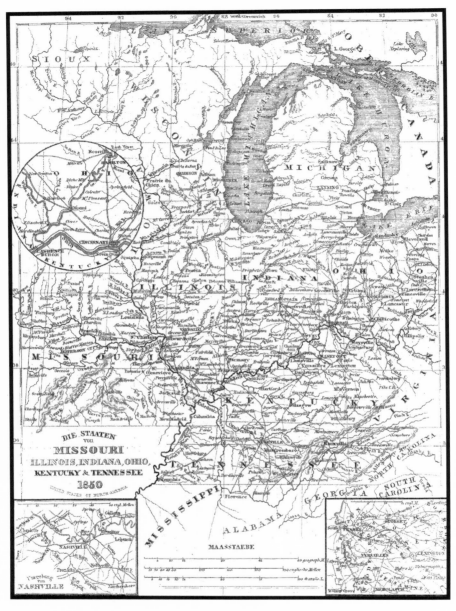

*T*he map above, published in Germany in 1850, shows the geographies of several areas involved in the novel *The Dark Line*. (See Author's Note.)

# THE DARK LINE

## Three Heroic Women
## of the Antebellum Border Country

a novel by

**Don Morrison**

This trade paperback original is published by:
Donmo Publications, 2102 Sylvan Circle, Maryville, TN 37803

This is a work of historical fiction. Although some of the characters
in this book bear the names of real people who lived in those times
and places, this story that involves them is fictional.

Manufactured in the United States of America
Printed by CreateSpace

First Edition: August 2014
ISBN-13: 978-1500958282
ISBN-10: 150095828X

Library of Congress Cataloging-In-Publication Data
Morrison, Don 1938 –
The Dark Line: Three Heroic Women of the Antebellum Border
Country, by Don Morrison - first Ed.

1. Underground Railroad – Fiction  2. Runaway Slaves – Fiction
3. Conducting Slaves to Canada – Fiction  4. Sexual Abuse of
Female Slaves – Fiction  5. Pre-Civil War History – Fiction

1. Title: The Dark Line

Front Cover Design by Donna Weaver
Back Cover Design, Editing and Formatting of text by Linda Weaver
Author Photo by Wynn Goodchild

*I visited Uncle Freman (Anderson, at Hanover, Indiana) for the purpose of interviewing him on aiding his fellow bondsmen (in Kentucky) to gain their freedom by piloting them to the Ohio River and ferrying them over to the Indiana shore where they would be taken charge of by under ground agents and ultimately conducted to Canada. The Ohio River was the dark line which defined the northern limit or boundary of slavery.*

"In the Days of Slavery: How Slaves Escaping
from Kentucky Got Through Indiana"

by George Woodruff Herrigo

*The Indianapolis Freeman,* October 31, 1891

# DEDICATION

*This book is dedicated to the memory of my grandfather, Howard Chauncy Morrison, 1870–1953. Not only was he my biological link to our ancestors, some of whom populate this book, but in spite of the demons that rode him, he imparted to me memories, words, cadences, even body language from those who had gone before him. When I was a child I saw glimpses of The Old Ways during the hours we spent together. I could not have foreseen that in later years some of these precious insights would reappear.*

# ACKNOWLEDGEMENTS

$\mathfrak{M}$any individuals, from the states of Kentucky, Illinois, Indiana and Ohio to southern Ontario, Canada, willingly gave their support, expertise, talents and time for this book. Many shared their knowledge with me, and some recommended books, historic sites, or told me with whom to speak for information on the Underground Railroad. Their assistance made the story become real for me and, I hope, for the reader as well.

The following individuals contributed to the project: Dr. Charles Robinson, MD (wounds); Helen Parks (History of Cotton Twp., manuscript reader); Cousin Mary Morrison Wiley (family photos and information); Barry Brown, Switzerland County Historian, (Hackney information); Cheryl Welch, President, and Penny Brinson, volunteer, Ripley County Historical Society (opened the Society's archives for my Hackney research, manuscript readers); Ruth Pickett, volunteer, Ripley County Historical Society (Morrison and Cunningham information and photos); Janice Barnes, historian and genealogist, Madison/Jefferson County Public Library (Hackney data, manuscript reader); Jim Sturgeon, Jerry Brown and Ellyn Kern (genealogical and historical support, manuscript readers); Martha Bladen, Executive Director of Switzerland County Historical Society (informative articles, programs and displays, manuscript reader); Donna Weaver, Director of Musee' de Venoge in Switzerland County (artisan programs demonstrating old-time crafts & music, advice on period clothing, front book cover design); Wanda Welch, secretary to County Commissioners, Courthouse, Jefferson County, Indiana, and Larry Vonderhaar, President, Universal Advertising

Associates, Inc. (permission to use maps); Canadians Bryan and Shannon Prince, Marlene Pierce and Rose Pierce (provided information and directed me to historic sites); my wife, Suzanne Morrison (helpful insights); and finally, Linda Weaver, retired University of Tennessee editor and writer (back cover design, manuscript reader and editor, manuscript formatting in both traditional and ebook form).

Much gratitude to all.

# CONTENTS

# PROLOGUE

The young woman, one hand on her round belly, purple spots swimming behind her eyes in the blazing August heat, leaned against the porch post. Rachel Morrison shaded her eyes and stared up the East Enterprise Road, awaiting a clearer view of the distant rider. His dark image approached slowly, moving toward her down the slope to the Sugar Branch ford. He passed out of sight for a few moments.

When his head reappeared, nearer now, she caught her breath. Even at that great distance, even before his shoulders and the horse's head came into view, she knew. The hat was wrong.

In place of Robert Sandlin's wide-brimmed frontier hat, the rider wore a skull-hugging Irish cap, and that silhouette revealed the truth. The rider was not the man whose ring she wore on a gold chain around her neck, the man she had promised to marry. In a flash of intuition the girl understood the message the rider brought. She knew in that moment she would never see Robert Sandlin again.

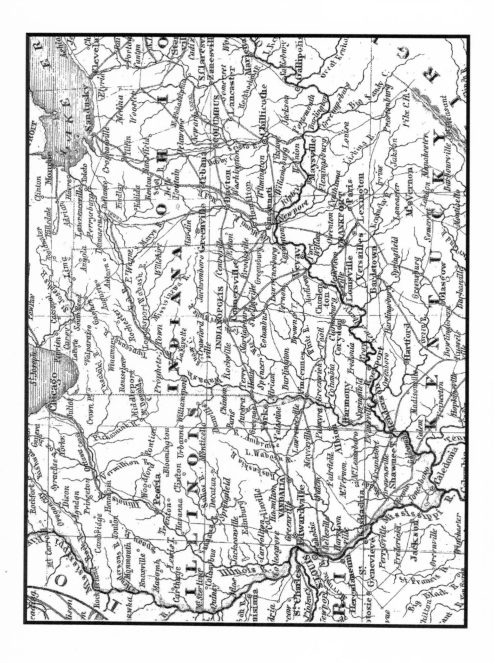

2

# PART I

---

# RACHEL

$\mathcal{T}$he map opposite, a segment of the 1850 map, shows the northern Kentucky/southern Indiana Border Country.

# CHAPTER ONE

*Y*oung Dr. Robert Sandlin gripped the railing of the *St. Augustine*, a packet steamer that had skidded down the ways at the Pittsburgh shipyard only a year before, in 1839. An hour ago, just after sunrise, the steamboat had left Louisville headed downriver. The progress of these boats depended on the number of stops at country landings. As he stood enjoying the morning sun and the warm wild smell of the frothing green water below him, Robert watched a lone figure step out of the forest on the distant Kentucky riverbank. When the boat came closer Robert saw a man standing on a rickety wharf in a loose shirt, wide floppy hat and dark trousers tucked into high boots.

Robert swore under his breath. "Damn! Don't you hail us to come about and take on your scruffy clutch of chickens or bushel of sweet corn. We've been delayed enough already at these two-bit landings. I'll never see Paducah at this rate."

As if to aggravate the doctor's impatience, the man on the dock lazily raised his hand and motioned the captain to land. Then he went back to his oxcart, barely visible under the trees near the landing, and began carrying heavy sacks onto the creaky wooden platform. The makeshift landing floated on sealed empty barrels and was lashed to trees on the riverbank in a way that would allow it to rise and fall with the river in times of flood or drought.

Captain Wilmer Pegg rang the bell to signal the crew, then ordered the pilot and engineer to bring the boat about, land and prepare to take on freight. The boat's clerk and several deckaneers stood by to record the transaction and stow the freight on board. Carney O'Sullivan, the new friend Robert had met just before the *St. Augustine* left Pittsburgh, came up to stand beside him. "It's only for them four sacks we're heavin' to?" Carney said. "Next, I'm guessin' it'll be a starvin' settler with a dozen eggs to sell, or a slack-jawed woman with a litter of pups to give away. Cap'n Pegg needs to pass up some o'these people and their triflin' treasures, wouldn't ye say, Robert?"

Robert expelled a sigh of frustration, then turned to the big Irishman with a resigned smile. "Well, it makes for slow travel, right enough, but steamboats are the only way these poor devils can get their produce to market. Here in the West we have yet to build a network of roads such as you've left behind on your Emerald Isle."

"Aye, 'tis true. This magnificent Ohio and the small streams flowin' into her are about the best roads ye've got. But I'll wager it won't be long ere proper roads'll be carryin' wagons full a'families and freight to the frontier. All the same, sure and I wouldn't wish steamboats an ill fate, much as I've enjoyed this journey. Your country's openin' before us like a flower at sunrise, she is." Robert smiled to himself. He'd heard Carney voice that exact description to Polly Mitchell just a few days earlier outside her cabin on this boat. This repetition was but another hint of his obsession with the girl.

Over the roar of the engines and the spray of the sidewheels thrashing water, Robert spoke to Carney and winked, laying a hand on his shoulder. "It seems you saw a bit of America you weren't expecting in the form of a certain cellist we left in Cincinnati."

"Aye, and for sure, mate. Not an hour passes that I don't spend a part of it dreamin' of my sweet Polly Mitchell. Had she not objected I might have lingered in Cincinnati longer than me bachelorhood could stand."

Robert's eyes widened. "She objected? I thought her to be thoroughly smitten by your Irish roguishness. And I couldn't help noticing that you two were, shall we say, keeping close company during the days, and closer at night, prior to reaching Cincinnati."

Carney grinned and gazed out over the river. "I'll admit to Polly and me bein' a bit indiscreet, Robert. Just before she and her kin left the boat she said as how we'd see if our feelin's for each other are still in high season after I've seen New Orleans. Give ourselves time

6

to think, so to speak. But truly me friend, were it not for my promise to stop at Paducah with you, after the first night without her I'd have hitched onto the next upbound steamer for Cincinnati."

Robert's laugh made Carney turn to him, grinning. "And I, as well, Carney. You've heard Cap'n Pegg and me talking of Rachel Morrison's and my wedding plans with the good captain officiating. That's why these confounded stops at country landings are so exasperating. I need to fulfill my social obligations in Paducah, then return to Vevay, Indiana, under full steam and claim the woman to whom I'm engaged to be married."

"Then you needn't make comments about Polly and me," Carney said. "I noticed you and Miss Rachel were warming to each other on the way down to Vevay. The looks and sighs that passed between the two of you at Rachel's teacher's party in Vevay and your confab with Cap'n Pegg and Rachel on the mornin' of our departure showed plain as day that serious plans were afoot between you and the young lass. You both could've done worse, if you ask me. I'm guessin' you'll make it official soon then, eh?"

# CHAPTER TWO

During the voyage's first nine days from Pittsburgh to Vevay, Indiana, Captain Pegg had invited Rachel, Robert and Carney to join him almost every evening at his table for dinner. The two remaining places were occupied by various other passengers. Polly Mitchell and her brother, sister and sister's husband provided dinner music, a recent innovation on the *St. Augustine*. Now that seventeen-year-old Rachel, her brothers James, fifteen, and Sylvester, twelve, and their Morgan horses had departed the boat at Vevay, Carney and Robert were left as remnants of the original dining group. So the captain invited different passengers each evening to fill the three vacancies at his table, which occupied the position of honor, closest to the stage on the right at the front of the hall. Each evening the captain would come onstage and offer a few cheerful words of welcome or brief announcements to the dinner guests. He would then descend three steps to the carpeted floor and welcome his tablemates for the evening.

On this evening, the six places were occupied by Mr. and Mrs. Buzz Charleton on either side of the captain, their teenage daughter Candace beside her mother, Carney and Robert taking the places across from the captain. After introductions and small talk, the captain said, "You may have noticed the last village we passed was Hendersonville, on the Kentucky side. Tomorrow we'll skirt Diamond Island, below Hendersonville. After that we'll be passing through a stretch of river rich in pirate history but, except for an innocent-looking ferry, and then Cave-In-Rock on the Illinois side, you'll see no signs of previous felonious activity now."

Robert leaned forward, listening intently. He tried to imagine a father's fears as he piloted his family's ponderous flatboat through and around all the obstacles in this wild river, avoiding the invisible shoals during times of low water, dodging treacherous sawyers and planters while being swept along on the spring flood. The spirited Carney might relish such an adventure, but as for himself, Robert considered the prospect daunting.

Wilmer Pegg went on to describe these features and some history of this section of river country. His listeners were enthralled by the tales he told.

"As you will see tomorrow, the Cave-In-Rock entrance yawns at the base of a high cliff of limestone that rises out of the flat riverbottoms with the river flowing past close to the entrance. The opening was partially screened in pirate days by saplings and brush."

Though he clearly had the guests riveted, the captain seemed to savor the suspense with a glint in his eye while the waiter brought their food. Mrs. Matilda Charleton, a first-time diner at the captain's table, nudged Candace. "Mercy!" she whispered, "I never dreamed the Wild West extended this far east."

Pausing a beat after the waiter left, the captain said, "This huge cavern formed a curiosity that many flatboatmen couldn't resist investigating. Early westering river travelers were a naïve bunch, by and large. Many of them had never traveled outside their own townships back east. They were easy prey to pirates at the cave or on islands such as Diamond above the cave and Hurricane below it. A typical ruse was to place a young woman at the head of Diamond Island and have her cry out in distress, begging to be rescued. The obliging family that stopped to take her on board often lost their boat, cargo, even their lives to the gang at the cave.

"Beginning a decade or so before 1800, Samuel Mason, and two later groups, the Ford Gang, James Ford and his sons Philip and William, and the Harp brothers, Micajah and Wiley, took a heavy toll on westering parties."

Smiling at the wide-eyed expressions of his audience, the captain paused, sniffed, and tasted his wine with deliberate care while the others held their breath.

Apparently satisfied with the wine, the captain smacked his lips, nodded for the waiter to pour for the other guests, cleared his throat and continued. "The cave became a place of congregation for all sorts of outlaws, and their mischief among the unsuspecting pioneers continued for years until flatboats became obsolete in favor of steamboats."

Carney spoke up to ask, "Cap'n, you told us earlier you've spent the better part of your life on these boats, beginnin' as a deckhand on the first steamboat ever to descend the river, the sidewheeler *New Orleans* wasn't it? Have you observed these rough fellows in operation? Did they ever attack one of your steamboats?"

The captain smiled. "In the early days we used to see wild-looking men gaping at us from the dark mouth of Cave-In-Rock, shouting and waving their rifles, but they weren't able to capture a boat obviously protected by a well-armed and watchful crew, and that moved under its own propulsion. We always tried to tell flatboat captains of the danger, but we couldn't warn them all.

"Meanwhile, the Ford Gang finally gained supremacy at Cave-In-Rock, and held it for years. But the successful voyage of the *New Orleans*, the first steamboat down the wild Ohio and Mississippi Rivers in 1811, on which I had the honor of serving as one of her six deckhands at the tender age of sixteen, signaled the slow demise of flatboat commerce in favor of this more efficient means of river travel. Also, primitive wagon roads were slowly being built, pushing the frontier ever westward. Both these innovations diminished the main source of income for the Cave-In-Rock operations."

Robert pushed his cup and saucer away and leaned on his elbows, his brow creased with concentration. "You've implied that the Fords continued at Cave-In-Rock even after these new developments in westward travel. Did they somehow adapt new means of waylaying the westering pioneers?"

"Astute observation, Doctor. Responding to this change in the workings of commerce, James Ford gradually converted the Cave-In-Rock business from flatboat piracy to wagon robbery, combining his business and road-building expertise.

10

"Ford commenced buying up the small ferries that dotted the riverbanks below Diamond Island and near Cave-In-Rock. He closed most of these enterprises in favor of his own ferry with the name Ferry Ohio, which he changed from Frazier's Ferry. The county court, on which he was a judge, granted him permission to open his ferry in 1823 and set the fares: 25 cents for a horse, 12½ cents for a man."

"He was a Judge!" Buzz Charleton, Matilda's husband, could stifle his incredulity no longer. "This man, the leader of a ruthless gang of outlaws, was a respected pillar of the community? Didn't the local citizens suspect what was going on?"

"Not for years, Mr. Charleton. You see, he had very carefully curried the favor of the local people, particularly those in county government. He was a prosperous landowner and taxpayer, a deacon in the Baptist Church, and the first to aid the poor with Christmas baskets every year. As for his clandestine activities at Cave-In-Rock, he left the day-to-day operations to his henchmen, and they consulted with him at his fine country home at 'Too-Loo,' spelled T-o-l-u, Kentucky, a few miles from his ferry, only after dark.

"James Ford used his wealth and influence efficiently to improve the local roads and approaches to his ferry on both sides of the river. He built a ferryhouse on the Kentucky side, in this case a large dog-trot log cabin, which sat about 200 feet from the river."

The spunky Candace Charleton was shaking her head in bewilderment. "Wait, wait, Captain, this all sounds like some far-fetched tale of the frontier. You're saying this James Ford managed to attain high office in the local government while also heading a large crime operation on unsuspecting travelers? And what, pray tell, is a dogtrot cabin?"

The group at the table relaxed into nervous laughter at Candace's outburst. The captain winked and reached past her mother to pat her hand. "It does seem a bit like some novelist's feverish dream, young lady, but the truth of the tale will be borne out should you ask any of the locals. James Ford did indeed lead a double life for years.

"By the way, a dogtrot cabin is two log cabins connected by a roofed passageway. There were multiple purposes and advantages of this type of frontier construction. The design obviously provided more space than a single cabin, yet it didn't require logs of extreme length that would be difficult to hoist to the upper tiers of the walls. Then there were other conveniences, such as separating the kitchen and living quarters for caution against fire. Also, a dogtrot provided a place to park, load or unload carriages and buggies in inclement weather. For whatever reason, it was a dogtrot building that Ford built as a ferryhouse at Ferry Ohio.

"Incidentally, James Ford also forged a sinister agreement with the Potts family across the river in southern Illinois who operated an inn about a day's journey along the road north of Ferry Ohio."

Carney said, "Let's see if I understand, Captain Pegg. Your well-respected bandit leader, Mr. Ford, switched his unsavory operations, then, from the cave to the ferry? Was that the end of Cave-In-Rock as a den for outlaws of murderous stripe?"

The captain stubbed out his cigar. "Not by a long shot, Carney. With the treaty of Ghent in 1814 that ended the War of 1812, the new nation began looking to the West for fresh opportunities. In the depression that followed, paper money could be issued by almost anyone, and most of it was worthless. You might say our young federal government had yet to learn how to launch secure banks and a solid currency.

"While the ferry trade was growing, Ford and his men sought new devious uses for the cave. Counterfeiting was rampant in those days, and became another source of revenue for James Ford and the Cave-In-Rock gang. As a countermeasure, one local bank issued raccoon skins of one dollar denomination, o'possum skins for 50 cents, mink for 25 cents and rabbit for 12½ cents. It was difficult to counterfeit this currency but some tried, sewing coon tails onto possum skins."

The dinner guests looked at each other, shaking their heads and laughing at the surreal nature of these tricks.

The captain ended his belly laugh with the declaration, "Believe me, ladies and gentlemen, I couldn't concoct a tale this amusing.

"There was even more devilment that came out of those economic times. Due to the scarcity of coins, silver dollars were cut into wedges, which invited even more trickery. One-fourth section of a silver dollar coin became a "quarter," or two "bits," each worth 12½ cents. Half a "bit" was a "fip," worth 6¼ cents. Being sharp on the sides, these wedges were filed smooth, further devaluing their worth. Unscrupulous traders sometimes cut silver dollars into ten pieces and passed them off as eighths, or "bits." The captain drew a tiny wedge of silver from his pocket and declared, "I defy any of you to tell me if this is a tenth or an eighth of a silver dollar. You'll see that without a dollar coin to compare, your sense of proportion doesn't hold." The group passed the coin fragment around the table, discussing the problem with animation.

After the silver piece had been returned to its owner, he said, "In 1816 the infamous 'Year Without a Summer' draped the Northeast in a frigid pall that lasted through the growing season. This weather aberration, bringing snow and frosts to the area all summer long, initiated a massive westward movement. More boats than ever followed rivers south and west. A new surge of ox and horse teams moved along the Wilderness Road through Cumberland Gap into eastern Kentucky. Young single men generally traveled by pack train, but families favored the more comfortable covered wagon. These wagons with their hickory bows and white canvas covering often had a bucket of tar or resin mixed with beef tallow hanging from the rear axle for use in greasing the wheels and kingbolt, for without lubrication, friction would soon burn the wooden parts and wear them out."

Mr. Charleton said, "Kingbolt. Isn't that the long iron bolt that connects the bed of a wagon to the front axle forming a pivot and allowing the wagon to turn? Critical part of the assemblage, I'd say."

"Exactly right, sir." Captain Pegg glanced about the room and discovered the diners from the other tables, having finished their dinners, were filing out into the passageways on either side of the room. He addressed his guests. "If anyone would like to continue this conversation, why don't we take our coffee and cigars and adjourn to the benches on the afterdeck. We can catch a breath of fresh air and allow the waiters to clear the table. The group rose, all of them following their captain to the stern, no one seeming to tire of his exposition.

# CHAPTER THREE

When the group had settled on the benches, Captain Pegg continued. "Now, with the roads beginning to improve across the region, more travelers used this new Ferry Ohio. Most parties were allowed to pass unmolested to protect the reputation of the ferry, but James Ford's men soon learned to read the signs. Certain prosperous-looking travelers were likely to have silver or gold coins hidden in their wagons or saddlebags. Some of the groups arriving at Ferry Ohio were en route to the salt wells in southern Illinois near the Saline River, and carried enough money to buy salt at $10 a bushel. They might have up to $40 in hard currency with them. To Ford's men the next step was obvious."

Robert said, "And you say James Ford was behind the whole operation, directing his men when, where, and against whom to strike?" If the captain's descriptions were true, this primitive land harbored plots as fiendish as the worst of those of the underworld in his native Baltimore.

"Indeed he was, Doctor. He received reports from his men of prospective victims arriving at Ferry Ohio. Then he'd decide whether to waylay the innocents at Ferry Ohio or at Potts Inn. Sometimes the gang would send a fast rider ahead of the chosen victims' wagon to Potts Inn by a shortcut forest trail, and the robbery would take place somewhere on the lonely road north of Ferry Ohio or when the unsuspecting party reached the inn."

Carney rose from his bench and went to lean back against the railing. He turned to the captain to ask an earnest question. "Sir, didn't you say earlier that Ford used his business and road-building skills to aid his crooked venture? If a ferry existed at this location before Ford arrived, wasn't there already a road leadin' to and from it?"

"Good question, my man. Ferry Ohio lies surrounded by hilly wooded land on both sides of the river. On the Illinois side, after leaving the ferry headed north, teams and wagons would move west right along the water for about a mile before the road ascended the bluff. This meant that in high water season the road would be flooded, forcing the travelers to seek a more convenient ferry. After Ford bought the ferry, he employed a gang of slaves in building a wagon road that switchbacked straight up the bluff from the ferry on the Illinois side. They then connected this bluff road to the existing network of forest lanes on high ground. This became known as the Ford Highwater Road."

"How did they pull the ferry across the river," Matilda Charleton asked, "particularly when the river was in flood? Did they pull it along a cable or rope?"

"Mrs. Charleton, ferries sometimes employed a 'teamboat' for river crossings, which used a sternwheel powered by a team of horses either walking on a treadmill or turning a sweep attached to a capstan. Ford adopted the sweep model, using four horses to turn the sweep.

"He dispatched riders to put up posters at crossroad inns, courthouses and village squares all across Kentucky urging westering travelers to avail themselves of the all-weather crossing at Ferry Ohio."

"Ah, the not-so-subtle power of advertising," Robert said.

"Thus, my friends," the captain continued, "with a good road to his ferry, an efficient teamboat and a sturdy ferryhouse that did double duty as an inn, James Ford launched his macabre business, and it continued in operation for many years."

Now it was the Charletons' daughter, Candace, who again voiced a concern. "The Fords were so well-organized they seem invincible. How did their evil enterprise finally come to an end?"

"Well, miss, law enforcement improved slowly during the first third of this century in the small settlements around Ferry Ohio. Still, frontier justice was often administered by vigilantes. Gradually

James Ford and his sons Philip and William came under suspicion for their murderous preying on travelers. Local citizens began to gather incriminating evidence against them. Then, in the span of a year, 1831-32, both of James's sons, Philip and William, were murdered. The nearby settlements sighed with relief as two of the major threats to the peace had been removed. The public awareness of these men's heinous crimes was so widespread that no one was ever prosecuted for their murders.

"Then, in midsummer, 1833, a posse of concerned citizens, called regulators, took James Ford himself into custody. Some of these men had lost relatives to the Ford gang. They took Ford to his own ferryhouse, offered him supper which he declined, and shot him in the back with a shotgun as he sat in the central passageway of the building. He must have been resigned to his fate, for he was within earshot of members of the regulators removing chinking from between the logs at his back, and might even have heard them counting the shot as they were dropped into the muzzle-loader.

"James Ford's body, which at this point in his life weighed 300 pounds and had quickly begun to reek in the summer heat, was taken to a burying ground the next night after the regulators hastily built a large coffin. Several slaves, under the supervision of a white man whose wife had been killed by the gang, dug Ford's grave and lifted the heavy coffin onto two rails across the hole. A thunderstorm rolled in, frightening the slaves, and one of the rails broke, allowing the coffin to come to rest with one end leaning against the side of the grave. The slaves, spooked by the storm, refused to climb into the grave to straighten the coffin, and so James Ford was buried head-down.

"Another negro in the neighborhood, an old man some regarded as a seer, had a dream that night in which he reported seeing James Ford falling head-first into Hell."

At this point, Mrs. Charleton, whose countenance showed a growing concern in the lamplight, asked the captain if there were any such river pirates still at large on this stretch of the river.

"There are still outlaws in the area, madam, but they aren't nearly so bold as the Cave-In-Rock scoundrels, as brazen as the Ford gang, nor as ruthless as the Harps. In fact, in this more enlightened age of 1840, Cave-In-Rock is deserted. Ferry Ohio is still in use, but with the demise of the Fords, it is now under the ownership of people who seem peaceable and honest.

"No, the current brand of hoodlum, Mrs. Charleton, is more likely to be involved in horse thievery and the kidnapping of freed and runaway slaves, all of which they sell to southern plantation owners."

"Has this bunch been honored with a name, and do they operate from Kentucky, or Illinois?" Robert asked.

The captain nodded. "They are known locally as the Pennington Gang," he said. "Ironically, they hail from a place called Christian County, Kentucky."

"Hmm," Robert said, "It evidently wasn't their kind from whom the county took its name."

"Right enough, Robert. The Pennington family live in the northern part of the county, closest to the river. The leader of the clan, Col. Francis Pennington, is a wealthy, upstanding citizen of Christian County, but he has two sons, Alonzo and Morton, of which the latter cannot be said. Alonzo and his ruffians occupy themselves stealing a stable of fine horses, and driving them south where they sell them to planters and traders. They then travel over into Illinois by the old Ford ferry and the Ford Highwater Road for a fresh supply.

"'Lonz' has begun to be suspected of questionable behavior, and he often has a number of strange men about him whose characters are subject to the same rumors.

"The Kentucky citizens have observed that about the time a drove of horses is taken south a few negro slave boys turn up missing from different sections of the county, never to be heard from again. The local taverns are full of whispered accusations that the Penningtons lure these negroes away from their Kentucky masters by the false promise of being taken north to Illinois and freedom. It would not be difficult to keep the blacks concealed until a drove of horses is ready for market. Then horses and slaves could easily be taken deep into the South and sold on cotton and sugar plantations."

The captain glanced away from his attentive listeners and summoned a nearby steward. "Abner, my boy, please bring a pot of coffee up to the pilot house." To the others he added, "Almost time to take my turn at the wheel." As the servant disappeared on his

17

mission, Captain Pegg regarded his five guests with a reassuring smile and said, "Lonz Pennington and his gang are still active in this area, but he has yet to interfere with steamboat commerce, so you needn't worry. Now I'll bid you all goodnight."

# CHAPTER FOUR

The next evening, Robert and Carney strolled on the open lower deck after dinner, taking advantage of the river breeze at sunset, still sharing memories of the ladies they missed so much, until Carney came up short and put his hand out to stop Robert. They paused along the walkway where they could see a small knot of men crouched in one of the empty livestock stalls.

"Would ye look at that worthless Jack Slater," Carney said, "up to his vile ways again. I thought I taught him a lesson when he cheated Rachel's brother James out of his money and was castin' greedy eyes at his Morgan stallion."

Robert remembered that Carney had given Slater a cuffing earlier in the voyage for shooting craps with Rachel's younger brother, James, using loaded dice. "Looks as if he has yet to see the error of his ways." As Robert spoke a disturbance erupted from the group of men, and one of them protested something Slater had done.

Slater's voice could be heard above the others. "If you're accusin' me of foul play you'd better be ready to put up or shut up, you miserable runt. Just because you're down on your luck's no reason to claim I'm cheatin'. Now hand over what you owe me and be on your sorry way." Slater stood up as if to threaten the other man.

"I'm leavin' all right, but I don't owe you nothin' after all the money you done took from me with them crooked dice."

As the man turned to leave the pen, Slater lunged and hit him in the face with a hard backhand.

Suddenly Carney was in the pen between the two men. "Avast, there, Slater. I see you're back at your tricks after our little set-to upriver."

"Stay outta this, you stupid mick. This is between me and him."

"Not anymore, it ain't. Hand over them dice and the ones in your pocket. We'll be seein' who's tellin' the truth."

Slater lowered his shoulder and tackled Carney, forcing him out of the pen and up against the railing of the boat. The other men, like a pack of hungry hounds, gathered round in ominous silence. Jack stepped back and brought up a knife from a sheath on his belt. He waved it in front of him. "I'll teach you to mind your own business, you scum of an Irishman. I'm gonna make fish bait out of you."

"Drop the skean, Slater," Carney said, " 'fore I ram it up your fundament for ye."

Slater feinted with the knife and moved from side to side looking for an opening while Carney crouched with his hands out in front of him, readying for the attack. Slater jumped forward, leading with the knife, but Carney slid to his left and arched his body so that the knife sliced through his shirt, barely missing his ribs. Before Jack could regain his balance Carney's fist hammered down on the back of his neck and he slumped to his knees, but bounced up with the knife still in a threatening position before Carney could pursue his advantage.

Slater sneered, cursed and lunged again, but this time Carney's reflexes were quicker. He grabbed the man's knife hand in both of his own, used Slater's momentum and brought his wrist down hard across the rail, dislodging the knife, which fell into the river. Slater screamed in pain, but before he could react, Carney twisted his arm up behind his back, and with his left hand behind the man's head, slammed his face hard into the rail once, then again. A gurgling howl came from Slater's throat, and he slumped over the rail long enough for Carney to thrust his left arm between Slater's legs and heave him overboard into the dark swirling water. Two or three seconds passed before Slater's face appeared above the water, mouth bleeding, screaming, "Help! I cain't swim."

By this time the circle of sinister observers had disappeared into the darkening passageways. A crewmember, having rushed to the disturbance, gave the alarm, "Man overboard, man overboard!"

Robert looked about the narrow passageway and spied a coil of rope hanging on the outside of a horse stall nearby. He threw one end into the water near Slater's head and shouted for him to catch hold. By this time the boat was slipping past the floundering man, but the crewman ran toward the stern, knelt and reached through the railing to grasp the man's collar and keep his head above water. Carney was soon beside him, and the two men lifted the gasping gambler back on board.

The captain appeared in time to see the rescuers on their knees tending the vomiting, sputtering Slater. "What's this all about?" Captain Pegg demanded. "Who's responsible for this?" Then his gaze fell upon Carney, eyes blazing. "O'Sullivan, is this more of your disruptive work?"

Carney did not hesitate. He looked the captain in the eye. "Yes sir," he said, "I found this man mistreatin' another passenger and felt it me duty to step in to protect the weaker man."

"Mistreating, is it? Appears it's you who's done the mistreating. Doctor, can you tell me what's going on here?"

Robert did his best to explain the situation and to add that there had been a previous confrontation between the two men when Carney protected James Morrison from the gambler Slater. "Now with your permission, sir, I need to get my medical bag and tend to this man's injuries. It appears his arm is broken as well as some of his teeth." Slater lay curled on the deck, moaning, writhing in pain.

The captain granted Robert his request, then ordered two of the crew to move Slater to his quarters. "Now, Mr. O'Sullivan, you will come with me."

The captain told Carney to wait in the captain's cabin while he instructed the pilot to carry on in his absence. When he returned he took a chair opposite the Irishman and glared at him across the table for several seconds before he spoke.

"So, Mr. O'Sullivan," he growled, "we now see that you've been involved in at least three episodes of violence since you boarded this craft. First, you bludgeoned one dockhand on the wharf at Pittsburgh, and shot another. Just now the doctor tells me of a previous incident I hadn't heard of between you and this man Slater before the Morrisons departed the *St. Augustine* at Vevay. Then there is this evening's fiasco."

Carney said, "Yes, sir. But with all due respect, sir, if I may explain . . . . "

"You, my boy, are a great disappointment to me. I have admired your witful table conversation and your gallant manners toward Rachel Morrison, her brothers and Dr. Sandlin. We did wonder briefly if you were taking advantage of Miss Mitchell before her party left the boat at Cincinnati, but it soon became evident that the young lady was quite capable of, um, holding her own, shall we say.

"Yet, after establishing those good impressions you seem bent on mayhem at critical moments. Why is that?"

"Thank you for the compliments, sir, but you yourself admitted after the Pittsburgh affair that I might have saved a greater misfortune by my actions against the Welshmen."

The captain nodded grudgingly. "Yes, but had I not relieved you of your pistol and ammunition after that scrape and made you recite the rules of this vessel to me the next day, what greater havoc might you have caused? As a matter of fact, I have had two aristocratic gentlemen with wives and young children on board come to me with complaints about the disturbances initiated by you, young man. One of those gentlemen is a partner among the owners of the *St. Augustine*. I can no longer stand idly by and watch you disrupt this voyage and endanger my defenseless passengers."

"Yes, sir, the rules of the ship took on a new meanin' after that fracas at Pittsburgh, they did. And, sure it is, sir, in the two events with Mr. Jack Slater I believed meself to be on the correct side of the rules, sir, and behavin' in a way you would have approved."

"Except that you exceeded your authority. I explained to you before that I am the only law enforcement officer on this steamboat, and you should have reported any rule violations directly to me instead of taking them into your own hands. You seem not to understand that, Mr. O'Sullivan, and now I must take action on behalf of the safety of my passengers."

At that moment Robert Sandlin knocked at the door and the captain let him in.

"And how is your patient, doctor?"

"I've splinted his arm and done what I can for his mouth, but he will need the aid of a doctor with better instruments than I have as soon as we reach a town."

22

"I'll see to that. Now, I'm glad you will be my witness, doctor. I am about to put Mr. O'Sullivan off this steamboat for repeated misbehavior that endangers my passengers. You have seen the violations that have precipitated this action, so you will be qualified to vouch for me in any future litigation Mr. O'Sullivan chooses to initiate."

Robert seemed surprised. "But . . . but Captain, surely you can see that Carney was protecting the rights and welfare of other passengers in what he did. Had he and I not stepped in on the wharf at Pittsburgh those Welsh rousters would surely have overcome the Morrison party and done them and their horses physical harm. The same reasoning should apply to stopping Jack Slater, who was by all means violating your ship's rules.

"In fact, sir, I was as much at fault as Carney in these incidents. If you banish him from the St. Augustine, you should put me off, as well."

"I see it differently, Doctor," Captain Pegg said. "You used no weapon, and it was you who made an effort to correct the damage that your friend here caused."

Carney asked, "Surely you won't set me ashore in the middle of the night, sir?"

The captain glanced out at the inky darkness. "No, but at our first landing tomorrow I will return your weapon and ammunition and ask you to leave the boat. It will be a sad occasion for me, to be sure, but I hope this will teach you to take a more reasoned approach to future altercations, my friend. Now go collect your things and prepare to disembark in the morning."

23

# CHAPTER FIVE

The next morning, not long after daylight, a few miles above Shawneetown, Illinois, the *St. Augustine* put in at a country landing on the north bank where two men on horseback hailed the boat. As the vessel came about, Carney and Robert appeared at the landing stage, Carney with his grip, Robert still hoping the captain would reconsider his decision.

The captain joined them and handed Carney his pistol and ammunition, then shook the Irishman's hand. "I'm truly sorry it's come to this, Mr. O'Sullivan. I wish you godspeed on your journey to New Orleans. You will find it slow going through the driftwood, vines and heavy forest near the riverbank. With any luck you'll find an old Indian path or buffalo trace on higher ground, but be mindful of your back, son. This is a country full of dangerous animals, especially the two-legged kind."

"Thank you, Captain," Carney said. "I hold no ill feelin' toward you, sir, and I wish you godspeed, as well." He turned to Robert, then, shook his hand and said, "Please give my best to your fair lady, Robert, and her brothers. I'll not be soon forgettin' the good times we shared on this voyage."

In that instant Robert made a decision. "Captain, please don't shove off until I retrieve my things. I'm going with him."

The captain's face went blank, then a ruddiness began to ascend from his collar. "Now see here, Doctor, I have already exonerated you from these troubles, and your services are still needed on board. I strongly advise against your leaving this vessel."

24

"I cannot argue against your decision involving Carney, but I have my loyalty to my friend to consider. Besides," he said with the hint of a smile, "Miss Rachel once suggested that Carney and I try our hand at overland travel at some point in our journey. This seems an opportune time for it."

The captain blinked, as if remembering something. "Wait, Robert. What about our plans for me to marry you and Miss Morrison here on board when you return from Paducah?"

Robert was already halfway up the stairs to the upper deck. He turned and gave the captain a mock salute and a grin. "I'm counting on it, sir. You'll not be hard to find; Rachel and I will be in touch with you soon."

While Robert was fetching his gear Carney approached the two riders who had just come up the landing stage. "Excuse the inconvenience, gentlemen, but my friend and I will be leaving the steamer here and tramping on west. Would you be knowin' as to the nearest town where we might avail ourselves of a ferry across to Kentucky?"

The two rough frontiersmen eyed each other, not hiding their condescending expressions. The taller one said, "Looks like we got us a city boy here, Charlie. Well, mister, if you can dodge the skeeters and the snakes, and the heat don't melt you down, you might make it to the river bluff where you'll find a trail on west to Shawneetown. I'd say it'd be a sight easier to stay on this boat and just have the captain drop you on the Kaintuck side."

"That won't be possible, sir, but I thank you for the information."

"Well, mister, if you're bound and determined to tromp this country I b'lieve I'd git me a hoss. This ain't no place for a man afoot."

As the pair of riders led their horses to a pen on the lower deck the first man said, "That rube's for sure a preacher man. Reckon how long he'll last out here in the hind end of nowhere?"

Robert appeared with his grip and medicine bag, and they walked down the gangplank. The captain rang the bell and the *St. Augustine* drifted to midriver, came about and headed downstream.

Carney regarded his friend with a regretful expression. "Looks like I've got us in a fine kettle o' fish, and for sure. Just look at this

25

tangle of driftwood, vines and muck. It's enough to bring back the horrors o'them jungle books me old uncle read to me when I was but a tyke at his knee."

"Take heart, Carney. We'll just press on to those bluffs yonder and find that trail you say your horsemen spoke of. We must buck up, now, and make Rachel and Polly proud of us." He turned and struck off bravely from the primitive landing where they stood.

They followed the tracks back along the narrow path the horses had trod through the swampy bottomland. For two hours they waded fetid sloughs, shouldered through dank willow brakes and slogged warily past piles of drifted logs that crawled with fleeing turtles and hissing water snakes, all the while slapping at their necks in futile attempts to ward off clouds of biting insects. When they finally reached the shading forest above the mile-wide lowland where floods had left their wreckage, they stopped to rest and partake of the canteen of water and packet of cornbread the ship's cook had shoved into their hands just before they departed the boat.

The sun had climbed halfway to its zenith when they came to the woodland trail and struck off to the west. The going was easier here, though the path was narrow and winding. Where their way crossed creeks in wooded valleys, they saw large depressions where Robert surmised buffalo had wallowed. As they skirted one of the huge mudholes he said, "Can you imagine a herd of buffalo rolling around in this mess?"

"A buffalo wallow, you say, Robert? Well, for a tuppence I'd cast off my clothes and wallow a bit meself." Robert chuckled and reminded his partner they'd better keep moving. The cook had told them they should make Shawneetown by midday.

By Robert's pocket watch it was ten past one when they stumbled into the dusty settlement of Shawneetown. A couple acres of forest, brush and driftwood had been cleared from the riverbank here. The landing lay at the foot of a sunbeaten north-south track that bifurcated the ragged collection of gray cabins, most with sheds leaning against them. Robert and Carney entered the ramshackle hamlet from their east-west trail, turned down toward the river and passed a trading post with a sign on the front that proclaimed one word, "MCDANIEL." Hounds, lazing on and under rickety porches, raised their heads only briefly to note the arrival of strangers.

The travelers' attention shifted to a woman berating a man who made a hasty retreat from a cabin over behind the McDaniel building. He escaped just ahead of the broom she brandished, scattering a flock of chickens. "You'll not talk to me thataway, Mont Honeycutt," she screeched. "I ain't a woman of that stripe."

A barn beside one of the cabins looked like a livery stable. Three horses stood in the lot with hind legs propped, heads hanging over the top rail with only their tails in motion fighting flies. The log stable's double doors hung open, revealing a wagon, and a buggy with a broken wheel leaning against it. Assorted saddles and tack hung on pegs inside.

Carney approached the stable and called out for the owner. A roughly dressed old man appeared, his mouth agape showing two irregular rows of darkened teeth. "Durned if you slickers ain't dressed too fancy to b'long hereabouts. What happened, you git throwed off a steamboat?" His mouth fell open even further as he hooted. The oldster looked back, seeming to evaluate his building through the eyes of his well-dressed visitors. "Beg your pardon for the common appearance of my place of business," he said. "As the feller says, I'm too poor to paint and too proud to whitewash." Carney and Robert did not respond to the man's broad wink.

Robert asked, "Where might we find a ferry? We're headed for Paducah."

The man wrinkled his brow. "Paducah! Ferry, you say? Why you need a ferry to get to Paducah? That's miles and miles downriver. B'lieve I'd flag a steamboat if I's you. They's several a day passes right by our front porch, so to speak."

Carney shifted his weight and squinted at Robert. "Well, sir, we're bent on gettin' to that fair settlement by an overland route, we are. But we're findin' ourselves on the inconvenient side of the river, don't you see."

"Well, why'nt you say somethin'? My name's Ebeneezer Steltenpohl, and you fellers're p'robly wantin' hosses, then. Got just what you need out there lookin' at you. Give you a good price on two of 'em and enough tack to git you where yer goin'."

"Now, about that ferry." Ebeneezer leaned over to peer past Robert and Carney toward the river. "Old Jeremiah's our ferryman most days when he feels like it, but he's takin' a nap tied up yonder

27

on the Kaintuck side now. Want me to raise him?" The man reached inside the barn door and fetched a long rusty bolt with which he approached the iron ring of a wagon tongue brace hanging by a string from a spike in the log wall.

Wincing in anticipation of the clang, Robert said, "Wait, wait. What sort of trail leads from the landing on the Kentucky side? We've had enough climbing through trackless tangles along the river for one day."

"Trail? Ain't much of a trail over yonder to speak of, mister, jest a wagon lane on down as far as the Caseyville settlement, across from the mouth of the Saline. Beyond that the trail peters out."

"What about this side of the river?"

"Well, now, I expect you'd have better luck takin' the trail on west from here, same one you come in on. That'll get you to Potts Tavern, though the Pottses don't run it no more. In the mornin' you'll take the Ford Highwater Road south to Ferry Ohio."

# CHAPTER SIX

Robert frowned. "In the morning? You mean we'd have to stay at the Potts tavern tonight? Can't we make it all the way to the ferry today?"

Eb squinted at the sun. "Well, sir, you'll be gettin' a late start. To get there today, even on horseback, ye'd have to travel the last few miles to the ferry at night. Now, you nor nobody else don't want to be on the Ford Highwater Road after dark. But from the landing across the river there you'll find roads enough to get you plumb to Paducah."

Carney said, "He speaks right, Robert. Remember Captain Pegg's tales about Ferry Ohio and the Ford Highwater Road?"

Eb nodded. "I see you've hear'd of the dark dealin's hereabouts in past years. Things ain't as bad now, but the Pennington Gang has been raisin' hell lately, stealin' hosses and kidnappin' black boys to sell down the river." Eb paused, looked around, then said in a confidential tone, "Don't let on to nobody I told you that."

The men turned their attention to Eb's horses. Upon inspection, Robert found the animals to be in better shape than their owner. After a bit of haggling, Robert and Carney bought two horses and tack for a little over half what Eb originally asked, after tossing their soon-to-be-empty traveling bags into the deal. When the horses were saddled and the contents of the men's leather grips had been transferred to the saddlebags, Carney said, "Hadn't you best tie the medicine bag on behind your saddle, Robert?"

"I thought of that, but it balances nicely here on the pommel."

29

The two travelers rode off into the hot afternoon, squinting against the blazing sun. They found this westward road in better condition between Shawneetown and Potts Inn than east of the village. Carney said, "You reckon that fella James Ford built this road to connect the inn with Shawneetown? Didn't the captain say he was a road contractor?"

"And a businessman," Robert replied. "He probably found a way to wring a profit out of his road building. Maybe it gave his outlaws better access to unsuspecting wayfarers."

"Can't say I'm sorry old Ford's gone on to meet his fathers."

The riders arrived at Potts Inn a little after sunset. They saw a two-story frame house with a tidy dooryard and two paths out back, one that led into the woods to an outhouse and the other, paved with flagstones, to a spring flowing out of a hillside between neat blocks of cut stone. Two saddled horses were tied at the hitch rail out front. A few rods past the inn lay the intersection of the Shawneetown Road with the Ford Highwater Road.

A matronly woman stepped out on the porch and addressed them. She wiped her hands on her apron. "Lookin' to put up for the night?"

"Yes, ma'am," Robert replied.

"Welcome to Potts Inn, the best beds, potluck and horsekeepin' anywhere in Illinois. Where you from?"

Robert and Carney chatted with the woman, whose name was Effa Seegers. She called for a negro man who appeared from the back of the house. After handing the men their saddlebags he took the horses to the barn. The woman introduced Robert and Carney to her husband, Nathaniel, who had been closing the hen house after the chickens had gone to roost.

At supper they met the other two horsemen who engaged Robert and Carney in conversation. The younger one, a blond boy of perhaps twenty, said, "You come from Shawneetown, I reckon. Where you bound?"

"Ferry Ohio tomorrow," Carney said. "Paducah in due time."

"Looks like you got some good horses there. I seen 'em as the nigger was takin' 'em to the barn. We hear tell they's certain folks around here'd be glad to relieve you of 'em."

30

Carney patted his pocket. "Aye, and it's for that I'm carryin' me little brother, here." All four men laughed.

"We bought the horses just today in Shawneetown," Robert said. "They've proven satisfactory so far. I have family in Paducah and my friend here will continue down to New Orleans after meeting my kinfolk."

"You gonna ride all the way to New Orleans?" the other man said.

Carney chuckled. "It's only a favor I'm doin' for Robert here, by trying the overland route for a few miles before boardin' a steamer at Paducah for the rest of me journey."

"And you, sir?" the younger man said.

"After parting ways with Carney I'll be catching another steamboat upriver to Vevay, Indiana, to announce my engagement to a certain young lady who lives near there."

Both of the other men beamed at Robert and shook his hand. "Bravo," the older man said. The conversation continued as Robert and Carney described how they had met at Pittsburgh and became friends with the Morrisons who were on their way home to Switzerland County, Indiana, with Morgan horses from their kinfolk in Rushford, New York.

After supper the two men shook hands with Robert and Carney, then left. Carney said, "Mr. Seegers, you seem to have dinner customers as well as overnighters."

"Them boys work for the Pennington family from down in Kentucky," Nathaniel said. "They ride through here and stop for supper now and again, usually on their way north to get horses for Lonz Pennington and his brother. They like to chat with strangers that stop by on their way through."

Effa Seegers carried a coal oil lamp as she led the men upstairs to their room. Just before they followed her up the steps, Robert saw Carney stop. He'd spied the black man sitting in a pantry just off the kitchen. He stepped forward, handed the man two bits and said, "Much obliged for your help with the horses."

The man reached to take the silver but he did not stand or speak. His expression remained stoic, his eyes somehow watchful and sad.

"You're our only patrons tonight," Mrs. Seegers was saying. "You can leave the windows up and your door open to catch a little

31

breeze. I'll open the door to the back stairs and that'll make it a mite cooler for you."

When they were alone in their room, Carney said, "Robert, I need to show you my pistol in case there's trouble. Don't suppose you'd stoop to carryin' a weapon, bein' a healer and all."

"With a gun I'd be more a danger to myself than anyone else. You expecting trouble on the road tomorrow?"

"I wouldn't be surprised. You heard Mr. Seegers say who them two gents work for. Now look here, Robert. I bought this piece in your City of Brotherly Love not long after I landed in this rough and tumble New World. People kept tellin' me I shouldn't venture into the West without a means of self defense, and you saw it borne out in that rowdydow on the wharf at Pittsburgh. Twas a shame it got the captain's nose bent out of joint."

"What kind of pistol is that?"

"The dealer called it a pepperbox percussion revolver."

"I see it has three barrels."

"Aye, three barrels that rotate, producin' three shots. The man showed me how squeezing the trigger rotates the barrel block, cocks the hammer and fires the weapon. He said this is the latest article in the business. They've only been on the market a decade or so."

"Is it European?"

"Some are," he said, "but this model is what he called an American Threebarrel Manhattan pistol. Don't know where they got the name, but you saw it was effective."

Robert took the pistol and examined it.

"Smooth bore, I see. How accurate is it?"

"Excellent point, me friend. These are designed for civilian use, primarily for self defense at close range, like in yer good old American gunfights. Ye'll notice there's no sights on the piece. They're designed to shoot from the hip as the feller says. You hold the gun low and point at your target's center of mass, like a man's belly."

"Ugh! In my business that's a bad wound to treat."

"Aye, Robert, but that's a sight better than bein' gut-shot yerself, wouldn't you say? Another advantage is its size, easy to conceal in a coat pocket, don't you see."

"Well, with a bit of luck, you won't have to use it again."

32

# CHAPTER SEVEN

As soon as the men finished their early breakfast, the negro had the horses ready at the hitch rail out front. Dust powdered the men's boots. The rising sun cast long shadows across the empty road intersection a few rods from the front of the inn.

The black man held the bridle while Carney mounted, then he cast a quick glance over his shoulder and said in a low voice, "Got your gun loaded, boss?"

"Right enough. I keep 'er ready."

The man's sad, steady eyes spoke eloquently. Carney gave him a long, questioning look, then drew the pistol from his coat pocket. "Well, I'm buggered!" he said. "Somebody took out me loads. Robert, did you empty my pistol?"

Robert's surprised countenance gave him all the answer he needed. Carney turned again to the negro, but his dark face had closed to the same expression he'd seen the previous night. Before Carney could question him further, the man turned and headed for the barn.

The cool air at sunrise was sweet with woodsmoke and birdsong. The wet grass had dampened the dust on the toes of their boots, but the young men did not notice.

They mounted up and started down the road, their horses walking, Carney quietly reloading his pistol, hoping not to further alarm his companion. "That Polly Mitchell must have me addled. Keep an eye on me, my man, make sure I mind me P's and Q's."

"I thought your pistol was loaded, too," Robert said, peering apprehensively at the surrounding hills, orange sunbeams now burning off mist in the wooded hollows.

They rode for two hours south on the Ford Highwater Road, passing few homesteads, grass growing between the wagon tracks, the road winding into deeper forest toward the distant ferry. In some places the way had been worn to a sunken lane between roadside crop patches or meadows, exposed tree roots making grotesque figures on banks to their right and left. It often seemed they were riding through a sylvan tunnel, with treetops intertwining above their heads. Robert said, "Now I understand why Eb advised us to avoid traveling here at night."

They had just forded a creek and rounded a bend, heading uphill, when two figures stepped into the road just ahead of them. Carney felt his jaw tighten, his heartbeat surge. The horses pricked their ears, but kept moving at their steady pace, their riders unmindful of stopping them.

The two men, one middle-aged and dark, the other younger with blond stubble and cold blue eyes, approached confidently and took hold of the horses' bridles. Carney was not surprised to see they were the same men they'd spoken with at the inn. "Howdy, boys," the older man said, patting Carney's horse. Last evening's smile had vanished from his face in favor of a deadly glare. Even at this distance it was evident from his breath and bloodshot eyes that he'd been drinking whiskey. He held the horse's bit and looked up at Carney. "Now, you need to step down. We're takin' these hosses."

The younger man grinned menacingly at Robert. "And I'm relievin' you o'that black bag, too."

Robert said, "No! I'm a doctor, I need this."

Carney drew his pistol and pointed it at the man holding his horse. "I say back off, there, ye worthless wastrels."

The man laughed derisively but did not reach for his own pistol, though both men were obviously armed. "That toy ain't gonna save your hoss, you stinkin' mick. Besides, you'll find it ain't loaded. Now dismount before I stick that thing up your hind end for you."

Carney slowly raised his pistol toward the man's chest. "Then have it your way, you gutter snipe." He fired and the man collapsed, blood gushing from his wound, eyes open and staring, showing only small jerking movements after he hit the ground.

At the report of the pistol the other outlaw gaped for an instant in disbelief at his dead companion, then in one motion he leapt up behind Robert, grabbed him around the waist and gave his mount's flanks a vicious kick. The horse bolted off, galloping up the hill with the thief's tan coattails flapping.

Carney shouted and pointed his gun at the fleeing outlaw, but did not pull the trigger. The chance of hitting Robert was too great. He pocketed his weapon and gave chase. Robert and his captor were now passing out of sight at the top of the hill. Carney kicked his gelding into a gallop, knowing he had to do something quickly, but having no idea how to save his friend from this hooligan.

Even before Carney came in sight of the other horse, when he was only halfway up the hill, he heard a shot, and an overwhelming feeling of dread coursed through his body. It couldn't be, it must not be.

When Carney topped the hill, he saw flapping coattails on a galloping horse far down the trail. His gaze shifted to the middle distance, and his mouth went dry at the sight of a dark unmoving shape by the side of the lane. He reined in his horse and jumped off, his momentum causing him to go sprawling in the road as the horse continued for a short distance. On his hands and knees now he found himself directly opposite the dark shape, and as he turned his head to look he saw with horror the back of Robert's hatless head. Blood had matted the scorched brown hair around a dark bullet hole. He had been shot at point blank range.

Uttering his friend's name in an agonized howl, he crawled toward him, took hold of his shoulder, turned him enough to see the terrible exit wound and the fact that Robert had held onto his medicine bag until the end, its handle still tightly gripped in his right hand. Carney screamed again, then released Robert's shoulder and buried his face in his hands among the dry leaves and debris at the roadside, weeping and retching.

# CHAPTER EIGHT

C arney was unaware how much time had passed when he finally summoned the strength to rise from his dead friend's side and face the next decision. As if in a stupor, and with tears flowing down his face, he removed his jacket and gently wrapped it around Robert's head. "I won't have people seein' you like this, me friend." Then he lifted Robert's body and secured it behind his saddle, leaning against the horse with his face hidden in his folded arms for a long moment before he was able to mount and ride slowly back in the direction of Potts Inn. He couldn't even pursue the man who had shot Robert. Despite the turmoil in his mind, as much as he craved revenge, his first duty must be to his friend, seeing that he was treated with respect and had a decent burial. He reluctantly put retribution out of his mind.

When he came upon the man he'd shot, still lying in the road with flies already at work, he spied the thieves' two horses tied to saplings a short distance from the road. Carney dismounted, walked into the woods and untied the horses, a bay mare and a gray gelding, and led them back to where his horse stood. He patted the mare's neck and looked down at the corpse. "You're both better men than this devil, you are. I won't leave you two mounts here. After seein' his partner dropped in his tracks that craven murderer won't be back for 'is horses for a while. There's people in Shawneetown could put you to better use." He rode off slowly toward the settlement leading the two horses, grimly aware of the irony of taking horses from horse thieves.

Turning toward Shawneetown and passing the Potts Inn, he thought he saw one of the curtains at a front window move, but otherwise all was quiet. He decided not to stop. In his present state of mind he was afraid he might kill both proprietors, regardless of their innocence or guilt. His wrath had already created too many disasters in this new country. Nothing could be gained now by killing two more people. He rode on toward Shawneetown in the sweltering August heat, slumped in the saddle, full of guilt and despair.

When Eb Steltenpohl observed Carney's approach, the old man hobbled out to meet him. With a confused glance at the horses, then at Robert's shrouded body, he said, "My god, son, what happened? Accident or somebody done it a-purpose?"

"Eb, would this place be havin' an undertaker?"

"Why . . . why yes, sir. Ephraim McDaniel does our undertakin' and buryin' round these parts. He works in the back shed of his store yonder." Then, the situation seeming to become clearer in his mind, he shook his head. "Damnable shame, it is, too. Them cussed Pennington boys, again, I'll wager. I shoulda gave you stronger warning, or sent riders with you . . . . How come them extry hosses?"

Carney spoke through gritted teeth. "It was no accident, Eb. It was a god-damned murder, and I'm as guilty as the man that shot him."

"Looks like you drove 'em off, but not in time to . . . . You need me to help you . . . with him?"

"I'd be much obliged. And I'll need to put these horses in your stable." Carney dismounted and waited beside his horse while Eb limped along leading the other two to his barn. He returned quickly and joined Carney. They made their way to the front of the trading post.

Ephraim McDaniel stepped out on the porch when he saw the two men approaching on their solemn mission. A couple of young boys had run up to gape at the proceedings. "Come around to the back," McDaniel said in a quiet, almost inaudible voice. "Boys, you run on home, now."

After the men exchanged quiet introductions and condolences by the back door, they lifted Robert's body down as gently as possible and placed it on a long table inside. After asking Eb's

37

permission, Carney took his horse to join the others at the livery stable. He removed the saddle and bridle and watched the horse walk a few feet into the dusty lot, lie down and roll, squirming to scratch his sweaty back. Carney took the saddle bags and Robert's medicine bag and rejoined the other men.

Ephraim McDaniel was just taking the coat off Robert's head, having already removed the boots, soiled jacket and shirt. He paled noticeably as he surveyed the horrendous head wounds. "I'll have to take care of him right away in this heat, and we'll bury him first thing in the morning. Eb, go get Willie and his brothers. Set 'em to diggin' a grave somewhere along the back row of the cemetery, over by the fence." Then, squinting at the sun riding low over the treetops, he said, "Give 'em a lantern or two if they need 'em."

Carney held his cap in his hand. "Should I be havin' a coffin made, sir? And shall I give you my change a'clothes fer'im to be . . . you know?"

"I got coffins in the shed out there. You can leave me the clothes, then clear out for a while. I reckon you'll want to sit a wake, so I'll have him ready here in a couple of hours. Don't expect you'll want the coffin open the way . . . he is." Carney shook his head in agreement. "It ain't that I'd expect anybody to come, you and your friend bein' strangers here, and all, but still it's the white thing to do. Eb, I'll need your help for a while after you set Willie and them to work."

Carney took a fresh shirt and trousers from his saddlebags and laid them on the long table at Robert's feet. Ephraim said, "I'll put anything I find in his pockets in this little basket for when you get back. I'll put it with his boots and suspenders. Now if you fancy somethin' to eat, Maudie Russell at that cabin catty-cornered across the road will fix you supper if you ask, and she can get you a bottle, too, if you need it. From the looks of you, you need that more'n food right now. Appears you've had enough of a shock for one day."

He wasn't hungry, but needing something, anything, to occupy his mind, even for a moment, to somehow dull the pain of his grief and guilt, Carney moved across the street, walking unsteadily, as if his feet were acting independently of his mind. The images of that crumpled shape at the roadside and the sudden knowing that Robert was dead came at him like repeated lightning bolts.

38

His boots clumping across the porch brought Mrs. Russell to the door. She was a tall trim woman with a ruddy complexion. He saw concern registered in a face that might once have been beautiful, but now, even framed in curly red hair going to gray, it had seen too many days of hard work, dust and blazing sun. Her eyes still shone bright blue with smile creases at the corners, but at this moment they focused on him with compassion. "I seen you with that . . . that man on your horse. You come right in this house and set down and let me git you somethin' to eat. You hungry?"

Somewhere in his head her voice struck a familiar note. Yes, she was the woman who had chased the man from her house with a broom yesterday. "No, ma'am, but I could use a wee sip of spirits, if you please. Then I'll thank you to let me sit here for a bit."

Maudie returned quickly with a glass and a stoppered quart bottle three-quarters full of whiskey. She poured him a drink and said, "You can set here just as long as you want, honey. I lost a husband over on the Saline River three year ago, and I know there ain't nothin' nobody can say to make it better."

Later, as twilight deepened the shadows and a breeze began to mellow the humid air, the creaking sound of iron hinges roused Carney from his thoughts as he sat on Mrs. Russell's front step. A few wagons had passed earlier in the evening and chickens scratched in the dust at his feet before going to roost. A dog meandered out from under the porch and sniffed at his boot, but after getting no response, wandered off toward the river.

Across the road, Ephraim McDaniel stood in the open door of his shed and Carney saw two lanterns hanging in the interior. Their light illuminated a coffin with the lid off where Robert's corpse had lain before. Ephraim nodded at Carney. He rose and started across the road.

"I done the best I could," Ephraim said. "I left it open for a minute. Thought you might want to see . . . ."

After one brief look in the coffin Carney, turning away from the grisly sight, said, "Yes, thank you. Now please close it." Ephraim gently placed a black cloth over Robert's mutilated face, then nailed the lid on the pine box.

"Besides the clothes," Carney asked, "how do you . . . did you prepare the body?"

39

"But for the face I just did the usual. Eb helped with movin' him and turnin' him. I washed the body, put on the clean clothes. Then I packed the coffin with aromatic herbs, we call 'em, before we lifted him in. Masks the odor, you know, and I used some of my homemade cologne. It helps, 'specially durin' the summer months. Even at that we'll need to bury him early tomorrow, before it gets too hot."

"And the grave?"

"It'll be ready in the mornin'. Me and Eb'll back a wagon in here and load up the coffin at sunrise. You want a preacher? Our circuit rider ain't due till next week, though old Hiram Olsen, he lives on a shantyboat down by the landing, he could say a prayer at the buryin'."

"No, I'll say a piece at the grave. What about a headstone?"

"Write down what you want on the marker and I'll have it cut into a stone or a riven oak plank. The stone'd take a while, have to order it from Elizabethtown away off downriver. I got a man here can fix the plank, take maybe two or three days."

"The plank will do. I expect Robert's kin will come soon to carry him home." Carney looked off to the distant hills, knowing he couldn't take much more talk. "So . . . I'll stay here with him tonight."

"There's a table and a pair of ladderback chairs there by the wall, and I'll bring in a couple of coal oil lamps. You want me to have Maudie bring you anything?"

"No, thanks all the same."

Ephraim brought a bundle of the herbs and laid it atop the coffin, then checked the doors and lamps before he said, "I'll be here early in the mornin'. The wife and I live up the stairs just inside that door. Give me a holler if you need me." Then he was gone and Carney sat for a long time with his head in his hands.

On the table, he noticed paper, pen and ink. He'd express his gratitude for Mr. McDaniel's thoughtfulness in the morning. Then he turned his chair to face the table and wrote the marker inscription. "Robert L. Sandlin, M.D." Carney didn't know Robert's exact birthdate, so he wrote, "1813 - 1840." After much thought, he added two lines. "Though felled by the dark hand of evil, his spirit shines on." Tears blinded him as he laid the pen down and lowered his head on his arms.

Some time later he was roused by a tapping at the outside door. In a moment, the door opened and Maudie stepped in carrying a tray with a small pitcher of water, a glass, a bowl of bean soup and a plate of cornbread. He nodded silently and ate a bit after she quietly sat down in the other chair and regarded the coffin meditatively.

After a few minutes Maudie said, "I hope you don't mind my bein' here. Just wanted to pay my respects."

"Fine, ma'am, I appreciate your kindness, and Robert would, too."

"Eb said a horsethief shot him. You musta been good friends. Grow up together did you?"

"No, but we had us some times together. Feels like I've lost a brother, and I shoulda done more to protect him, gentle soul that he was."

"Lord, I know that feelin', but you can't go on that way. Hard as it is to understand, it was just his time to go, and you nor nobody else coulda changed it."

"Mayhap in time I'll see it that way."

"Where was you headed?"

"Paducah, at the mouth of the Tennessee first, then we would've parted, him heading back to his lady love in Indiana, then to his home in Baltimore. Me, on down to New Orleans. Now all that feels like a bad dream."

"But you've got to see New Orleans someday. Your life cain't stop, your friend wouldn't want that for you. You just make up your mind that after your duties is finished, you'll come back down this old river all the way to New Orleans."

"That may be, but it's beyond my thoughts right now."

Maudie got up to say goodbye and took Carney's hand. "And when you come back this way, you stop and say hello, for I'd like us to get better acquainted, you hear?"

Carney rose to see her off at the door. Before she turned to cross the dark road Maudie smiled up at him and said, "I'll be with you at the funeral tomorrow."

41

# CHAPTER NINE

The early sun cast long shadows across the dew-laden meadow grass as Carney, Maudie, Eb and Ephraim followed the wagon up the lane to the cemetery that lay on high ground at the edge of the settlement. The place commanded a magnificent panorama of the river.

Hanson's Mack, an old freed slave who had not changed his slave name, rode on the wagon seat speaking gently to the horses. He raised a hand when he saw Willie and his brothers already sitting by the grave with their shovels. They had placed locust rails across it to receive the coffin and long ropes underneath to lower it later.

Nobody spoke as the men laid the coffin on the rails. They all stepped back as Carney removed his tweed cap and moved to the head of the coffin.

After a long silence with his head bowed, Carney spoke reverently. "We're here on this sad occasion to bid fare thee well to a fine man who was taken too soon from us and from this life. He had read medicine and even before beginnin' his own practice in Baltimore he saved lives and soothed the suffering of many after a steamboat explosion on the Ohio River below Wheeling. I had the honor of laborin' at his side during those calamitous hours. I was with him when he fell in love and became engaged to a beautiful girl on the same river voyage.

"Now, Robert, though it's a responsibility I'll be dischargin' with a heavy heart, I'll find Miss Rachel, and your family at Baltimore to give them these tragic details. Hearts have been and will be broken at our loss, my friend, but if ever there was a man bound for a better life in Heaven it is surely you, lad. Ye've set a high bar in your life toward which all of us, your fiance, family and friends shall strive, Robert. We shall work with diligence to do honor to your memory."

Carney paused with his head bowed, then slowly turned to the others assembled there and said, "Anyone wish to add a word?" He didn't expect a response, but Ebeneezer Steltenpohl stepped forward.

"I cain't say I knowed young Robert, but durin' the short time I spoke with him and Carney I could see in his eyes and from the words he spoke that he was a man of high value. May he rest in peace." Eb nodded to Carney and stepped back into the circle of onlookers as Carney signaled the boys to lower the coffin. Ephraim asked Willie and his brothers to lift the coffin slightly so he could pull out the rails, then motioned for them to lower it into the grave. When it had settled gently at the bottom and the ropes had been withdrawn, Carney threw the first handful of dirt onto the coffin's top. Others followed suit, and then the boys went to work with their shovels.

The group made its way back to Maudie Russell's front room. She walked beside Carney, tenderly holding his arm. He looked back twice at the grave, then daubed his tears with a handkerchief.

Ephraim made a quick detour to his store for the medical bag, the little basket of Robert's personal items and the boots that he'd promised to keep safe for Carney. Eb and Ephraim sat at the table with Carney while Maudie served coffee and whiskey. Carney gave Ephraim the paper with the inscription for the grave marker, then counted out the money he owed him for the funeral with something extra for the gravediggers. Eb asked if he'd like to sell the three horses and tack back to him. Carney thanked him and took him up on his offer, saying he needed to travel with all possible speed back upriver. Eb said, "I'll put the thieves' horses on the next boat headed downriver. Won't do to have 'em here when the Pennington bunch comes snoopin' round." Maudie said she'd help Carney hail the first upbound steamboat.

With the transactions complete, the men shook hands. "You boys move on, now," Maudie said. "I'll feed this young man a hearty breakfast before he leaves. I'm determined that he'll have at least one decent memory of old Shawneetown." That brought a faint smile from the Irishman.

While he waited for his breakfast, Carney composed a letter to Robert's Paducah relatives explaining the tragedy and informing them of details such as Ephraim's name and the location of the grave. He looked at the personal items that Ephraim and Eb had removed. They were few: coins, pen knife, tie pin, pocket watch, wallet, handkerchief, suspenders, boots. Robert's killer had made off with everything else.

Except for one item, he put the things in the medicine bag and carried boots and bag to the trading post and asked Ephraim to give them to whichever of Robert's relatives reached him first. "I don't know these people at Paducah," Carney said, "but I'd say they'll appear at Shawneetown before many days pass. His kinfolk from Baltimore will no doubt be here in due time, as well."

When he returned to Maudie's cabin he asked her to put his letter to the Paducah relatives on the next downbound packet boat. During his breakfast, with Maudie nursing a cup of coffee across the table, Carney kept looking out the door toward the river. "Don't want to miss the next steamboat," he said.

"You won't miss it. See that team and wagon waiting at the landing? The wagoner's headed upriver, too. He'll hail the boat, no need for you to worry. Everybody in Shawneetown will know when she arrives, anyway. She'll be clangin' the bell and swooshin' water and them big engines'll shake the very ground we walk on."

Just before noon they heard a steamer approaching from downriver. Young barefoot boys ran past the cabin on their way to the landing. Dogs barked and followed the boys. People came out of the scattered cabins, and stopped working in their gardens to watch the steamer *White Eagle* as she eased up to the landing.

Maudie walked with Carney down to the river. "I can't thank you enough for all ye've done, Miss Maudie. Sure, if ever I set out for New Orleans again I'll bide a wee hour hereabouts to say hello."

Before he saw it coming, Maudie hugged him and kissed him on the lips. She smiled as she released him. "I'll make you welcome, Carney, and that's a promise." He took her hand and thanked her again, then tipped his cap, said goodbye and boarded the boat as the bell clanged three times to signal departure. He turned to wave at

44

Maudie, but she walked briskly toward her cabin without looking back.

After having spent only a few minutes to offload a team pulling a cultivator and take on the wagon that had been waiting, the boat churned away from the landing and began plowing upriver. The *White Eagle* was a proud craft, freshly painted with her brass fittings shining, but much smaller than the *St. Augustine*, on which he'd descended this river with his new friends.

Carney leaned on the rail at the stern gazing back across the roiling brown water at the tiny Illinois settlement of Shawneetown. He could not avoid his obsession with the recent devastating events. Confused thoughts spun in his head. How had it come to this?

He'd been in America for only a few lustrous weeks, having come here on a bold impulse seeking adventure. He had met Robert Sandlin, Rachel, her brothers, and had become enamored of Polly Mitchell, a woman the likes of which he hadn't known existed in the world.

But now, he'd been jerked up short, as if awakened from some delightful dream to find he'd been breaking laws, shirking responsibilities, inflicting pain on his friends. Yes, he'd betrayed them all. He struggled with the reality that he'd just buried his best friend, and incredibly, he must now explain Robert's death to those closest to him, his fiance and his family. How could he do that? What could he possibly say that would make the truth any less horrible? He shook his head, trying to divert his mind to less painful thoughts, but it was of no use.

How could he face these people when the cause of Robert's death was so transparent, could be so easily traced to his own criminally negligent behavior? And the final maddening question: What vital part of himself was missing, what heinous exclusion from his character had resulted in this unthinkable tragedy?

It was his hotheadedness, of course, his lack of self-control. Perhaps it had been his growing up without the discipline imposed by a father, or his raging against the inhibitions forced on him by the Catholic Church. He'd heard some men were subject to episodes of violence as the evil offspring of the Irish penchant for drink. Then again, it could be just a quirk in his brain he was born with, some hereditary darkness occurring every third or tenth generation in the

45

afflicted family. He heaved a heavy sigh and reviewed the deadly chain of events leading to the murder of his friend.

It had begun with a fight in Dublin's Greystone Pub. Carney relived that night as he leaned on the rail in his stricken state of guilt. That disturbance had resulted in the death of an old drunk and had prompted the young man's flight to a ship bound the next morning for America. Then a couple of men in a Philadelphia pub had persuaded him to purchase a pistol for his westward journey into an untamed land. He had used the weapon for the first time at the Pittsburgh wharf when a mob of Welsh roustabouts was on the verge of attacking the Morrisons and their outfit as they tried to board the *St. Augustine*.

Then Carney had become enraged at the gambler Slater, the man he caught cheating James Morrison in a game of craps. Later, after the Morrisons had left the steamer, the second run-in with Slater had resulted in his expulsion from the *St. Augustine*, and Robert's decision to go with him. This altercation had set off the course of events that left Robert dead on a remote country lane. Carney had no doubt that had he and Robert never met, his friend would still be on that steamboat headed for Paducah.

# CHAPTER TEN

arly on the morning of Wednesday, August 5th, 1840, the *White Eagle* landed at Vevay. Carney O'Sullivan rented a horse and saddle from old Wiley Campbell at the livery stable and asked directions to the Morrison place at Sugar Branch. Then with a heavy heart he made his way to Mrs. Dumont's house in town, dreading her response to the terrible news he carried.

He was surprised to see several people converging on her front door. When he stepped up on her porch, Julia gasped, "Why Carney O'Sullivan! So soon back from New Orleans? Where's Robert, pray tell? Do come in, young man, and share your adventures. As you can see, I'm entertaining a few friends at morning tea."

Carney held his cap tightly in his hands, his smile stiff, his face pale. "Aye, Mrs. Dumont, so good to see you, but I must have a word with you privately, and I shan't stay long."

Julia seemed to see now the distress in the young man's countenance. She glanced behind her. "Come into the kitchen."

She led him to the inglenook just inside the kitchen door. There she turned and looked up at him expectantly. He paused and swallowed, trying to calm himself in order that the story would make sense to Rachel's beloved teacher. He forced himself to speak slowly, being careful to keep events in proper sequence, sparing the lady all but the most rudimentary details of Robert's death. At the end of his tragic story Carney said, "Now, Mrs. Dumont, you'll have to excuse me. I must make haste to Sugar Branch to tell Rachel, a task I would give anything in this world not to do. Then I shall be off to Baltimore, for Robert's family must be informed, as well."

"Oh, you poor boy, and poor Rachel! Please tell her and Fanny that I will come tomorrow to offer what help I can."

He squeezed her hand in his cold fingers. "I will, Mrs. Dumont. May God bless you, ma'am." Carney turned, rushed through the collecting guests, bolted out the front door, untied his horse and swung into the saddle.

Julia composed herself for a second by the fireplace, then she moved through the door into the front room where her guests were mingling. She nearly bumped into Isaac Stevens, editor of the *Vevay Times*, who had evidently been listening at the door to the kitchen, which stood ajar. She appraised him with teacherly suspicion. "Isaac, did you overhear what that gentleman just told me?"

"Why, ah, beggin' your pardon, Mrs. Dumont, but I couldn't help catchin' a few of his phrases. It seems that Dr. Sandlin, Rachel Morrison's . . . close friend, has met with foul play downriver, is it?"

"That is sadly true, Isaac, and I know your paper comes out tomorrow morning, Thursday. I won't ask you not to print this, but I implore you to swear your staff to secrecy and to not mention it to anyone until your paper appears. That will give Carney time to ride the fifteen miles to Sugar Branch and talk with Rachel before the public becomes aware of this. May I have your promise, Mr. Stevens?"

"Why, ma'am, I couldn't possibly get this item into tomorrow's paper, having only just heard it. Still, I shall keep the story to myself until this gentleman has had ample time to reach the Morrisons."

Carney put his horse into a gallop from Mrs. Dumont's house through the town until he reached the foot of Vevay Hill, a distance of some sixty rods, then he allowed the animal to slow to a brisk walk. He needed time to collect his thoughts for Rachel's sake, but all that came to him was more self-recrimination.

He rode with growing despondency, recalling that he'd left his poor widowed mother in Dublin without even a goodbye. Then on his voyage down the Ohio River aboard the *St. Augustine* he'd bidden farewell to Polly Mitchell at Cincinnati, the girl he now realized was the love of his life. At Vevay, Indiana, the Morrisons had departed; Rachel, James and Sylvester, another goodbye to dear friends.

By his own unrestrained behavior against the Welsh rousters and the gambler Jack Slater on the *St. Augustine*, he'd been forced to leave yet another friend, Captain Wilmer Pegg of that fair vessel.

And finally, Robert, who in the short space of but a few weeks on the *St. Augustine* and during their overland jaunt had become his best friend. Now he, too, had been left behind, but unlike the others, Robert was now in his grave, and Carney felt his friend's death might as well have been by his, Carney's, own hand.

In fact, he realized, over the past three months he had left not one, but three dead men in his destructive wake. First was the drunkard in the Greystone Pub in Dublin, who, though Carney couldn't be certain he'd died, had at least suffered injury when attacked by the drinking mob that Carney led. There followed the recent pernicious events that had taken the lives of the horse thief and his dear friend Robert.

For the first time in his life, Carney began to question his own character. Was there some flaw in him that precluded compassion for his fellow man? How had he become so unfeeling, so unconcerned with the welfare of others around him? Did his easy wit and gregarious nature draw people to him only to suffer dire consequences because of his lack of caring?

He rode on toward Sugar Branch, reliving each lost opportunity or hurtful action, the voices in his head torturing him. He probed his thoughts, desperate to understand how he had failed each of those who'd become close to him.

There just seemed to be a sinister creature within him that eventually caused hurt to anyone who came near him. Frantic to avoid this poison, this insanity, Carney knew he must find a way to escape the pall of melancholia that smothered him.

The only escape he saw was to find Polly Mitchell and make her his forever. After all, hadn't she called him a man of substance, so much more mature than the frivolous fellows she'd trooped with in her Cincinnati music school days? Even now, the very thought of her gave him a measure of peace.

He was certain that in partnership with her he could fend off his demons, if he could find her and somehow convince her to be his wife. If only she had not already promised herself to another.

# CHAPTER ELEVEN

Noah Taylor, having ridden to Vevay to pick up some liniment and a hog ringer for his parents back at Sugar Branch, learned at the Schenck Store that a young stranger had walked up from the wharfboat this morning. The visitor had rented a riding horse from Wiley Campbell, the livery master, and asked directions to the Morrison place at Sugar Branch. Noah hastened to the livery stable and quizzed drunken old Wiley about the newcomer. He learned precious little, other than the man's destination and that he had to see some unnamed folks before going to Sugar Branch. With that, Noah took off at a gallop for the Morrison place, knowing they awaited the arrival of Rachel's young doctor friend.

After Noah shared his news, venturing that the rider would probably be there around midday, Fanny shooed the menfolk out of the cabin so they wouldn't scare Robert off. She and Mariah started preparing dinner. Rachel stayed on the porch peering up the East Enterprise Road through the shimmering August heat.

She felt her spirits begin to sink when she saw the figure approaching up the near slope from the Sugar Branch ford. Even at this distance she could see the rider was wearing an Irish cap like the one she had seen Carney O'Sullivan wearing every day on the *St. Augustine*. For what seemed a lifetime she watched the silhouette grow larger. She was drawn as if in a dream toward the road, peering into the withering heat, supporting herself on the gatepost, her fears becoming more real with each step of the approaching horse.

51

Carney stopped in front of her, dismounted, dropped the reins and removed his cap, then stood still as a stone looking at Rachel. His mouth moved, but no words escaped him, and she saw his chin quiver. She stood for breathless seconds, her hopes powerless against the truth in his sad eyes and mournful demeanor.

Her scream brought John Wesley and the boys from where they'd been watching in the barn. Her arm, which had supported her against the post, sagged and her head lolled back exposing her death-white face to the sky. Carney's strong arms caught her as she fell. Fanny and Mariah, with little Emerson peering between them, stood frozen for an instant in the cabin door, then came running.

Carney, following Fanny and Mariah, carried the unconscious Rachel through the dogtrot to her bedroom where the women laid her down and loosened her clothing. The men huddled in the passageway of the double cabin while James introduced Carney to his father, brothers and Noah Taylor. John Wesley glanced apprehensively at the cabin door and said, "Mr. O'Sullivan, we need to get some things straight, here. We'll set in the shade of the porch. You must be dry. Em, bring him a cup of water." The men and boys swabbed tense faces in the sweltering heat. John Wesley and Carney sat in the two rocking chairs; the others lay about on the porch floor or leaned against the posts.

Carney hung his cap on his knee, thanked Emerson for the water, drank it down in one draft then looked at John Wesley. "It's sorry I am to be bringin' ye this woeful news, sir." He then described for them in a halting voice the events that culminated in Robert's death. John Wesley and the others remained fixed in stunned silence when he finished. Carney leaned forward and put his face in his hands, releasing a pent-up sigh.

At that moment Mariah appeared at the door of the dogtrot and called for water. Sylvester sprang to answer her request while the others slowly gathered in front of Mariah where she stood, one step above the dusty ground in the doorway. "We'll bathe her and do what we can. They's boiled pork and taters and beans on the crane. Go ahead and eat. When you're finished bring Mr. O'Sullivan over. She may be able to listen by then, and she'll want to . . . know."

As the group filed into the cabin, James asked, "Can you stay with us for a little spell, Carney? It'd be a godsend for Rachel to

52

have you here for at least a day or two, seein' as how you and her and Robert was real close friends."

"I'll stay as long as she needs me, James. Tis the very least I can do."

Late that evening Rachel recovered enough to ask Carney for the tragic details. He sat in the dim golden lamplight near her bed, hat in his hands. Fanny and Mariah stood near the door. Rachel listened stoically, eyes gazing at the ceiling. After several minutes, during which Carney shared the dreadful facts in a soft and halting voice, Rachel brought her handkerchief to her face and held it there with both hands, sudden sobs racking her body. Mariah moved close and gently caressed her arm.

Fanny whispered, "That's enough for tonight, Carney. She'll have questions tomorrow." And later, to Mariah outside she said, "We must be watchful for the safety of the unborn child."

Rachel slept in the glimmering light of a low-burning lamp on her dresser, under the watchful eye of Mariah. Noah had gone home and Fanny told the boys to double up in the cabin loft so Carney would have a bed. Nobody felt like sleeping, so all except Rachel and Mariah congregated on the porch, sitting on chairs, benches or the floor.

To avoid moths and bugs they lit no lamps, and in the long silence a screech owl's mournful whinny lent a mood to their reflections. Somewhere off in the woods a fox yapped, and Bud, the ancient bluetick hound, could be heard struggling to sit up. He sniffed the air half-heartedly, then with a soft whine he folded his arthritic bones back down, and dropped his chin to the floor with a wistful sigh.

A breeze stirred, bringing late-summer scent from the corn patch and Fanny's withered kitchen garden. The outer darkness, relieved only by starlight and the occasional firefly, slowed their thoughts, mellowed their grief.

James began slowly, "I hear'd Rachel tell Robert and Carney they oughta travel on foot for a piece, see how lucky they was to be on a boat, but if it hadna been for me gettin' drawed into Slater's crap game Robert woulda been alive today."

Sylvester shifted on his bench. "But if I'd of let you learn your lesson without snivelin' to Carney about it, that whole Slater thing woulda slid by with no trouble."

"Aye, but lads, sure and it was my nature in the end that done poor Robert in," Carney said. "I could've handled Jack Slater a hundred ways better'n I did. But no, I had to vent me hot blood on his scruffy hide, and look where it got us. No, gentlemen, it was me played the role of the idjit and now we're all payin' for it, especially poor Miss Rachel."

John Wesley let the sorrowful silence grow long before his resonant voice came forth like a benediction. "I reckon they's enough fault to go round. Several of us can look back and find somethin' in this that lays heavy on his conscience. I never met the young man but from what I've hear'd, we could all do well to live by his example, and he's done left that as his gift for us, if we'll but use it. The Lord expects each of us now to earn a little of what Robert's give us."

Carney stayed three days with the Morrisons, spending time at Rachel's bedside, alone and with her kinfolk. He shared Rachel's tears, answering her questions with truth and tenderness.

Mrs. Dumont arrived early on the second day, helping where she could. She made soup, washed dishes, hung the washing on the line and took her turn sitting with Rachel. John Wesley took Julia back to Vevay in the evening. There would have been hardly any place for her to sleep.

On the fourth morning, Carney shook hands with John Wesley and the boys, hugged Mariah and Fanny, and went to spend one last moment to say goodbye to Rachel.

She asked him to help her out of bed, and she saw him to her bedroom door. Just before leaving he pressed a small object into her hand. In answer to her bewildered look, Carney said, "It's a small token to be sure, dear Rachel, but he'd want you to have his pocket watch." He bent to kiss her forehead, squeezed her hand and went out the door with tears leaking down his cheeks. Nodding to the menfolk gathered at the hitch rail, he donned his cap, mounted his horse and departed on the first leg of his journey to Baltimore.

Rachel brought Robert's watch to her lips, then removed the chain with his engagement ring from around her neck. Closing her

54

hands over these, her only earthly amulets touched by his life, his presence, she sat on her bed, tears flowing unchecked.

She spoke prayerfully in a barely audible voice. "Oh, Robert, Robert, you're gone so suddenly, before we could begin our life together or truly know each other. Gone . . . . So unreal this dark stroke, as if you'll come and wake me from this nightmare that draws the very life from me."

She was silent, then, for several moments. When she continued, whether conscious of it or not, she spoke with greater resolve, as if she was turning to face a decision.

"The flood of life will carry me from this time, my love, but I shall never be without you. You will be near me every day and every night of my years until at last I shall join you in a better life on high. Your name will grace my every prayer, Robert. This is not a goodbye, not an end. It is but a pledge, my oath that I shall never leave you, Robert, never forsake the memory of your handsome face, your golden kindness. Though our love was never consummated, you shall live within me as long as I draw breath, and I shall love you forever, Robert Sandlin."

She rose, then, and slipped the ring and watch into a drawer of her dresser. She was again sitting on the edge of her bed when Mariah came through the door, stopping abruptly, seemingly taken aback at her sister's firm countenance. Rachel nodded and reached for Mariah to help her to her feet.

# CHAPTER TWELVE

The sisters walked across the dogtrot to the kitchen, Rachel blotting her puffed eyes, unsteady on her feet, Mariah holding her arm. Rachel asked her to find Sylvester. When he arrived she said, "I want you to hitch up the team and wagon and take me somewhere."

"Where?"

"I'll tell you after we've started." Mariah and Fanny looked at each other, then intently at Rachel.

Sylvester soon drew up the team and wagon in front of the cabin. Rachel came out of her bedroom in a different dress with her face washed and powdered, her hair combed and pinned up in a bun under her bonnet. Sylvester said, "You look nice, sis," then he helped her up to the seat. As the horses approached the road he gave her an enquiring glance and held up both hands in which he held the lines, his thumbs pointing east and west.

"Turn east," she said.

Sylvester drove slowly as they made their way toward the Sugar Branch ford, then started up the slope on the other side. "Turn up Sugar Branch Lane here."

The twelve-year-old eyed his older sister. "I reckon you're goin' to see Samuel Cunningham. I'd be obliged if you'd tell me what you got up your sleeve, for I ain't ready fer no fussin' nor killin'. Should I of brought the shotgun? Seems more a job for Pop, don't it?"

56

"Don't be silly. I have some serious questions for him to answer, though he doesn't know it yet." Sylvester's eyes opened wide, but he returned his gaze to the road and kept quiet.

Sylvester went to the Cunninghams' cabin door while Rachel waited on the wagon. Sam's mother directed the boy to the barn, then she spied Rachel and called, "Won't you come in, child? You'll take a sun stroke out there."

"Thank you, Mrs. Cunningham, but I just need a word with Samuel."

Sylvester turned to fetch Sam, but came up short when he appeared at the barn door, his face showing slack-jawed surprise. After a moment's hesitation Sam walked slowly toward the wagon, his eyes fixed on Rachel.

Rachel's voice was subdued, but she held her back straight, her gaze riveted on Sam. "Good morning, Sam. I need to speak with you privately. Where can we go?"

He had reached the wagon and now stood looking up at her, his eyes still confused. "Well . . . ah, Pa's in the barn and Ma's in the cabin. I guess we could go . . . uh . . . ."

"Get on the wagon. Sylvester, drive us on down by the creek to a shady place." Without a word, Sam climbed up to sit beside her on the seat, neither saying a word until Sylvester stopped the horses with their front hooves in a shallow ford where they could drink. Tall sycamores protected them from the blazing sun. "Sylvester, hand me the lines, then walk on up the creek for a few minutes." When he stepped down, she moved to the far edge of the seat from Sam, wrapped the lines around the brake handle and turned to face him.

"Have you heard about Robert Sandlin?"

Sam took his hat off and turned it in his hands between his knees. His long black hair was shining with sweat where his hatband had pressed it down. He did not look at her. "I reckon everybody in the county's heard about it by now."

"Robert and I were engaged to be married."

"Your brother told me that, too."

"And then you gave him a beating when he tried to defend my honor."

"That's a damn lie! He come at me and I just grabbed him. He still head-butted me in the mouth, split my lip and loosened a coupla teeth. I shoved him away then but it weren't my fault he hit his head on the door frame."

"Just like it isn't your fault I'm pregnant with your child? James said you called me a loose woman and claimed I asked for everything I got that night in the Gibbs barn. You even said Robert is the father of this child."

"Look, Rachel, I don't want us to go on fussin' like this."

"No, Sam, I want you to hear this. At first when Robert asked I refused to say I'd marry him. He insisted I tell him the reason, and I had to admit I was pregnant by you. Do you know what he said? 'Do you love that man?' After I said I did not, and the baby was the result of your forcing me, he said, 'Then I'll be a father to the baby and love it as much as I love you.' That's the kind of man he was, Sam. That's the kind of man I was going to marry, but now he's gone."

Sam raised his head and gazed off into the trees with an anguished expression, then spoke in a penitent voice. "Aw, Rachel, I was just angry when I said them bad things that wasn't true . . . and I'm sorry to hear about your Robert."

"So, where are we now? Because of us, but really because of *you*, there are now three where there were two. What are you going to do about that, Sam?"

"Well . . . what do you want to do about it?"

"It isn't what I *want* to do, it's what we *have to* do, Sam."

Sam remained quiet for a few moments. Then he straightened and met eyes with her. "You can ask anybody in Cotton Township, Rachel, I ain't been courtin' no girls since way back when you went off to New York with your brothers. Now, I said somethin' else a while back, somethin' true and good, somethin' you prob'ly don't even remember. Last time I saw you I told you I loved you, and that I wanted to be your husband. I said you'd come to love me and we'd be married someday. All that speech got me was your showing me the door of your pa's cabin, but that ain't changed the way I feel."

"Let me make one thing clear, Sam Cunningham. I do not love you, but I love and will always love this child growing inside of me. Going through Cincinnati on our way to New York we saw a girl drown her newborn baby in the river, and I still see that in my nightmares. I will do anything I have to do to bring my child into the world and help it grow.

"In this day and time a young woman can't go it alone with a child, yet I refuse to ask my folks to take us in. God knows they've already raised nine young'uns and that's enough for one lifetime. So that leaves you, Sam. We have to take responsibility for what you did in the Gibbs barn, and make things right for this child. Now, Sam, are you man enough to face your obligations and marry me? For if you're not . . . ."

Sam interrupted her. "Yes, Rachel. It's what I wanted all along." His eyes brightened and he said, "We'll sure'nuf make things right for the child and right for each other. Let's go tell Ma and Pa."

"No, Sam. We'll have a proper meeting between your folks and mine. Today's Saturday. We'll come over here to discuss the marriage tomorrow afternoon. No need to give voice to wedding plans to anyone but family. There will be time enough for prideful talk after the baby comes."

"I'll have Ma fix Sunday dinner, then."

"Don't do that, Sam, this will be strictly business. We'll get here after dinner and leave before supper."

Rachel waved for Sylvester who had been sitting under a Sycamore chewing a grass stem, gazing off across the creek. They dropped Sam off at his parents' cabin, then continued west on the East Enterprise road. Grasshoppers scattered in the dry weeds at the roadside, the straight-up sun casting no shadows in the noonday heat. Sylvester mopped his face with a sleeve, then stopped the team in the shade and leaned forward to slap a horsefly dead before it could deliver its painful bloodsucking bite into Jill's rump.

Rachel sat in grim silence on the wagon seat with her hands clasped tightly in her lap. Her eyes never met Sylvester's shy glances.

On the way home, Rachel's mind buzzed with the awareness brought by her pregnancy and now the impending marriage. She realized that in her youthful naïvete before that evening in the Gibbs barn she had assumed human beings to be somehow superior to "lower animals."

For as long as she could remember she had casually observed the life cycles of pets, farm animals and wildlife. They'd once had a little terrier, Trixie, that Rachel considered hers. After Trixie mated with the Oakses' Jack Russell she grew larger, gave birth, nurtured her puppies and produced milk for them. Yet, not once did it occur to Rachel that both she and Trixie belonged to the same family called mammals. She never sensed her mammalian sisterhood with cows, mares, sows and ewes.

Rachel had learned from overheard conversations between women and girls, that when a woman's episodes of monthly bleeding stopped, and she became afflicted with morning sickness and sore breasts, she was likely to be with child. Only when this happened to her on the journey to Rushford did she begin to wonder about her place among God's creatures.

It was simple enough to connect her condition to Sam's attack on her in the Gibbs barn, when he forced himself inside her. In one lightning flash of comprehension she saw for the first time that her body obeyed the same laws of reproduction as the other animals with which she was so familiar. She talked to her mother after her return from New York, and Fanny expressed regret that she'd never broached the subject with her daughter. She told Rachel she didn't have the words for it.

The wagon bounced along as new questions occurred to Rachel. Could dogs, cats, rabbits communicate, each with their own kind, like human beings? Could bears and deer feel pain, just like people? Years ago, Uncle David Morrison in Rushford told her that when he shot a deer the animal felt no pain. "It's like they expect to be hunted, killed and used for our food," he'd assured her. At the time his answer satisfied her, but now the question was framed in a different light for Rachel, of being personally involved in the creation of new life. Could mankind and animals be members of one huge family of life on earth?

Could animals think, foresee danger and learn ways to avoid it? She'd seen animals protecting their young, like the time she and James had found a mother robin dead on her nest having shielded her hatchlings in a hailstorm. Another time she'd seen a vixen crouch snarling at the mouth of her den rather than abandon her kits.

60

Speaking of these ideas to her Sugar Branch neighbors would be futile at best. The uppermost concern of these families of the soil was to keep their annually-increasing brood of children fed and sheltered for another season. To them, Rachel's esoteric dreaming would be naught but girlish fancy. Were she to give voice to her ideas and her questions, they would be met with glazed eyes, and minds as worn-down as the latch of a cabin door. Her less generous neighbors might sneer down her ideas as folly, even blasphemy, but Rachel had discovered a compelling thought, a larger frame of reference in which to place her life and that of her unborn child.

The dread of approaching motherhood now seemed mitigated for Rachel by a new understanding of the world, a new sense of belonging to the larger family of life. Dared she expect these thoughts to provide solace in the approaching dark hours of labor?

# CHAPTER THIRTEEN

The Morrisons gathered round the kitchen table, Rachel, Mariah and their parents sitting, the boys hovering nearby to hear what Rachel had to say. Fanny said, "Honey, are you sure marrying Samuel is the right thing to do? You just said you don't love him, and with Robert so recently passed . . . ."

"Mother, marrying Sam is the only practical course for us and our families. Yes, I still grieve for Robert, but I will grieve for him the rest of my life. Sam and I have to think of the baby now, and act quickly to make a secure home for it."

"The Cunninghams are Baptists," Fanny said. "Don't you think we ought to take Preacher Seals with us? He's their pastor."

"He isn't a proper preacher, Mother, no more a man of the cloth than you, Pop, or one of the boys here. He's vowed he was called to the Lord's work, but I'll venture he can't even read the Bible. Besides, Mother, I want just you and Pop to go with me to the Cunninghams." At this last pronouncement, Philander winked at James, then made a pretend gesture of clearing sweat from his brow and flicking it on the floor. Sylvester nodded and grinned.

After greetings were exchanged on Sunday afternoon, the families seated themselves on benches at the Cunninghams' long kitchen table. Sam and Rachel each sat beside their parents and faced each other across the wide polished board with a sugar bowl on a diamond of rough-woven cloth in the middle, cups and matching napkins at each place. Mrs. Cunningham poured tea, having brewed

62

it beforehand and chilled it in an unglazed earthen jar. A sprig of mint leaves decorated each glass. The sweltering guests gratefully accepted.

After Sam's mother took her place at the table next to John, the Cunninghams nervously looked to Sam to begin the discussion. He scratched his arm and avoided meeting eyes with Rachel, reluctant to launch upon what to him must have been a thorny subject. He finally cleared his throat, looked in her direction and said, "How you think we oughta do this?"

Rachel scanned the faces before her, then asked her mother, "Do you and Pop have anything to say first?" Fanny's face tensed with surprise before she collected herself and said, "No, just say what you told us."

The girl sighed, glanced down at the table before she said, "First I'll explain everything that went on between Sam and me. There must be no misunderstandings about this."

Elizabeth Cunningham, her body bent and shriveled by arthritis, leaned forward with her elbows on the table, winced briefly at the pain, then directed a kindly expression at Rachel. "That'd be a good idea, sweetie. We hardly know a thing about your courtship, Sam bein' a poor hand to confide in his old parents, ain't that right, John."

Sam's father only grunted and nodded. He briefly lifted his gaze to glance at John Wesley and Fanny, then resumed scratching the white sun scabs on the back of his hand. Sam seemed embarrassed, leaning an elbow on the table, cradling his chin in his palm, eyes downcast.

Rachel started speaking in a low voice. "Sam, if I say anything untrue, feel free to correct me, won't you?" He nodded without looking at her.

Rachel began then, slowly weaving the story of how she and Sam flirted and spoke briefly with each other at the Morrison cabin-raising, then, almost a year later, their walk in the forest after supper when the neighbors gathered for a log-rolling at the Cunningham place. "He let me wear his coat because it was chilly that night. We stopped in the woods and Sam leaned against a tree and pulled me to him. He kissed me and touched my breasts, and I allowed him for a little while. I had a girlish crush on him then, but had never learned what such things can lead to."

She told how they sat by the burning log pile before they went back to the gathering at the cabin where people were singing. She paused and noticed that Sam seemed to have lost some of his shyness and was looking at her with the beginnings of a smile. "Do you remember those times, Sam?"

"I do," he said. "I remember the feelin' I had for you then, and still now."

Rachel glanced from one to another of the listeners. "Those were days of innocent bliss for me. I thought Sam hung the moon, like many other girls around Sugar Branch. I'd heard them talking about him at church before ever I laid eyes on him. They were giggling trying to guess what those initials 'C.V.' in Samuel C.V. Cunningham stand for. I still don't know. Tell me, Sam."

"Carson Victor, after some of our people in Carolina." Sam's eyes had brightened, and Rachel needed him to be alert for what was coming.

She related the story of starting school in Vevay that fall, studying with Mrs. Dumont, rooming with the Dufours on Ferry Street. She didn't see Sam again until old Ned died in March and she and the boys were set to go to New York for the Morgan horses. The Gibbses had a going-away party for them on Saturday night before they left on Monday morning.

Rachel said she'd hoped to see Sam at the party, and her heartbeat surged when he walked in late. Rachel met Sam's eyes across the table, but she did not smile as she concentrated on the next part of her story.

At the party everyone was prancing and swirling. She remembered her father playing the fiddle with Ira Vanosdol calling the dance. John Wesley grinned. "We played and danced up a storm," he said. John and Elizabeth nodded.

Rachel continued, saying Sam seemed in a hurry that night, and he asked her to come outside to talk. He admitted to having another girlfriend since she'd last seen him, and he asked if she had taken up with some boy in Vevay.

Sam told her that courtship didn't go anywhere and the other girl was now planning to marry someone else. Rachel assured him she had no boyfriend in town. It seemed their feelings for each other had grown stronger than before.

John Cunningham said, "S'cuse me, Miss Rachel, this is a cute little story, but what's it got to do with you and Sam marryin'?"

"Bear with me Mr. Cunningham. I think you'll have your answer in a moment. It was at that point Sam took me to the barn," she said, "to get away from the noise he said. Young boys were racing about in the dark playing games, and I recall Sam telling me about his plans to become a blacksmith or some such. Do I have it right so far, Sam?"

Sam said, "Yeah," but his face had tensed again.

Rachel continued her story. She had been caught up in the romantic feeling of being alone with Sam in the mysterious darkness of the barn. He kissed her and she kissed him back. Then he took her into a granary where Thomas Gibbs kept clean wheat straw for bedding the stalls. They sat in the straw and she heard him reaching in his pocket. Sam gave her his grandmother's ring, saying he wanted them to be engaged to be married. He tried to slip the ring on her finger, but Rachel told him she'd have to think about it, and they'd decide after she returned from New York. Sam told her to just keep the ring, then, and Rachel agreed, tying it into her handkerchief.

Sam's mother seemed surprised at the mention of her mother's wedding ring. She turned sharply to Sam and said, "You should have asked me before you took Mother's ring, Samuel."

"Do you recall what happened next, Sam?" Rachel said.

Sam ducked his head and mumbled, "Ain't no use in tellin' any more. Cain't you just leave it be? I thought we was goin' to plan our marriage today, not rehash all this."

"That's what I thought, too," echoed John Cunningham.

"It's important for both our families to know these particulars, Sam, Mr. Cunningham." All four parents leaned forward.

Rachel folded and refolded a napkin in her hands on the table, but her voice remained steady as she continued. "In the barn that night, after I said I'd keep Sam's grandmother's ring tied in my handkerchief, he kissed me roughly and touched me again, saying that when two people are engaged the man can have his woman whenever he wants. I protested that we were *not* engaged, but he forced himself on me. I tried to stop him, but he was too strong. He entered me then, and did as he wished. He left me stunned and in pain, my dress soiled and torn, the one my New York grandmother had made for me."

Fanny turned to stare at Sam and seemed ready to say something, but Rachel spoke first. "When I regained my senses I heard the distant sounds of music and dancing coming from the cabin and the hoofbeats of a horse galloping away."

"Mercy, child," Mrs. Cunningham said, "must you describe all this . . . this ugliness so vividly?" She turned to her son. "Samuel, did you really harm this poor girl in that way?"

Her husband said, "Now, Lizzie, little missy was playin' with fire. What was he s'posed to do?" Elizabeth's pleading eyes did not turn away from her son. Her question hung in the air like a storm cloud as Sam squirmed on the hard bench.

Sam could not respond to his parents' words. He only bowed his head in silence, his cheeks reddening and a hank of his long hair falling across his damp forehead. Mrs. Cunningham brought her hand to her mouth. Her eyes filled with tears as she turned back to Rachel.

"I'm sorry, Mrs. Cunningham. I'm sure you raised him to be a gentler person than that."

Fanny and John Wesley sat with stricken faces and clenched jaws. The lingering pause was filled only with audible breathing around the table. Finally, Rachel spoke again.

"Now, everyone here knows what went on during what I shall loosely call our 'courtship,' and you know my feelings. Sam, do you still want to marry me?"

Sam looked at Rachel for the first time in a while. He said, "I already told you I was sorry for what I done in the Gibbs barn, and that I think the world of you, Rachel. Now, we'll have to work out our differences, but I still want you for my wife."

"Our 'differences,' as you call them are considerable, Sam, and only some of them are being aired here today. Where did you gallop off to that night, Sam? And what about the baby? Do you still seriously think it is Robert Sandlin's child?" Sam's parents had not been prepared for this final shock.

"Who? What's this about some other man?" John Cunningham sputtered, then looked at his wife. "Did you know 'bout this?"

"Mr. and Mrs. Cunningham, Robert Sandlin was a young man I met on the steamboat coming home from New York. I was in love with him, but he's dead now. Sam?"

"Nah, now Rachel, I just said that 'cause I was mad. I know it was me made you with child, and I'm willing to do my best to provide for you and the baby."

Rachel stared at Sam, her eyes burning into him. She wanted to tell those seated before her that if her Robert were still alive she wouldn't give this rough-hewn young savage a second look. She would shun him, and would never, ever consider marrying him.

Instead, she said, "Sam, it is for the baby and the baby alone that I will marry you, and if I knew any other way to provide for this child I would take that course, but I don't."

Sam could not meet her eyes. His only response was a sullen nod.

"Having said that, I will enter into this marriage intending to carry out my wifely duties, to be a helpmeet and a support to you."

Sam eyed her hopefully, as if expecting her to say more. The two older men gazed intently at their hands folded on the table. The mothers blotted tears from their eyes.

When normal breathing resumed around the table, and slow conversation commenced, the group got down to the business of planning a wedding. An hour later the plans were laid out to the satisfaction of all. The ceremony would take place two weeks hence, on Saturday, the 22nd of August, to be held at the Sugar Branch United Methodist Church, where John Wesley and Fanny worshiped. Reverend Allen Wiley would conduct the service, with Reverend Russell Bigelow assisting.

# CHAPTER FOURTEEN

*F*anny and John Wesley were proud of their church, though for want of a Presbyterian church in Sugar Branch, and it being too far to Vevay to attend the Presbyterian church there, Fanny had joined her husband's chosen house of worship, honoring the Morrisons' long-held religious preference. Just before they left Rushford, New York in the spring of '38, Fanny had been among the charter members at the organizational meeting of the Rushford First Presbyterian Church.

The Methodist church at Sugar Branch had been organized in 1816 and services were held in the Macedonia log school, later known as Morton School, about a mile northeast of the village. When they arrived at Sugar Branch, John Wesley and Fanny became loyal members, as did Charles and Eunice Gary when they came to the settlement. Soon, both John Wesley and Charles were serving as trustees of the church.

Their families were close friends, for both had immigrated to Sugar Branch from Rushford, the Morrisons around 1838 and the Garys a couple of years later, first residing briefly at Rising Sun, Indiana. It was on Charles and Eunice Garys' flatboat that the Morrison teenagers, Rachel, James and Sylvester, with their three Morgan horses, had floated down to Pittsburgh on the Allegheny River in the spring of 1840. The teenagers had then booked passage on the steamer *St. Augustine* for the voyage down the Ohio to Vevay. This was the same Eunice Gary who had betrayed the Morrison youngsters at Pittsburgh.

After both families settled at Sugar Branch, the Morrison teenagers had made an uneasy truce with Eunice. She condemned Rachel, in particular, for allowing herself to become pregnant by the Cunningham boy. She'd discovered this fact from Rachel's morning sickness on their earlier flatboat journey together.

Charles Gary was a much more amiable person than his hard-bitten wife. He signed Rachel and Sam's marriage license as a witness before Arthur Twineham, Justice of the Peace.

Rachel's wedding Saturday was like all the other Saturdays in August, hot and humid. Jane Lee lent Rachel her own wedding dress that she'd worn when she married David in the Baptist church out at Versailles. It was an eggshell white satin gown, full cut with a high neck and accompanied by a wide-brimmed white hat adorned by Fanny with a veil and a small bud bouquet of wild roses, lillies and a sprig of English ivy on one side. The outfit drew exclamations of approval from the assembled guests, but Rachel found herself nearly smothered in its heavy folds. She learned later that Jane had married in December, not August.

All the families of Sugar Branch were represented among the sweaty audience in the schoolhouse. Women's fans accomplished little in moving the fusty air. Laura Craig, a classmate of Rachel's at Mrs. Dumont's school, sang two songs with Marilee Morton accompanying her on the piano. While Laura sang, Rachel and her bridesmaids, Phoebe Cotton and sister Mariah sweltered in the anteroom, fanning themselves furiously. Rachel prayed she wouldn't faint before the ceremony even began.

Sam, his best man Dewey Sexton, and attendant Luther Pavy entered with the preachers. Sam's thick black hair had been shorn to a length considerably above his shoulders. He and his seconds wore black suits and cravats in fresh white collars. They wore their best boots that showed shining evidence of having been recently rubbed with stove black.

Rachel's thoughts during the ceremony were as much of Robert as of Sam. When she repeated the vows, "I Rachel Morrison do take thee . . . take thee Samuel Cunningham to be my lawful wedded husband," she had almost said Robert's name.

Fanny had mercifully thought to bring a more comfortable dress and shoes for her daughter to change into after the ceremony. Everyone gratefully fled the schoolhouse for the fresh air and faint breeze in the grove of towering tulip trees behind the church to enjoy a picnic dinner.

The two old men, Dicey Cole and Frank Bascom, who had roasted the pig at the Cunninghams' log-rolling, received so many compliments from their earlier success that they were enlisted for an encore at the wedding. All the families in attendance brought baskets of side dishes and table service. Children scampered about soiling their go-to-meetin' finery while men gathered out by the horses and wagons and passed around flasks of shine. A few old women cast them scathing looks for desecrating the ceremony.

As the women vacated the schoolhouse following the men, Rachel tossed her bouquet over her shoulder in the direction of the gaggle of young women and girls on the schoolhouse steps, and Laura caught it. The others kidded her about being the next to marry and asked who the lucky boy would be. Laura blushed an appropriate shade of pink.

Eunice Gary went about among the female guests whispering that Rachel's wearing of the white veil, which Sam raised when the minister said he could kiss her, was a slap in the face of Christian marriage tradition. Everyone knew they'd already consummated their marriage and there would soon be a baby to prove the point.

Near the end of the wedding dinner, when the bride and groom were going through the food line, Eunice came up to Rachel, and in a stage whisper asked, "When is your due date, dear?"

Rachel had anticipated what Eunice was up to, and she had an answer ready. With a wide smile she said, "Why, Mrs. Gary, so good of you to come. You do so brighten the day for everyone." Sylvester, close behind them in line, sniggered through his nose.

In late afternoon Nell Leatherbury cast a wary eye at the greenish-black cloud approaching from the northwest. "That's a juberous-lookin' cloud yonder. Get the kids inside a'fore they get blowed away."

One of the crones who'd cast mean looks at the men imbibing by the wagons said, "Let the men stay out there and reap God's fury. It'll serve 'em right!"

The air grew deathly calm except for distant lightning and thunder. Presently a breeze picked up, sending large raindrops to puff the dust in front of the steps to the schoolhouse door. Hailstones rattled on the building's oak shingles and the breeze became powerful gusts. In minutes, all the celebrants had crowded back into the building, laughing, shouting, the men threatening to shove the children and young girls out into the downpour. People scurried to close the windows.

Sam and Rachel, finding themselves crowded into the anteroom, had a moment to catch their breath and take stock of how far they'd come this afternoon. Rachel felt as if the two of them had somehow made their peace for the time being.

Sam said, "Well, we're finally married. It's all over but the hollerin', now."

Rachel looked up at him. "Yes, the first part is over."

"You ain't feelin' sick are you?"

"No, but I'm anxious to get home and rest a bit before I take stock of what Mariah and Mother and them left us in the way of food. I'd hate for my husband to go hungry for our first meal together." Her own words teased a wan smile from her lips, and Sam took the opportunity to kiss his bride again. She noted that his touch this time was smooth and gentle. For an instant she relived the moment when he'd first kissed her as they leaned against that tree long months ago. She could not deny the small sunbeam of happiness she felt, now that they were married and she had done all she could this day to secure their baby's future.

Her thoughts were quickly wrenched back to the concerns of the moment for, even above the roar of the storm, they heard a sizzling sound instantly followed by a sharp bang louder than a shotgun. Everyone rushed to the windows in time to see mist, bark fragments and small limbs exploding from the tallest tree in the grove. Through the driving rain they saw a zigzagging yellow crack left on the tree trunk by the lightning bolt as it raced to ground, ripping bark off the tree. The crowd groaned in awe as the huge trunk divided with loud splitting sounds, one half of it teetering in slow motion before crashing down, barely missing the schoolhouse.

Mariah, her face pressed close to a window pane watching the storm, drew back in fear at the lightningbolt. With her hand upon her

71

heaving chest she said, almost out loud, "Lord, God a'mighty! That was Robert Sandlin, sure as the world, lettin' his feelings be known from Heaven, and he almost come right through the roof!"

Aaron Cochran, Mariah's fiance standing close beside her, said, "What'd you say, hon?"

The newlyweds spent their honeymoon night in the cabin on a claim owned by the Cunninghams at Melville, near Sugar Branch. Sam's parents had invited them to make their home there.

Fanny and John Wesley shared whispers in bed that night. Fanny said she was sorry that Rachel felt she had to marry Sam, and she hoped he would be gentler with Rachel in their nuptial bed than he had been in the Gibbs barn.

"Last summer I passed by the swimmin' hole down on Indian Creek on my way to Madison," John Wesley said. "I stopped to rest the horses in the shade and watch the boys swim and play in the deep pool under that big oak. Some of the kids was swinging on a rope hanging from a high limb and droppin' into the water. They was swimming naked, and Sam come backstroking across the stream from the far bank, his stiff manhood creatin' a wake of its own. Oscar Ramseyer yelped, 'Sam you oughta tie a flag on that bruiser and enter it in the Fourth of July parade.'"

Fanny stifled a giggle and said, "John Wesley! Shame on you and your smutty stories. This is no time for jokes."

His voice, more serious now, came from the darkness. "Hit weren't no joke, Fan. It's a calcified fact."

"Poor Rachel!" she said. "I've said many a prayer for our little girl, and you should be praying, too, instead of talking such tom-foolery."

"From the way she talked at the Cunninghams a week ago Sunday," he said, "I reckon she can take care of herself tonight. Now, sweetheart, why don't you slide this way an inch or three, and let's talk this thing over." All he got for his trouble was a playful punch in the ribs.

72

# CHAPTER FIFTEEN

The neighbors referred to the beginning of Sam and Rachel's country married life by saying, "They went to housekeepin' in a little ol' cabin down on the creek." Often a young married couple would move in with one of their families, but in the Morrisons' case they already had a houseful, and the Cunninghams had a better plan. Sam's parents owned a small empty cabin on the back of their place that they gave to the newly married couple.

Life was not easy for the young Cunninghams starting out. Rachel was confined to her bed almost from the beginning, unable to do much housework or cooking, which frustrated both of them. Sam had to be occupied with the heavy labor of farming, both for himself and for his aging father, maintaining the buildings and fences, feeding the horses, cow and pigs. He found little time to ply his blacksmithing trade, which he was learning from his father. As for pursuing runaway slaves, which required a network of informers, careful planning and quick response, Sam had to put off this dubious, though lucrative occupation indefinitely. Even when he and his father did discuss Sam's planned return to the clandestine business after Rachel gave birth, when he would have more help in the house and could spare the time, they were careful to keep their conversations from Rachel.

Fanny sent over a pot of beans, a baked chicken or a pie now and then. John Wesley occasionally loaned his son-in-law tools, a bucksaw, a twitch, or split rails to repair fences. Mariah came to help two or three times a week, washing clothes, cleaning and cooking, and Sylvester dropped by every day to feed chickens, gather eggs and milk the cow, appropriate chores for a kid of twelve. On most days he walked the quarter-mile to Rachel's place, but the trip became easier and more enjoyable when "his" mare, Genessee Jill, was available.

The other Morrison boys of working age, James, fifteen, Philander, thirteen and Johnny Jr., nine, often came to help Sam with the hardest labor, though Philander's club foot limited him to driving the team for haymaking and corn-picking while the others did the heavy work.

James and Sam had buried the hatchet, Sam apologizing in his own crude way for giving James a thumping when the smaller boy had attacked Sam over his treatment of Rachel in the Gibbs barn back in March. Still, after they made their peace, Sam could not resist reminding James, "See? I told you we'd end up bein' brother-in-laws." James didn't share Sam's loud horse laugh.

Egg and milk production dwindled as the season turned toward fall and winter. When the cow came in heat Sam led her to the Mansers' place to their Durham bull. He allowed the cow to go dry some weeks after weaning her calf to restore her energy for the next freshening.

Rachel earned a bit of pin money from eggs and cream that Sylvester took once a week to Madison. In this way pioneer wives could provide themselves with household incidentals, needles, thread, salt, or coffee if there was any money left over. Widowed farmers too old to work in field or forest could use their egg and cream money for amenities such as tobacco and a bottle of whiskey now and then. Their more basic needs were often provided by the daughter's or son's family with whom they lived.

The weather brought relief to Rachel. In September a rainy spell arrived, followed by a harbinger of autumn, a cool wave in which the air became milder, drier, sweeter. From that time onward the days glowed warm and bright but the nights grew chilly, allowing Rachel more restful sleep beneath her blankets. Sam's appetite for Rachel had abated a bit after their first weeks of marriage.

One Sunday afternoon Sylvester took Rachel and Mariah out for a wagon ride in the crisp fall sunlight. Common treasures like goldenrod, tansy, ironweed, ground ivy, peppermint and the orange berries of bittersweet briars transformed unkempt roadsides and fencerows into fragrant fall bouquets. Leaves of maple, dogwood, oak, beech, ash and sumac had reached their brilliant peaks, transforming faces of distant woodlands into spectacular tableaus. Rachel, shading her eyes, remarked over and over at the beauty of the scene and the smell of autumn in the air. "Rachel, you been living cooped up in that cabin like a dainty princess," Mariah said, "everyone scurryin' round lookin' after you. When that baby comes you'll be so spoiled you won't know how to do nothin' for yourself no more." She winked at Sylvester, then petted her sister's shoulder as if caressing a cat. Rachel said, "Oh, pooey!" and shoved Mariah's hand away with a grin.

Sylvester drove the wagon down the road toward East Enterprise and turned off on a small lane into a grove of shagbark hickories where Rachel could sit in the shade with a book while he and Mariah gathered hickory nuts off the ground.

When the boy and his older sister returned to the wagon with their baskets full of nuts, Sylvester evidently decided it was time for a story. "Gatherin' nuts puts me in the mind of what Lot Mitchell said at dinner time at school last week. You know him and his family is poor as church mice. Well, he looked in his dinner bucket and said all he had was a handful of hickory nuts and a hammer."

Rachel giggled, but Mariah showed him a wry face and said, "That's a pitiful joke, squirt."

"Teacher thought so, too, when he started crackin' 'em on top of her desk."

During her confinement indoors through the dreary days of November, Rachel could vary the tedium and eyestrain of reading, knitting, darning and mending by cracking and picking nuts. She sat for hours in her big chair surrounded by pillows, her swollen ankles elevated. Bathing now required a greater effort than before, and those ever more frequent trips to the drafty outhouse were a nightmare.

Some weeks before her expected delivery, on a cold day in November when the men were occupied with hog butchering, Rachel and Mariah bundled up for the ride over to see Lucy Littleton, the midwife, and her daughter Maryann. The Littletons lived near the Old Dutch Settlement in Pleasant Township, west of Sugar Branch. Their place lay up a lane off the main road, almost to Avonburg.

They had asked Lucy and Maryann to come to Rachel's cabin at the time she went into labor, probably the last of November or early December. Rachel was surprised when Lucy sent word that they should come see her before the middle of November.

When their wagon pulled up in the lot, Maryann came onto the porch and welcomed them into the Littletons' small cabin. The neatness and herbal fragrances inside reminded Rachel of her grandmother Kendall's home back at Rushford, New York. Lucy took their shawls, offered them seats at the trestle table in front of the fire in the kitchen and gave them hot tea. Lucy and Maryann then joined them at the table under ceiling beams hung with sheaves of drying herbs. The Morrison girls felt at ease in the cozy warmth and fragrance of the room. The Littletons' rosy cheeks and cheerful banter complemented the ambience.

Rachel made a quick introduction. "Mrs. Littleton, I'm fortunate to have three mothers, my real mother, Fanny, whom you already know, Mrs. Julia Dumont, my teacher in Vevay, and my sister here, Mariah. I don't know what I'd do without any of the three."

Her hostess chuckled. "I'm so glad you came, Rachel," Lucy said, "and you're kind to bring her, Mariah." After Lucy enquired about Sam and Rachel's families, she said, "Now we'll want to have us a little woman-talk." The sisters nodded.

Rachel licked her lips nervously and asked, "What do we need to talk about, Mrs. Littleton?" She had heard of Lucy's pre-delivery meetings with mothers-to-be, but she was unclear about the questions to come.

"Whatever's on your mind, honey." Lucy smiled in a way that made Rachel feel the most important thing to Lucy was herself and the baby she carried. Rachel slowly turned her attention to the worries she'd been keeping bound up inside.

"Well, I guess I wondered why you wanted to see me even before the baby comes," she said.

"So that when it's your time and I come in your cabin and start ordering people around and acting like I own the place, we'll already be friends and you'll know you can trust me. Today I'll explain to you what we'll be doing to help you and your baby."

Rachel sat quietly for a moment trying to comprehend Lucy's heavy responsibility for the lives of the women and newborns so dependent on her skills. How long had Lucy been doing this? From whom had she learned? Was she training Maryann to become a midwife herself one day? She gave voice to these questions.

"I'd been catchin' babies for three years with my Aunt Betsey when I hear'd about 'em offerin' a new midwifery course up in Cincinnati. My husband Abraham, may his poor soul rest in peace, sold a horse for the money, and I went, took the steamboat up from Vevay. I stayed with a cousin and we had night classes in a schoolhouse."

"Were you taught by doctors?"

"Lord, no, honey, and it's just as well. In these times, when it comes to catchin' babies, medical doctors don't have the best record. American doctors ain't been at it all that long, where with midwives, we're talkin' hundreds and thousands of years. Colleges in this country started teaching child birthin' recently, following the European example. American doctors thought they might as well have the extra money, same as their brothers overseas.

"We was taught by a young city-trained midwife and an old granny woman who'd been at 'catchin' rabbits,' as she called it, for years and years. The younger woman said we oughta call ourselves doctor women, for that's what we are."

Rachel said, "I've heard tell of midwives reading books like *Pierce's Medical Discovery Book*, which has information about herbal medications and medical procedures. I saw Mrs. Dumont's copy at her school in Vevay."

"Yes, sweetheart, they taught us from that book, and about the herbal remedies such as tobacco, elderberry, horehound, the white and the black, and lobeelee. The city midwife taught us things like boiling the bedclothes. In the old days midwives didn't know that helped cut down on sickness in the mothers and babies. She said even the Romans knew to boil bedclothes for the birthin' bed, but later generations somehow forgot it.

"At the end of the course they give each of us a black medicine bag with the things we'd need at the birthin'. This proved we had a midwife's license. In that bag we carry items like blank birth certificates, and the many tools of our trade. I also found me a little set of scales to weigh the newborns."

"Will we need to come get you in the wagon when she goes into labor?" Mariah asked.

"No, child, just send a fast rider to let us know. Sometimes people wants to bring an extry horse for us to ride, but we got old Berthy, our mule. If we have to come at night we'll wrap oily rags round the end of a stick and set it ablaze to keep the wild varmints off and to light our way."

Rachel looked at the black bag sitting under Lucy's table. "So you'll fill out the birth certificate after the baby's born. Do you take that to be recorded down at the courthouse?"

"That's right, sweetheart, and I keep a record in my own little book, here. Maryann, hand me that book." The girl reached into her mother's bag and laid two leatherbound books on the table, one black and one red. Lucy leaned over and quickly dropped the red book back in the bag. Then she opened the black one and riffled the pages, showing Rachel. "See, I put a note of every baby I've delivered in here, when I come, how long the labor lasted and how hard, what herbs I used, weight of the baby and its name, how long me'n Maryann stayed afterward, things of that nature. Every midwife keeps some kind of a record like this."

Mariah's brow furrowed when Lucy so casually dropped the little red book back in her bag.

# CHAPTER SIXTEEN

$\mathcal{L}$ucy continued speaking to Rachel. "Me and Maryann will stay with you as long as we're needed after the delivery, takin' care of you and the child, helping start the breastfeeding, cooking, even doing laundry and housecleaning if necessary. I see you got plenty of help nearby, so we prob'ly won't have to stay long. We'll sleep on a pallet that we'll bring with us, so we won't be no bother."

"How soon will I be able to get up and do for myself?" Rachel asked.

"You don't want to try it too soon. I'd say you'll need to stay in bed a few days till the bones come back together. Then you can start bein' up a few hours every day."

Observing a short lull in the conversation, Mariah spoke up. "Miss Lucy, I wonder if I could talk with you alone for a minute. They's other things the family would like to ask, but we don't need to bother Rachel with it."

Lucy looked from Mariah to Rachel. "Why certainly, child. Let's see. Maryann, you and Rachel go on into the front room and set by the fire. Get her another cup of tea if she'd like it."

After the others had left the kitchen Lucy turned to Mariah with a gentle smile. "It's so good that Rachel has the help of you and your family at this early time in her married life, Mariah. What can I answer for you?"

"Miss Lucy, what do you keep in the little red book? You only showed Rachel the black one."

Lucy's smile evaporated and her face drew tight as she looked from Mariah to the open bag on the floor. She leaned back in her rocking chair, folded her hands across her abdomen and said in a gentle voice, "I'm glad you wanted the others to leave. This is a part of my work that I usually don't get into with the mother before their labor starts."

"Why not?"

"Because they need to get to know me and trust me first, before the hard choices come."

"Hard choices? I don't understand."

Lucy took a deep breath and leaned closer to Mariah. "Rachel's probably not gonna have to know about the red book at all, and don't you tell her, or she'll worry herself to death."

"Lord," Mariah said, "just tell me."

"When I go to the mama after her labor's started, I make her as comfortable as I can and talk real gentle while I'm gettin' things ready, tellin' her everything's gonna be just fine, tellin' her what to expect during the next step of our work. Then at some point I'll ask her if she's lookin' forward to having that baby in her arms, sucklin' it, lovin' it. If the baby's welcome, in other words."

"What's that got to do with the red book?" Mariah said, a hint of annoyance edging her voice.

"I'm comin' to that. Patience, child. This is a delicate matter, something that could affect the lives of the mother and child forever. Now, after I ask the question whether the baby is welcome I watch real close how the mother acts. I listen to what she says next, and I watch how her body moves. Does she smile? Does she say she cain't wait, or that she's been lookin' forward to holding her baby for a long time? She might even cry and say she dreads the pain, but wants to get on with birthin' the little one so she can see it, hold it.

"Or does she look away from me with a sad face, turn to the wall so I can't see her tears? Or does she just lay there lookin' at the ceiling sayin' nary a word? Then I might gently ask another question or two."

Mariah looked at the woman intently. "Miss Lucy, I can guarantee you that my sister is eager to have that baby and help it grow up safe and well. She's already faced that question, and she would die before she let anything bad happen."

80

"I can see that in Rachel, but there are some who feel different, though it may be hard for you to believe. What if a close blood relative made the woman pregnant? Is the mother in danger of losing both hers and the baby's life if the pregnancy continues? Maybe the unmarried woman is pregnant and the father is not willing to face his responsibility? You and I both know a woman without a man or a family to support her in this day and time has a poor chance of raising a child.

"Also, what if the family already has more children than they can feed? You've seen that babies come every year or two regardless of their parents' situation. So there's a lot of things for the pregnant woman and her midwife to consider."

"And you . . . you . . . ."

"I help them any way I can. It's called midwife's mercy. That's why I need to know the herbs, use 'em to knock a baby loose when it's necessary. It's better that way, easier on everybody."

"Which herbs do you use for . . . for that?"

"Pennyroyal, though you have to be careful of the dose. Too little and it don't work. Too much and the mother dies, too. Tansy tea is good. Nothing like tansy tea to ease a woman."

"And what about the ones that are already born? How do . . . . "

"With a pillow."

Mariah was almost in tears. "But how . . . how can you do a thing like that?"

"I done explained it to you, child. It ain't necessary but for a very few, maybe one in a hundred or more."

"And these are the ones you put in your red book?"

"Yes, here." Lucy handed Mariah the red book. "Open it up. See, the entries are almost like the ones in the black book, including family names. I'm trusting you to never tell what you seen in this book, you hear?"

Mariah silently nodded. Then she said, "There's family names, followed by a B or G. What's the D for? I see it wrote after every second or third name."

"Deformed," Lucy said. She sighed and looked at the floor. "It means the baby come out and there was something wrong with it."

"What if there's no D?"

"Then there was nothing wrong," Lucy said.

"And?"

"The baby wasn't welcome."

Mariah showed her distress. She cited the Bible's teachings, "Aren't we taught to value life and do all in our power to save baby's lives?"

The midwife responded in a tired voice. "Mariah, I've read many times what the Bible says on the subject, and I've picked the brains of preachers and doctors about it. What I learned is the teachings can be taken either way, depending mostly on what you believed before you even read the Bible. And depending on the circumstances that each expectin' mother faces.

"There are reasonable arguments, both for doing away with the child if need be, and for saving it at all costs.

"We have to remember, the Bible was written many long years ago, and by men who never had a baby. Yes, we still have to work hard for our food and shelter, and that's why boy babies are sometimes wanted more than girls 'cause the boys will grow up bigger and stronger, able to do more hard work. That determines the situation for some families, whether it's a girl or boy.

"But it's a different world today," Lucy said. "We have more choices, we have more herbs and know better how to use them. A woman no longer has to save a baby where there's no chance for it and its mother to have a normal life.

"Ain't you playing God here?" Mariah said. "Couldn't some of these babies be saved? We're supposed to treat each other with merciful kindness, especially babies."

The midwife went to the fireplace, took the teakettle off the crane and poured two fresh cups of tea. She sat down and remained quiet a long moment while the tea cooled and she fussed with spoons, napkins and sugar. Finally she raised her eyes to Mariah and spoke.

"Yes, some of these babies in the red book might of lived, maybe for years in a crippled state. But say they've already got ten children, and they're about to starve, what's merciful now? Maybe they don't feel they can afford to keep a crippled child that'll draw down the mama's and the whole family's energy, food and money.

82

"These is hard times, girl. Look how many children dies before their first birthday, even if they was born healthy. Death lurks in every household, even under the best of circumstances.

"So, I ask if the baby's welcome, and I get the woman's answer. They almost always let me know they want the baby, just like you and Rachel was sayin'. So at that moment we are in agreement, and I do my best to carry out their wishes."

Mariah leaned forward in her chair. "But what do *you* believe about the Bible's teachings?"

The woman looked directly at Mariah and said. "I'll tell you what I believe, but that don't mean I'll make Rachel's or any woman's decision for her."

"I believe life enters the baby when the mother first feels the quickening. So it becomes a living thing at that point, but that ain't the end of it. The *soul* don't enter the baby until it draws it's first breath. According to Genesis, 2:7, 'And the Lord God formed man of the dust of the ground, and breathed into his nostrils the breath of life; and man became a living soul.' That's the moment the baby becomes a living *human being*."

Mariah struggled to comprehend what Lucy was saying. "So, if the baby is born dead and never takes a breath, it ain't considered a human being 'cause it has no soul?"

"Yes, the family that believes that way usually buries it out somewhere near the cabin. There's no grave marker. After a while they forget about it. It's just like some other animal that died, it ain't a human being. They'll often give the next child the name they'd picked out for the dead baby.

"Now, in my work, after I've talked about all this with the expectin' mother, the decision is totally in her hands. I'm there to serve the mother. Nobody is playin' God. We do what we have to do."

"So that determines if the birth is recorded in the black or the red book?" Mariah said.

"Yes. But remember there are very few entries in the red book."

The young girl leveled a look at Lucy and said with quiet conviction, "My sister's baby will not die and be buried as if it never existed, left to wander lost through eternity."

# CHAPTER SEVENTEEN

At six-thirty on the morning of December 3, 1840, Rachel's water broke. She lay alone in her bed, Sam having risen a few minutes earlier and carried his lantern to the barn to do the chores. When he came back Rachel was trying to clean herself and the bed, apologizing that she hadn't made his breakfast.

Sam took her in his arms and said, "You rest easy now. I'll wrap you in this dry blanket and you just set still here in your easy chair by the fire. I'll go tell your folks and Sylvester'll ride to tell Lucy and Maryann. I'll be back here inside of a half hour to help you, get you somethin' to eat."

Sylvester put Genessee Jill into a long, loping canter and was knocking on the Littletons' door in the dawn light. Presently he saw a dim yellow streak under the door. The door opened and Lucy held the lamp high, blinking the sleep out of her eyes. "Sylvester. Is Rachel ready?"

"Yes, ma'am. Sam said her water's done broke."

"When?"

"Just this mornin', around six."

"Tell 'em we're on our way. Most everything's already packed up."

They arrived just after mid-morning. Lucy took charge, directing Sylvester and Sam to clear out, starting Maryann heating water, laying out the things she'd need later on, telling Mariah to make Rachel comfortable.

Out on the porch Sam told Sylvester, "I ain't much use at this business. I'll be workin' in the barn."

Later, as he brought in more wood for the fire, Sylvester asked Lucy if he could stay inside and help in some way. Lucy said he could go get an axe, then stay in the kitchen until they called him.

When the boy came into the kitchen with the axe, Maryann stepped in to get it. To Sylvester's raised eyebrows the girl said, "To lay under the bed. Cuts the pain."

John Wesley brought Fanny over with a pail of soup and a basket containing some cornbread and honey. Fanny stayed but John Wesley went back, saying to send Sylvester when they had news. He spent a few minutes talking with Sam in the barn.

Lucy, Maryann, Mariah and Fanny busied themselves around Rachel's bed, asking how she was doing, adjusting her pillows, talking to ease her nerves. When the serious pains began, Mariah held her hand and noted time between spasms, Lucy telling her when to push or relax. The women took turns having a cup of soup and a piece of the cornbread, then went back to Rachel's side. Maryann joked that they'd save some for Rachel, but just then the pain came again and she didn't answer.

Around two o'clock Sylvester heard Rachel's first groan, which started him pacing the floor. Two hours later the groans had become screams followed by low voices of the attendants. He went out on the porch where he found Sam sitting on the step, whittling. The young man and the boy talked in muted tones, about hunting, farm work, horses, anything to occupy their minds.

Mariah put her hand on Lucy's arm when the midwife picked up a boiled straight razor after a hard contraction. Lucy looked up at the big girl's worried face and said, "Won't be long now, but she's small, got to cut her a little."

"She's already in fierce pain," Mariah said.

Lucy Littleton's face showed wet in the firelight as she looked up at Mariah. "Some people say birthin' pain is women's atonement for the Original Sin, or that the more pain a woman feels, the more she'll love that child. Now, you can believe what you want, but I got to cut her a little, get her through this. I'll sew her up afterward, fix it so's Sam won't hurt her once she heals up."

Sylvester, back in the kitchen feeding the fire, heard another scream, but this one longer, drawn out, becoming a sob at the end. Then louder voices from the women, and the sweetest sound he'd heard all day, a baby's squall. Sylvester felt his lungs fill with air and his shoulders relax as if a load had slid off. He laid his crossed arms on the mantle, head on arms, lips moving as if he were saying a prayer. He was drying his eyes when Maryann burst into the kitchen and said, "It's a girl! Go tell her daddy."

In the bedroom, Lucy laid the child, healthy and whole, on Rachel's stomach. She, still breathing hard, her body drenched with sweat, her hair plastered back from having cold wet cloths on her face all day, raised her head enough to see her child. Her hand came up to touch the wrinkled red head with its thin wet swirls of dark hair. Then Rachel lay back, smiled and closed her eyes.

Lucy expertly cut the umbilical, dried the child and swaddled it in a soft blanket. As she laid it on the bed in the crook of its mother's arm, Mariah moved a pillow from the bed to a nearby chair. "Won't be needin' no pillows today," she said. The sister and the midwife exchanged tired smiles.

# CHAPTER EIGHTEEN

**M**aryann came into the kitchen to find Sam and Sylvester standing there looking hopeful. She told Sam he could come in for a few minutes.

He knelt by the bed where Rachel lay on her side facing the baby, sheltering it in the crook of her arm. "How you feelin', hon?"

She looked up at her husband with a weary smile. "Fairly well, Sam," she said. "Look here what we've got." She lowered her gentle gaze back to the baby.

"I reckon she'll smooth out some directly," Sam said. "Already got a start on some hair, ain't she? Is she gonna be Frances Elizabeth or Elizabeth Frances? You still want to name her after her grandmothers, don't you?"

"Your mother is feeling poorly, Sam, and it was her idea to give us this cabin. I think the name ought to be Elizabeth Frances."

"Well, I'm glad you got through it," Sam said. He held Rachel's hand and touched the baby as if afraid she would break. "I hope you ain't gonna be like your mama," he said after a quiet moment, "no boys till you've practiced with four girl babies."

Rachel looked up at him, then kissed the baby's forehead. "You can argue against nature all you want, Sam, but God chooses, not us. I couldn't be more pleased with my Elizabeth Frances."

Lucy and Maryann stayed only until Elizabeth was nursing well, then went home after ordering Rachel to stay confined to the cabin for the better part of a week. Mariah slept on a pallet on the floor in the front room, but after three days Sam had become more irritable

87

than usual and everyone was feeling crowded in the small space of the cabin.

Rachel got up on the fourth day and helped Mariah fix dinner for both of them, Sam and Sylvester, then she told her siblings to go on home for a while. Fanny and Mariah had laid in enough supplies for a few days and Rachel assured them she could manage. Sylvester continued to do the small chores for a few weeks, but Rachel eventually took over the egg gathering and the milking.

Sam made it clear that he wanted Rachel to wean Baby Elizabeth as early as possible, being impatient to fill his house with sons. Within a few months Rachel was supplementing the baby's diet with mashed soft food. Not long afterward she resumed ovulating, and she was soon pregnant again.

As that first winter of marriage dragged on the reality of running a household of three people brought new expenses and hardship. Sam had to help inside the house as well as do the farm work. The baby needed blankets, powder, mild soap and other supplies. Sam's blacksmith training had stalled due to Sam's father's failing health. At first Sam borrowed money and provisions from his parents, but they were in no condition to do this for long, and his pride wouldn't let him ask Rachel's family for help.

Sam began to relive the memories of that night last spring when his father had led Sam, Homer Miller and Dewey Sexton on a slavecatching foray up to Oliver Cain's stone house on Tucker's Run back of Lamb. Cousin Cyrus over in Kentucky had signaled them that a party of runaway slaves was shoving off in a skiff for Lamb on the Indiana side. Cyrus operated out of Carrollton, formerly known as Port William, a village on the Kentucky side of the Ohio at the mouth of the Kentucky River, a major tributary of the big river. The village had been called Port William until 1838, when Gallatin County was split forming the new Carroll County with Carrollton as its seat. Considering how reflexively suspicious of government decrees the denizens of the Kentucky frontier were in those days, the old name of the village persisted in use for several years.

Now, reminiscing with his mates about that exciting night, Sam's hands would sweat, and his eyes would glow fiercely as he recalled subduing the two fugitive slaves and their free black conductor in the old stone house in the dark. Later, after asking the constable at Lamb to lock up the black men overnight, his father found the owner of the runaways and an agent who would later sell the conductor on down the river. Sam and his partners made good money on their catch that night.

After only a couple months of marriage, Sam was drinking too much, hanging about with his rowdy friends, Homer and Dewey, at their old campsite in the cane brake down by the river. There, on dreary overcast winter afternoons, listening to the wind rustling dry leaves around them, they would chew tobacco and spit into the fire as they honed their sheath knives. They'd peer out through pallid winter light at the dark wooded hills of Kentucky across slow-moving water that smelt of dark things below. Their conversation often turned to ransom money from catching runaways. But even this lucrative activity had passed its peak for the year. Most slaves with freedom on their minds chose the autumn season for their escape. The weather usually mellowed then, and living off the land was easier. Sam and his friends were impatient for the seasons to turn.

One late February day with the northwind beating sleet against their backs, Sam and his friends rowed a skiff over to Carrollton to speak with the old man they called Cuddin Cyrus.

Living near Sam and Rachel's cabin, the Morrisons would have had to be blind not to see what was going on over there. Sam spent ever more time away from home, neglecting his chores of cleaning stables, mending fences and harness, repairing machinery and laying in seed for planting season.

Mariah, still a frequent visitor to the young Cunninghams' cabin, spoke seriously to Rachel on a day after Mariah had found Sam lying sick drunk in the barn. "Sis, why don't you let me tell Pop so he can come talk some sense into Sam's head."

Rachel looked up, wide-eyed as a deer, as if caught in her own self-deception. "Oh . . . oh Mariah . . . it's nothing. He's just worried that we're poor and there's not much he can do till spring. We started out from scratch, you know, and he's just taking things hard. He'll brighten up when warm weather comes."

"They's plenty of work needs to be done before plantin' time, sis. He could be clearing more land this winter, and a lot of other things. I agree you and Sam didn't start off with much, but both our family and the Cunninghams has been helping all they can. Sam ain't showed much gratitude to 'em if you ask me. If the feller needs help, Pop and the boys'd be glad to lend him a hand. Pop and Mother could even come over on a Sunday for a visit and both of 'em try to get his head right so he'd face up to his responsibility."

"Oh, that won't be necessary," Rachel said, affecting an air of confidence. "I'll speak with him. He's just not used to people depending on him. We can work things out, no need to bother Mother and Pop with it."

"But that drinkin's a bad sign, Rachel, 'specially drinkin' enough to make him sick. You think you can talk him outta that? All by yourself?"

"Let me handle it, Mariah. I appreciate your concern, but he'll listen to me. I'll get him to stop, you watch."

"I hate to see all this making it harder for you, sis. Looks like he'd take more interest in lookin' after you and 'Lizabeth. I've been worried about you marryin' Sam ever since you and Sylvester went to see the Cunninghams in the wagon that day. I know it ain't none of my affair, but you sure you done the right thing?"

"Now, Mariah, you just mind your own business! Things aren't perfect around here, to be sure, but in spite of it all, I got what I wanted, and that's a secure home for Elizabeth. Now I've taken your meaning about Sam's drinking and I'll have a sit-down with him over it, but beyond that, it's my concern, not yours."

The next day at noontime Rachel dished up the food and they ate a silent dinner. Sam had already got up from the table when Rachel took a deep breath and said, "Sam, I'd like a word with you."

He turned back to the table, with a look of mild annoyance. "About what?"

"Would you please sit down for a minute? There's something we need to talk about."

He scraped the bench back and sat down, regarding her with sullen eyes, as if suppressing a burst of anger. "What is it?"

"Sam, you're drinking too much and I'd like you to stop."

"Drinking too much! How you know how much is too much? I'll take a drink now and then, but that ain't nothin' new, I drank a little before we was married, too."

"It isn't just a little anymore, Sam. I'd like you to cut back, or stop it altogether, considering the baby and all."

"How you know it ain't just a little?"

"Mariah found you passed out drunk in the barn yesterday, and you'd been sick on yourself. I washed out your shirt this morning."

"So, your sister's been spyin' on me! I'm about to get plumb tired of her and Sylvester and them wandering around here under my feet. I'm gonna tell 'em to stay home for a spell and let me breathe."

"You need to talk to somebody, Sam, somebody who can help you. Something is troubling you, and if you get help with it, you won't feel the need to drink."

"There ain't a thing wrong with me, Rachel. You and your family is just trying to tell me what to do, and it ain't gonna work."

"I'm *asking* you, Sam. Asking you to consider your drinking and stop it. Would you go see Reverend Wiley, our minister, if I went with you? He knows how to help people with their problems."

"I don't even know him, and I ain't got a problem."

"Now, Sam, if you drink till you get sick and pass out, that's certainly a problem. What if we went to see Preacher Seals? I know he's the one you talked with after our . . . that time in the Gibbs barn last March. I don't consider him a real minister, but if that's what it takes, I'll go with you to see him, or whoever you want."

"Look, Rachel, I know I ain't the husband you wanted, but I'm the one you got, so you'll just have to make the best of it, like I'm doin'. You think it's fun knowing how you grieve over your doctor? It ain't my fault he's dead!" Sam got up and stomped out of the cabin.

A mounted horseman had been waiting outside. Rachel looked out to see Dewey Sexton on a chestnut gelding talking with Sam, who came back in the cabin to get his coat and hat, then left again without a word to Rachel.

Sam and Dewey went to the barn where Sam saddled his horse, then they rode back past the cabin toward the creek. As they passed, Rachel listened at the door and heard Dewey chuckle before saying, "Sounded like you and her was havin' a fuss when I rode up."

"It ain't nothin'," Sam said. "She'll get used to me and my ways. All I got to do is keep her knocked up, and she'll finally get over it." Both men laughed as they rode off.

Hearing Sam's words, Rachel gasped. She turned her back to the door and brought her fists to the sides of her face, breathing hard to dispel her rage.

Sam came home earlier than Rachel expected that evening. As he walked past her to hang his hat and coat on the peg she noticed the absence of liquor smell. He turned to her. "Hon, I'm sorry for the way I talked at dinner. Times is tough for both of us, but things'll look up in the spring."

Rachel moved to stand directly in front of him. She showed him a stern expression, her worry smoldering in her eyes. "What you said to me at noon wasn't the worst," she began. "You can say almost anything to my face and I can come to some understanding with you over it. What I can't abide, though, and what I shall not tolerate, is your saying mean things about me to other people behind my back."

It took Sam a moment to overcome the shock of her words. He finally spoke, but with a stricken expression. "Now, Rachel, here I am tryin' to make up with you, and you ain't havin' none of it. What am I s'posed to do?"

"What you're *not* supposed to do is make hurtful statements to your friends about keeping me *knocked up*. And right outside the cabin where I'd be sure to hear it."

Sam's jaw dropped. "Ah, Rachel, I didn't mean nothin' by it. It was just man talk. We say things like that to our sidekicks just to get a laugh. You jest took it wrong, that's all."

"I took it exactly the way you meant it, Sam Cunningham! You said it to be disrespectful to me. Honestly, Sam, I sometimes don't know how I can go on living with you the way you are. If this continues I'll have to take Elizabeth and go somewhere else." Despite her resolve not to weep, Rachel's voice was breaking, tears beginning to stream down her face. "Living in the poorhouse scrubbing floors would be better than the way you treat us sometimes." She hurried into the other room and flung herself on the bed, her sobs waking the baby in her cradle, causing Elizabeth to send up a howl of her own.

Rachel turned over on her back, trying to wipe her tears away with her sleeve and find the strength to go pick up the baby. The sun had just set, filling the room with somber half-light. Rachel had

92

reached rock bottom, completely depressed, out of patience with Sam, frustrated by Elizabeth's frequent crying, mindful of her own body sinking into exhaustion. After a moment she rolled to a sitting position and, wearily turning to look at the cradle she noticed a shadow in the doorway.

Sam stood there looking at her. He moved to the cradle and gently picked up the baby, wrapping the blanket around her, then coming to the bed and stretching out beside his wife with the baby on his chest. As he patted Elizabeth's back the sounds of her crying began to diminish. Both parents laid gentle hands and soothing words upon her.

In a few minutes Rachel took little Liz in her arms and held her close. Sam moved toward them and, with his rough fingers, tucked a loose strand of Rachel's auburn hair behind her ear. He lay looking at her a few moments while she cooed to the baby. "Me and Dewey rode down to the river camp this afternoon," he said. "We built us a fire and talked about things. He's been courtin' that Stepleton girl from over at Allensville, and wonderin' how he can afford to marry her. I told him he better watch out 'cause marryin' ain't for sissies."

Rachel looked up at Sam with a tired smile. "I appreciate your not drinking today," she said.

"I been considerin' my ways on that and how I've treated you lately. And you're right about what I said to Dewey when we left today. That was not a thing to say about a man's wife anytime, whether you hear'd it or not, and I'm sorry about it. I was raised better'n that."

More tears leaked from her eyes, and she snuffled before saying, "Thank you. That makes me feel a bit softer toward you. I know things haven't been easy for you around here, either. We married not far ahead of winter with no crops to harvest, and I said some terrible hateful things to you in front of our folks even before the wedding. If we both try hard we can make a life for this girl and for each other, don't you think?"

"Peerin' into that fire down on the river I decided I was gonna try to fly right, start bein'have like a decent feller ought to when he's got him a beautiful wife and little girl." He grinned. "Dewey thought I was sick 'cause I wouldn't drink with him."

She smiled up into his face, drying her tears. "We'll work on it together, then." She looked down at the baby, fast asleep now. "Hold her while I go warm up the bean soup."

"Just a minute, hon. I need to say somethin' else 'fore it gets lost." Sam was quiet a moment, as if putting his words in order. "I pondered what you said about speakin' with Preach . . . uh, Reverend Wylie, and I've decided it's a right good idea. I figure maybe the best way to get acquainted with him is to go to meetin' Sunday. On our way out the church door at the handshakin' we might ask to see him on an evenin' during the week. Whattaya think?"

It was dark in the room now, and Rachel's only reply was to reach over and pull Sam's head close and kiss him on the lips. Then she put her damp cheek beside his and held him as tight as she could without waking the baby.

# CHAPTER NINETEEN

During that first brutal winter of Rachel and Sam's life together an unexpected stream of stimulation began to arrive every few days at their cabin. As a gift to the young Cunninghams at the birth of their child, Mrs. Julia Dumont made sure a roll of one or more *Cincinnati Enquirer* newspapers occasionally made its way to Rachel's cabin. Julia knew her former student would appreciate being able to keep abreast of events in the world outside Sugar Branch during her new life of wifely and motherly obligations.

The *Enquirer* became a daily paper in 1841, having been a weekly up to that time. The papers were delivered a day or two late to Vevay on packet steamers. Mrs. Dumont saved them and sent bundles at least once a fortnight to Rachel at Sugar Branch. Sam didn't appreciate the value of the gift, but Rachel found it a preserver of her sanity. Among the first of Julia's parcels, Rachel read with interest the stories of political fulminations going on in Washington in the early months of the new year.

Following the most hotly contested presidential campaign in the nation's history, "Tippecanoe and Tyler Too," the ticket of William Henry Harrison and John Tyler, of the Whig party, defeated the incumbent Democrat Martin Van Buren, and were elected President and Vice President on November 3, 1840. President Harrison, after giving the longest inaugural speech in history to that point, outdoors in bitter cold weather on March 4, died of pneumonia on April 4, 1841, only a month after taking office.

95

John Tyler turned out to be a disastrous successor. He vetoed a law establishing the Second Bank of the United States, thus aligning himself against his own Whig party's position. The veto caused an angry riot of Whig party members on the White House grounds and Tyler's entire cabinet, except Daniel Webster, resigned.

One day, as she read newspaper accounts of these proceedings in Washington, Rachel fondly recalled a dinner conversation at Captain Pegg's table on the *St. Augustine*. It was then that she learned she and Robert shared the same political views and the same feelings of empathy for those less fortunate in society. She sighed. How well they would have complemented each other as a married couple in Robert's hometown of Baltimore, he a distinguished medical doctor, she perhaps becoming a teacher or writer.

Then her eyes fell upon little Elizabeth, happily discovering her toes in her cradle. Rachel regarded her baby with a loving smile. She could forge a fulfilling life for herself right here in Sugar Branch, too. She would turn her efforts to making a good life for this child and those to come.

One morning Sam looked up from his breakfast in surprise when Rachel burst into laughter. She sat cradling the baby with one arm and holding the folded *Enquirer* in her other hand. The walls of their tiny cabin hadn't echoed with Rachel's laughter since their wedding day back in late summer. "What's so funny?" he asked.

She lifted her bright face to him after finishing the paragraph. "Washington D.C. must be full of unusual people. There's a sculptor named Horatio Greenough up there, and he made a statue of George Washington. I'm sure everyone was in favor of honoring our American hero, but Horatio created the statue in what they call the Neoclassical style. Listen to this last sentence. 'Public outrage at the sandaled and semiclad depiction of the first president prevents the statue from being placed in the Capitol Building.' You know my mother still remembers attending a memorial service for George Washington in 1799 when she was a child of four or five. Washington was such a hero there were services for him in every small town in the country."

In answer to Sam's expressionless eyes, Rachel giggled again and explained, "The sculptor made George look like an ancient Greek instead of an American soldier and diplomat!" She returned to

96

the paper with a chuckle, while Sam's only response was a weak uncomprehending grin.

With the aid of Mrs. Dumont's newspapers, Rachel was able to keep abreast of more serious events such as the buildup to the Mexican-American War, which erupted in the 1840s. The charges and threats exchanged between the two countries seemed of remote interest to most residents of Cotton Township, but to Rachel the territorial implications of the conflict were monumental. She read of Democratic Party politicians beginning to trumpet slogans that culminated in the term "Manifest Destiny" by mid-decade.

# CHAPTER TWENTY

In early January of the year 1845, Mariah and Aaron's families and friends gathered at the Methodist Church to christen little Marietta Cochran. Her sister Lucy Ann would be born later that year, to be followed later by John Wesley and Sarah Frances. By this time Rachel had three little girls, Elizabeth Frances, Prudence and Mary. Edith Tinker, a neighbor lady, and her daughter Missy stayed with Rachel's babies while James took her to the ceremony.

Sam did not attend the christening. He and his cohorts Dewey Sexton and Homer Miller had spent the dark hours of the previous night supposedly "night fishing" on the big river. Unbeknownst to Rachel, they had spent the night pursuing and capturing two runaway slaves, a pair of negro brothers from Carroll County, Kentucky, who for some reason had chosen to run away in the dead of winter. Sam and his sidekicks sent the white conductor back over the river after a severe cuffing. They asked Elisha Bardwell, the constable at Lamb, to lock up their captives until Sam and the others could contact the owners back in Kentucky the next day. Sam came dragging in muddy and tired just before Rachel left with James for the church, telling her he'd given his share of the catfish to Dewey. He immediately fell into bed. Rachel's protests that he was expected at the christening were met with loud snores.

Even before the minister had sprinkled the baby's head, whispers began to circulate among the guests at the ceremony with the news that Dewey, Homer and Sam had caught a pair of young negroes last night. Sam's absence put an exclamation point on the story.

Eliza Hallgarth made it a point to sashay up to Rachel afterward and ask in a too-loud voice why Sam hadn't come to the service. Rachel mumbled an evasive answer to her busybody former friend, then maintained her composure just long enough to complete her sisterly duties before asking James to drive her home.

For most of the residents in and around Sugar Branch, capturing fugitive slaves was a distasteful business and those who did it were labeled unsavory characters. Several families in Cotton Township, including John Wesley and Fanny Morrison, let it be known that if black fugitives appeared on their doorsteps, they would protect them from their pursuers. Their differences over this issue kept relations cool between the elder Morrisons and Cunninghams.

Rachel did not reveal her anger at Sam to James on the way home. She understood the hard feelings that had existed for many months between the two young men. Besides, she remembered her brother's mixed feelings about slavery and slavecatching that he expressed on their long overland trip to Rushford for the horses. Instead, she asked James to send Sylvester over to see her after breakfast the next day. Sylvester, by now a rapidly growing young man of seventeen, still routinely took Rachel's eggs and cream to market at Madison every few days, so her request did not raise James's curiosity.

As Rachel expected, Sam was gone when she got home from the church. She would learn soon enough that her husband had gone back down to Lamb that night to meet with his partners, retrieve their captives from old Elisha at the jail, tie them up and take them back across the river. Over in Kentucky they had the Carroll County sheriff lock up the black men while they sought the slaves' owner and collected their bounty.

Sylvester arrived at Rachel and Sam's cabin bright and early the next day. He said he'd seen a weasel around her chicken coop, so he'd set a trap next time he came over. Then he and Rachel had a long talk during Sam's absence. She learned her younger brother had known about Sam's marauding before most of the others at the christening got wind of it.

As the siblings sat at Rachel's kitchen table, Baby Mary in her arms and the toddlers occupied with their homemade toys, she voiced her frustration about Sam's behavior, namely the fugitive-chasing. She poured out her thoughts to her trusted kid brother whose ideals and preferences tended to parallel her own. "We must find a way to intercede for these poor black folk, Vess, both to save at least a few of them from Sam and his rascals, and to face our own consciences."

The boy rubbed his chin thoughtfully, in the manner of a young man wise beyond his seventeen years. After a pause he said, "Well, we cain't just follow Sam around and holler a warning to the slaves when they start crossing the river. And I can't be camping out down by the river skedaddlin' back and forth in a johnboat trying to keep tabs on Cuddin Cyrus and Sam and them. Besides, we couldn't do any good just by ourselves, stuck out here in the woods ten mile from the river. We need us a good line-up of scouts, better than theirs. We'll have to fix up somethin' they won't notice, so's we can get to the runaways before they do and bring 'em across by a different route.

"Won't that take several people?" Rachel asked. "Who can we trust to help us?"

"We'll have to be slick to beat 'em at their own game," Sylvester said. "Old Cyrus knows Carrollton and its people like the back of his hand, and he's well acquainted with the Kentucky River and most every boat that comes down it. That old drunk Billy Higgins in his shantyboat down at Lamb watches for Cyrus's lantern signal that they's freight comin' over the river, then gets the word to Sam and his sidekicks."

"But we can't let on that we're working against them," Rachel said, "It might be easy to sink old Billy's boat or do something to foil Cousin Cyrus, but it would be too easy for them to find out who did it. Oh, it's so complicated."

Sylvester studied a moment. "Who do we know that feels the same way we do about slavecatchin'? Our close neighbors is again' slavery, too, but if they threw in with us wouldn't it be a hard secret to keep? You know gossip flies around Cotton Township like a flushed covey of quail. For our own good we dassn't let anybody in Sugar Branch in on this, even our own family. It'll have to be just me and you, and maybe others way off somewhere, like in Kentucky, that's willing to help us."

"Good lord, that makes it even harder."

"Wait a minute, sis. What about Adam Coulter? Didn't he say he'd be glad to send you the names of Quakers in our neck of the woods, them *Friends*, as he called 'em? Seems like most of them folks is again' slavery and sometimes helps runaways move on north. I know Adam was as sweet on you as a bee on honeysuckle. Didn't he give you his post office address in . . . where was it, Clairsville . . . no, St. Clairsville, Ohio?"

Rachel sat up straight and gazed off into the corner, concentrating. Adam Coulter, a road builder who sometimes assisted the Quakers in protecting runaway slaves, had given the three Hoosier travelers a lift in his luxurious chartered stagecoach on the National Road. That was back in Ohio and Pennsylvania in the spring of '40 when they were trekking to Rushford. "He did give me his address, as a matter of fact. Let's see, I stuck the paper in my journal book, but then I gave it to Mrs. Dumont. Would I have taken his address out first?" She rose from the table and went to the china cabinet whose doors were glazed with wavy glass panes separated by mullions. As she turned the wooden keeper and opened the door she said, "She gave the journal back to me a few weeks later." She took the leather-bound book off the shelf and riffled its pages. Finding no papers, she took down the wooden fruit bowl from the same shelf. After a moment of shuffling the clutter of papers in the bowl she said, "Here it is! But by now Adam will surely have married. After all, it's been five years. Would he still be willing to help us?"

"Only one way to find out," Sylvester said, "If you write him a letter right now, I'll take it to the post office."

Rachel looked apprehensively toward the cabin door. "Sam may be home any time now, but I'll write a quick note to Adam. Hand me a pen and paper from the drawer over there." She shifted the baby in her arms and began to write quickly. "If Sam comes in I'll finish the letter while he's not looking and give you that empty pie tin to take back to Mother. Put Adam's letter under it so he won't see it."

"How long you reckon it'll take to reach Adam?"

101

She looked up from the paper. "Lord only knows," Rachel said. "He may not even be in St. Clairsville anymore. He was on furlough from a job in Indianapolis when we met him, remember?"

"This is a shot in the dark, sis, but it's the best chance we got, far as I can see. I could look for Quakers round here myself, but considerin' these times, they'd likely be suspicious of my intentions without a note from Adam, or somebody else known to the Friends."

"Adam seemed sincere when he offered to help us," Rachel said. "We'll pursue this as far as we can, and keep our eyes open in the meantime."

Sylvester grinned impishly at his sister. "Old Adam was sincere, all right, sincere about doin' anything under the sun to make a favorable impression on you, I'd say. But I won't be lookin' a gift horse in the mouth if he gets your letter, answers it and agrees to help us."

After a few minutes of silence while she finished and sealed the letter, she said, "You'd better go on now before Sam comes in and starts asking questions. If he sees me writing a letter he'll get suspicious."

It was true. Sam didn't often respect her privacy, in her letter writing or in the bedroom. As Vess rose to leave she said, "You come back later, let me know the letter's mailed, then set the trap behind the chicken coop."

"Good. We're set, then. See you this afternoon, sis."

Just as Sylvester rose from the table, heavy footsteps sounded on the porch. Rachel hid Adam's address in her skirt pocket as the door opened. Sam's massive frame filled the doorway. "What're you doin' here, squirt? You're gonna have to start payin' for your keep over here."

Sylvester flashed his disarming grin. "Just tellin' sis 'bout a weasel I saw out behind your chicken coop this mornin'. I'll set a varmint trap out there this evenin'. Got to be goin' now, see you'uns later."

Sam had already turned away from them and began putting wood on the fire. When Sylvester was a couple of minutes gone with the pie tin and the letter he said, "Better go check on the cow, 'pears she's fixin' to be fresh soon."

102

While he was gone Rachel washed herself and the baby, then dished up oatmeal for the other two children. Rachel's two toddlers' diet now consisted of hot cereal or mashed food. One day when Sam saw Rachel using a potato masher to process solid food for them, he told her most women in his family chewed food in their mouths, spit it into a spoon and fed it to their babies. "That may be," Rachel said, "but I prefer doing it this way."

When Sam returned she was putting the baby down for a nap in the bedroom. She asked about the cow. "Already got a bull calf," he said. "I helped it suck the first time. Looks like we'll have plenty of beef in a few months and fresh milk after the calf gets a good start. He's a fine big calf, and with a decent crop this summer there'll be feed enough to take him and his mama through the winter. Things are startin' to look up around here."

From the bedroom Rachel saw Sam walk to the fireplace. A premonition flashed in her mind, and she continued to watch him through the open door. He took what looked like folding money from his pocket and placed it under the earthen jar on the mantel, the one with the fall bouquet she'd collected months ago. She knew this would be another boost for Sam's spirits, slavecatching money.

In the next moment she saw him take something heavy from his back pocket and slip it down into a corner of the woodbox. She quickly turned her attention back to the baby when Sam turned and told her he wanted a cup of coffee.

She covered the baby with a blanket and came to the kitchen. "Where've you been the past two nights? You missed Marietta's christening." Her voice was flat and hard, causing Sam to stop and look at her.

"Uh . . . me and Dewey and Homer built us a campfire down on the river and cooked them fish we caught. I'm sorry I wadn't at the shindig."

She saw through his flimsy lie, but she only smiled ruefully to herself and turned to her work with a silent vow to do whatever she could to frustrate his heinous attacks on fugitive slaves. The next time Sam was out of the cabin she went to the woodbox. There in a corner she found a pair of handcuffs under the firewood.

103

# CHAPTER TWENTY-ONE

$\mathcal{A}$round mid-afternoon, after setting the trap, Sylvester waved at Sam at the barn, then paused a moment in the kitchen to kneel and take Elizabeth and Prudence in his arms. He jollied them, pretending to bite their ears. "Gonna get me a mess of ears," he said, which sent the little girls into shrieks of pleasure. He kissed their cheeks and stood up, quieting their protests by handing them each one of Grandma Morrison's sugar cookies from his pocket, then he winked at his sister. "Got her mailed, slick as a whistle," he said.

Years later, Sylvester would learn how great a risk he and Rachel had taken in sending or receiving mail that dealt with aiding fugitive slaves. In that era of inflamed emotions over this issue in Border Country, it was a chancy enterprise to entrust such mail to strangers, neighbors, even the U. S. Postal Service.

Thus began what promised to be a long hopeful wait. Knowing Adam Coulter, Sylvester was sure he wouldn't waste a moment's time answering Rachel's call for help, *if* he received her letter at all.

Later that afternoon Rachel put the baby down to sleep with a full tummy, and she saw that Elizabeth and Prudence, bundled up against the cold, were playing on the porch with Popcorn, the calico cat, and her litter of kittens in a straw-filled basket. Sam came in from the barn, and Rachel asked him to sit down at the table a moment. She began to vent her frustration.

She told Sam that shortly after she and her brothers returned from New York she had learned what else he did on that fateful night when he hurt her in the Gibbs barn. Afterward she'd heard hoofbeats as she lay dazed and bleeding. He was off at a gallop to join his father, Dewey and Homer. Later that night, they'd pursued and captured two runaway slaves and their colored conductor. The fugitives had just crossed the river, fleeing from their master in Kentucky. The confrontation took place on the Tucker's Run Road at Oliver Cain's abandoned stone house in the woods above the river.

"Those black men haven't been heard from since. Folks around here assume that you returned the slaves to their owners in Kentucky for a ransom and that the conductor, a free black man, was sold back into slavery down the river. You and your friends had quite an exciting and profitable night, didn't you, and all at other people's expense and suffering. I'd hoped you'd stopped that hateful business when we married, but I see you went back to it last night."

She paused then, as if waiting for his reaction. When he remained sullen and silent, she continued. "Sam, you know that my family and I are strongly opposed to and offended by this wicked slavecatching. We and others who have emigrated from New York to this settlement, the Oakses, the Mansers, the Garys and others are united in our anti-slavery views."

Sam objected. "Now, Rachel, I know this here slavery question sticks in your craw. But you know my folks comes from South Carolina, and down there the whites and negras takes a different view of things.

"The whites has had many generations of livin' together with the nig . . . black folks and we've all learnt how to get along. The negras needs work and the whites wants help on the farms and plantations with all the hand labor it takes to raise cotton and other crops, so the system works for everybody. You might say the negras would be helpless without the whites providin' food, clothes and shelter for 'em, takin' care of them, so to speak. They ain't got the brains nor the spunk to survive on their own. They're shiftless and lack common sense, so slavery helps 'em get along in the world."

Rachel, barely able to control her anger, fixed Sam with a cold stare. "But you're no longer in South Carolina. This is Indiana, a free state."

"I don't give a rip where we are. It's a matter of a man's property. When a slave runs away to the North, his owner is out a lot of money, so when we catch him and return the property to where it come from, his owner is pleased to make it worth our while, and we feel we done the man a service. Besides, it puts money in our pockets, money we need for ourselves and these young'uns till we get on our feet."

"Yes, and it's tainted money," Rachel said, "money that was gained through human suffering. Besides, no man can belong to another man as his property. That goes against the principles most people live by around here."

Hearing only a resentful silence from Sam, Rachel got up and began clearing the breakfast dishes.

Almost before Rachel and Sylvester dared to begin hoping for an answer from Adam Coulter, Philander rode up to the cabin after a trip to the Sugar Branch Post Office on a dark and drizzling morning in late February. He carried a folded and sealed letter addressed to Rachel and bearing a St. Clairsville, Ohio, postmark.

She could hardly contain her excitement, but took time to ask after the family and to thank her brother for his trouble. Then she watched with pounding heart as he returned to the hitch rail, mounted Sadie, one of the New York mares, and rode off toward his parents' place.

She closed the door, rushed to the table, picked up a flatware knife with trembling fingers and broke the seal on the letter. Sinking onto a bench, elbows on the table with the open letter held close to the coal-oil lamp, she read:

*My Dear Rachel,*                                        *February 13th, 1845*
*It was with joyous heart that I read your letter of January 25th, which I received in good time yesterday. Times innumerable, my dear friend, have I thought of you across the long months since we spent those luminous spring days together with your brothers journeying along the National Road.*

*In response to your request I now hasten to take pen in hand to do my humble best to support your efforts in aiding fugitives of the dark race as they enter your stretch of Border Country there along the Ohio.*

*An urgent consultation with my acquaintances of the Quaker persuasion has produced information I hope you will find helpful. There be a family of Friends living in your nearby town of Madison by the name of Calloway, who reside in the second street above the river at number 240. I'm told their house is two stories, and of a gold-brown color. Squire Judd Calloway is being alerted to expect word from you. He and his family have been faithful to Freedom's Cause on previous occasions, both officially in his office as Justice of the Peace, and in their everyday lives. I wish you godspeed, and my hope is fervent that we shall meet again someday in less troubled times.*

*I remain ever your faithful and obedient servant,*
*Adam F. Coulter*

# CHAPTER TWENTY-TWO

*A* few days after Rachel received Adam's letter, Sylvester found himself nervously knocking on Judd Calloway's door at 240 Second Street in Madison. The boy had waited until his normal market day for his ride to town so as not to arouse Sam's suspicion.

Having sold his cream and eggs at the farmers' market, Sylvester now stood peering up at the facade of one of the largest and finest homes he'd ever seen. This place made Papa and Mimi Kendall's roomy family farmhouse at Rushford, New York, look like a homesteader's cabin. What kind of people lived in such houses as this, standing stately among its handsome peers along this fine street? He'd heard Madison described as the largest town in Indiana, but since he was acquainted with such a small corner of the Hoosier state, that grandiose declaration held little meaning for the boy.

After Sylvester doffed his hat and stammered his request to the impatient maid at the door, Judd Calloway finally appeared, a frown etched on his broad bearded face. He seemed a bit rumpled, somehow off kilter to be the purse proud owner of such an edifice. The boy refrained from further speculation and forged ahead with his mission. "Top o' the mornin' to you, sir. My name is Sylvester Morrison, of Sugar Branch, upriver a piece. Could I have a word with you in private, sir?"

Calloway, a balding older man of modest height with rust-colored hair and a bushy beard, was dressed in a wrinkled white shirt, loose collar with a cravat draped loosely around his neck. His uncreased flannel trousers seemed much in need of the braces that prevented their slipping off the man's comfortable girth. Mr. Calloway put his thumbs in his waistband, stood to his full height and said, "I'm very busy, young man. State thy business and then be on thy way." Sylvester felt his stomach cringe.

"Well, sir, I was wondering if you might of received a letter lately from a friend of ours, Mr. Adam Coulter, sir?"

"Coulter, thee says? No, I'm not acquainted with anyone by that name. Thee has the wrong house, son. Run along now, I have work to do." As he spoke, Mr. Calloway stepped back and reached for the door, as if he were about to close it.

"Mr. Calloway, my business is about savin' runaway slaves, and Adam give us your name as a person who might help us."

The hand on the door paused, and Calloway's heavy body inclined back toward the open doorway. "Saving slaves? This man gave thee my name?" Judd Calloway stepped outside on the stoop, closing the door behind him, looking up and down the tree-lined street, then at Sylvester. "Now see here, who is this . . . Coulter thee speaks of? And what does thee mean, coming up to my door assuming I've received a letter from someone I've never heard of?"

"Adam told us you're a Quaker, Mr. Calloway, a Friend, as he calls it, and your talk sounds like the few Quakers I've seen. But he said you're a person what can help us, and he's s'posed to of sent you a letter."

Calloway still seemed puzzled and suspicious. "I don't know anything about this. It's time thee went on thy way. I'm very busy, as I said."

"Mr. Calloway, we know of some people who lay in wait to catch runaway slaves when they cross the river up in our neck of the woods. We're again' slavecatching, and you're the only one we know of that might help us out of this fix. Ain't you Quakers again' slavery, too?"

"Yes, but . . . . "

"Adam's letter has done been on its way for some time, and it should be in your hands by now, sir. Have you got your mail lately?"

"Well, no, I haven't been to the post office for a while."

"Why don't we hop along up there, then, and see if Adam's letter ain't in your cubbyhole. That'll prove I ain't a picaroon, and that we need help savin' these people."

Calloway quickly donned his coat and top hat, which in the boy's opinion only increased his comical appearance. On the way to the post office Sylvester queried the older man about the Quaker religion. He observed that Mr. Calloway sounded a bit like Buford and Angeline Hartley, the Friends who had helped Rachel, James and Sylvester to save Enoch Paisley, a fugitive slave, on their way to Rushford a few years ago.

Judd Calloway gave Sylvester a long look as the pair walked along a gravel path under the trees, as if deciding whether to trust this upstart youth with his earnest beseechment for information and help. At length he said, "In the first place, our group prefers to be called the *Society of Friends*, as opposed to *Quakers*. That derisive name was given to us years ago by non-believers based on their ignorance of our religion and way of life.

"Also, when it comes to aiding our brethren of the dark race, there are many suspicious non-believers about with their ears pricked up. So, as thee can see, many of the locals are opposed to us on both counts."

Sylvester's heart thumped as Mr. Calloway peered into the array of individual patrons' mail slots covered by a pane of glass. The postmaster retrieved several sealed foolscap letters from the pigeon hole with Calloway's number in gold paint on the glass and handed them to Judd with a humorous comment about the weather. Sylvester couldn't help looking over the man's shoulder as he shuffled his mail. The next-to-last letter bore a St. Clairsville postmark. Sylvester exhaled so hard that Calloway redirected his gaze to the boy for a split second. "That's it," Sylvester said. "I'll just step over yonder for a minute whilst you read it." Calloway nodded absently, for he had already broken the seal and was unfolding the letter.

Mr. Calloway appeared to read the letter at least twice while Sylvester looked on from a bench, trying not to seem too anxious. Then the older man came to the bench, wordlessly reached out, took the boy by the arm and guided him outside. After again glancing both ways up and down the street, he whispered, "We'll go back to my house. We need to talk."

110

Sylvester's only experience with a room as elegant as the library in Judd Calloway's house had been the carpeted dining room of the steamer *St. Augustine*, on which he and his siblings had returned from Pittsburgh to Vevay five years ago. The bearded older man seemed ill-at-ease after the twin shocks of Sylvester's appearance at his door in broad daylight and the contents of Adam Coulter's letter.

Calloway launched a barrage of questions concerning everything from the identity of Sylvester's family and their place of residence to the boy's knowledge and description of the slavecatchers he had mentioned. Judd asked if Sylvester and his family had first-hand evidence of the actions of slavecatchers in Switzerland County, or just rumors. Sylvester answered every question, being careful not to divulge too much information about his family members, either the ones helping slaves or those trying to catch them. Upon more intense interrogation, the boy told the older man of the capture of two male slaves and their black conductor five years ago as they made their way into the Indiana hills from the village of Lamb. Now, he said, some of his family members had observed these same people and their cohorts preparing to resume their clandestine attacks. "And the exact crossing point of which thee speaks?" Calloway said.

"Mouth of the Kentucky over to Lamb, sir, seven mile downriver from Vevay."

"God help us," Mr. Calloway said, gazing off into the distance with a distressed countenance.

After a fifteen-minute discussion and more probing questions, Judd Calloway leaned forward and confided to Sylvester that he had Quaker accomplices in Kentucky at Milton and Carrollton who often became actively involved in helping parties of runaways cross the river.

His face clouded in a frown, Sylvester said, "Carrollton?" Judd explained that Carrollton's old name had been Port William, and many local citizens had clung to it. Officially the settlement's name was now Carrollton.

Mr. Calloway said, "Our group has been aware for some time that the mouth of the Kentucky River offers fugitives a most convenient place to cross to the Indiana side at Lamb.

"There's a man there by the name of McKay who is very trustworthy and efficient at hiding fugitives and moving them on up the line.

"Also, the sparse population in the hills behind Lamb make it easier to move fugitives on north from there rather than from Madison. Some of our negro and white brothers bring them down to Carrollton on a steamboat from the Bluegrass, sometimes as far up as Frankfort and beyond. Then we get a message to our partners on the Indiana side when there's a group coming over."

"And at Milton, too?" Sylvester said. "Right across the river from Madison, here?"

"Yes," the older man said. "This was a good crossing point until recently, but now it's too dangerous. Kentucky slaveowners have been losing so many slaves to the north that they're up in arms and guarding the Milton-to-Madison crossing point so tightly we can't use this route for a while. In fact, the Kentuckians have begun coming over and raiding Madison's negro district, Georgetown, capturing runaways and punishing anyone caught helping them. We're afraid they may burn the blacks out of Georgetown, and as a consequence of that fear many of the dark race are leaving for safer precincts to the east and west."

The boy looked up at Calloway with a puzzled expression, rubbing his peach-fuzzed chin. "So where are you crossing them these days? I've hear'd tell that some have crossed from Cooper's Bottom, a few mile west of Port . . . uh, Carrollton. Maybe the conductor with the slaves could get off their steamboat, say a mile or so upstream from Carrollton and high-tail it west over to Cooper's Bottom, then cross over to South Hanover without nobody knowing they'd changed course."

Judd Calloway smiled ruefully and shook his head. "Son, has thee ever traveled overland, going west from Carrollton to Cooper's Bottom? That land is so rugged it'd take an Indian a week to get through there. That's one rough tract of land, and that's saying something for Kentucky. If the runaways were to get off the boat above Carrollton and go west, they'd have to walk right along the river on the narrow beach below the hills, and they'd be sitting ducks exposed like that. We'll have to do it a different way, somehow.

112

"That's why the news thee brings is so distressing. We had hoped to shift more of our bands of runaways to Carrollton, but from what thee has told me it seems that route is becoming as perilous as ours here at Madison. I'll have to confer with my Quaker friends to choose another route, though any new route won't be as convenient as the two I've mentioned. Lord knows none of our pathways is easy in any case, with patrollers and bounty-hunters and their bloodhounds gaining in strength and determination every week."

# CHAPTER TWENTY-THREE

**S**even days later, as Rachel Cunningham dished up hash, fresh dandelion greens and cornbread shortly before noon, she saw Sam lift his rifle down from pegs above the mantle and set it by the door. He told Rachel he'd be away hunting for two or three nights with Homer and Dewey, and that he'd asked Johnny, Jr., one of her younger brothers, to come over to do the chores.

When Sam had gone she checked the woodbox and found the handcuffs missing. She knew something was going on with the slavecatching and that one or more runaway slaves would soon be in peril.

Rachel lost no time informing Sylvester of her discovery. They had set up a system of line-of-sight signals between her cabin and the Morrisons' a quarter-mile away.

That night, after a hurried trip to Madison to inform Mr. Calloway, Sylvester learned that Judd's free black contacts in Carrollton were preparing to receive a party of two young slaves, a man and a woman. This pair was being conducted down the Kentucky River on Hiram Easterday's sternwheeler, the *Sally Preston*, and would put in above Carrollton near the settlement of English to await further instructions.

Sylvester questioned this move. He asked Judd Calloway, "You surely cain't hide these people for very long, can you? Ain't the slavehunters bound to be pokin' around all the hidey holes and the tied-up boats on the Kentucky River?"

114

Calloway said, "Yes, Hiram will have to pretend his boat's had some sort of breakdown and make it look real to anyone suspicious that fugitives are on board. Thanks to thy information of last week a plan is in motion to save these runaways by a different route, and the reason for this delay is to get people ready to receive them when they disembark from the steamboat on the Indiana riverbank at Hanover."

"So, you'll have a man there to meet them?" Vess said.

"Yes, but we have a further problem in that our man at Hanover, James Hackney, who happens to be a mulatto, is away from home training horses for a person at Scottsburg, farther west, away from the river. We're trying to reach him, but we haven't been successful so far."

Judd then explained to Sylvester, there would be no "crossing-point" in the usual sense of the word for this party of fugitives. Hiram Easterday's steamboat would not be stopping at Carrollton as scheduled, but would move on out into the wide Ohio, proceed downstream and put in at the Hanover Landing just long enough to drop off the fugitives. Then the steamer would return to Carrollton and conduct business as usual. "All that remains to complete the plan is to have someone waiting at Hanover Landing to conduct the slaves the ten or fifteen miles out to Lancaster under cover of darkness. Jim Hackney is usually the man who does that job for us."

Sylvester saw his chance to become a part of the slaves' escape to freedom, and he broached the subject with Mr. Calloway. "How long you reckon it'll take the steamboat to reach this place you call English?"

"We heard he's already enroute downriver from Shaker Landing near Pleasant Hill above Frankfort. I'd say he may be at English within three days, then he'll tie up and wait for word from us."

"No time to waste, then. Mr. Calloway, I'll be your man at Hanover."

"What! Thee's just a boy. Jim's over thirty year old and lives in that area. He knows those rugged hollows leading up from the river like his own backyard, and he's led many a runaway slave up through there over the years."

"But you said he ain't there now, and we cain't be waitin' around to move them people. Me and my friend Jess Wagner up at

North Madison has hunted them woods and hollers together, and I can scout that area over the next day or two to scope it out, see what the slavecatchers is doin' and get things ready."

Judd Calloway paced the floor, hands clenched behind his back, breathing audibly, beard jutting forward, brow knitted above his red nose. Then he stopped and turned to look intently at the young man before him. "They'll be informing me when Hiram's boat has stopped at English. How would thee let me know when thee is ready, and how will thee know when Hiram's due to arrive at Hanover Landing?"

"Won't be hard. After I've scoped the area a day or two I'll come and tell you, then I'll ride back down there and camp close to Hanover Landing till the boat comes. The landing ain't but five mile or less from here. But how you gonna make connections between here and English?"

Calloway smiled in spite of himself. "Our Society of Friends has a contingent of riders scattered about the area, mostly farmers' sons, boys about thine own age, wild as March hares. They delight in racing up and down the country relaying our messages. Paul Revere had nothing on these fellows, but like Revere, these brave boys are in constant danger of being intercepted on some lonely nocturnal byway, never to be heard from again."

"But they cain't ride across the river," Sylvester said.

"True, but the young riders make occasional use of the Madison ferry, the *Prairie Bird*, to negotiate the river, and we also have brethren living along the river ready to send and receive signals, of both the sound and the visual variety."

"Like Cuddin Cyrus, I guess."

"Who?"

Sylvester grinned. "Never mind. Can I bunk here tonight, get a early start to Hanover?"

"Certainly, but won't thee need equipment for this mission? And won't thy family need to know what thee is up to? Will thee have to ride all the way back up to Sugar Branch?"

"First thing in the mornin' I'll stop for grub and gear at Jess Wagner's place on the hilltop, then go on to Hanover."

"We'll send someone to tell thy kinfolk, then."

116

"Don't need to. If I don't show up at Sugar Branch in a few days one of my brothers'll be knockin' on your door. My sister Rachel knows where you live. Best to keep this to ourselves, anyway, right?

"My sister Rachel's the one married to the headman of the slavecatchers at Lamb. She's done read the signs and seen him and his rascals was about to go slave huntin'. Then she told me and I told you not to cross 'em at Lamb. Don't know how her husband found out about these slaves comin' down the Kentucky River, but him and his outlaws has scouts, too."

Judd Calloway cast the boy a worried look. "I see. If it weren't for thy sister these fugitives would have been led right into a trap at Lamb. When you see her, please tell her we're grateful. Still, I'm not resting easy with this decision for thee to meet the *Sally Preston* at Hanover, Vess, though it appears to be our only way out of this spot. May God be with thee, son." He offered his hand to the boy.

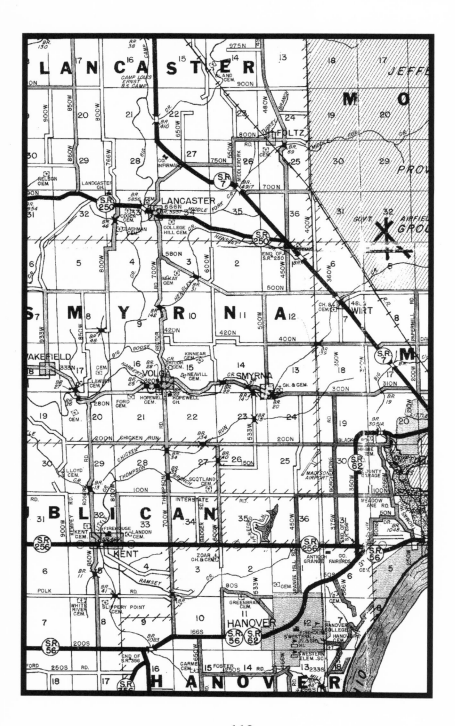

# PART II

## IVY

The map opposite is a segment of a 1983 Jefferson County, Indiana road map used by written permission of the Jefferson County Commissioners, Wanda Welch, Secretary. The area from Hanover to Lancaster was much less developed in 1845 than this map shows.

# CHAPTER TWENTY-FOUR

### Binford Plantation, near Pleasant Hill, Kentucky
### February, 1845

Three black slaves came driving a wagon down out of the woods and across the muddy hemp field that lay fallow now in the chill of February. They came at a gallop toward the cabins of the slave quarters, wagon wheels and horses' hooves slinging mud. They whooped for the women in the quarters and the big house to come take care of the injured man they carried, Jacob Brown, an eighteen-year-old lad whose leg had just been crushed by a tree they'd felled in the forest.

Ivy Mays, rising from her barn frame loom, came to look out the door of the shed with another slave woman, Edina Ditto. The two of them worked in this small board-and-batten structure, Ivy as weaver and Edina as her helper, on the Binford plantation. The lumber for the weaving shed had been salvaged from the wreck of a flatboat on the nearby Kentucky River in the flood of '39.

They ducked back into the shed to lay down the things they carried, scissors with the points blunted, balls of yarn. Ivy lifted her skirt above her worn homemade shoes and hurried with the other women to the big house, scattering chickens and joining black children as they ran over the bare earth of the slave quarter alley.

The wagon stopped between the mansion and the cabins in the quarters, the horses lathered and lolling their bits, the driver shouting for help with the injured man. Old Mistress Martha Binford came to the kitchen door, leaning on the arm of her black house slave, Bessie. Martha ordered the men to carry Jacob into the summer kitchen, just a few steps beyond the rear entrance of the great house.

Tate Binford, old Master John Binford's nephew and only acknowledged blood kin, late of Lexington, viewed the commotion from the window of his bedroom on the second floor. Just yesterday he had finally convinced his ailing Uncle John to deed ownership of the plantation, its thirty-seven slaves and their children, to himself.

Evidently wishing to exert the importance that came with his newly-acquired property, Tate charged downstairs, across the veranda and out toward the summer kitchen, shoving slave children away from the door. "Get out of here, you woolly heads!" he shouted. Without even looking at the injured man being laid on the large table with his left leg hanging limp and bleeding, he said, "Get that nigger off the table, for god's sake. Take him to the quarters."

"But he been hurt, Marse Tate," Bessie said, eyeing her new master with a beseeching look. She was in charge of the house slaves, three other kitchen women and two male servants. White plantation supervisors were called overseers, their subordinate black counterparts referred to as overlookers, or drivers. The Binford Plantation hadn't enough slaves to employ a white overseer, so the plantation owner discharged the overseer's duties himself, patrolling the slaves' field work and administering punishment when necessary. But as Master John Binford had aged over the years, he made fewer appearances in the fields and barns, and so Clay Jeter, the black driver, gained increasing authority.

Except for Bessie's supervision of the housework, Clay was driver of all the other slaves. He did not hesitate to make his own rules for the underlings, especially in recent years, and he did not spare the whip. But now, with Tate Binford having just arrived to assume ownership, the plantation hierarchy would be shifting.

"Get him outta here!" Tate shouted, and the slaves gingerly lifted the groaning Jacob back onto the wagon sideboard they'd used to carry him in.

Ivy, at the edge of the group of women gathered round the injured slave, stared at the white man in disbelief. She turned to Edina to whisper, "Who make that white boy boss of this plantation all a sudden? Missus done told 'em to put Jacob in here."

"He mus' be the new marse everybody talkin' 'bout. They say he the nephew of Marse John and Miss Martha. The way he be yellin' and stompin' round, look like we's in for big trouble."

Tate ordered the field slaves back to their woodcutting, then told Clay to ride to the village of Pleasant Hill, two miles distant, and fetch Doc Matthews to look at the injured man. Only Clay among the Binford slaves was allowed to leave the plantation without a pass.

Tate roared at the women to get back to their chores, except for Bessie, whom he commanded to stay with Jacob. Ivy and the other women slowly filed out of the cabin directing worried looks back over their shoulders at Jacob, who lay on the pallet groaning.

As the women left, Clay, taking his time heading for the stable where old white-headed Perry would saddle his chestnut gelding, pulled Ivy aside for a quick word. "I'll be comin' round to see you, gal, one of these first nights. You come when I give you a sign, 'cause me and you got some bidness to talk over." His hand moved to brush Ivy's breast before she saw it coming. She gasped and recoiled a step backward as Clay chuckled. He moved close to her again and said, "You follow my meanin', gal?"

Ivy dared look up only as far as the black giant's barrel chest, with its sweat-stained chambray shirt open at the collar. "Yassuh."

Young Master Tate observed this short conversation, then took closer notice of the slave girl, Ivy. Tate had been told that her white grandfather, Master John Binford, who had owned this large acreage in Woodford County for decades, was fond of the girl and treated her kindly. Because of the elder Binfords' benevolence toward her, Ivy remembered many happy hours playing in the big house as a child. Martha Binford, herself barren of children, seemed to accept her husband's mulatto grandchild.

Old John hadn't been so kind those decades ago when he'd forced himself on some of his more seemly slave women. But passing years and failing health had weakened him, mellowing even further his treatment of the slaves and allowing a climate of careless leniency toward them. In recent years he had been heard several times to declare, "I'll sell a slave before I'll use a whip on him." Then Marse John had suffered a stroke three weeks ago, giving

123

nephew Tate the opportunity to take over the plantation and its thirty-seven slaves.

Now, watching the short one-way conversation between Clay and Ivy, Tate suspected that the driver had already forced, or was about to force, Ivy to his own dark purpose. The new master decided to intervene.

Ivy was indeed a handsome slave girl. Those who had seen quadroons, or quarter-blood slave women, noted their unusual style of beauty, the rich olive tint of the complexion, the large bright eyes, often of green or amber color, the flawless features, the long black wavy hair. Many romantic fancies and mystical associations centered on those individuals in the South, often the property of their own grandfathers.

When the crowd dispersed Tate went inside the cabin and addressed Bessie who was slitting Jacob's bloody pantleg. "Come out here, you gonna do somethin' for me."

Outside the cabin the trim, well-dressed white man pushed his hat back revealing a high forehead and thick black hair. He took an initialed handkerchief from his pocket and mopped his face, which streamed with sweat, a peculiar sight considering the brisk weather. Tate saw Bessie regarding him warily, her head wrapped in a calico rag and her ample form draped in a brown skirt of rough material. "Startin' tomorrow mornin' I want you to train that Ivy to be a housegirl." The new master did not care that Bessie, and soon the others too, would understand that he wanted Ivy for something more sinister than housework.

The older slave women had seen this before. Years ago Marse John had taken the tall athletic Mattie and moved her into the slave cabin nearest the big house as "kitchen help," when all the blacks knew how he would use her. The fruits of that biracial union had been James, a boy who died in infancy, and Jane, a light-skinned girl who grew up to jump the broomstick with Daniel Mays, one of the field slaves. Jane and Daniel had named their first and only child Ivy. She was born three months before Daniel died of a kick to the head by a greenbroke mule while he was hitching the beast to a harrow. Her mother died of consumption when the child was twelve.

"But Marse Tate, Ivy be our bes' weaver. The other one out there, Edina, jus' more or less learnin' from Ivy. What we gone do if you take her off the loom? Edina cain't do all the weavin'. 'Sides, we got all the house help we needs."

"Put somebody with the woman and tell 'em they got to do it. You take Ivy to the kitchen tomorrow and make a house servant out of her like I told you, damnit."

Bessie only shook her head, looked at the ground and turned to go see about Jacob. Tate saw disrespect in her actions, resentment of him as her new owner and master. He had to set a tighter rein after the loose discipline imposed by old Master John and Mistress Martha Binford in recent years. "You hear me!" he shouted.

With her head still bent low and her back to him she muttered, "Yassuh!"

Now, unbeknownst to Ivy, she was about to become a house slave, one of the personal attendants of her new master, Tate Binford, and his elderly aunt and uncle. Every plantation had five or six trusted slaves trained to do the work of cooking, serving, cleaning, washing and generally tending the needs of the white folks who lived in the big house. Some house slaves had learned their tasks as children from their mothers and fathers who'd held the same jobs before them.

House servants lived in quarters near the great house, and were given slightly better huts, food, bedding and furniture than other slaves. Their white owners could ill abide having starved and dirty slaves serving their white friends at dinners.

Ivy at twenty would be younger than most of the Binford house slaves, but to carry out her most important duties youth was one of the primary requisites. Henceforth she would have to labor neither in the weaving shed, nor in the broiling sun under the constant threat of the lash, like most other slave women. But had she known what lay in store for her, she would have felt keenly the added degradation of her position, and she would have wished even more ardently to be free.

It would take a long time for Jacob to be able to walk again. The white Dr. Matthews from town saw him but once and did what he could, but the thigh bone was badly broken. "Looks like a spiral break, and it's compressed. Must have done that gettin' him out," he said as he straightened both of Jacob's legs on the pallet, paying little attention to the boy's groaning. "See how that leg's a little shorter than the other one? It'll swell up, but the bone didn't break the skin. Those scrapes and bruises are from the weight of the log and them gettin' him out from under it. I can't set a break like that. The bone will have to heal on its own, in whatever shape it chooses. That's why you need to keep him here with his leg splinted straight but not too tight, and keep him quiet for two weeks.

"When the swelling goes down, tighten the splint a little. Doctor him for pain and the cuts and abrasions." He splinted Jacob's leg, gave Bessie some laudanum and ointment, then went to the big house for his payment from Master Tate and left.

Ivy moved into the cabin that she was to share with Bessie and her family. It was the hut nearest the big house, and not far from the cabin where Jacob lay on his pallet.

In the days that followed Ivy took the lead among the other women in bringing Jacob back as close to good health as possible, and came to anticipate with a smile her morning and evening walks to see to the injured boy. This kept Ivy from dwelling on what was to become the darker side of her life at the hands of Master Tate.

Jacob had been moved in amongst three other young unmarried men, and by the time Ivy arrived every morning the others had left for the fields or woods, usually permitting Ivy and Jacob a few minutes alone. She enjoyed sharing news and flirtatious conversation with this bright-eyed young man who seemed so eager to get well.

Ivy saw that Jacob was no fool. They both knew his survival on the plantation depended on his recovery to a point where he could do useful work. If he didn't, his value on the market would fall to nothing and the master might summarily manumit him, especially this new Marse Tate who seemed not to be cut from the older Binfords' moderate cloth. In that case, manumission would not be an occasion for rejoicing. Rather, it might become a sentence to starvation.

The cruelest slave owners also sometimes freed elderly male slaves, after their productive years had passed. The infirm black men found themselves driven away, suddenly cut off from the plantation, their source of food and shelter. The lucky ones were sometimes

126

retained to perform small tasks such as mending harness, leaky buckets or sharpening tools. Aged females were occasionally kept as babysitters for field slave women.

During Jacob's convalescence Ivy became a cheerful comfort to the boy she suspected of being a bit younger than herself. As he began to heal they chided each other over the season of the year when each was born, as if one season were preferable to the others. Jacob had not the faintest idea of either the season or year of his birth. Old Master John had told Ivy her birth date, but she decided not to let on to Jacob.

After pretending to study the matter for a while, she announced, "I's decided this here black chil' was borned in corn shuckin' time."

"Why you say that, woman?"

" 'Cause he be so used to havin' all the womenfolk buzzin' round his good-lookin' self like they do at a shuckin' bee, gals talkin' all at once, makin' eyes at him, toadyin' to his every need. You be spoilt rotten, boy."

"What 'bout you, miss granny woman? I thinks you musta come along at Christmas time, 'cause you actin' like you the savior of this here poor nigger with the busted leg. You been layin' down the gospel law to everybody roun' about this here cabin." This brought laughter to them both, and Ivy thought the glow of humor in Jacob's sad eyes might be his best medicine. That, plus the open flirtation that brought them closer and lighted their smiles.

Ivy and the other slave women nursed and encouraged the young man for weeks until he could walk with the aid of a wooden crutch. Perry, the old white-haired slave who took care of the horses, had whittled it for him from a forked tree limb. Jacob told Ivy he was determined to learn to walk without the aid of the crutch, so eventually by painful practice, clutching onto stall gates, harness pegs, wagons, even the horses themselves, he managed to get around on his own after a fashion. Thereafter he became Perry's helper.

With the passage of time, Jacob, benefitting from the strength and resilience of youth, began moving about more easily. Later, he would take over for Perry in the horse barn. The old fellow had been a faithful livery man for Master John and Mistress Martha for many years, but now he was falling victim to his hunched back and sore knees. Back when the elder Binfords were running things, the slaves

127

understood from long practice that the old folks would usually allow them to make common sense decisions around the plantation without John and Martha's involvement. With Tate Binford taking over as the new master, that situation seemed likely to change.

# CHAPTER TWENTY-FIVE

essie made her way to the weaving shed early on the morning after Master Tate had given her orders. The male slaves spoke to her in sleepy voices, trudging past her toward the woods, carrying axes and saws, squinting against the orange glare of the new-risen sun. Their shuffling steps left tracks in the muddy lane, the procession snaking double-file behind the wagon into the misty distance between split rail fences toward the hills and the dark line of timber. They cut trees into short lengths during these damp cold days before planting time in order for the chunks to cure by the first frigid days of November. Then they would split them for firewood.

"Marse Tate say I has to make a house slave out'n you, but it don't take no witchy woman to see what that mean. Has you been paradin' in front a'him in a flippy tail skirt and a tight blouse showin' yourself?"

"No ma'am!" Ivy said. "I don't know nothin' 'bout what Marse Tate say, and no, I ain't been shinin' up to no white man, not even to Jacob, though he act like he want to keep company with me. All this gossip goin' on 'bout me, I ain't fixin' to take up with no man, white or black. Why they after me like this?"

Bessie looked at Ivy and shook her head. With a wan smile she said, "Child, all you got to do is peek at a lookin' glass to see what they thinkin'. Look around. Clay pick him off a cute slave gal now and again, make her his sweetheart for a while, and you seen the black chilluns that come of it, ain't you? You don't smarten up quick, gal, you's in for a rough education. Tonight after supper get old Nettie to tell you how Marse John took over her sister Mattie, your own gran'mammy, back in the old days. Nettie be your great aunt, you know.

"Can't figure what we'll do 'bout the weavin'." Bessie said. "I's goin' send old Nettie down to help Edina in the weavin' shed. Years ago Nettie done some weavin', but she almos' blind now and her hands all twisted up. All she good for mostly is scrapin' dirty dishes into the hogs' slop bucket. Lawsy mercy! Marse Tate fixin' to drive niggers crazy roun' here."

Ivy walked with Bessie to the big house kitchen. She was glad to be out in the sunshine, breathing fresh sweet air after long days in the dark weaving shed with its two small windows. She gazed off across fields and valleys where morning mist rose to meet the warming sun. The girl breathed in the sweet smell of wood smoke, the redolence of recently-cooked breakfast fatback, potatoes, onions and cornbread in the slave cabins they passed. She shivered and rubbed the goose flesh on her arms, responding to the chill in the air and the innate vigor of a healthy young woman, but her exhilaration was to be short-lived.

As they neared the big house Ivy felt a cold stab of fear for what awaited her there. What would Marse Tate do to her? She'd heard the sordid tales of abuse, women's lives ruined by the wanton cruelty of their owners. Her brow wrinkled as questions formed in her mind. She turned, still frowning, to the older woman. "Bessie, I's scared. Don't know nothin' 'bout bein' with no white man, 'cep it be sinful."

Bessie stopped at the foot of the steps leading up to the kitchen of the big house and looked intently at Ivy, then took her hand and patted it. "Old Bessie hep you best she know how. Come on up in here."

The older woman sat the girl down at the kitchen table and gave her sassafrass tea. "We talk a minute firs', then get to work. Even though you's to be a house slave now, you still gonna live in the quarters. You be takin' old Nettie's place with me an' my Owen and the chillun. As you know, we lives in the cabin closest to the kitchen here. You gonna have that little lean-to off the side of our cabin.

Give you a place to be by yourself. Nettie be stayin' in your hut from now on.

"After we talk you go get your things and take 'em to my cabin. I'll get Uncle Eddie to take Nettie's things out to your sleepin' place close to the weavin' shed."

Before teaching Ivy the labors of cleaning, washing and cooking for the white folks, Bessie told her some of the unspoken rules she'd learned from observing white men's treatment of their black mistresses over the years. "Firs' of all, you ain't to pay no mind to what other black folks say to you. Jus' remember none of this dirty bidness is your fault. Hold your head up high, gal.

"Now, when it come to white men, don't do no good to beg for mercy. If they sees somethin' they wants from a nigger, they takes it, and now Marse Tate want you. It ain't right, but if you do somethin' he don't like, even lookin' at him the wrong way, he have the driver cut you with the rawhide and throw salt water on your back. You got to be strong. No cryin' or wheedlin', just take it and go on or you gets the whip."

# CHAPTER TWENTY-SIX

*L* ate the next evening Ivy found herself standing bewildered in Tate's bedroom to which she'd been brought by Clay. In the low light she looked around. She saw the chairs, the washstand, the bed, the small fire in the grate. Clay closed the door and left her alone standing there. She heard a sound and turned frightened eyes to see Tate stepping from behind a screen. Her impulse was to run, but she remembered Bessie's warning that to attempt escape from white men only made things worse for a slave woman.

The thin dark-bearded man walked past her without a word, locked the door behind her and pocketed the key. He came back to stand before her, and she saw for the first time that he held a long knife, its blade gleaming in the dim light. His voice was low and slurred when he said to take off her clothes. She stood motionless, daring not to breathe until he took a step toward her, eyes dilated and shining, mouth twisted in a wet-lipped grin. When her blouse fell to the floor exposing her young breasts, the brown aureoles contrasting darkly with her olive skin, he motioned with the knife and she stepped free of her skirt and shift. "Them, too," he said, pointing again with the knife. She stood in her rough-woven drawers, which reached halfway to her knees. The garment was open at the front showing an inner linen ribbon wrapped twice around her waist, between her legs, then tied to the waist strap in front, holding the dry absorbent moss in place.

She struggled to ease her tight muscles, but the trembling remained in her voice. "I be bleedin', suh, my moon time."

He cursed, and after a moment he ordered her to her knees. He moved to stand close in front of her, free hand loosening his clothing, talking, calling her a comely nigger wench. He held the knife behind her head, its blade touching her neck. She tried not to look, but saw his hand moving, the unbuttoned flap, the opened trousers, his evil intent . . . . She closed her eyes.

Afterward, choking and retching into his chamber pot, Ivy heard Tate Binford tell her he owned her now, had taken her over with the other slaves from his aged and failing uncle. He said that now she would be his personal servant. "Did Bessie move you outta the weavin' shed and give you a place with the kitchen women?"

She struggled to control her breathing and speak. "Yuh . . . yassuh."

"Good, now get on back to the quarters and don't be talkin' about this."

It was late when Ivy crept down the back stairs from Tate's bedroom and out toward the dark slave quarters. A dog barked way off somewhere, causing her to look around with frightened eyes. Her faint moon shadow glided along Bessie's cabin wall beside her like a goblin ready to scream out to the night watchman. Tongue working in her cheek, desperate to make no sound by her movements, her thoughts voiced a silent mantra, *Sweet Jesus, don't let nobody catch me out here. Hep me, Jesus, ease my torment.*

She stopped, peered round the corner, able to see all too well along the bare earth lane between the two rows of slave cabins. *Lord, sail a cloud 'cross that ole moon. I be standin' out like a white ghost in the firelight.* Her bare feet soundless on the hard ground, she reached the door of the cabin, creaked it open and slipped inside. She listened to sounds of sleep-breathing from the pallets on the floor, alert for the slightest sound indicating someone following her.

"Bessie?" she whispered, even as she dreaded her mentor's questions, aware and ashamed of the white man's filth and stench upon her.

"Ivy," came the soft answer. The girl saw Bessie sheltering the tiny flame of a lily stalk taper that she'd lighted from a dying coal in her fireplace. Bessie took her arm, led her into the lean-to and drew the frayed hook rug back across the opening. Using the taper she lit a small lamp on a shelf. The older woman's form turned and loomed

133

in front of Ivy, blocking for a moment the light from the lamp. She folded the girl in her arms, whispered, "Marse Tate hurt you, or was it that no-good driver?"

"Marse Tate. He done make me do things . . . awful things." A sob broke forth now, and she heard a movement in the next room. Bessie shushed her.

"You need to wash, gal," she whispered. "Then you tell old Bessie what happened. Talkin' the onliest way to let the shame out."

Later, both women sat on the wash bench after the basin had been moved to the earthen floor. Ivy had wrapped herself in her nightgown and blanket, then sobbed again as she struggled to describe the violation of her body at the hands of Tate Binford.

Slowly the girl quieted. Bessie let the silence grow long, her hand caressing Ivy's back. Then she spoke in a low, sorrowful voice. "Gal, they ain't no peace for us women of the dark race in this world. It be like the Lord testin' us, makin' us walk through fire to earn our peace in heaven. We has to do our bes' and pray to God to bring us all home to that golden city on high one day.

"If a slave woman ain't killin' herself in the fields she be sweatin' in the kitchen gettin' whupped for the least little thing go wrong. God forbid, she break a cup or somethin'. Or when a black girl child like y'all grow up showin' a pretty face she get claimed by a white man for he own scandalous and sinful use."

Bessie paused again, and in the quietness Ivy heard the crickets chirping around the cabin's foundation heralding the coming of spring to these rolling Kentucky hills. She envied those tiny insects for their simple existence. They seemed oblivious to cares, especially the cares that now tormented Ivy.

All she wanted at this moment was sleep, the long nightmare sleep of one too traumatized to face what new violence the world would bring tomorrow. She felt humiliated, defeated, defenseless, unable to protect herself from this new master's wanton ravagement. A wave of nausea swept over her again. She longed for unconsciousness.

After a moment floating between sleep and wakefulness, Ivy became aware of Bessie moving, taking something from the folds of her nightgown. "I's gonna give you somethin', child. It be one thing that'll ease your mind no matter what he do to you. Hide this here little pouch somewheres in your things. It got seeds inside."

Ivy drifted back toward sleep. Bessie abruptly turned to her with searching eyes. "Brace up, child. We gonna do something to protect you. I done seen too many black gals took the spew of a white man and birthed his baby. This here'll keep that from happenin' to my precious Ivy. Now you listen good, 'cause this here Queen Anne's lace seed gonna hep you, even with Marse Tate doin' his foulness on you."

Ivy spoke from her dreamlike torpor. "I cain't, Bessie. Please, let me go to bed and forget this evil. I just wants to sleep."

Bessie shook Ivy's shoulder. "You got to fight, gal, like all us black women got to if we gonna live another day. You wake up, now, 'cause I got somethin' right here that fix it so you can save a piece of yourself from him. You take and chew up two of these seeds every morning and night for two days after you been with Marse Tate, you hear? They for every time he get up inside you. The seeds tastes bad, and they gets all greasy in your mouth, but chew 'em up good 'cause they'll keep you from havin' his child."

The girl rose slowly from her nightmare, staring down at the seeds in Bessie's hand. "I chews 'em every day?" she said.

"No, just two every mornin' and two in the evenin' for two days after Marse Tate been with you. It be two, two and two, easy to remember. And don't try to go out by yourself and get more seeds. They's other weeds that looks like Queen Anne's lace, but some of them seeds is bad poison. You come tell Bessie when you run out, you hear?"

# CHAPTER TWENTY-SEVEN

A few days later, Clay came in the back of the great house after breakfast, saw Ivy washing dishes by herself and called her outside, away from the house. He spoke in a low growl. "I'll be at your lean-to before sunrise tomorrow, take you up to Marse Tate's bedroom. He said for you to wash up, get ready for him." The overseer spoke with a lop-sided leer and a smirk. She smelled chewing tobacco on his breath, he being the only slave allowed such a luxury. "What you reckon he gonna do to you?"

Ivy stood with her eyes downcast, tremors beginning in her legs. She clenched her abdominal muscles, clasped her hands so tightly together they turned numb, prayed not to break down in front of this man. "Don't know, suh."

"He goin' to work you over, use you till you cain't walk straight, like he did last time. He told me I better not lay a finger on you, for you his woman now. You tell him what I said to you that other time?"

"Nahsuh, I ain't said nothin'."

"Well, if I ever hear you did I'll catch you when nobody ain't lookin' and you'll feel a *real* man on you. Then I'll whip you for talkin' outta turn."After he left, she felt so dizzy and nauseous she barely had time to stumble around the corner of the summer kitchen before she vomited.

On their way up the back stairs next morning, Clay put his hand low on Ivy's backside and kept it there though the girl flinched and nearly fell. She tried to move away from him but he followed, his hand making contact, caressing slowly, moving lower. At Tate's door, Clay growled in her ear, "You remember what I told you. Not a word."

Though tears were forming, she replied in a small quavering voice, "Yassuh."

Inside the room, she barely had time to wipe tears away with her hands before the master appeared from behind his screen. "You done bleedin'?" His voice was cold and brittle as ice on the horse trough.

After a brief pause she sniffed, drew a shuddering breath, "Yassuh."

He again locked the door, then stepped toward her, looking closely at her in the gray morning light that crept around the drawn drapes. Tate's voice rose in intensity as he spoke. "You been cryin'? That damned Clay say somethin' to you? He been messin' with you? What'd he do?"

Caught between the demands of two abusive men, the girl could contain her tears no longer. Her face crumpled and she brought her hands to her mouth to stop the tears and snot, unable to stifle the gasping sobs of a frightened child. Her knees buckled and she slipped to the floor.

Tate stood over her a moment, then reached down and touched her shoulder with one hand. "Here, stop that squallin' and tell me what that son-of-a-bitch did."

She was beyond words, lying on her knees face down, like a pilgrim in supplication before an idol, sprawled forward with her hands covering her face, sobbing uncontrollably.

Lying there crying and defenseless for long moments, unable to overcome her hysteria, she fully expected to be punished. Then slowly, slowly, feeling no reaction to her collapse, her sobs abated and her breathing came under control. She wiped the mucous from her face with her sleeve, opened her eyes still expecting a kick, a blow, at the very least angry threatening words. Instead, nothing. No footsteps, not even the sound of his breathing.

Had he left the room during her outburst? She turned her head enough to peek at the door. It remained closed. Her heart jumped when she caught sight of Tate's feet, clad in soft slippers, standing where they had been the moment she fell.

The knife! Was he standing over her ready to kill her when she moved? Terrifying images flashed through her mind like lightning. She had violated Bessie's rule in the most flagrant way. Was she now going to die for her mistake?

Several more seconds passed before the girl dared move from her prone position. She crawled backward a few inches and spoke fearfully into the silence. "Marse Tate?" No response. "I . . . I's sorry for what I done, Marse Tate."

Then a new thought occurred to her. "You all right, Marse Tate?" Ivy had continued inching backward as she spoke, and now she dared to push her upper body from the floor so that she was on all fours and could take in more of the room. She now saw Tate Binford's legs standing perfectly still in front of her, clad in pajamas. She stared straight ahead at him, then gradually raised her eyes to his face.

The man stood there transfixed, no movement, his eyes staring straight ahead, looking at nothing, his hands held slightly away from his sides, motionless. It was as if the girl were looking at a statue.

Ivy rose, first to a squatting position, then she straightened her legs little by little until she was standing before him, her gaze never leaving his face. He had not moved, nor even blinked.

Was he testing her, waiting for her attempt to escape? Would he then catch and whip her, or worse? She looked behind her. She knew the door was locked with only Tate having a key. Her confusion and fear had her at the brink of calling out for help when she caught a movement at the edge of her vision. Had he moved?

As she watched in horror his hands moved haltingly, sluggishly toward each other. When they met they moved together in a rubbing motion, as if he were washing his hands. Then his head turned slightly and he moved his feet, as if to adjust his balance. His eyes seemed to roam about the room before settling on Ivy. "Is you all right, Marse Tate?"

Her presence seemed to register with him at last and he mumbled, "Garlic . . . . You been eating garlic?" He continued rubbing his hands together.

Still afraid this was some sort of trick, Ivy held her silence a moment, then whispered, "Nahsuh, I ain't et no garlic."

138

Tate turned then, and went unsteadily to sit on the side of the bed. He stopped rubbing his hands and motioned for her to sit beside him. She sat near the foot of the bed, leaving space between them.

He spoke in a subdued voice, his speech indistinct, rubbing his neck. "Tired, bad headache. You been here long?"

"Nahsuh, not long."

After a long silence he gazed about as if awakening. Finally he looked at her and said, "Go on now, you be here in the morning. Don't say nothing."

"Yassuh. You . . . you let me out, Marse?"

He fished in the pocket of his robe and found the key. "Here."

She took it and rose to go, as eager to get away as an escaping prisoner, for in reality that's what she was. But desperate and frightened as she felt, halfway to the door she stopped and turned to face her master. "Beggin' your pardon, suh, I sho'nuf do as you say, suh, but . . . could you . . . not . . . ." Ivy gripped the large key so tightly it bruised her fingers. She peered at him in the dim light, watching his face, fearing an expression of anger that would send her running. She was breaking the rules again, and her timing could not have been worse, but the words came out in spite of her, revealing her greatest fear.

Tate turned his head slowly to look at her, squinting, trying to focus his eyes. "Not what?"

"Not have Mistuh Clay bring me up here, suh." She paused and took a deep ragged breath, then, "He say things and touch me, suh. I's 'fraid of him, sho'nuf."

"You just be here early in the morning, you hear?"

"Yassuh, I be here." She was gone in seconds, leaving the door ajar with the key still in the lock.

# CHAPTER TWENTY-EIGHT

𝐼vy was confused by Tate's spell and his answer to her plea as she was leaving. What had caused his illness? Did he not remember his rant about Clay? Would the overseer come get her in the morning, as before? Had Marse Tate even understood her request about Clay?

In the chilly blue light of predawn with frost on the stubble fields and smoke rising straight up in the windless air from breakfast fires in the quarters she waited for Clay. Whether the driver appeared or not, she knew she'd be whipped if she didn't go to her master's room, or he might send the overseer looking for her. She had not told Bessie what was going on, she just slipped out of the lean-to and walked with hurried steps across the cold bare ground to the big house, being careful to avoid chicken droppings, peering about with frightened eyes. She climbed the stairs to his room, stepping lightly near the wall to avoid squeaking the treads.

She knocked softly. He was waiting for her, made her undress as he watched and told her to get on the bed. She lay on her side in the fetal position facing him with her arms across her breasts in a pitiful attempt at modesty. He told her to turn over, lie on her back. Then he took off his robe and pajamas, his hungry eyes never leaving her.

Ivy was so shocked her thoughts burst out in spite of her, violating Bessie's advice again. She begged him not to violate her. "Please, Marse Tate. Don't . . . don't hurt me, I's . . . jus' a girl."

He ignored her plea, got into bed with her, instructed her as he rolled onto her. "Bring your knees up." He entered her roughly,

140

without prelude. She cried out in pain, then sobbed, bitterly but not as hysterically as she'd done before.

She felt him meeting resistance and her pain intensified. He lunged against her several times, and finished in seconds. He withdrew. "So, you ain't been keepin' company with no man?"

The shaking came again, and she could barely speak, but whispered between gasps and gritted teeth, "No, Marse . . . ain't been with . . . no man 'fore now."

"Good, because if I ever see or hear of you fornicating with a nigger, I'll sell him South in a minute, you understand?"

"Yassuh."

When he began putting on his clothes she again folded herself into a protective position on the bed, shivering, breathing irregularly. She followed him with the eyes of a cornered animal.

Tate waved his hand, as if shooing flies, and dismissed her, then turned to stir the fire in the grate. He had not locked the door this time. Dressing quickly, hurrying down the stairs she realized he hadn't mentioned his spell of yesterday morning. Did he not remember it? And what of his tirade against Clay, and her begging him not to send Clay to fetch her? At least Clay had not come to force her to his bedroom this time. Did Marse Tate just forget about Clay?

Thereafter, Tate used different ways to give Ivy the sign when he wanted her in his bedroom the next morning. He would tap on his window when he saw her crossing the yard to the back door of the big house, or drop a word to her as he passed her clearing dishes from the dinner table or sweeping the kitchen. He ordered her up to his room on several occasions over the next few days, each time forcing her to disrobe, then taking his pleasure with her on the bed. Each time she cried and begged him not to force her, to no avail, but she did not see the knife again, and he did not send Clay to fetch her.

By this time Ivy was confiding in Bessie after each attack at the hands of Master Tate. On these occasions the older woman would hold her close, make sure she was using the Queen Anne's lace seeds and would sit talking with her in the kitchen until the girl's tears subsided. "Ivy, when you in his bedroom, you bound to notice things, things he don't want nobody to know 'bout him. But you got

141

to act like you ain't seen nothin', for it come back to bite you. All us slaves round the big house comes to know things. And niggers what knows things 'bout white men is dangerous to the men, but more dangerous to theyselves. Be watchin' yo back, gal, you hear?"

More than anything besides Clay, Ivy feared that Tate would summon her during her next moon time, and that he would force her to kneel in front of him again. She knew her time was approaching and that Marse Tate would want her again soon. The girl briefly considered ending her life rather than face that horror again, but she knew the sorrow, and eventually the added abuse that act would inflict on Bessie, Jacob and the others, so she abandoned the idea.

The next time Tate came up to her she was beating a rug that hung over the clothesline. He took the heavy wire rug beater and pretended to inspect it as he spoke. "What you beatin' rugs for?" he said in his drawling indistinct voice. She felt his cold stare.

"Spring cleanin', suh."

"You be in my room in the morning. Before daylight, you hear?"

Ivy gazed down at her hands clasped tightly at her waist and said, "Yassuh, but . . . ."

"But what?"

"My moon time fixin' to start again, suh, anytime now."

"Godamnit! I ain't doin' it like that again. How long your bleedin' last?"

Trembling and fearing the whip, she said, "Only 'bout a week, suh."

"Shit!" He threw the rug beater to the ground and stomped up and down the clothesline with his fists clenched. "You damn well better not be lyin' to me!"

"Nahsuh, Marse Tate. Time come 'bout once a month, suh."

"Looks like you'd get with child so I wouldn't have to put up with this bleedin' stuff."

"Yassuh, maybe soon, suh."

"You ain't been with no other man, have you? That damned Clay?"

"Nahsuh, nobody, suh."

"That's the way it better stay."

"Yahsuh. I know that be right."

Ivy watched as Tate Binford marched off toward the big house muttering obscenities under his breath.

Ivy's moon time never came. Could the seeds have stopped her monthly bleeding? Had it just been delayed? Had she taken some terrible illness? Was she already with child? After a week had passed Tate ordered her to his room three times the next week. She learned to keep herself under control and not cry out or beg for mercy while he made preparations to assault her.

On the third occasion he had just told her to take off her clothes and lie on her back on the bed when another seizure came upon him. She saw him standing, having just kicked off his slippers, starting to take off his pajamas, when he went rigid. He stared into space as he had done the first time, but now his body jerked, and he soon lost his balance and fell hard against the bed rail, striking his shoulder, rolling onto the floor where he continued to  convulse and thrash about, striking his head against the foot of the bedpost.

Ivy sprang off the bed, standing over him wringing her hands. "Oh, Marse Tate, you gonna hurt youself." It was as if he couldn't hear her. His eyes were open but rolled up into his head, fixed, unseeing. She dropped to her knees, grasping for his arm, which was flailing against the leg of a chair. Before she could stop him his fist struck her across the face, knocking her away.

She came back to him with renewed determination, throwing herself on his thrashing body. Ivy was a tall, strong girl, her muscles conditioned over the years as a slave. She finally caught his arms while keeping her face near his chest to avoid his blows. For all the suffering and fear he had put upon her, Tate Binford was not a large man. The weight of Ivy's body on top of him succeeded in limiting the violence of his flailing. She managed to slowly move him away from the furniture into the middle of the room. "Oh, Marse Tate," she said, "you head be bleedin'! If you don't come outta this Mistuh Clay gone kill me for doin' this to you, suh. Please, Marse, wake up."

Just when the girl thought he would throw her off and continue injuring himself against the obstacles in the room, his wild thrashing began to weaken. He grunted and gasped for air, finally saying, "Get off!" in an unclear voice.

When she saw it was safe to do so she rolled off his body, taking care to hold onto his nearest arm to protect herself from another random blow. Then she stood on all fours at a safe distance, breathing hard, watching him as he quieted.

Tate awoke from his seizure as if coming out of a nightmare. He groaned, shook his head, looked around as he had done the first time, then struggled to get up. "Here, Marse, let me hep you," Ivy said. She managed to get him to a sitting position, he barefoot, still in his rumpled, twisted and bloody pajamas, she totally nude. "We got to get you on the bed, suh. But wait a minute, Marse. Firs' I got to get you somethin' to lay on, so the blood won't mess the bed." She lowered his upper body to the floor. He closed his eyes, still breathing irregularly, but he appeared to understand what she said.

Ivy looked wildly about the room trying to find a suitable blanket or cloth to lay him on. She went to a dresser on one side of the room, intending to pull out the bottom drawer, hoping to find a blanket. Just before she stooped to touch the drawer pulls something bright caught her eye on the dresser top. There in the dim gray light lay the long knife that Tate had threatened her with the first time she'd come to this room.

She looked back at her master lying on the floor with his eyes closed, groaning softly, defenseless. An idea surged into her mind, and she watched her fingers creep toward the knife handle.

# CHAPTER TWENTY-NINE

*I*t took only a moment for Ivy to realize she was in too deep to work herself out of this dilemma by herself. She might easily kill this man, or flee from this room, but in the end it would cost her life. Even though her master had treated her more cruelly than he would a lowly farm animal, her thought evaporated instantly. Bessie's warning about knowing white folks' secrets rang in her ears.

Her only hope was to help him. Better to tolerate a mean dog than be thrown to the wolves. Even with Tate Binford lying there semi-conscious on the floor it was clear to her that she was the powerless one.

After a moment's rummaging in the bottom drawer, she found an old frayed counterpane. She quickly spread it double on one side of his bed, then approached him again. At the last moment she realized she was still naked, so she clothed herself as fast as she could before helping Tate to his feet, where he stood unsteadily, leaning heavily on her. She guided him to the bed where he sat down clumsily, and with her steadying him, he lay back. His legs were heavy as logs as she lifted them onto the bed, trying to make him as comfortable as possible. She straightened his body as best she could before she said, "Marse Tate, I got to get some water and a washrag to clean up your bleedin', suh." His only reply was a soft groan.

She brought the bowl with some water and a cloth from the washstand, then climbed up on the bed beside him to wipe away the blood and get him out of his bloody pajamas. She observed that he'd bitten the inside of his cheek or tongue, for blood trickled from the corner of his mouth. She quickly inspected his arms and legs where he had struck the furniture, and saw that ugly bruises were forming.

While Ivy busily tended Tate's wounds he seemed to be regaining full consciousness. She noticed him watching her as she worked over him. "You feelin' better now, Marse Tate?"

His voice seemed to come from far away. "What happened?"

"You done had a spell, suh, rollin' round on the floor hurtin' yourself. Ivy have you cleaned up shortly, suh."

"I'm sore all over."

"Yassuh, you like to beat yourself up, suh. You got somethin' I can put on this here cut on your head?"

He raised his hand and Ivy guided it to the place she indicated. He winced, then looked at his fingers. The flow of blood had stopped but a knot was forming there. "It's in my hair. Won't show much, will it?"

He made no resistance as she took hold of his head and turned it gently to see the injury more clearly. "Nahsuh, won't show at all, but I say you sho' gone feel it for a few days. Them other bruises, they be covered by your clothes, suh."

Tate told her to look in the top drawer of his dresser for a tin of salve. When she returned and applied a small amount to the place on his head, then fluffed his hair so it wouldn't show, he looked at her and said, "Tell me what happened. Did you hit me with something?"

"Oh, nahsuh! I get on the bed, like you say. Then it be like you pass out on your feet and fall down, beatin' yourself again' the bed and chair 'til Ivy hold you down so you won't hurt youself no more."

"How long was I out?"

"Don't know, suh. Reckon it wadn't no more'n a few minutes, suh. Then you start wakin' up."

He lay looking at the ceiling a moment, rubbing his bruised arm. "Did I pass out when you was here before?"

"Yassuh, but you didn't fall down. Scared me though, sho'nuf."

"I been blacking out some lately. Far as I know me and you is the only ones knows about it. You better not be tellin' anybody."

"Oh, nahsuh, I never do that, suh."

"The last thing I need is for Clay to hear about this."

146

Ivy made a quick decision. "That other time you had a spell, you was talkin' 'bout Mistuh Clay sayin' mean things to me, sayin' he gone hurt me. That be just 'fore you pass out, suh."

"He been botherin' you?"

"Nahsuh, not since you stop havin' him take me up here."

"So, you been coming without Clay bringin' you?"

"Yassuh, I done axed you not to have him bring me, and you see I come when you say. Mistuh Clay ain't had nothin' to do with it. I thanks you for that, suh." She wondered again, could he have just forgotten to tell Clay to bring her these last few times?

Tate sat up in the bed and leaned forward, elbows on his thighs with his hands on either side of his head. He began to talk. "Good. That pushy bastard wants to take over this plantation and all the slaves. He knows as a nigger he can't ever own the place, but he thinks he can get control now. With Uncle John and Aunt Martha getting older and weaker, they couldn't stop him.

"Before I came from Lexington he had it figured that Uncle John would die soon, and Aunt Martha would be even more helpless to get rid of him. So he'd keep on bein' the big boss around here.

"Then I offered to come live with my aunt and uncle, keep the place goin'. They said the plantation would be mine eventually, anyway, seein' as I'm their only kin. "The nigger never expected me to show up and take over the place. That's killed his plan. Already I seen what he's been up to, carvin' out his little kingdom around here. So, if that sneaky hoodoo knew I been havin' blackout spells he'd look to take advantage, maybe even try to kill me."

It would never occur to Ivy, but as Master John's granddaughter, his direct descendant, she should have a stronger claim to inherit the plantation than Tate. Except, that is, for a few problems. This was the South, it was 1845, Ivy was a female and she was black.

Ivy had chosen sides, whether she wanted to or not. "Oh, Marse Tate, I hopes you feelin' better now, 'cause I's 'fraid of Mistuh Clay."

"You tell me if that sonofabitch messes with you again."

"Yassuh." She felt her legs growing weak again, her heart pounding. "Suh, you want somethin' to eat directly, cool cloth for your head? Maybe you wants to rest, suh, Ivy come back later?"

147

"What time is it? Hand me my watch. Damn, goin' for eight already. I got to get up, check on things out there."

"Yassuh. S'cuse me, suh, but be careful out yonder. That old sun mighty bright today. Ivy come back this evenin', bring you somethin'?"

"No, just be here in the mornin', same time. Don't tell nobody."

"Yassuh, I be here."

# CHAPTER THIRTY

Thus began the pattern of Ivy's next few weeks of life on the Binford Plantation. Tate expected her to appear in the early morning several times a week. Most mornings he would take his pleasure on her and she would leave. But changes crept into the routine.

The next morning after Tate's severe seizure he made her go through the same sordid ritual of disrobing, except that this time he remained calm and did not black out. He lay down beside her and fondled her briefly, but she was still tense and unlubricated when he abruptly entered her. She whimpered, but fell silent a few moments later as he spent more time than usual upon her before he finished. Afterward he seemed in no hurry for her to leave.

Thereafter when she came to his room he initiated one-sided conversations with her as they lay naked together after he finished. Tate's desire would be sated, Ivy still recovering from the discomfort and tensely awaiting his next demand.

One morning they lay side by side on their backs with daylight brightening around the closed drapes and morning sounds seeping in from outside. After Tate had finished with the girl he pulled the sheet over them, then turned to her and caressed her breasts and abdomen as he spoke. "You're afraid of me, ain't you, gal?"

She turned only her eyes to look at him, her body still tense under his touch. Then she realized he wouldn't allow her to remain silent. "Yassuh, I's scared of you and Mistuh Clay, 'fraid of the rawhide, suh, like all the other niggers is."

149

"Well, you ain't like all the other niggers 'round here. You think you deserve the whip? What you done to get a whippin'?"

"I's cried and begged, suh. Slaves in the quarters done tol' me the least little thing bring the rawhide. I seen it before, suh. I's always 'spectin' it, and the saltwater after."

"You talk about whipping. Clay ever whip you?"

"Nahsuh, but I seen a poor slave get a unmerciful whuppin'."

"That must of been before I got here. I didn't know Uncle John and Aunt Martha whipped their slaves."

"It weren't Marse John, but Mistuh Clay, suh. He whip a field slave name of Ike near to death, he did. Marse John don't hear 'bout it 'til it be too late."

"Why'd he whip him?"

"Way I hear'd it, he axed to leave the barn a few minutes one mornin', go see 'bout his sick wife in the quarters. Mistuh Clay say no, get back to work, nigger. Ike, he start walkin' to the hut anyways. Clay send three more slaves to get him, say he shoot 'em if they don't go."

"What happened?"

"They brung Ike back, Mistuh Clay say take off his shirt, tie him to a tree. They's a lashin' ring on that tree, still there yet today, suh, bark 'bout growed over it. Tell all the slaves to come see the fun, he say. Me an' Edina, we come out the weavin' shed. Whippin' tree close by.

"I close my eyes, but still hear them terr'ble lashes. I feels ev'ry stroke in my stomach, all over my body. Ike, he cry out, make awful sounds. Mistuh Clay, he don't stop. Ike groan till he get so weak, cain't holler no more. Clay beat him way too long, then say cut him down, let him lay in the sun, throw salt water on him.

"Then the bell ring, dinner time. Wadn't no nigger et no dinner that day."

"Did the slave die?" Tate asked.

"Slave women gather roun', even his sick wife, put a poultice on his back, put his shirt on. Blood soak through, anyways. After dinner Mistuh Clay make Ike carry tater sacks like them other slaves. He fall, niggers pick him up. Mistuh Clay standin' there with his whip an' his gun."

Tate lay silent a long moment. Then he heaved a long sigh. "I see why you're so scared of the whip."

"*All* us slaves scared, Marse Tate. I still has bad dreams 'bout it."

"Listen, Ivy, you're my personal servant now. If anybody took the rawhide to you it'd be me, and I ain't gonna do it, understand? Think about it, gal. Ain't you done things to help me since you been comin' up here?"

"Can't rightly say, suh."

"When I blacked out, you stayed with me, cleaned up the blood, and then didn't tell nobody."

"Yassuh, but I's the onliest one here, had to hep you, suh. And 'sides, I tells one person, Mistuh Clay be after me."

"But you *did* help me."

"Yassuh, I did."

"So, you help me and I help you. You keep my havin' spells to yourself, do like before when you see me havin' one, and I won't let Clay bother you. Long as it stays that way, won't be no whippin', understand?"

"Oh, yassuh! Thank you, Marse Tate."

"If you come up here every time I say, Clay'll never hurt you. He better never touch you again, or that bastard is dead."

"Oh, yassuh, I sho'nuf be here when you say."

"It's late now, you go on, help Bessie. I'm ridin' into town tomorrow, you don't need to come up here, but you be here early on Thursday, all cleaned up, you hear?"

"Yassuh."

The days following Tate's trip to town were busy for Ivy. Master Tate wanted to see her nearly every morning, and then she had to appear in the kitchen for instructions from Bessie. Even though Jacob was almost healed now, and able to get around on his own fairly well, she often needed to check on him, seeing to his painful leg and taking food to him along with the home remedy medicines the other women had prepared. Seeing Jacob also grounded her, his good humor and kidding never failing to make her smile, no matter the worries of the dark side of her daily existence.

151

A couple of weeks later, Bessie frowned at the young girl and told her to sit down a moment. "Ivy, what be goin' on 'tween you and Marse Tate? I sees you comin' from the back stairs mos' every mornin' now."

"Same as before. He just gettin' to like me better."

"You still chewin' the seeds?"

"Yes, ma'am, two and two and two. They tastes bad but I takes 'em mos' every day now that Marse Tate . . . ."

"And you likin' Marse Tate pretty good, too?"

"He treat me better now. I ain't so scared of him no more."

"He still force you, don't he? Or you gettin' to like it?"

"It ain't so bad now, he more gentle with it, and he don't force me no more."

Bessie leaned on the table, opposite Ivy. "Let me ax you somethin'. So, tomorrow he want you but you say, 'Nahsuh, I don't want to do it this time. I b'lieve I go on back to the quarters.' What he say then?"

Ivy showed a sheepish grin. "Oh, Miss Bessie, I can't never say that. When he want me I got to go."

Bessie leaned over with one hand on the table, one finger in Ivy's face and fire in her eye. "You listen here, gal! You still his slave, he still your marser, and he still be forcin' you, even you ain't got sense enough to see it."

Later, Ivy saw Clay watching her as she left Jacob's hut, headed for the big house to help Bessie. She pretended not to see him and ducked as quickly as she could into the kitchen, then stayed close to Bessie the rest of the morning.

The next day Ivy climbed the back stairs of the mansion in the foggy predawn, her knitted brows showing she remembered Bessie's scolding of yesterday. The older women had all given the girl the same message. Her great aunt Nettie had said it as well as anyone when they talked a few days ago. "Be careful, honey, they's nothing more treach'rous than a white man holdin' power over you in his bedroom. I'd druther live with a nest of rattlesnakes."

Ivy found the door unlocked and Tate tending the fire in the grate. He turned and said, "Come warm yourself." Then he locked the door.

"Mornin', suh." Eyeing him, she cautiously approached the flames and gratefully spread her hands to the warmth. They stood quietly for a few moments before Tate reached to take her hand. She tensed, but he only caressed her pale palm with his thumb, watching her as he did so.

His hands came gently to remove her blouse. "I'll help you this time." She held her breath, not knowing what response he expected. He touched her arm. "Here, step close to the fire," he said, and moved behind her, cupping her breasts with his warm hands. Goose flesh stippled her arms and legs. He slid her skirt and shift down, letting them fall to the floor. She felt the fire's radiating warmth on her legs, then his hands roamed over her front and downward until he had removed her drawers, as well. She shivered, and felt him move close behind her to fold her into his arms, his beard prickling her neck and shoulder. Her eyes widened with a new awareness. Without Master Tate's boots or slippers on they were the same height.

He stepped away toward the bed, then came back holding a soft white robe open to the fire. After a few seconds he folded it around her from behind, tying the belt loosely. "Stay here." When he returned he held a small box.

"That day I went to town? Got some medicine from Doc Matthews. Haven't blacked out since. Bought a coupla things for you, said they was for Aunt Martha." He opened the box and took out a silver charm hardly bigger than a pea on a silver chain delicate as a thread. "This and the robe is for you to wear while you're here in my room."

He moved behind her again and, holding both ends, dropped the necklace in front of her face, fastening it behind her neck. Her hand came up to hold the tiny disc, showing a woman's head in delicate relief. She gasped at its beauty. "Oh, Marse Tate, this be too fine. This be for some rich white lady, not me."

Tate chuckled. "It's for you and nobody else, it and the robe."Ivy looked at her master, unaware that tears streamed down her tawny cheeks. "Oh, Marse! I thanks you, thanks you, suh, but it be too much."

"I waited a few days to be sure I wouldn't have another spell before I gave you these, didn't want to spook you again. I believe the medicine's working."

He approached her then, and took Ivy in his arms. Her hands came up hesitantly only far enough to touch his sleeves as he hugged her. Her eyes closed, squeezing out large tears. As Tate moved back his lips rested for an instant on hers, the first time he had kissed her.

The startled girl brought a hand to her lips and stared at him with wide eyes. This was the first kiss of her adult life. Not even Jacob had ventured this far in their flirtations.

"One more thing," he said. From his pocket he produced a rounded bottle of white liquid the size of an egg, with a cork stopper. "This is something to make your skin soft. I'll show you how to use it; I watched my mother do this since I was knee-high to a toad."

Ivy looked on in amazement as he removed the cork, and said, "Hold out your arm." He pushed up the sleeve of her robe, bent her arm and smoothed a drop on the dry outer skin of her elbow. "After I rub it in it won't show," he said. "That feel good?" As she watched, smiling, he did the same on her other arm. He told her to sit in a chair facing the fire and cross her legs. He pushed up the hem of the robe and applied the soothing liquid to her knees. "It's good for knees and feet, too, 'specially your heels. They get all rough in this weather."

He took Ivy's hand and she stood up, wide-eyed and watchful, but with a broad smile. He put a drop in each palm and told her to rub it on her hands and wrists first, then smooth it lightly over her face. Her eyes misted again as she did so, feeling the luxurious softness spread over her skin. "You can use it all over your body, wherever the skin feels dry or you see those white chafe marks that itch or get sore. You can use this anytime you're here in my room. It's got no odor so the others won't know you're using it if you don't tell 'em.

Tate stood watching her rub the lotion into her skin, enjoying the luxurious sensation so much she seemed to glow. "Hold out your hands again," he said. He placed a tiny white drop on the fingertips of each hand. "Rub a little into my face above my beard."

Ivy looked at her master and suddenly felt the old fear returning, the cold tightness in her stomach. Slaves did not initiate contact with

154

their masters, even though she'd done so during his spell when he was in great need. Now, incredibly, he had told her to touch his face. She hesitated, even stepped backward still holding her hands open. "Oh, Marse . . . ."

He smiled. "Don't be afraid. I want you to do it."

She paused a moment, then with a shy grin she came forward and extended her right hand to cautiously touch his cheek. She noticed he must have shaved this morning, for his skin was smooth above the black bristles of his beard. Her hand moved in a small circle, barely touching his face. After a moment her left hand moved to the right side of his face. He closed his eyes, still smiling, and uttered a sigh, "Umm. Feels good." She moved her hands gently over his cheeks, up across the cheekbones, up to his temples and down along his thick black sideburns. She felt his breath on her face.

She smoothed the lotion into Tate's cheeks for a long silent moment, observing his calm expression, the hint of a smile on his lips. Then he opened his eyes, took her hands in his and kissed them.

He replaced the stopper in the bottle. "Now," he said, and stepped back to admire his slave girl in the necklace and robe that contrasted so elegantly with her smooth olive skin and dark hair, highlighting her white teeth. He moved forward, his cheek brushing hers as he seemed to sense her new softness. She felt the trembling begin again, caused not by fear, but a much different emotion.

She saw he had turned back the bed covers, and now he helped her slip out of the robe. He stood close in front of her and cradled the silver charm in his hand a moment, then released it to hang above her firm young breasts. He kissed her again and motioned for her to get in bed. He pulled the covers over her, then took off his pajamas and joined her.

In the moments that followed Tate proceeded slowly with her, caressing her, murmuring soothing words. He kissed her lips lightly and tasted her erect nipples. He touched her face and told her she was his woman now, and that he would protect her from Clay or anyone else who threatened her.

In the warmth of the bed and under the influence of his tenderness her muscles began to relax. She closed her eyes and heard his smooth phrases assuring her that she would be safe with him. He gently fondled her, and in spite of herself her body responded. She turned her face to him when he said she had become his best friend on the plantation, and that he would make her his helper in running the place. He told her how much he'd been touched by her caring for him when he blacked out, and how her new robe and necklace accented her beauty. He said that applying the lotion to each other had made him want to make love to her.

He moved on top of her and kissed her more deeply. She felt his rising passion. This was so different from the times he had taken her brutally. She found her hips moving in rhythm with his. She'd never known, even thought about such intimacy with a man. Now it was as if she'd always known.

For a time she floated detached, neither fearing her master nor conscious of her squalid existence as a slave. This moment filled her mind, nothing else mattered in her world except holding and being held by this young white man who had terrified her before, but who had now escorted her into this world of pleasure. She only knew that nothing had ever made her feel this way . . . .

"Ohhh, Marse!" She breathed in great gulps of air and clung to him as he lunged above her, matching her movements with his, riding an incredible wave.

Afterward they lay in each other's arms, breathing hard, voicing senseless exclamations, each lost in their own reverie. Slowly they became aware of each other again.

Ivy suddenly realized their actions in these last few moments had been all too familiar. It was a sinister thought. When she was able to speak coherently, she said, "Oh, Marse, is them spells catchin'? I's 'fraid I done catched it from you."

He chuckled and tried to ease her fears. "No, you ain't got the spells. You're just fine, nothing wrong with you, gal. Did you like it?"

"It scare me, Marse." He held her close and kissed her cheek, and though she held him in her arms she stared off into space, bemused, remembering, reliving the experience, trying to understand what had just happened.

"I went slower this time, so's I could feel you enjoying it too, and I saw you was keepin' your pleasure locked inside, growin' and tightening inside you till you couldn't hold the feelings no longer and it all busted out. When that happens people say you *came*. You

156

broke loose. We came off together that time. How you feel now? Still scared?"

She focused her attention on him at last. "Oh, I don't know, suh. I think it be too much commotion for me."

"Well, you were good, gal. Let me take off your necklace now. I don't want the niggers, 'specially Clay to see you wearin' it, or even knowin' that you have it. And don't never say what we done when you come up here, understand?"

She was already on her way to the washstand. "Yassuh."

# CHAPTER THIRTY-ONE

$\mathcal{F}$rom that time forward, Tate made Ivy his exclusive personal servant. None of the other house slaves were allowed into his bedroom. Ivy was soon serving his needs in the roles of chambermaid, mistress and confidante, duties which grew to consume most of her time.

She found herself watching over her master and guarding against others learning of his spells. Even when he went outside the big house, Ivy tried to watch him from a distance in case he should become sick.

Tate continued to have occasional epileptic episodes, despite the doctor's medicine, but working together he and Ivy learned to recognize the signs of approaching illness. Ivy improvised methods to protect him from injuries during the spells, a dry washcloth between his jaws, getting him on the bed where she could better restrain him once he lost consciousness.

In spite of his illness, Tate was a young man with a young man's appetites, so in addition to Ivy's frequent early morning visits to his bedroom, he began summoning her occasionally in the evenings, as well. He would repeat the ritual he'd initiated with the robe, necklace and lotion every time she came to his chamber. After he'd taken his evening pleasure with her, Tate would often make her stay and talk a while, since at that hour she hadn't the urgency of other duties.

They sometimes sat on the floor wrapped in a quilt, gazing into the fire, leaning against a wingback chair. They spoke of his

158

adventures on riverboats, her happy memories of playing as a child in this house under the affectionate supervision of Mistress Martha. In those soft hours with Tate, Ivy struggled not to indulge the stirrings of affection she felt for this man.

The fire's warmth against her face lulled her, and she wondered in her heavy-lidded reverie if this serenity was something white women might experience every day in their lives of ease and comfort. She looked at her master beside her, his smooth white cheeks above the immaculately trimmed dark beard, the sensuous lips whose touch had so enchanted her. She savored the image of his profile warmly lighted against the darkness beyond, then his face turning toward her, his eyes looking deeply into hers and the sound of his voice speaking intimate words meant only for her. Basking there in the warmth of the fire it would be so easy to surrender herself completely to this man.

These serene moments by the fire were hypnotic for the girl. After being in bed with her master more often now, and his becoming more considerate of her feelings, she had begun to consider him her protector, her trusted friend, even her lover. His early brutality, the physical and mental pain, the paralyzing fear, the humiliation—all that now seemed from a past life, a distant nightmare.

After the lovemaking, for that's what it now seemed to Ivy, an expression of love more than sexual abuse, she felt at peace. She learned that intimacy with this man who held absolute power over her was strangely exhilarating. It was almost as if in those moments Ivy viewed the world through Tate's eyes, seeing threats coming from outside, and she understood that she was important to him in keeping those external threats at bay. While in this room, this cocoon with all danger closed outside, both their lives were peaceful and secure.

She saw it in the fire, the flames licking the dark logs, consuming the inner space. Stylized human forms writhed and danced, disappearing to reappear in different colors. Shimmering dark and bright images dazzled the girl, darkness on shining water, shadows against a blazing sunrise.

After one of their intimate times together, Tate said, "Ivy, you know I think the world of you. If it wasn't against the law I'd marry

159

you. All the same, I'll always consider you to be my wife, and I'll treat you as such. And you should regard me as your lawful husband. If we have children, I'll make sure they're raised free and given an education."

Ivy could only say, "Oh, thank you, Marse Tate, thank you." But no matter how hopeful her dreams, how wondrous the images conjured by his promises, Bessie and Nettie's words always came back to Ivy. Suddenly there by the fire she would again find herself peering at Tate across the same chasm of contradictions: master vs. slave, European vs. African, education vs. illiteracy, man vs. woman, light vs. dark.

Bessie, seeing occasional signs of ambivalence and torment in the girl, drew from her the truth concerning Tate's promise of marital obligation. The older woman had already cautioned her about becoming pregnant, and given her the means to prevent it. She now explained forcefully to the girl that, though a white man might live with as many colored women as he pleased without damaging his reputation in southern society, it was against the law in the slave states for anyone of European descent to marry a person of African extraction.

Any babies produced from her union with Tate would be condemned to a life of slavery, for the laws of Kentucky dictated that the condition of the children followed the condition of the mother. Only on the rarest occasion, Bessie said, was there a master to be found true to such pledges. And should the white father become hopelessly involved in debt his mulatto children could legally be sold as slaves, regardless of his promises to the black mother, especially if he died in debt.

In those idyllic moments when Ivy felt Tate's arm come round her shoulders as they sat before the fire she could almost forget those warnings. But the conflictions would not be denied, stark and rigid as ever. She would have to be watchful. Good times were gone quickly, she'd heard Bessie say.

One morning in the kitchen Ivy listened as Bessie voiced her frustration over the girl's arrangement with Master Tate. "Miss Bessie, I's just doin' anything I has to do to get along," Ivy said. She dared not tell the older woman about Tate's illness, or that she and

160

Tate had found a measure of common purpose, or about the things he'd given her. She had to keep her mentor and kitchen boss at arm's length.

Yet Ivy knew very well that the older woman had a point. In effect Bessie had one less house slave now to help her manage all the household chores, Ivy's personal service for Master Tate notwithstanding.

That evening Ivy summoned the courage to mention Bessie's problem to Master Tate even as she feared punishment for speaking out of turn. She raised her downcast eyes in slow amazement as she observed him giving the matter careful thought for a moment, then calmly telling Ivy to bring Ellie, Edina's child, to Bessie for training. "The gal's reached the age of thirteen and needs to be put to work," he said.

Ivy was shocked. He had actually responded favorably to her small test of the trust she'd felt growing between them. Had he really meant what he said earlier about Ivy becoming his helper in running this place? As much as she relished today's small victory, as much as she had been influenced by his attentiveness and kindnesses, she knew that would be unthinkable.

Even while Bessie was being placated by this new strategy, Jacob protested that Ivy's visits to his cabin and the stable were becoming less frequent. Ivy feared Jacob's reaction if he were to discover how Marse Tate used her, but she knew he would never hear it from Bessie.

The kitchen boss and the other house slaves were always circumspect about divulging the habits of white folks to the outside slaves. This was not only to protect the whites, but to avoid rumors circulating about the white men's abuses of slave women, and those rumors' inflammatory effects on the slaves in the quarters.

If a black slave could not take out his anger and shame on the white man who was abusing his woman, he would often vent his frustration on the woman herself. Bessie and others remembered how the blacks had shunned and mistreated Ivy's grandmother Mattie to the point that she was forced to relate to and depend on her abuser Marse John Binford more than to her black friends and family in the quarters. She had suffered great moral and physical anguish over it, and it was from this that Bessie and the others tried to shelter Ivy.

But they could not protect her from Clay.

# CHAPTER THIRTY-TWO

Clay had watched Ivy go to Jacob's cabin every morning that she wasn't with Tate, and she kept going long after the boy's leg had healed. He assumed Ivy and Jacob were lovers. He also observed that Tate was demanding more of Ivy's time lately, not that he could blame the master.

There hadn't been a slave girl that well put together on the plantation in all the years he'd worked here. She'd grown up right before his eyes, and it rankled him that Tate had intervened at the very moment when he was about to take her for himself. That added more fuel to the fire of Clay's resentment of this young upstart from Lexington. He'd horned in and taken advantage of the elder Binfords and thrown a monkey wrench into Clay's plan to become the big boss of the plantation after the old folks finally passed on.

Clay suspected that by now the girl had developed a kind of loyalty to Tate. His suspicion was confirmed the day he watched from a distance as Ivy hurried out of the kitchen and down the steps toward Tate, who had been leaning motionless on the back fence a few moments. He saw her speak to her master, then take his arm and walk him toward the house. By the time they had climbed the back steps to the verandah it appeared she was supporting most of his weight. The overseer saw instantly that Tate was not well, and that the slave girl must be conspiring with him to appear strong and competent as the man in charge of the plantation.

In Clay's eyes Tate and Ivy's behavior followed a natural progression, up to a point. The "chosen" slave girls, after an initial

163

"breaking in" period, usually realized they had no choice but to give up their bodies and their pride to their white masters. In return they received protection, easier work and the occasional bauble. Clay had enjoyed his own personal experience in such transactions with young slave girls. He realized he'd been fortunate, for not many black drivers were allowed to molest the negro girls with impunity as did the white men. But the scene Clay had just witnessed revealed a vulnerability in his adversary than he had not suspected.

Now he suddenly saw Ivy, and by association her black boyfriend Jacob, as the only barriers between him and his prey. He began spending time laying out a plan.

On one of Ivy's morning visits to Jacob's cabin, after they had joked and laughed a few minutes, he hugged her, and kissed her for the first time, allowing his hands to slide down her back to caress her buttocks. His eyes came wide open. "Umm, I sees you got some hard muscles down by the fork of the road. I guess that come from sittin' round all day takin' it easy." He showed a sly grin. "You strong 'nuf down there to give your boyfrien' a good long ride, ain't you, gal?"

She replied with a playful slap. "You quit that crazy talk, young fool! Old Marse John made that barn frame loom for the weavers what come before me a long time ago, but he build it too wide for women, so we has to reach far out to throw the shuttlecock through the warp back an' forth. We makes wide runs of cloth that way, but it like to wear out what we sittin' on. You try it all day long ev'ry day an' see if old mistuh hiney ain't sore in the evenin' times. Same go for shoulders an' backs. I ain't even tol' you 'bout dressin' the loom and workin' your feet. Weavin' ain't no easy way a'goin' like you think, boy."

"I's findin' out lots of new things 'bout my gal frien'," Jacob said. He came back to Ivy and took her in his arms, his hands roaming more freely now. She was reluctant to indulge him, considering her dark relationship with Tate, but she found herself giving in. It was true that she had warm feelings for this handsome young man who had fought so bravely to overcome his crippling injury, and who seemed infatuated by her. Jacob pulled her down on his pallet, kissing and fondling her. She felt herself becoming aroused, but couldn't help noticing Jacob's inexperience and

164

awkwardness. Unfair as it may have been, she saw clearly the difference between the amorous fumblings of young Jacob and her practiced and proficient Master Tate. She silently scolded herself for judging unfairly this young man of her own race who was so obviously smitten by her.

Suddenly they heard a sound just outside the cabin. Ivy straightened her clothing and rushed to the door in time to see Clay's black form step quickly around the corner. Lord, how long had he been watching? Ivy didn't doubt that Clay would tell Marse Tate what he'd just seen. Jacob, of course, didn't understand how serious this unguarded moment would turn out to be.

Later that day Clay came to the stable and called Jacob outside. When the boy stood before him, the overseer spoke in a low growl, barely audible. "I seen what you and that nigger wench was doin' this mornin' in your hut. Gettin' kind of uppity with your marse's woman, ain't you?"

Jacob couldn't hide his surprise and anger. "Marse's woman! We's *all* Marse Tate's slaves, why you say that 'bout her?"

"You must be the only one round here so dumb you don't know she been sleepin' with him, doin' what all he wants anytime he wants it for a few months now."

Jacob flushed and his jaw muscles clenched. He looked off toward the hills, breathing hard, desperate not to lose control in front of this man of his own race, yet who held absolute power over him.

Clay leaned in and growled through a lopsided grin, his face close to Jacob's. "Guess you ain't such a proud cocksman now, after all." After a pause he shouted, "Are you!" Jacob flinched.

"You know all I got to do is tell Marse Tate 'bout this and he'll sell your crippled black ass down the river. What about that, boy? How you think you gonna like pickin' cotton or cuttin' cane in the hot sun down in Lou'siana with your bum leg an' all?" Clay casually moved his hand to rest on the revolver he wore at his hip. He spit a stream of amber juice into the dust and wiped his mouth on his sleeve, then leered at Jacob again.

The boy tried to disregard the ugly charge Clay had made against Ivy and the master even though it roared like a cyclone in his brain. Instead, he said, "We . . . we wadn't doin' nuthin', suh. Just

165

funnin' each other, jokin' round. Ain't no call to tell the marse 'bout it. Won't do it no more."

"Bullshit! I seen you had her down on your pallet goin' at it, and it late in the mornin' when you both s'posed to been workin'. I oughta whip you both, just for that. We'll see what Marse Tate wants to do about this."

The driver continued, warming to his subject. "You don't know what you messin' with, nigger. He'll put you in his pocket quick as a wink when I tell him what been goin' on out here, though there ain't much of a market for cripples like you. Nobody never tell you what it means to be sold South?

"I'd pay to see it when they first get a'hold of you down on a Lou'siana plantation. First day pickin' cotton, they'll whip you up, make you pick fast as you can. Nighttime they weigh your cotton. You pick less the next day, you feel the whip. You pick more than that the next day, you got to make the same weight every day or you get the rawhide. You break off branches with bolls that ain't ripe, the bolls die and you get whipped again. Niggers on a cotton plantation always workin' scared."

Clay was talking fast, his sweating black face close to Jacob's, relishing the effect he was having on the frightened young man. "After all day pickin' cotton, even at night if they's a moon, you got to do your chores, feed the mules, feed the swine, cut wood. Then you go to your quarters, make a fire, grind your corn, make supper and dinner for the next day. Carry food and water to the field in gourds.

"If you get to sleep by midnight you're lucky, up before daylight. Every Sunday overseer gives each nigger a week's ration of three and a half pounds of bacon and corn enough to make a peck of meal. No tea, coffee, sugar, salt. You got no knife, fork, plate, kettle. Lucky if you got a calabash. You make ash cakes in the fire, cut your bacon with the axe at the woodpile, cook the meat in the fire. In summer time, if it ain't smoked enough, bacon likely be full of worms. Eat off a board, sleep on a board with a block of wood for a pillow. You get one blanket. If you use moss off the trees for a soft bed it'll breed a swarm of fleas.

"Reckon you'd like them fixin's, eh nigger? You niggers don't know how easy you got it on the Binford plantation. Think I'm

166

lyin'? I done seen it for myself. That and worse is what's waitin' for you once I tell your marse what I seen you and that whore doin' there in the cabin. You and her best be thinkin' 'bout that."

Clay spat again at Jacob's feet, turned and strode toward the big house.

Jacob stood still after Clay left, unable to control his confusion, his fear, the tremors in his arms and legs. Being separated from Ivy was one thing. That alone would break Jacob's heart, but if the master sold him South into the conditions Clay had just so graphically described, it would likely be a death sentence.

The boy assumed Clay would waste little time telling Tate what he had seen, and especially what he had wanted to see this morning. Jacob spent the rest of the forenoon distraught and pacing in the barn with old Perry doing his best to calm him.

Jacob returned to his cabin that evening by a back way. In case anyone was waiting to capture him, he'd have a chance to escape. He sent one of his cabin mates to the big house kitchen with a message that he wanted to see Ivy immediately. As dusk approached he confronted Ivy with harsh words and wild eyes as she neared his cabin door. He scanned the alleyway, then took her arm and led her out to the woodlot behind the cabin. When they were hidden among the trees with day turning to night, Jacob turned and put his face close to hers. "Gal, that damn black overseer say you an' Marse Tate been keepin' comp'ny. Now you better say he lyin', for if he ain't, no tellin' what I's gonna do to you."

Ivy shrank back a step in shock at the look on the young man's face, then she sat down on a stump, eyes downcast. Slowly she brought herself under control and looked up at Jacob, a stricken expression on her face. He stood still, eyes blazing, breathing so hard spittle formed on his lips. His face shone, fists clenched at his sides. She spoke with a clear voice, but could not hide the shaking in her hands and legs. "Jacob, I won't lie to you. Marse Tate been forcin' me to come to his room an' . . . his bed. All my cryin' and beggin' don't make him quit. He hold a knife on me an' make me do awful things, he do. I cain't no more stop him than hold back lightnin'." She could not tell Jacob all the other things that had happened, the strange feelings that had grown between her and her master. The young man would never understand.

Even her partial confession was enough to spur the desperate youngster to action. He said, "Clay done seen us together this mornin' and he make it soun' like me 'n you was fornicatin'. I tol' him we only playin' but he done have his mind made up. Woman, how long you reckon it be 'fore I be sold South? Clay come 'n grab me tonight, in the mornin'?"

Tears of anger and fear streamed down his face now, but he quieted enough to say, "You get ready, gal, for we's goin' away this very night." He leaned his head on his crossed arms against a tree. Then he turned, eyes flashing, almost shouting, pointing his finger at the big house, "'less you druther stay here an' be his whore!"

He came close and took her arm, whispering, "We goin'. Get your things. I be outside your door a half-hour after full dark."

"Goin'? We cain't go, Jacob. Ain't no place we can go."

The whisper became a low snarl. "Step quick. We goin'."

As much as the choice frightened her, Ivy was forced to acquiesce to Jacob's plan, for she saw no other way out. Running away would put them both in extreme peril. She could not have read the laws of Kentucky that pertained to slaves, even if a copy had been laid before her. Still, all slaves were drilled from infancy by their masters and overseers on the state slave laws, and punishments for violating them.

*"Any slave, for rambling in the night, or riding horseback without leave, or running away, may be punished by whipping, cropping, and branding in the cheek, or otherwise, not rendering him unfit for labor."* This was but a mild example of Kentucky slave law, and Kentucky was considered one of the more lenient of all the slave states.

Ivy assumed Clay would tell Tate he'd seen her and Jacob fornicating, and that he would lie again, saying they'd been lovers all along. Even if Clay didn't betray them to Marse Tate right away it would be too dangerous for Ivy and Jacob to remain at the plantation with Clay holding this guillotine over their heads. After Jacob had been disposed of, Clay might blackmail Ivy into a sexual liaison with him, or any number of other heinous possibilities.

Should Ivy immediately take the initiative, try to explain to Marse Tate that she and Jacob were merely friends, not seriously involved, contradicting what Clay already had, or would later tell him? If Marse Tate's jealousy convinced him to believe Clay, and Ivy's explanation failed to change his mind, it might be too late for them to escape.

Ivy worried for their safety should she and Jacob attempt to run away, but she also feared that after they were gone Clay would learn of Tate's illness, crush him and take over the plantation. God help the other slaves if Clay gained more power over them. She realized all too clearly that Clay had successfully played the three of them off against one another. Ivy knew this decision taken by her and Jacob in their moment of urgency would haunt her for the rest of her life.

At twilight that evening, about the same time Jacob was wrangling with Ivy in the woods behind his cabin, Clay stopped in front of old Raymond's hut. The frail cast-eyed night watchman sat outside his door whittling a toy for the naked grandchild at his knee. Clay said, "They's trouble with a couple of Amos Johnson's niggers. Been sneakin' round the neighbors' plantations at night stealin' stuff."

"Yassuh, Mistuh Clay. I be watchin' good tonight, come tell you if I sees somethin'."

"No, I'm takin' the watch tonight. If I see them bastards I'll drop 'em in their tracks. They know if you see 'em they got time to get away while you come runnin' to tell me."

"Yassuh. What I do, tonight then?"

"You sleep tonight, stand watch again tomorrow night."

With Raymond out of the way, spending the night with his family, Clay retired early. He knew that by morning two obstacles to his taking over the plantation would probably have disappeared. And if Ivy and Jacob didn't have the sense to run off, Clay would simply tell Tate his lie about the two young slaves being lovers.

169

# CHAPTER THIRTY-THREE

The wagon bumped along the rough road in the dark of the moon, drawn by a team of sorrel mules, driven by Pearl Selvey. Familiarity with the road, starlight and a few lamplit windows along the way were her only guides. The two young people lay under a canvas in the wagon bed among boxes of sawdust that cushioned jars of Shaker jams and jellies. Ivy's body was numb, yet her mind remained alert to the fear of punishment she and Jacob would suffer if caught in this dangerous escape. Coupled with that fear was the thought of those she was abandoning by running away from the plantation, her fellow slaves and especially Marse Tate, whom she feared would be no match for the conniving Clay.

Ivy must have slept then, for when she woke she saw gray dawn light and heard pigeons cooing somewhere. The wagon had stopped, no longer on the road. Jacob and the older woman moved around the wagon, checking the mules, speaking in low tones.

Jacob came and spoke to Ivy. "Where we at, Jacob?" She looked about, rubbing her eyes as if in a daze, half expecting Tate or Clay to burst in on them at any moment.

"We's in a barn, Ivy, not far from the river. Pearl brung us here. We hides in here till nightfall, then light out for the river. She gone come back an' take us."

Ivy had been so frightened that she hardly remembered getting on the wagon in the dark with her small bundle of clothes, or seeing the woman who drove the team. "Ain't we bound to be catched and sent back to the rawhide?"

170

"Pray God we don't. Pearl say we got a good chance if we can make it to the river."

"You know this woman?" Ivy asked. "Where she come from out the middle of the night?"

"She a free black washerwoman, live by herself at Shaker Village after her chirren growed up. Them Shakers gen'ly acts kindly towards black folks. She got to be careful, though 'cause she lose her freedom if the pattyrollers catches her heppin' us."

"How she know 'bout us lightin' out?"

"Pearl make the rounds mos' ev'ry Wednesday sellin' Shaker jams an' jellies to neighbors, kinds mos' folks don't make, like quince and fig. She keep her ears pricked up for blacks needin' hep. I had old Perry slip her the word when she stop by the big house today."

"Why she don't take us all the way to the river?"

"She need time to tell Hiram Easterday to get ready to take us. He make steamboat runs downriver, haulin' stuff from Shakertown to market. He gone wait a extry day for us this time." After a pause, Jacob voiced another concern on his mind. He faced Ivy squarely, his face close to hers. "Now listen here, Ivy. Las' evenin' you say Tate Binford been forcin' you into his bed. Why ain't you tol' me 'fore now?"

"What good it do to tell you?" she said. "What you gone do 'bout it, 'cept get your black self killed?"

"Even you don't tell me 'bout Mistuh Clay and Marse Tate I seen the way they been lookin' at you. I knowed if we don't go soon I kill one or two of 'em and that be the las' anybody see of me round here, for I soon be one dead nigger. I's jus' sorry we didn't go off before they hurt you, Ivy."

They had stepped down from the wagon and waited there while Pearl watered the mules. Sparrows flitted through dusty slanting sunbeams that brightened the space high above them under the barn roof. Jacob took Ivy in his arms. "They ain't gonna hurt you no more, gal."

Pearl soon came back with a small packet of food and an earthen jug of water stoppered with a red corn cob. She showed them the dry cistern in a corner of the barn where they could hide till

171

nightfall. "Y'all get down in there outta sight. I be back after dark. Hiram gone make a hidin' place ready for y'all on the boat."

Jacob let himself down into the brick-walled vault first, grimacing silently when his weight came down on his bad leg. Then he lifted Ivy down with his large hands on her waist. "I'm slidin' this here 'baccer basket over the top now," Pearl said. "Don't make no fuss; they's white folks close by."

The hours dragged past after Pearl left. Ivy and Jacob whispered to each other of their fears. What if Pearl failed to return for them? Would she be captured by patrollers who'd seen them entering the barn? Would Clay and his slavecatchers stop them before they reached the boat?

The cramped space in the cistern became warm, then stuffy. The rounded brick bottom of the hole made it impossible to rest comfortably. Finally Jacob found a dusty burlap sack that he wadded under his head for a pillow and lay on his back with his knees bent. Ivy tried to rest in a sitting position with her back against the bricks. "We's got to get some rest 'fore night come," Jacob said. In spite of their discomfort they were soon asleep, no longer able to concentrate on their fear of all the unknowns swirling in their heads.

Ivy woke to see Jacob's hands moving, scratching his neck and chest. She saw that the light in the cistern had changed. It must be late evening now. She listened for sounds of movement up in the barn, but heard only the listless cooing of the pigeons and the sparrows' occasional chirping. She sat up and looked at Jacob. "You doin' a lot of scratchin'. Reckon they's lice down in here?"

"Somethin' sho is chewin' on me; I be itchin' real bad. You see anything on my neck?"

Ivy turned so she was facing him up close. "Here, set up so's I can see. Mercy, child! They's *spiders* on you." She reached out and brushed three or four of the tan and brown creatures off his neck and shoulders. "Reckon they bites what makin' you itch? That sack must be full of 'em."

"You see any bites on my neck? Feel like a hundred chiggers been after me." He was scratching his upper body now with both hands. "My lips an' tongue feel like they goin' to sleep."

Ivy looked more closely. "Move your hands. Oh, lord yes! They's red spots on your neck an' all up under your chin. You needs

172

some of Bessie's calamine lotion. Try not to scratch too hard, make it bleed."

"Cain't hep it. Never had no itch like this befo'. They commencin' to burn, too. Whoo law!"

During the hour or more until Pearl arrived with the wagon, Ivy frantically tried to make Jacob comfortable, moving him away from the sack, even desperately rubbing her saliva on the ugly bites on Jacob's neck and chest. The wounds were now becoming angry black places surrounded by red rings, and she saw with horror that her efforts at soothing him were in vain. His condition seemed to be worsening rapidly. It was all she could do to keep him from screaming and betraying their hiding place.

By the time Pearl moved the tobacco basket from the top of the cistern Ivy was in tears with Jacob thrashing about, fighting the pain and struggling to breathe. "What on earth, chile?" Pearl said when she saw the gravity of Jacob's condition. Between sobs Ivy related the story about the spiders having bitten him. Pearl said, "What color was them spiders?" When she heard the answer her dark eyes widened and she said, "Fiddle-backs! We got to get him outta that hole an' on the boat quick."

The young man was nearly helpless in his agony. He groaned and tried to help by grasping the rim of the cistern to pull himself up, but he collapsed back into Ivy's arms. Pearl and Ivy had to lift his dead weight out of the cistern. By the time they had him in the wagon and covered with the tarp they were almost totally spent. Jacob, his eyes rolled up in his head, was slipping in and out of consciousness, suffering from the excruciating pain and lack of air.

"Hiram got black gunpowder on the boat," Pearl said. "I seen it used for spider bites. Jus' pray it ain't too late." She snapped the lines and spoke to the mules. The wagon rattled down the lane into the dark gorge. Their destination was Shaker Landing on the Kentucky River where Hiram Easterday waited impatiently in the pilothouse of his sternwheeler, the *Sally Preston*.

When Pearl's wagon reached the landing Hiram directed his son Caleb and another deckhand to assist the fugitives and show them to the locker below the pilot house where they would be hidden. But when Pearl described to the young men Jacob's dire condition, they laid him gently on the deck near the landing stage and summoned the captain.

After Pearl's brief introduction of the captain and Ivy, and his quick appraisal of Jacob's injuries he ordered Caleb to prepare to cast off while he tried to help the injured man. Pearl said, "I got to be gettin' off the boat, but he done been bit by a passel of them brown spiders, Hiram. You got any black powder? I's hear'd of folks treatin' spider bites with gunpowder."

"You say brown spiders with dark marks on their backs?" Hiram asked. "Them's the worst of the lot. You said a 'passel.' How many bites does the boy have?"

"I ain't had no good look at him, bein' anxious to get him here 'fore he dies, but Ivy say he got into a whole nest of 'em down in the dry cistern where I made 'em hide, that right, gal?" Ivy, her eyes wide with fear, simply nodded.

At that point Pearl had to hurry back across the landing stage so the *Sally Preston* could shove off. They had learned from long experience that when hiding and transporting runaway slaves, it would not do to tarry. Speed and elusiveness were imperative.

Caleb ordered the landing stage raised and powered the boat to midstream where he brought her about and soon had her headed downstream under a full head of steam. Meanwhile the captain knelt beside Jacob. "Edward, bring the lantern," Hiram said to a deck hand. When it was delivered he held it over the boy who was now unconscious and wheezing with each struggling breath. "God help us, gal. Look close and you can see the tiny fang marks. There's more bites on this poor devil than I've ever seen before." Without moving his eyes from Jacob's ravaged neck he said, "Edward, fetch my powder horn and a cup of drinking water."

Ivy, who had been watching in wide-eyed terror, holding Jacob's motionless hand, now wept openly and bowed her head low onto her friend's chest. "Oh, Jacob," she sobbed. "You got to fight for your life and pray with me for Jesus to save you. Please don't leave me, Jacob, please don't leave me." Hiram gently moved her away from the boy so he could view the wounds more closely. Edward was back in seconds with the powder and water. The captain told Edward to hold the lantern while he began mixing the powder

174

with drops of water to make a paste, which he then daubed on each of the bites.

"Each one of these bites has put a drop of venom into the boy's body. The poison eats the flesh and the wounds grow fast. See the black center of each bite? Them's the dead spots and they're gettin' larger."

Ivy spoke through her tears. "Gunpowder gone stop the poison, suh?

Hiram kept applying the paste to Jacob's wounds. He gave her a brief look, and the sadness she saw in his eyes conveyed the awful truth. "It may help some, child. It's the charcoal in the powder that does the work, but only a doctor or a pharmacist would have the best kind, called activated charcoal. Ain't none of them hereabouts, so this is the best we can do."

When he had treated all the bites he could find, the captain ordered a pallet laid on the floor of the crew's quarters. "We can't leave him exposed out here on the deck. Too many slavechasers roamin' the country. You think you and the boy will be missed right away?"

"Don't know, suh. Jacob an' me, we don't show up at the stable and the kitchen come sunrise, they start lookin' for us, turn the dogs loose."

Now that the *Sally Preston* was headed downstream and the landing stage had been secured Hiram climbed the narrow stairway to the pilot house for a quick word with the first mate, his son Caleb. Then he returned and ordered the three deckhands to help him move Jacob inside. Ivy walked beside her friend holding his hand, speaking softly to him. After they had settled Jacob on his pallet inside the cabin one of the men brought blankets. Ivy made sure Jacob was warm, then spoke a few words with Hiram and thanked him for his help.

"I'm mighty sorry for you and the boy. We'll keep dosing him with the powder, and we'll bring drinking water for you, and him in case he wakes, but it sure don't look good for him, gal." Jacob had now slipped into deeper unconsciousness. His chest heaved with each labored breath and the gasping sounds made Ivy cringe. "The number of bites and the amount of poison in his body may be too much," Hiram said. "I'll have one of the hands stay close by to be of what help he can. Otherwise about all you and all of us can do is pray for his recovery. He's young and strong, so he's got that in his favor. Try to get some rest yourself, child. You'll need strength for what's to come."

The *Sally Preston* moved on down the Kentucky River under a new moon, her stacks billowing smoke, engines thrumming, the sternwheel making pat-pat-pat sounds against the frothing green water. The sound and the vibration lulled Ivy into a troubled sleep. Her last thoughts before slumber were a prayer for Jacob, but not only for him. She had no idea how she could survive in this strange world without him.

# CHAPTER THIRTY-FOUR

At first light, Hiram came and gently touched Ivy's shoulder. She awoke still holding Jacob's hand, but now it was stiff and cold. "Jacob!" she wailed, and flung herself across his body, still covered by the blanket.

The captain spoke softly to her and helped her to her feet, then tried to console her as a father would a grieving daughter. "I'm so sorry. There just wasn't nothing to be done for him, too much poison for him to fight off."

She would not be comforted. "*I* be the one shoulda died!" Her sobs came with renewed bitterness. "This here trouble all 'cause of me. Jacob jus' tryin' to hep me an' now look what happen. Lord, I never forgive myself."

"You mustn't think like that, child. You know they say God works in mysterious ways his wonders to perform. Just because we can't understand this young man leavin' us don't mean we done somethin' wrong. Near as I can tell from what Pearl said, you both done the right thing by runnin' away. Now, we're gonna get you on down the river to a safe place.

"We run under full steam all last night, 'cause we didn't want Tate and Clay and their men to catch up with us. I know the upper stretch of river like the back of my hand. We also had a bit of starlight and a tiny sliver of a moon, but tonight we're gonna lay by. Looks like clouds is movin' in and it's too dangerous to navigate through treacherous water with no light."

177

"But what 'bout Jacob?" Ivy said. "How we gone give him a Christian buryin'?" She looked up at the captain with beseeching eyes and anguished countenance.

"We'll have a funeral for him right here, Ivy. I've got a prayer book and as captain I can lead a service for him. Would that be all right? We dassn't take the time to tie up to the riverbank and bury him there. This close to the Binford place Clay and them might be on us in no time. And where we're gonna tie up tonight there ain't enough space for a grave, nohow."

"Where we gone bury him, then?"

"After we have the funeral me and the crew will bury him in the river. We'll wrap his body and do it with respect. You don't have to watch if you druther not."

"I be watchin', fo' sho. Jacob and me be bes' friends on the plantation, suh. He always smilin' an' funnin' with me. The leas' I can do is say a last goodbye an' see him off to a better life with Jesus."

A short time later, even before the sun had burned off the morning mist over the river, the crew had the body carefully wrapped and weighted and the captain conducted a short service for Jacob. With a final prayer he was gently lowered into the water and sank immediately. After a moment of silence broken only by Ivy's muted sobs, Hiram went to her again and said, "Now, child you come in the cabin and rest on my bunk. Caleb will be in shortly to bring you something to eat. Later we'll show you where to stay during the daytime in a locker right under the pilothouse."

The time required to reach Hiram Easterday's destination of Carrollton, Kentucky, on the Ohio River, would be uncertain. The distance along the river was something like 130 miles, but there would be several sets of locks to get through, and the time delays would depend on river traffic. The dams and locks had been built beginning in 1833, designed to make the river navigable as far up as Shaker Landing, which was about halfway up to the river's headwaters at Beattyville. These structures had transformed the river into a series of lakes rather than the wild-flowing stream that had once existed there. But even the dams could not prevent floods from interrupting commerce on the Kentucky, and the times of high water were as unpredictable as the weather.

Later in the morning, while Ivy was eating the food Caleb had brought, Hiram came to sit on the bunk across from her. "I can't say exactly when we'll reach Carrollton, but it usually takes three or four days. When we get close we'll haul up to the riverbank near a settlement called English and wait to hear from the Quakers. They keep a close watch near the mouth of the Kentucky for slavecatchers or over-eager lawmen lookin' to cash in on the reward for any runaway slaves bein' smuggled down the river before they cross over to Indiana. You might say it's a game of our scouts against theirs. When we find out what we're up again' we'll decide what we got to do, then wait till nightfall and run the gauntlet one way or t'other."

"Is you and Caleb Quakers, too?"

"No, but when it comes to slavery, we're on the same side of the fence with them. Now, in a few minutes we'll be comin' to a set of locks. We'll have to slow down, stop and wait for the lockmaster to lock us through. We'll be sittin' ducks at that point, but me and all hands on deck will have our rifles nearby. Caleb will be at the wheel with the engineer and fireman doin' their jobs in the hold. If Tate and Clay's nearby I expect 'em to make their move at the lock. They's been many a runaway slave captured at these bottlenecks on the river but we're here to protect you. I'm tellin' you this so you won't be scared when we're stoppin' and movin' slow into and outta the lock. If you hear gunfire, just stay put."

"They catch me, they jus' up an' shoot me dead?" Ivy said.

Hiram showed a sad smile and shook his head. "No, Ivy, from the way Pearl talked, the last thing Tate would let 'em do is hurt you, but they'd tear this old *Sally Preston* apart lookin' for Jacob, never mind we tell 'em the truth about him. They might even set the boat afire, or worse."

"You gone hide me now?"

"You'll be in a locker right under the pilot house. I done put a little stool in there and you can lean back on the bulkhead when you get tired. They's some food and water and a blanket in there, too. It ain't fancy, and there'll be engine noise and vibration, and it'll smell like oil, but it'll be locked and under guard by my boys. At night we'll let you out if the coast is clear."

179

"You a open man, Mistuh Hiram," Ivy said, "but you puttin' youself an' your men in bad danger doin' this for Jacob an' me."

The older man chuckled. "We do it several times a year. There's people who pay us a little somethin' for packin' you folks downstream, though we call you 'freight,' like the stuff in them crates and bales on the lower deck. The Society of Friends, or Quakers, is involved like me in what they call the Underground Railroad, which ain't neither underground nor a railroad, just some of us boatmen and teamsters and homesteaders and the like passin' you on from one to another, protectin' you till you get to a free state or Canada. We ain't gettin' rich on this enterprise, but for most of us it's a matter of principle more than money, anyhow."

"Ain't you li'ble to get catched for doin' bidness, handlin' money for takin' me an' Jacob on this here boat?"

"This business is done accordin' to a code of honor, Ivy. Ain't no written bill of lading nor no such a thing. Nothin' the slavecatchers could grab and string somebody up for. It's strictly the honor system between honest men and women, and it's all done by word-of-mouth. We get to Carrollton the Friends will likely slip me maybe thirty dollars, so you see after I give somethin' to my crew, it won't amount to a ball of lint in my pocket. Now come on, gal, we got to get you hid."

Ivy talked to herself and tried to avoid panicking in the small locker. She cried and longed for Jacob's company. Time crawled slowly as she listened for strange noises. The vibrations and bad air nearly made her sick. An hour later, from her cramped hiding place Ivy heard the engines stop and calm voices of conversation between Captain Easterday and Lemuel Carr, the lockmaster, as the *Sally Preston* eased into the small lock and the watertight gates closed behind her. During the next few minutes the boat was lowered by water flowing out of the lock on the downstream side. Then the lower gates opened and the steamer's sternwheel began sloshing water again and she headed downriver. Ivy had expected to hear shouts and gunfire, perhaps even someone breaking into her locker, but there was nothing like that. She could hardly believe that after the apprehension expressed by Hiram their passage through the lock had not been challenged.

180

That evening at dusk Hiram came to her door and spoke softly looking off into the distance. "I'll let you out in a minute when it gets full dark. Don't see no signs of trouble. You makin' it all right in there?"

"Yassuh, I's tol'able well. I's expectin' a big commotion back at the lock, but it seem real quiet. What happen, suh?"

The captain told Ivy he was surprised there'd been no trouble at the lock or elsewhere on their voyage so far. "Tate and them surely must have knowed you and Jacob would try to escape by way of the river, and the *Sally Preston* was the most likely boat to take you. It don't figure that they wouldn't come after us."

Ivy was quiet a moment, thinking, wondering if Clay had already acted out her worst fear. "They woulda knowed we's gone by sunrise or a little after, suh. The overseer, Mistuh Clay, he always lookin' to get rid of Marse Tate. Maybe us skedaddlin' give him the chance he lookin' for. The more I thinks 'bout it, an' what he say to Jacob yestiddy, that could be jus' what he do now. Maybe he *glad* we run off. He might of planned it thataway. Oh, suh, I's 'fraid what he gone do to the other slaves now." She did not go on to express her fear for her master Tate's well-being.

Hiram opened the door of the locker then, darkness having fallen quickly in the deep river gorge. "I thanks you, suh." She took several deep breaths of fresh air, then looked out at the blackness with fearful eyes. "You sho nobody be shootin' at us now?"

"They won't shoot at somethin' they can't see." Hiram said. "We're gonna tie up down here to a sycamore on the right bank that's growin' right outta the base of a cliff," he said. "There ain't no space for a road, even a trail down to the water there, so it'll be safer for us than most places. You can walk around on deck if you want, or sit in the cabin. I'm goin' up to help Caleb pull her in to tie up for the night. We'll have a bite to eat after we land."

That night Captain Easterday seemed to note Ivy's melancholy attitude as he and his crew sat in silence in the cabin after supper. The table around which they sat was lighted by a single lantern. The running lamps had not been lit, and the lantern would not have been visible to observers viewing the boat from the clifftops.

Hiram cleared his throat and spoke into the silence. "Ivy, we understand your grievin' over Jacob and his tragic passing. I thought

181

we all might find it agreeable to rest our minds list'nin' to Samuel Cummings's description about this old Kentucky River that's takin' us down to the Ohio. Samuel wrote this here book that tells some interestin' details of river life." He held up the small book and read its title: *The Western Pilot and Gazeteer.* Ivy still seemed lost in a world of her own.

"I'll commence readin' the most interestin' parts, on page 47." He cleared his throat and began to read aloud. *"Kentucky River: This beautiful river rises in the Cumberland Mountains, and interlocks with the head waters of the Licking and the Cumberland rivers. Its length is about two hundred miles. For a great part of its course, it flows in a deep channel, cut out of perpendicular banks of limestone. Nothing, says Mr. Flint in his Geography, can be more singular than the sensation arising from floating down this stream, and looking up this high parapet at the sun and the sky from the dark chasm, down which the waters float the boat. Stone coal is found in its banks in several places and a species of marble, which receives a fine polish. Port William is situated at its mouth, where it is one hundred and sixty yards wide.*

*"Frankfort, the seat of government for the state, is situated on the east bank, sixty miles above its mouth. It stands in a deep bottom, or valley, surrounded by precipitous hills. It is not as large as Lexington, but receives importance from being the political metropolis of the state. A chain bridge across the Kentucky connects the town with the beautiful country on the west bank. It contains about 400 houses, and 4,000 inhabitants and is twenty-four miles from Lexington."*

By this time Ivy had raised her head and was listening to Hiram as he read. After a pause she said, "I do 'preciate y'all takin' me on this boat, an' your kindness." She timidly looked around at the blank expressions of the six white men and one negro. "Everything here so diff'rent from the plantation. I feels lost and 'fraid without Jacob. Maybe I feel better directly."

Hiram closed his book and laid it aside. He leaned his elbows on the table and looked at the girl. "Ivy, we all feel the loss of Jacob, too. And we know you've been through troubles that we can't imagine, but we're here to help you, so you ask if you need anything. I know you could use some rest right now. We're gonna fix you a place to sleep where you'll have privacy. Try not to worry, 'cause we're here to keep you safe." She looked up at the captain and smiled her gratitude.

# CHAPTER THIRTY-FIVE

The next morning, with still no indication of danger, or that anyone was following the boat, the captain escorted Ivy out to the railing for a few minutes and called her attention to the cliffs on either side of the river and the deep emerald color of the water. She felt the warm sun and gentle breeze on her face. The girl had never been on a boat before, never even seen the river, but for a moment she forgot her fear of the unknown and absorbed the beauty of the spring morning. "Ivy, some of these limestone cliffs is two hundred feet high. They're called the Kentucky River Palisades, 'cause they reminded the earliest explorers of forts with their high walls. The Palisades stretch from Clay's Ferry behind us all the way down to Frankfort ahead of us. That's the state capital I read about last night. If you look ahead or behind us right now, this river looks almost the same as it would have looked hundreds of years ago when only the Indians lived here."

As Ivy peered in wonder at the beautiful scene a great blue heron took flight from a small gravel bar ahead of the boat. "Oh, look, Captain, a shikepoke. We seed 'em sometimes in our little cricks on the plantation. Only this one the biggest I ever seed."

"That's a blue heron, Ivy. Shikepokes is what people round here call the smaller green heron. There's all kinds of wild critters that live in the river gorge. We've seen bears, wolves, deer, panthers and all kinds of smaller game along here, like turtles and snakes on the logs we pass by. We usually see animals in the early mornings or late evenings. This country is about as wild now as when the good Lord created it."

"They ain't many landings along here, is they Mistuh Hiram?"

"Once we get down to Frankfort and the riverbanks level out into bottom lands, we'll be stoppin' at landings to take on and offload freight. Up along here, it's still mostly wilderness and the Palisades keeps people from doin' much business along the river. We'll have to hide you again when we go through locks and when we get near Frankfort because there's likely to be slavecatchers hangin' round the river at those points watchin' out for runaways on boats like ours. Right now, though, you can stay out on deck and enjoy the fine weather for a little bit. We ain't likely to see anybody, much less slavecatchers on this stretch of the river."

Just then, as if in answer to Hiram's over-confident words, a rifle shot rang out, raising a small geyser of water near the bow. Its sharp report reverberated between the limestone walls of the river course for two or three seconds. Even before the echoes died Hiram had grabbed Ivy and shoved her into her locker, slammed the door and stepped back to the railing to scan the high cliffs on the port side, from where the shot had seemed to come. The deckhands appeared with their rifles in hand, also looking upward at the imposing ramparts. They heard a cackling laugh and some shouted words they could not make out, except for a liberal sprinkling of curses.

Taking cover behind a barrel of salt pork on the port side, the captain cupped his hands and replied, "Come out in the open, you yay-hoo, and we'll have us a little target practice on your sorry bones."

"There he goes!" shouted Cecil, one of the hands. "He's hightailin' it back into the trees up on top."

"Don't show yourselves." Hiram said. "There might be others."

After they waited for a couple of minutes with no more firing from the cliffs the captain and his deckhands began to relax. "What you reckon that was all about?" one of them asked.

"In this country it could be anything," Hiram said. "Some crazy hermit that thinks he's guardin' his territory, a bored hunter, some kid tryin' to be a man by scarin' somebody."

185

Ivy stayed hidden the rest of the day, which included passage through two more locks without incident. That night the captain again invited her to join the crew for supper in the cabin.

As planned, the *Sally Preston* reached the settlement of English, a short distance above Carrollton, in the wee dark hours of the third night of their journey down the Kentucky, and Captain Easterday tied up there. He carried only freight, mainly the products grown and crafted by the Shakers at Pleasant Hill. His only passenger was Ivy, thus he wouldn't have to deal with questions or complaints about his change in itinerary.

Just after daylight the captain ordered the crew to remove two of the wooden buckets from the sternwheel. Hiram hoped this would make it appear to any suspicious pro-slavers watching that the equipment had been damaged on the voyage down the river. The men carried the buckets inside the cabin on the lower deck and made hammering sounds as if they were repairing the broken parts.

Hiram was relieved when, just after noon, a young rider came galloping down the road to the English Landing. He tied his horse and trotted up the landing stage. Captain Easterday met him on the lower deck, took him into his cabin and poured both of them a shot of whiskey. "Don't tell your mama nor the Quakers you been drinkin' with me, son, but I figure you done earned it. I hope you're bringin' news from Judd Calloway."

The boy looked around, apparently expecting to see runaway negroes. "That I am, sir. They've had a change of plans, though. They hear'd tell of a bunch of patrollers a'waitin' across the river from Carrollton at Lamb to catch these slaves thee has on board."

"Well, they's only one fugitive on board now, a mulatto girl. She had a partner, but he died on the way down. But go on, son," Hiram said. "Where we s'posed to land this gal, then?"

"They said for you to pass on by Carrollton, head out into the Ohio and drop her downriver at Hanover Landing. Ain't safe for no slaves to cross the river here at Carrollton right now, 'cause Cyrus Stenigal, an old codger that's in cahoots with the slavecatchers, he'll be watchin' for you to haul up at Carrollton, and he'll signal his cronies that's waitin' on the Indiana riverbank to look for somebody bringin' her across in a small boat."

"Hanover Landing, you say? I ain't done much navigatin' on the Ohio. Hold on a minute whilest I grab my navigation book." Hiram went to a locker and brought out his copy of *The Western Pilot and Gazeteer*. After studying the text and maps he said, "I see we'll have to be on our toes to dodge them little islands and sandbars, then we'll pass Madison and a couple of creek mouths and put in on the Indiana bank at Hanover Landing. I see it here on the map. Looks like about seventeen mile downriver from Carrollton."

"The outlaws may light out after thee from Lamb on horseback when they see thee headin' downriver," the boy said.

The captain laughed. "If we run on down to Hanover, they'll play hell catchin' us. That's a long hard ride from Lamb to Hanover, and they won't know where we're headed once we disappear down the big river. For all they know we could be headed for Louisville, even New Orleans. Now, you say they'll be a man waitin' there to take charge of this gal?"

The boy nodded and said, "Yes, sir." Then he grinned, raised his shotglass to Hiram, who joined him in knocking back his whiskey. The boy grimaced and suppressed a cough in spite of his manly pretenses and said, "I hear'd the wife of one of them slavecatchers that's waitin' over at Lamb has outfoxed her husband. She seen some way that he was fixin' to go on a patrol and sent word to Judd Calloway in time for him to change the plans like I done told thee."

"That's good, but they better be somebody at the Hanover Landing to meet this gal and move her on north. We'll be in a hell of a fix if there ain't nobody waitin' when we get there. We can't afford to hang around for the outlaws to show up."

"Judd'll have somebody there, don't worry thyself about it, sir."

# CHAPTER THIRTY-SIX

That evening Hiram's crew replaced the undamaged buckets on the sternwheel. They waited till after dark to shove off from the English Landing. The captain brought the *Sally Preston* up to speed, then he steamed down past the Carrollton Landing and out into the powerful current of the Ohio. He chuckled as he set her course downriver, imagining the look on Cyrus Stenigal's face, sitting on his hilltop above the mouth of the Kentucky River. He would have positioned himself where his lantern signal could be seen by Sam Cunningham and his henchmen across the river at Lamb. But Cyrus would not see the *Sally Preston* tie up at Carrollton and drop off any fugitives tonight, so his cohorts on the Indiana shore would have to wait and wonder. The slavehunters at Lamb, as well as Cyrus at Carrollton, would be flummoxed by the sight of the steamboat passing on out into the Ohio and disappearing downstream.

Even if Sam and the others took off overland on horseback in pursuit of the steamboat the distance was too great and there were too many land obstacles like ravines, creek crossings and fences in their way. They would have no chance of following close enough to see where the *Sally Preston* deposited her passenger on the Indiana side miles downstream.

Caleb came down from the pilothouse to Ivy's hiding place in the locker under the stairway. He brought her into the cabin where he spoke to her, explaining their plans and revealing the dropoff point for her journey northward toward freedom.

A little less than two hours and seventeen downriver miles later the captain put in to the Indiana shore at Hanover Landing. The packet boat's engines labored to bring the small vessel about and nudge her up to the landing on an upstream bearing, so as to maneuver more efficiently against the current. The crew of the *Sally Preston* did not even tie her up to the wharf. The boat bumped gently against the rickety structure and the pilot kept her there for only a minute or two. Caleb told Ivy to step quickly and bring her belongings, for the boat would not be lingering at this unprotected place. It was far too vulnerable to attack by patrollers. Caleb led the slave girl down the partially-lowered landing stage. They did not take time to celebrate the girl's freedom, for it was by no means certain at this point. Caleb scanned the darkness for the conductor who was supposed to be there to meet the boat. No signal was needed. The engine noise and the sternwheel roiling the water could be heard for a mile or more.

Then in the feeble light from the lone running lamp on the boat's bow a human form appeared waving a white rag. Caleb whispered, "There's your man." They jumped off the gangplank and he led the girl from the tiny wharf up the incline to meet Sylvester Morrison, who took the girl's arm and hurried her back to the treeline. He stopped only long enough to turn to Ivy and whisper, "Just one? Nobody else with you?"

Her voice trembling, she said, "Yassuh, jus' me.

"Surprised by her voice he said, "You a girl?"

"Yassuh."

"Come on, then."

There had been no time for introductions among the three young people. Caleb whispered into the darkness toward where the two forms had just disappeared, "God be with you," and jumped back up on the landing stage. Two deck hands were already cranking the winch as Hiram steered the boat forward against the current into the main stream where he ordered full power to push back upstream to Port William.

Sylvester had spent two days scouting on foot and horseback the territory between the Hanover Landing on the river and the Lancaster settlement, some ten or twelve miles from the head of Dead Man Hollow, out across the Hanover Plain. The hollow rose from the level of the river at 420 feet to the tableland on top at an elevation of about 750 feet, according to the crude map Judd Calloway procured for him. The boy made several trips up and down the hollow on foot during both daylight and dark until he knew the course so well he could almost have found his way up through the dense woods and rocky creekbed with his eyes closed.

His observations included the fact that Cooper's Ferry, operated for the Cooper family by old Jack Johnson, plied the river between Cooper's Bottom on the Kentucky side and the Hanover Landing in Indiana. Sylvester learned the ferry did not run after sunset. When the ferry passengers landed in Indiana during daylight hours, Sylvester observed from his hiding place that they made their way up the road through Crowe Hollow, which lay to the west of the aptly named Dead Man Hollow. This was for good reason. Local residents he'd cautiously spoken with said even if a person could make the strenuous hike up Dead Man Hollow from the river they would be stopped at the two waterfalls looming where the deep gorge forked at the head of the ravine. Dead Man Falls and Horseshoe Falls both rose nearly eighty feet above the streambed.

Sylvester had stabled his mare in Jess Wagner's barn on the flatland not far from the head of Dead Man Hollow. He climbed down into the hollow and camped there so he could continue his scout during nighttime hours and in the early morning. He kept track of the times of sunrise and sunset, first light and full dark. He noted the phase of the moon and the condition of the muddy soil on the talus slopes at the upper end of the hollow near the falls.

Sylvester's sister Rachel had told him the valley of the Ohio River marked the southern extremity of the advance of the glaciers in the last ice age, and that the numerous steep ravines that drained into the river were the subsequent result of erosion. How she'd come by all this information was a puzzlement to the boy, but then he and his family had learned not to question her authority on most subjects.

He tried to anticipate the effect of weather on his mission, and he hoped the runaways in this party, unknown to him in both identity and number at this point, would be physically able to do some rugged climbing. If not, or if it turned out there were more than two or three fugitives, he'd have to choose one of the easier, and therefore more dangerous, routes up to the flatlands.

After he had scouted the Dead Man Gorge to his satisfaction he rode his mare across the Hanover Plain to Lancaster at night, learning the network of lanes, shallow valleys and woodlands that would afford him the quickest and most secure route to the abolitionist village.

By the time he met Ivy at the riverbank, he had been outfitted by his friend Jess Wagner at his saddle shop in North Madison. Aside from hardtack and jerky in his pockets, Sylvester carried a two-pronged grapple hook lying flat against his back with a length of strong cordage attached to it and coiled over his shoulders. Jess' corn knife in a homemade leather sheath was tied to his belt and secured to his left leg by a leather thong, its eighteen-inch blade having been blackened so as not to reflect light. His own small sheath knife also hung from his belt at his right hip. Slung across his shoulders was a small canteen of clean water, for he knew the water in the creek downstream from the settlement of Hanover would make both him and his fugitives sick.

In his coat Sylvester always carried his prized possession, a small pistol like the one Carney O'Sullivan had showed him. He'd seen it when the Irishman brought the sad news about Robert Sandlin to the Morrisons at Sugar Branch five years ago. The boy decided he had to have a similar weapon. He looked long and hard around Switzerland and Jefferson counties to find such a piece, which Carney had called a pepperbox percussion revolver.

The boy finally found a similar model that belonged to Karl Mote, the owner of a livery stable in Madison. Karl wasn't in the mood to part with his treasure until Sylvester offered to trade him a stud fee for Allegheny Messenger, the only Morgan stallion in southeastern Indiana, to service his mare. When his handshake sealed the trade the boy had no idea how he'd be able to repay the fee to his father, but he hoped John Wesley would be generous with the terms of his loan.

To save weight Sylvester carried no extra ammunition for the revolver. The three loaded barrels would have to suffice for this nocturnal mission.

The boy was pleased that the only people he'd seen in Dead Man Hollow during his two days of scouting were a couple of kids hunting mushrooms. He'd watched them from the rim of the ravine until they disappeared down the trail.

# CHAPTER THIRTY-SEVEN

$\mathfrak{S}$ylvester led Ivy through the trees and about ten rods up a slope that rose gently from the river bank into the mouth of Dead Man Hollow. He found his way by faint moonlight and by peering upward to see the outlines of trees against the sky. In the edge of the forest he drew Ivy inside a giant hollow sycamore with a cavity large enough for them to stand.

The boy whispered, "My name's Sylvester, but folks call me Vess. What's yours?"

"Ivy."

They could hear each other breathing in the confined space, but Sylvester still had hold of Ivy's arm and her hand tentatively touched his sleeve. In this total darkness, besides their voices and breathing, they had no other way of keeping contact with each other and this would be a critical necessity for both of them on the coming trek through wild terrain.

"You're wearin' britches, ain't you?"

"Yassuh. Jacob make me dress like a man when we run off."

"Jacob?"

"He a slave, too, but he done died on the Kentucky River."

"Your husband?"

"Nahsuh, jus' a . . . jus' a frien'."

"That's too bad about him dyin', but britches'll make things a lot easier for you tonight. There's a trail we can follow most of the way up this holler. You walk behind me and keep your eye on this white rag I'm tyin' on my belt. We got a little moonlight, so that'll

193

help. When we get to creek crossings or rough spots I'll help you across."

"How far we got to go? This be Canada?"

"It ain't Canada by a helluva ways, but you done got the Ohio River behind you. We got to go 'bout a mile up this holler, then maybe ten more mile up top. That'll be the easy part, unless they see us."

Ivy's voice tensed. "Who see us?"

"Slavecatchers aimin' to shoot me and take you back to your master for bounty, but that ain't gonna happen tonight. Hiram dropped you down here at Hanover to dodge one bunch of slavecatchers I know about upriver at Lamb. We had to find this safer route up Dead Man Holler, not that they ain't other bands of freebooters round here, too, lookin' to make a little bounty money.

"I s'pose to know all them places an' names? I be lost as a blind man at midnight."

"Don't fret about that. I done scouted this place. Fugitive parties used to go up the easier Clifty Hollow to the east or Crowe Hollow west of here but these days them hollers is sometimes watched by slavecatchers. I've heard 'em brag when they catch runaway slaves out of them hollows."

"Other folks gone hep us, too?"

"You bet, Christian people, abolitionists. You'll be safe there at a place called Lancaster. Now, let's get movin'."

They moved out, able to see a little better now, after their moments in the dark tree cavity. A small animal scurried up the trail ahead of them, then off into the woods to the left. Ivy evidently didn't see it. Sylvester started slowly, allowing time for the girl to get used to walking on the uneven trail. Most of the leaf buds hadn't burst yet and they could see the wooded tops of the ravine skylighted high above them. The ascending hollow gradually narrowed as they walked. The trail crossed the creek four times, and each time Sylvester let the girl come up from behind him, then took her arm and helped her across. A sprained ankle or knee could drastically affect their chances of success.

They were moving more quickly now and Sylvester was impressed by Ivy's strength and agility. At a point he judged to be about halfway up the hollow he stopped, reached back to take her arm and draw her alongside. "You doin' okay? Need water?" he whispered.

"Toler'ble well Mistuh Vess. Ain't thirsty, but I hears a dog barkin' up above. He gone git after us?"

"That ain't no bloodhound, if that's what you're thinking, just somebody's porch dog. Nobody's expectin' us to be comin' up through here."

"Why not?"

"It's too rugged. You'll see soon enough. And don't call me mister, just Vess, like I said."

"It be a hard habit to break. You white an' I be black."

"I'm just a kid, but call me what you want. Come on."

The trail slowly vanished and another twenty minutes of climbing over bushel basket-size rocks brought them to a place that seemed to be surrounded on three sides by towering walls. The sounds of a high waterfall ahead pulled them up short. "Dead Man Falls," Sylvester said.

"Lordy, mis . . . uh, Vess, that be so high, what we gone do now?"

"We're gonna rest a minute, then go up this slope on our right. Better take on some water."

After a short rest they began to climb the steep side of the canyon, grasping hold of small trees, brush and fallen logs to pull themselves up. Saplings had grown up among the small stones and mud of the talus slope. Sylvester turned and said, "Right up there is where we're headed, not too much farther now."

He heard scrambling sounds as she came up even with him and braced herself against a tree next to him. She spoke as soon as her breathing would allow. "Look like this go straight up. I's 'fraid I'll slip in this mud, kill my weary self on them rocks down below."

As Ivy spoke the boy took the rope and grappling hook off his shoulders. "I want you to set next to this tree and hang onto it with both hands."

She did as he said, then whispered, "What you gone do?"

"Try to hook that next tree up yonder. Can't cross this little washout up ahead without a rope. We get a-past this place we almost got it made. Keep your head down. I got to swing this hook now."

195

All was quiet except for Sylvester's climbing, slipping steps to separate himself a little from the tree where Ivy sat, and then the woop-woop of the hooks swinging in the air. When the sound stopped it was followed by the hook banging against a tree a few feet past the dark slide area. "Damn! Missed it." He reeled in the rope, and on the second throw the hook caught at the base of the tree. He tested it with his weight and found it had made secure purchase among the roots.

"Here we go. I'm tyin' this end of the rope around my chest. You get in front of me and both of us gonna pull hand-over-hand and walk up till we get to that tree. From there it's just a little ways farther."

"Mercy! What if the hook come loose?"

"It won't, I tested it. Come on, now." They climbed again, both of them pulling themselves upward along the steep slope toward the tree.

Suddenly Ivy's feet slipped from under her, causing loose rocks to slide and tumble down the slope, clattering into the creekbed far below. She managed to hang onto the rope and Sylvester grabbed her under the arms just as he lost his footing, too.

With the rope now supporting both of their dead weights, their bodies having swung down to hang directly beneath the tree, Sylvester felt the rope tightening around his chest, cutting off his wind. "Grab the rope, pull, get your feet back under you," he gasped.

Ivy was sobbing, her breath coming in ragged bursts, but after struggling a moment she had herself braced with her feet on the slope and a firm grip on the rope. As she lifted her weight upward off of him, Sylvester felt some of the pressure ease from his chest and he finally managed to recover his own footing. "Rest a minute," he said. "Let your breath and your heart calm down. We're gonna be all right."

# CHAPTER THIRTY-EIGHT

As they rested, Sylvester talked to her calmly, reassuring her that they had not much farther to go. Then they began to walk themselves up the rope again inch by inch. After resting twice more Ivy was able to grasp a root of the tree. When she had scrambled upward, free of the rope, she turned, braced her feet on the base of the tree and reached for Sylvester's hand. In a few moments the rope hung loose, dangling from its hook over the steepest part of the slope they had just traversed. The two young people lay in a heap with their feet against the tree, sprawled on the upper slope, Ivy holding onto Sylvester as if she would never let go.

When the trembling had left their limbs and they found the strength to cautiously stand up supported by the tree and each other, Sylvester said, "Now, can you see that sapling setting on the roots of the big tree up ahead? I sawed the little one off the day before yesterday, and scooted its butt over so the larger tree would brace it. Had to use a saw, for an axe would of made too much racket. Never know when somebody will get curious and come lookin' round down in here."

"Seem like we make enough racket just now to bring a whole army lookin' for us," Ivy said. "How many time you bring black folks up in here?"

He hoped she couldn't see his sheepish grin in the dark. "You're lucky," he said. "You got to be the first."

"Lawsy mercy! I's sho' glad you didn't tell me that down by the river! How old is you, Vess? Seem like you ain't but a boy."

"Seventeen. You?"

"Sweet Jesus! I's twenty, and here I is, puttin' my life in the hands of a chil'."

"Now don't you worry, Ivy. We're gonna be fine. You watch."

"Watch! Cain't bear to watch, scare me to death."

Though Sylvester's leaning tree was only a large sapling, it had grown straight and tall in the deep hollow reaching for the sun. After he'd cut it two days ago Sylvester wondered if he had the strength to maneuver the butt over the few inches to rest it against the larger tree to keep it from sliding downhill. Finally, by working for over an hour lifting and prying, using all his strength, he had the base of the smaller tree secured. He had tested the sapling and found it strong enough to take his weight as he climbed to the top of the cliff.

When they left the tree where the hook was fastened, Ivy said, "Want me fetch the hook an' rope?"

Sylvester looked back. "Just leave it. I'll come back for it later, but it won't be anytime soon, maybe never." Ivy muttered to herself that she never wanted to see another rope and grappling hook as long as she lived.

They moved slowly up the slope to the sapling that leaned against the cliff. "We s'posed to shinny up that thing?" Ivy asked. "Look to me like we's gone fall and bust our mis'able self to pieces."

"Look close and you'll see they's limbs sticking out along the trunk, places where you can catch hand and foot holds. I sawed off all but the ones that's spaced just right for us to climb."

"That take us all the way to the top? Where it end up?"

"I made this tree ladder in the daytime when I could see. It reaches up the steepest part of this cliff to where the ground levels out some. It'll be easier to get from there on up to the flatland."

"How you know that thing won't break?"

"I done climbed up and down it two or three times, once in the dark. It'll bend some, but it'll hold us if we go up one at a time."

"Lord, you fixin' to send me firs', ain't you?"

"No, Ivy. I'll go first, but you got to follow me. You ready?" Without waiting for an answer, Sylvester set a boot on the first limb and moved up the slender sycamore using his spaced hand and foot holds. When he'd almost reached the top he looked back and said in a stage whisper, "Ivy, come on. You can start now." He felt the sapling move as it gave under her weight. She came up slowly, feeling for the hand and foot holds.

Sylvester was glad for the darkness. Even if Ivy looked down now she wouldn't be able to see clearly the precipice they were scaling with the aid of this crude ladder. One misstep could send one or both of them plunging to their death on the rocks below.

When he reached the wide flat rock at the top he turned around, sat down and braced himself to pull her up when she reached the ledge. He heard her labored breathing and an occasional whimper, but she came on steadily.

She finally reached the top of the tree where he made her stop for a moment. Her hands were level with the rock ledge, still holding onto the limbs of the tree. "Catch your breath a second while I tell you what to do."

"Oh, I's scared, Vess! My legs be shakin'."

"I'm braced real good, so you take my hands and keep pushing with your feet. I'll pull you right up on top of me. You crawl over me and get behind where it's level. Then we'll rest a minute."

On his signal, Ivy did as Sylvester said, but as soon as she reached the safety of the ledge behind him she burst into tears and wrapped her arms around him, clutching for anything that felt safe after her nightmarish climb. It was several moments before her shivering stopped. He patted and warmed her hands that she had clasped tightly in front of his chest, and he spoke soothing words to her, praising her for her bravery and strength during the long ordeal.

"Now, Ivy there's one more thing we got to do before we head north." As he spoke, he unsheathed Jess' long corn knife, originally fashioned for cutting fodder in a corn field. Jess had hardened the steel in a blacksmith forge that his father kept in his shop, and now the boy found it useful as a multi-purpose tool and potential weapon when he'd come out in these woods on a "scout" as he called it. He'd heard from his father that the term had been used by Sylvester's grandfather Ephraim, who'd been a scout near his home in upstate New York in the Continental Army back in the early '80s.

Ivy had released him by now and moved back away from the rock ledge, but she still sat huddled in fear. "I needs to get away from this place. I's afrighted half to death."

199

"We'll leave in a minute, Ivy, but first I got to get rid of our ladder. Now you hold onto my left hand while I reach out and whack off the top of this sapling so it'll fall and nobody else can use it."

Groaning and sobbing softly, the girl did as she was told, bracing her feet and holding Sylvester's hand while he reached far out over the edge of the cliff. After a few expert blows with the heavy corn knife the top of the tree separated and they heard the long lower part crash to the bottom of the gorge.

Sylvester quickly sheathed his corn knife, pulled the girl to her feet and helped her dry her eyes with the white rag from his belt. Then they set out at a brisk pace up the gentle slope through the woods toward the flat land ahead.

# CHAPTER THIRTY-NINE

They came out of the woods, crossed a lane and then moved into a fallow field. "Can you see that log barn over by them woods?" Sylvester whispered, walking beside Ivy now. In the watery moonlight the barn's shingle roof blended perfectly with the forest behind it.

"Where? I don't see no barn."

"See the direction I'm pointing? It's a short walk, less than twenty rod."

"Don't make no never-mind if I sees it or not. We gone hide there?"

"It belongs to a friend of mine, Jess Wagner, and his dad. He's been known to help runaway slaves now and again. You about wore out?"

"I know that be right. Don't never want to see that hole back yonder no more."

"You won't have to. I got my mare, Genessee Jill, in that barn. I thought if there was just one of you we'd ride the mare. More than that, some of us would have to walk, and that would slow us down. Since it's just you and me, we're gonna ride for a while. You're ready, ain't you?" He hoped she could hear the grin in his voice.

Sylvester had the mare saddled and bridled in no time. When he put the bit in Jill's mouth he took care to touch her teeth with his forefinger first, not wanting to bang her teeth with the cold metal bit before she opened her mouth. "I'm tying this little burlap sack with straw in it behind the saddle for you. You'll be ridin' pillion." He

201

mounted, gave Ivy a stirrup, and told her which foot to put in it. He reached down and helped her up behind him.

"I be ridin' what?"

"Pillion, it means behind me. Hold onto me till you get used to ridin'. You comfortable?"

In answer he felt her arms come around him, and she shifted her weight a little. Her voice was sober with apprehension. "Ain't never rode no hoss before. Clay say he catch a slave ridin' a horse he gone feel the whip on his sorry back."

"Who's Clay?"

"He the black overseer on the plantation I come from. Bessie say he the devil's firs'born son. You fixin' to run her?"

"Not unless somebody comes after us, but that ain't likely."

They rode from the barn out to a lane that meandered between crop clearings and large tracts of forest. In a few minutes they came to a wider mud road heading north. Jill walked smoothly along the berm to avoid the ruts, making it easy for the riders to accommodate themselves to her gait. Sylvester noted with satisfaction that Jill's hoofbeats were silent on the dead grass. The surrounding countryside was flat as a tabletop, though that would also help anyone trying to follow them. "This mare's a Morgan, got a easy way a'goin'," he said, hoping to allay Ivy's fears on tonight's venture that had already frightened the girl enough. "Can you see the North Star up there?"

He could feel her small movements as she looked upward. "I done hear'd 'bout the drinkin' gourd."

"Can you see it? We goin' north? Tell me how you find the north star from the gourd."

"You looks for the front lip of the biggest gourd, then follows that d'rection three times that far an' there be the Freedom Light. Ain't but a puny-lookin' star, but it lead to freedom, they say." She paused, then her voice took a skeptical tone. "You know that, you jus' playin' with me, ain't you?"

Ivy couldn't see him grinning. He said, "Had to be sure you knowed which direction to run, in case somethin' happens to me."

"Oh my lord a'mercy! They better not be nothin' happen to you."

"I don't mean to scare you, Ivy, but this here's a chancy business we're up to tonight." The mare took several steps before he continued. "And I was joshin' you a little." He patted her hands that she clasped around his chest. "Thought we both needed to loosen up a bit. Feelin' better now?"

After a pause, "Yassuh . . . I means . . . yes."

They rode on in silence for a while, Sylvester feeling the girl's shivering arms hugging him for warmth. She let go of him only once to blow her nose on the white rag he'd given her. The boy guided Jill off the lane into the edge of a woodland where he reined her around and scanned the brighter horizon behind them. The air was cooling rapidly. The frosted fields glowed silver-white in the faint moonlight. He looked upward at the luminous dome. The Milky Way spread its frigid high road toward infinity.

Satisfied there were no riders following, he took off his coat and handed it back to Ivy. "Put this on." She shrugged into it, turning up the collar, then her body came close to him again and he felt her warmth.

"I 'preciate it, Vess, but how you gone keep warm now?"

"I got my gloves, and my long handles on underneath my clothes, plus I got you to keep the wind from blowin' up my shirttail. B'lieve I'll be all right." He felt her arms grasp him a little tighter and she shrugged her shoulders as if luxuriating in the warmth of the coat.

The boy nudged the mare with his knees and Jill stepped forward again. Based on his scout of the area he decided to take a shortcut through the forest and pick up another north-bound lane on the far side. Unbeknownst to the two riders, danger lurked both behind them and ahead.

They had just crossed a creek called Chicken Run when the mare suddenly threw her head up and snorted. A large shadow hurtled out of the darkness and lunged for Sylvester's leg, growling ferociously. Jill pranced sideways, momentarily carrying the riders away from the attack. Ivy screamed and nearly fell off until Sylvester reached back to steady her and she grabbed the cantle of the saddle.

By this time he'd been able to identify the beast as a large dog or wolf, not a bear or wild cat. It was of a gray or black color, perfectly camouflaged in these dark woods.

The animal came at them again, snapping at the horse's prancing legs as well as those of the riders. "Lift up your feet!" Sylvester shouted, and Ivy did so. He kept his own feet in the stirrups, but felt strong jaws scrape down across the outer part of his right stirrup, saving his foot. On the creature's third jump the teeth caught his britches leg and he felt it rip.

He couldn't kick the mare into a gallop. Ivy might lose her balance, and in these dark woods they could easily be knocked off their mount by low limbs. There was the corn knife, but he knew that swinging it would endanger the mare's legs.

The pistol was in his coat, but Ivy was wearing it. Should have bought a holster. He frantically reached his right hand back and into the coat. Ivy leaned forward, but the small pistol was hard to locate and grasp in the large pocket. With his left hand holding the reins of the frightened mare, he finally brought out the revolver, cocked the hammer and swung the piece toward the lunging beast.

Having only three loads he needed to aim carefully, but the movement of horse and attacker in the darkness made that impossible. He remembered Carney O'Sullivan's instructions: the weapon was built for close-range combat, round lead ball, no rifling in the barrel. Just push the muzzle toward the target's center of mass and fire.

Just then the creature leapt high enough to grasp the edge of the saddle blanket and hang on. An inch either way and the teeth would have ripped into the thigh of one of the riders. Sylvester pushed the revolver's muzzle toward the hollow between the creature's shoulder and neck and pulled the trigger. Smoke rolled and the pistol's report came simultaneously with the "chock" sound of ball entering flesh. The animal yelped and fell to the ground. Sylvester reined the mare in a circle round the beast with the pistol ready for the next shot. He could see the thing flailing on the ground, trying to rise. When it managed a sitting position, front legs splayed wide, he thought he saw blood pulsing from the mouth. It turned its head, tongue lolling from the open mouth, eyes seeming to glow following the mare as she circled. It tried once, twice to come up on all four feet, but its strength was gone and it flopped onto the ground where it convulsed a moment and lay still.

After he caught his breath Sylvester said, "That bruiser's a serious hunter." "Sneak attack, no barking. He wadn't no durned blood hound for sure. Only one, not a pack thank god. Reckon this is the outlaw that spooked that barking dog back yonder? Let's go look."

They dismounted and Sylvester wrapped the reins around a sapling. He had his pistol drawn and cocked. Nudging the thing with his boot brought no reaction. He bent to inspect it more closely, but still couldn't be sure. The creature might be a mixed shepherd breed, but the color wasn't quite right for a shepherd, uniform dark gray or black with no white markings or brown points that he could see. The shapes of body and head were similar to those of a wolf, but no matter, the beast was dead and they had to be moving.

They walked back to the mare and Sylvester checked her legs for wounds. After rubbing his hands up and down all four legs and finding her sound as far as he could tell in the dark, the boy turned to Ivy. She was badly shaken. She leaned against a tree with her hands beside her head, breathing hard. He spoke gently to her.

"Lord, girl, you've had enough excitement for a lifetime on this here ramble tonight. We'll soon get you to a place where you can rest. They's one thing for sure about this fracas," Sylvester said. "You don't need to worry about me bein' cold for a good little while." He leaned toward her to touch her shoulder and she reached out to cling to him again, sniffling as they moved back to Jill's side. "It's late," he said. "The Lancaster folks'll be ridin' out to find us before long."

205

# CHAPTER FORTY

They remounted and Jill moved on through the woods and out onto a lane again. "You think pattyrollers hear'd the shot, be lookin' for us?"

"Could be, but I doubt it. No cabins close by and it's late. Even patrollers got to sleep sometime. Don't think we got as many of them night riders up here as you have in the South."

It suddenly occurred to Sylvester that he knew nothing about Ivy. Being young and inexperienced as a conductor, the boy didn't know that for safety's sake sometimes the less the actors in these dramas knew about each other the better. But he'd become curious about this brave girl.

"What part of the South you from?" he said. Ivy explained that she'd been a slave on the Binford plantation up the Kentucky River near Pleasant Hill. Sylvester told her about Sugar Branch and his people, both the anti- and the pro-slavery factions. "That's why we couldn't bring you across the Ohio from Carrollton to Lamb. We knew they was slavecatchers waiting to grab you there."

In the small hours after midnight the mare moved along easily across the plain, through flatwoods and over gently rolling hills toward Lancaster. Their adrenaline having receded, the young people were unaware that fatigue was taking its toll on their bodies and dulling their watchfulness. But having more time now to reflect after their dash from the Ohio riverbank, they began to share with each other details of their lives.

"I can't imagine bein' a slave," Sylvester said. "Did they have you working in cotton fields and such?"

"Kentucky ain't no cotton country, leastways not aroun' Binford Plantation. We growed corn an' hemp an' hay, mos'ly. 'Baccer, o'course, some wheat an' oats. They was cows, horses. Hogs to butcher in cold weather. Slave families made kitchen gardens an' all. Some raised they own chickens."

"You said hemp, what's that?"

"It grow tall like corn. Take lotta slave work to grow hemp, rot it an' mash it to get the lint out. Lint be the hemp fiber. Then we cleans the lint, spins it an' weaves that into cloth. In old-timey days slave women wove the hemp into goods for slave's clothes, but now the marse, he buy rough cotton cloth an' slave women sew up clothes for the niggers. Cheaper, he say.

"Sometime they growed hemp jus' for seed. We et the seed or pressed it for oil. After they get all the lint an' seed out they burn the fodder. Some'a them nigger boys like to breathe the hemp smoke, make 'em crazy. Just pretend, mostly. If driver catch 'em he break out the rawhide."

"Did they make you work with the hemp?"

"Not in the fields. When I gets old 'nough to work they teach me to weave hemp into cloth. Make small pieces, mos'ly. Horse blankets, mats, pallets. Then a new marse come an' he make me a house slave."

"So then you cooked and cleaned house?"

Ivy was silent a moment. "Yes, and the marse make me he own . . . slave."

Sylvester paused in puzzlement. "But you was already his slave, right?"

Just then the riders were thrown off balance by the mare easing downhill to cross a creek. Ivy took hold of Sylvester again. Jill splashed through the knee-deep water, then climbed the other bank. "This here branch is called Harberts Creek," he said. Upstream they saw a scattering of log buildings through the trees in the distance. The houses sat dark and silent in the pallid moonlight. Sylvester had skirted the settlement and its shallow ford to avoid raising the alarm. "That's the Volga settlement," he said, "named after a river in Russia where them people come from, I heard."

207

Back on even ground, Sylvester turned his head to hear Ivy's words more clearly. "What was you sayin' back there . . . about your master?"

"I'd druther not talk 'bout it, Mistuh Vess."

"Oh. So them's *your* chickens, as the feller says." He could feel from her stillness his attempt at humor hadn't worked. They rode on in silence.

Soon the boy began to feel her sobbing, leaning against his back. Her arms slipped around him again. He tried once more to draw her out.

"So . . . uh . . . your master was mean to you, is that it?"

He heard her snuffling and she moved, blotting her tears. "He make me *his* woman . . . force me to . . . ." Another sob ended her sentence.

"Oh, sh . . . ." The boy was speechless for a moment, moving in the saddle to the rhythmic gait of the mare, yet cringing inside with each new sob from the girl behind him. He understood her anguish, having observed his sister Rachel's trauma over being abused in that way by Sam Cunningham just before they started to New York several years ago.

Her weeping became more intense now, like the gasping frightened sobs of a child who has just revealed a shameful secret. Sylvester felt he needed to do something for her. But what?

"Listen, Ivy, we're gonna haul up here for a little bit, get off and set down to rest. If we don't you're gonna get sick."

He helped her down in a small clearing and settled her at the base of a tree. He reached into the pocket of his coat she was wearing. "Here, try some of this dried beef and these hardtack crackers. Be careful or it'll bust your teeth. Better take some water with it. Hold it in your mouth a minute before you try to chew." She took the dry food he offered and did as he said. Thus occupied, at least she stopped crying.

She finished the food he'd given her. He reached forward with more but she declined. She sat with her knees drawn up and her hands holding her bowed head. After a few quiet moments the peepers in a nearby marshy lowland resumed their springtime chorus. A nightbird set up a strange song of quavering calls in a scrubland at the edge of the woods. The girl turned toward the sound. "Reckon that be some kinda signal?" Ivy whispered.

"Just some old nightbird. I think my sister Rachel called it a screech owl when we heard it one night on the trail to New York. I guess it's well named, but I wanted to shoot it that night"

"You say New York? That be north?"

"Yes, it's up north, but that's a long tale that don't need tellin' right now. Maybe later."

After a moment, Ivy dried her eyes and looked up at his silhouette against the sky. "I's sorry for holdin' you up. You been good to hep me, but I's got a hateful tribulation on my mind."

"We'll soon be with our friends at Lancaster. It'll be more comfortable there, and maybe you can talk with Sarah Tibbets about it. She's a young, gentle woman, minister's new wife. I b'lieve they married just last year."

Ivy's voice became tremulous as more tears started. "I's got to find my own peace with it."

"You've run away from your master now. Don't that feel better? Or is it your grief over losin' your friend Jacob?"

"I does grieve for Jacob, but . . . "

Sylvester sat down beside the girl and spoke softly. "Ivy, are you carryin' your master's child?"

"No, but . . . but Marse Tate be sick with the spells and fits. If the driver find out he maybe kill Marse and take over the plantation an' all the slaves. I done my bes' to hep Marse Tate keep his secret, but I ain't there now."

"But you got away from all that. It ain't your worry now."

Ivy took a deep breath. She looked at Sylvester and he could see, even in the darkness, her anguished expression. "You a gentle man, Mistuh Vess. You an' them other folks on the boat done took up for me, else the slavecatchers be after me like a cat on a field mouse. But I got to tell you it ain't easy as just runnin' away from the plantation. Marse Tate save me from Clay, that black devil overseer, an' I hep him keep his secret from the others. We hepped each other an' now I's 'fraid my marse be dead or terrible sick, and the slaves be whupped now 'cause of me leavin'."

"Then why'd you run off if you feel that way?" Sylvester said.

209

"Jacob foun' out what Marse Tate be doin' with me. That hateful Clay done tol' him. Clay seen Jacob and me together an' we 'fraid he tell Marse Tate 'bout us keepin' comp'ny. So Jacob he get mad an' scared of bein' sold South an' say, 'We leavin' tonight.' Jacob didn't know Marse Tate need me and treat me better after I hep him with the spells. Marse even give me presents and talk to me almos' like a white woman, not a slave. But how I tell Jacob all this? How he gone understand? So I run away with him."

"Sounds to me like Jacob loved you. Reckon you come to feel a spot of love for your master, too?"

He could see Ivy slowly shaking her head. "That be dang'rous country for a slave gal. Don't need to be talkin' 'bout no love. Jacob be dead now an' I done run away from them that needs me. This here nigger woman ain't fit for no love."

"Damn! You're too hard on yourself. You're a friendly, kind-hearted girl, and I might as well say it; you're flat out beautiful, girl. You got a big bright future in front of you if we can get you to Canada. I'm sure you done all you could for them other people before you had to leave. People have to take care of themselves, like you did by leavin' there. Once my sister Rachel read something to us from the newspaper. It said, 'He who would be free, himself must strike the blow.' "

"But Vess, I's brung more pain on they heads, an' that be eatin' on me," Ivy said. She slumped back against the tree, looking exhausted, miserable. Sylvester began to stir, dejectedly preparing to move on toward Lancaster, but he was brought up short when Ivy spoke again, so softly he could barely hear her, "Y'all ever have a runaway slave ax to go back?"

# CHAPTER FORTY-ONE

Sylvester was dumbfounded. It took him a few moments to formulate an answer. "Ivy, you been through a sight of trouble but I can't cipher what all's goin' on in your head. All I know is it's my job to get you to Lancaster, and I'm gonna do that. Now, we can talk more later, but right now we got to get on this mare and move out. We're already overdue at Reverend Tibbets's house and they'll be worried about us."

He was about to help Ivy to her feet when the peepers suddenly fell silent in the marsh and they heard horses moving through the woods, hooves thumping the ground, twigs snapping, leather creaking. Sylvester's Jill mare gave a soft whinny. The boy put a hand on Ivy's shoulder and peered into the darkness until he could make out riders coming toward them from three sides, closing in. Someone yelled, "Don't move!"

They heard a man's deep voice say, "Hank, light that fatwood." There came the sound of a metal container opening. They were evidently carrying live coals in a can slung off the pommel of a saddle. Sounds of breath blowing a coal to life, a wad of tinder bursting into flame. With it a rider lit a fatwood splint and from that a pine knot torch. Then he handed the torch to the man who had spoken. The leader held the torch high. The boy saw a tall bearded figure sitting his horse not more than thirty feet away with a rifle in the crook of his arm pointed at Sylvester.

"Take out your pistol, boy, and any other weapons. Let me see 'em, then drop 'em on the ground. They's three rifles trained on you, so don't try no funny business." Sylvester did as the man said and dropped the revolver, then the corn knife and his sheath knife.

Stalling for time, Sylvester said, "How'd you find us?"

The leader laughed, sliding his long gun into its scabbard, switching the torch from his left hand to his right. "That steamboat made a big racket puttin' in at Hanover Landing. We heard it up on the flat where we was patrollin'. We waited at the head of Crowe Holler thinkin' we'd see if you was conducting slaves when you come up the road. When you didn't show up after a while we rode down to the river to find you. Then we rode up along the river bank till we seen from your tracks you took the hard way up Dead Man Holler.

"We followed you and seen you'd already made it out of the holler so we had to backtrack several miles. When we hit your trail headin' northwest we knowed where you was bound. We caught up with you after we heard the shot. What was you doin', shootin' at shadows? Then we heard you splashin' across the creek at Volga. After that we just trailed you and waited till you give us a easy chance to grab you.

"You only got one nigger with you? That ain't gonna be much of a payday, boys." Sylvester didn't answer.

The man who'd been talking dismounted and said, "Now you move real slow, nigger, and get over here."

Sylvester stepped in front of Ivy. "You don't want this one. He's got the fever and we're headed to a doctor. You're liable to catch it if you take him with you."

"Sick, huh? Come over here, nigger. Take off that hat. You get outta the way, young feller, or I'll put a hole in you."

After hesitating a second, Ivy took off her hat, which freed her long hair, and stepped closer to the man who was doing the talking. He held the torch higher. "Well, now, what have we here? Looks like we done got us a handsome amber-eyed mulatto wench." He approached her more closely and put a hand on her forehead. "Your boyfriend lied, didn't he? You ain't got no more fever than I do. Looks like we'll have us a little fun with this one boys before we take her back."

"Don't you touch her," Sylvester said.

212

The man chuckled deep in his throat. "Don't seem like you're in no position to be layin' down the law, nigger lover." The man mounted his horse again, then held the torch high. "We're fixin' to relieve you of your nigger slut, and you cain't stop us. How's that make you feel, white boy? Tie him to a tree, Curt, and Hank, hoist the wench up behind me. We'll have your horse, too. You won't be needin' it for a spell."

Hank came forward to grab Ivy. She tried to run, but he caught her even before she had escaped the circle of torchlight. "She's a feisty one ain't she," the leader said. "That's the way I like 'em. Havin' a little fun with her oughta make up for the miserly pay she'll bring."

Ivy screamed. "Vess!"

Sylvester moved forward, but stopped when Hank said, "Hey! One more step there, son, and I'll blow your ass to kingdom come."

The boy stopped. "You'd best leave her alone. We got riders comin' to meet us, and they ain't gonna take kindly to you two-cent hoodlums botherin' her."

Curt had taken a coil of rope off his saddle and now he approached Sylvester. "Oh, we're gonna do a whole lot more'n *bother* her, sonny boy. We may even let you watch. You'll see this ain't Sabbath school." Suddenly he swung the knotted end of the rope, striking the boy across the neck. He whipped the rope backhand, delivering a second lash to Sylvester's face. "How you like the old salt eel, son? Seem like you ain't got much to say now, eh? Time for you to cork that smart mouth and quit tellin' stupid lies, you towheaded pissant." Two red welts were already rising on Sylvester's face and neck, the stinging pain blinding him with tears. "Now unless you want more'a this, back your butt up again' yonder tree."

Hank spoke up as Curt took hold of Sylvester's arm. "Will, before I put her up behind you, we oughta have our fun with her right here in front of her smart-ass conductor. It'd serve that mouthy little bastard right, don't you reckon."

Curt having turned to look at his two partners said, "Yeah, whattaya say, Will? I'm ready to have me a piece of that."

213

Will looked down from his horse. "No, we're clearin' out now," he said. "We been here too long already. Tie the kid up, Curt. Hank, lift her up behind me like I told you."

Hank was not ready to give in. "I don't see why we got to wait," he said. "I say we take her now and maybe have another go-round later. We can draw cards to see who goes first."

Will switched the torch back to his left hand and drew a pistol with his right. "Now godammit we ain't gonna waste no more time here. Do as I said right now or somebody's gonna get hurt."

Suddenly a shot rang out. Will grunted and toppled off his horse, dropping his pistol and torch. The torch fell into the duff of the forest floor, near where Ivy stood, almost going out and reducing the light in the clearing nearly to darkness. Sylvester took three steps and grabbed Ivy, then instinctively hit the ground and lay flat, shielding her with his body.

The two young people heard the other patrollers scrambling to find cover, then all was deadly quiet for a few seconds. A figure came out of the dark woods and picked up the faintly glowing torch. The area was again cast in a brightening orange glow, but whoever held the torch high was shielded by Will's horse, its rider now groaning and writhing on the ground, holding his bleeding side.

A calm resonant voice came from the opposite edge of the clearing. "Hank and Curt, you're surrounded. Throw your guns out where we can see them in the light."

Curt hollered from his hiding place. "I ain't doing no such a god-damned thing. You cowards need to show yourselves and we'll fight it out like men."

In the seconds that followed Sylvester heard the distinct clicks of three rifles being cocked. The sounds came from the woods beyond the edges of the small clearing. The two patrollers were apparently surrounded by the two men already heard from and three more riflemen in the forest nearby. After a couple more seconds of silence the calm voice said, "I'm John Tibbets. We're five men from Lancaster and we aim to save these young people. We saw your light, left our horses back a ways and crept up here. If we have to hunt you other two down we'll do it. Now, what's your pleasure, gentlemen? You can come out into the light and give up, or face the certain consequences."

214

Hank's shrill voice came from the darkness. "Don't believe 'em, Curt. If you bastards is really from Lancaster you're Quakers, and I happen to know it's again' your religion to be usin' guns. Who the hell are you?"

"You've been misinformed, sir," the calm voice said. "We're from Lancaster, all right, but we're New England Baptists, not Quakers, though we work hand-in-glove with our Quaker brethren when need be. We Baptists have no compunction against using firearms when necessary to uphold justice and freedom, in particular against the likes of you sneaking slavecatchers."

Curt spoke up from his hiding place. "I'm fixin' to run for it, Hank."

"That would not be advisable, mister. We're five men with five horses nearby and weapons. You two are now on foot. Need I point out that you'd be at a severe disadvantage? Your leader here on the ground can tell you we're serious, gentlemen."

After a long silence Curt's quavering voice came from the woods. "Don't shoot. I'm comin' out. Come on, Hank." Two rifles landed in the light of the clearing. Presently Curt and Hank's dark forms emerged into the torchlight to stand with their hands raised. Three men with rifles leveled at them came out from deeper in the forest.

The calm voice, now embodied in a tall man dressed in black, stepped out to face the group and their prisoners. He said, "Vess, you're guiding but one fugitive tonight?"

Sylvester helped Ivy get to her feet. He brought forth the frightened girl. "Yessir, Reverend Tibbets. They would have been two, but the other one, a young man, passed away on the journey down the Kentucky River."

"We're sorry for your loss, girl. Now, Sylvester, please collect these outlaws' weapons and stack them here in the center of the clearing. Also, take the saddles and bridles off two of their horses and add them to the pile. Hand Lyman here the reins of Will's horse. It is now our property along with their weapons and tack. We'll leave Joseph and Leonidas here to guard our possessions until we can send for them with a wagon later this morning."

Before collecting the weapons, Sylvester carefully positioned himself in front of Curt. "Looks like you ain't gonna have your fun with the girl, huh. That mightn't of been no easy trick, anyway. She's a better man than you'll ever be, you low-life scum."

Curt sneered. "It's easy to talk big now that y'all got the drop on us. You out here runnin' niggers through the woods thinkin' you're a bigshot. Why, you ain't nothin' but a . . . ."

Sylvester interrupted. "Now, as for your rope tricks I got an answer for you right here." The outlaw bellowed in pain as Sylvester's boot came up hard between his legs. Curt grabbed himself and bent double. Sylvester put both hands on the top of his head and smashed Curt's face with a swift knee. The outlaw fell backwards and didn't move for several seconds, blood oozing from his nose and mouth. The boy stood over the dazed man, fists clenched. "Now what was you sayin' you sorry blackleg? Speak up, I cain't hear you."

"That'll do, now, Sylvester," John Tibbets said.

Will, the other injured man on the ground, found his feeble voice and protested between grunts from the pain. "Take the other mounts, but . . . leave me my horse. I . . . I just swapped for that saddle last week . . . come from out west, Santa Fe. It's . . . one of a kind round here."

"Ah, another of your ill-conceived ideas, Will," the reverend said, "pursuing this dicey game with equipment and animals you can't afford to lose. Our pleasure at unhorsing and unsaddling you is now even greater, sir.

"Now, Hank, I trust you know how to ride a horse bareback. Gather your fallen comrades. I believe them able to sit a horse in spite of their injuries. If not, they can walk. Round them up and begone. While you're at it, throw your white hats and boots in the pile, as well. We'll take pleasure in burning those articles so they can no longer be used to strike fear into the hearts of our fugitive friends. Know that if you ever show yourselves in Smyrna or Lancaster Townships again your lives shall be in serious danger."

After Sylvester had collected the weapons, tack, hats and boots, the five Lancaster men, along with Sylvester and Ivy, stood silently watching the sock-footed Hank struggle to get Will on Curt's horse. Curt moved slowly, spitting blood and walking bowlegged. He struggled to mount his horse and sat behind Will. Hank fashioned a crude rope halter for his gelding, then mounted and urged the horse forward. The second horse with Will and Curt aboard dutifully followed its mate. They were last seen moving eastward through the forest, already complaining of cold feet.

With but little added conversation, the Lancaster party mounted up and moved out, their horses' breath condensing in white puffs in the pre-dawn air. John Tibbets and the two older Lancaster men led the way, the posse now including Sylvester on his Jill mare and Ivy on Will's horse, the one that had just been expropriated from the patrollers. The girl rode just ahead of Sylvester and Jill, holding onto the horn of the fine western saddle with the reins tied together and looped over it. This heavy saddle was the first of its kind Sylvester and the Lancaster men had ever seen.

The five from Lancaster had successfully saved Sylvester and Ivy this night, and relieved the patrollers of a horse with three saddles, tack and several weapons. This they considered fair punishment for the night riders' determined pursuit and capture of fugitive slaves. But the clandestine war between proslavers and abolitionists was to continue unabated for years to come. A few weeks later arsonists slipped into the village at night and burned two Lancaster houses to the ground. These newly-completed structures were to have been occupied by biracial families seeking to move to Lancaster for safety.

# CHAPTER FORTY-TWO

Ivy struggled to fathom the changes that had been wrought in her over just these few dark hours, the miles and hazards she and Sylvester had traversed on this night of peril. She relived the harrowing events they'd shared and the new ideas she'd absorbed from their conversation. Sylvester had given her courage to face new challenges, and he'd done it with a gentle persuasiveness that made her want to please him almost as much as to escape to freedom. He made her feel as if she was a full partner in delivering herself from the threat of capture, the foul disease of slavery itself. For this girl of the subjugated slave culture, her first hours of freedom had been full of revelations, yet she did not fully comprehend the concept of her personal freedom, perhaps would not for years to come.

After the better part of an hour the five riders came in view of lamp-lit windows and smoking chimneys of the Lancaster settlement, a thriving village and surrounding community of some one-thousand souls. Robins heralded the new day, and people were just beginning to rise to face the day's work in the fields, forests, shops and homes of Lancaster Township.

As they approached the Tibbets house, Ivy looked through the naked branches of tall maples at a scarlet iridescence across the eastern horizon. She was mesmerized by the brilliance of the light, shading upward to orange, yellow, finally to aquamarine before being engulfed by the dark blue vault of a frigid cloudless sky. In her near exhaustion she was struck by the thought that she'd somehow been here before, observed this intense light, but where, when? This

218

thought soon gave way to curiosity as she and the other riders began to move among the houses of the Lancaster community.

Lancaster was home to a unique group of abolitionists, primarily of the Baptist faith. They had formed an organization in 1837 called the Neil's Creek Anti-Slavery Society. The dedication of their Eleutherian Institute, to be devoted to the education of students regardless of gender or race, the first of its kind in Indiana and one of the few in the nation, lay three years in the future from this cold spring morning in 1845. The institution would be housed in a great three-story stone building on the highest hill in the village. In 1854 it would be renamed Eleutherian College.

On this morning a few anxious folk at the two-story white clapboard Tibbets home awaited the return of the search party. Upon hearing the horses' approach, three women and two teenage boys came out to welcome the riders. When John Tibbets told Sarah why David and Leonidas were not in the group the reverend's wife raised a loud shout of thanks to the Lord that the Lancaster men as well as Sylvester and the fugitive he led were safe. John sent the boys off to the barn with the horses. When they returned he instructed them to grab a quick breakfast, then hitch up a team and wagon and return down the trail to the forest for Joseph and Leonidas with their confiscated weapons and tack. Sarah, along with her two female domestic servants, welcomed the travelers and ushered everyone inside where the fire crackled and the kitchen was redolent of hot coffee and fried bacon.

After coats, hats and mufflers were shucked and hands warmed by the fire, the black-clad Reverend Tibbets asked everyone to join hands while he led the group in prayer. Afterward, he said, "And now, my compatriots, it's time to introduce everyone to our guest whom Sylvester Morrison has rescued and conducted to us from the Ohio River. Sylvester, would you do the honors, son?"

The boy shyly turned to Ivy and brought her forward to stand beside him. She had removed her hat upon entering the house and now, tired and muddy though she was, the mellow light of the room set off her quadroon features to good advantage. Some in the group, in fact, caught themselves staring agape at the girl's considerable beauty. Even Sylvester, seeing the others' response to Ivy, felt himself blushing. He recovered just in time.

"Gentlemen and Ladies, this girl's name is Ivy, from the Kentucky Bluegrass. She has proved herself a real trooper on her perilous journey down the Kentucky River, down the Ohio to Hanover, and 'specially on the way up here tonight. Ivy, these fine gentlemen that came to our rescue are," and he pointed to each in turn, "Reverend Thomas Cravens, Lyman Hoyt and Reverend John Tibbets. The two young men we left back in the woods are Reverend Tibbets's brother-in-law Joseph Nelson and the Tibbetses' nephew Leonidas Cushman. The fine lady who welcomed us at her door is Mrs. Sarah Nelson Tibbets, that I've done mentioned to you, and her two helpers are, uh . . . . "

Sarah Tibbets smiled and said, "This is Mabel Henry and over there is Vivian Baker."

Ivy bowed her head bashfully and said, "Pleased to meet y'all, and I thanks you for what all you done for me." Then she raised her eyes to Sylvester, seeming to hope the group's attention would be directed to him.

Before the reverend invited everyone to take seats at the long trestle table in the middle of the room he intoned, "Ivy, we of the Lancaster community and the Neil's Creek Anti-Slavery Society welcome you. We have supported many other fugitives from slavery and have exerted ourselves to move them on to freedom farther north. We do this work as a labor of love and good conscience toward our fugitive brothers and sisters.

"This morning we rejoice at Sylvester's success in bringing you to safety here with us. James Hackney will take you on to Vernon tonight. He returned just last night from training horses at Scottsburg. May God bless and keep you in the continuation of your journey." Then with an expansive gesture Rev. Tibbets indicated the guests should be seated.

Vivian, one of the black servants, quietly invited Ivy to eat with her and Mabel after they served the others, at a place in a corner of the kitchen by the fire. Sylvester, saying he needed to speak with Ivy, joined her at the small table. Just after they were seated and while Mabel and Vivian were serving the other guests Ivy reached up to touch Sylvester's face. "You has ugly marks on your face and neck from that evil man's rope. I's gone ax for some salve to put on them stripes."

"That can wait till later, Ivy. Right now we need to talk," he said.

The older people at the large table in the dining room were digging into scrambled eggs, bacon, fried potatoes, porridge, maple syrup, milk, cornbread and coffee served by the two girls. The room was warmed by the fire and lighted by oil lamps in sconces around the walls.

After breakfast the men retired to sit around the fireplace in the front room, awaiting the return of the rest of their party. The girls served Ivy and Sylvester's food, then ate quickly at the same table and departed to clear the large table and start washing dishes, under the supervision of Sarah Tibbets.

Ivy and Sylvester remained seated near the kitchen fireplace. While the boy's voice droned on about how he and Jess Wagner had met the Tibbets group and become acquainted with their work here at Lancaster, Ivy's attention was drawn to the fire. Vivian had just put two more chunks on the coals, and now the bright flames were leaping voraciously for the dry oak. Like the times she and Marse Tate had sat in front of the fire in his bedroom, the girl was mesmerized by the dark wood being overcome by the engulfing flames.

Sylvester was still talking. "Ivy, Mrs. Tibbets will take you to a sleeping room directly, and you can rest for tonight's journey to a town called Vernon. You'll stay there tomorrow in the cellar of the Sanford Tavern close to a river, the Muscatatuck. There'll be somebody nearby to protect you while you rest."

"You goin' with me, Vess? We go on horseback again?"

"No, Ivy. A different conductor will come here tonight and take you on to Vernon. He's a free colored man, Indian and negro mixed, by the name of James Hackney. I don't know if he'll take you by wagon or on horseback. I do know he's a good man with horses, makes a living training 'em."

"But I be scared if you ain't there."

"You needn't worry. James is a better conductor than me. He's older and has took many runaways on up the line. He's never lost a one of 'em to slavecatchers."

221

Sylvester could tell Ivy was becoming more nervous and frightened. He knew she still considered going back to the Binford Plantation. "The futher I gets from home the more I worries. It 'bout to make me sick."

"Still thinkin' about the overseer taking over the plantation and doing away with Tate?"

"Yes, that an' . . . an' what Canada be like, Vess? It take a mis'able long time to get there an' too many dangers 'tween here and there. I ain't got no idea of goin' to a place where I's got no frien's, no kinfolk. It be cold there, I hear'd, and some of them people hates black folks jus' like in Kentucky. I hear'd the driver say them Canada people sometime *eats* nigras. I's still thinkin' maybe I needs to go back . . . cain't hep it."

"Ivy I never been to Canada, but I know they don't eat black folks up there. From what I hear it's a sight better than where you come from. At least you'll be free there. You can walk down the road and nobody's lookin' to catch you and send you back South. No master to tell you what to do and whip you for not doin' it. You can decide where you want to live and what you want to do. Theys good people up there in churches and the like that'll help you get settled with a new start in life. They have schools for fugitives from slave country so they can learn to read 'n write. I'm sure a girl as smart and strong as you will do good there, Ivy."

Ivy pondered Sylvester's words a moment. Gazing into the fire she spoke dreamily, as if to herself, clasping her fingers together, opening them, intertwining them again slowly. "Binford plantation be long gone behin' me now. Maybe I never know how things turn out back there. Maybe Marse Tate and the slaves be doin' fine, maybe they ain't. I has bad dreams 'bout leavin' my frien's, even Marse Tate. He treat me bad at firs', but he never whup me an' he give me nice things, take care of me, like I hep him in his time of need. They be other folks needin' me there, too. I still got to study on it." The fire was coming alive before her eyes. Figures leapt and writhed like tormented human dancers. Flames consumed the logs as her tortured thoughts consumed her mind. She remembered the ominous feeling she'd had at dawn this morning, the colors of the sunrise appearing like the colors of Marse Tate's fire of a few days before. What did it mean? The visions tormented her.

222

Vess and Ivy stood up and moved to the kitchen fireplace so the girls could clear their table. Gradually she emerged from her introspection. Sylvester was talking. "Yes, you have to make your own decision, but don't worry about Canada. If it's cold up there you can wear warmer clothes. I'll venture they have a summertime, too, like we do. You can make friends with whoever you want. You're a beautiful girl that can make friends just by smilin' at people . . . like me. See, we ain't knowed each other but a few hours and already I feel like I'm your good friend, maybe more than that. In fact, I already know I'm gonna miss you bad when you go. You'll have all kinds of friends up there before you know it."

Sylvester was not ready for what Ivy did next. She grasped him in a tight hug and clung to him for a few moments. The boy looked into the dining room to see if any of the older people were looking. "Oh, Vess, we *is* good friends. What I do if it wadn't for you savin' my hide all them times comin' up here from the river? You talkin' 'bout leavin' me now make me feel lost again, like when we's comin' down the river after Jacob died. Make my mind play bad tricks on me."

"We both got to think ahead, Ivy," he said. "I'm seventeen and you're twenty year old so we got our lives ahead of us, as the feller says. I think the world of you, and I'll do anything to help you get what you want. But just ask yourself, do you want to be free or a slave? You know the life of a slave, people workin' you hard, liable to whip you, your master forcin' himself on you, worryin' that if he's killed you'll be at the mercy of the overseer. Could you really stop somebody if they was bent on killin' him? That ain't no life for a beautiful girl like you, Ivy."

A tired smile crept around the corners of Ivy's mouth. "You sounds jus' like Bessie. She be my kitchen boss on the plantation. She always talkin' 'bout Marse Tate might be nice to me, but he still my marse, an' he won't let me do nothin' but what he want me to do, keep me livin' in sin."

"She was right," Vess said. As for me, how could I ever look in a mirror the rest of my life if I took you, the way I feel about you, back to that life, the life of a slave? It'd be like me takin' a friend to prison for the rest of her life, almost like killin' my friend. Well, girl,

I ain't gonna do that to you, and if I can stop it I ain't gonna allow nobody else to do it, neither.

"You need to get on up the road to freedom in Canada. Even Indiana or anywhere in this country is too dangerous for you. They's raids all the time of slavecatchers comin' over the river lookin' to catch or kidnap people of color livin' unprotected around here, even farther north, be they runaway slave or free. Maybe someday when this hateful time is over you can come back to Kentucky, but not now. You understand, Ivy?"

Just then Sarah Tibbets came and touched Ivy's arm. "Time you got some rest, girl. Here it is going on noon and you've got a long night ahead of you. I'll show you where to sleep." Ivy looked back once to meet eyes with Sylvester, as if to ask if she'd see him when she woke.

# CHAPTER FORTY-THREE

S arah drew the blinds before settling the girl in the back room, but Ivy could not sleep. The room was now shrouded from the brightness of the day outside, and voices from within the house had been reduced to distant murmurs, but the girl still felt the lingering claw of fear in her stomach.

The surroundings, even in this anteroom, were more reminiscent of Marse Tate's big house than of the place where she had slept in the lean-to at the side of Bessie's cabin on the plantation. The blankets on the daybed where she lay were rough, the furniture crude, but the framed images of old white men she'd seen on the walls of the dining room, even the smell of the house evoked only thoughts of strangeness and uncertainty. She had been welcomed, warmed and fed by these apparently devout people, devout both to their god and to their mission of abolitionism, but still Ivy lay distracted from her rest.

So many concerns whirled in her head that even the dilemma of whether to return to the Binford plantation was momentarily thrust into the background. What were her chances of successfully making this long journey to Canada? She had no concept of the distance or the time required for the trip. Would she be strong enough? She would be alone without the comfort of Sylvester's company, even the companionship of other pitiful refugees like herself with whom to share her fear. Would there be people at every stop as gracious and caring as the Tibbetses?

And what of the men who would conduct her? Would they all be as trustworthy and considerate of her bewildered state as Sylvester had been? He had said her conductor on tonight's sojourn would be a black man. Would this man be as vulnerable to capture and return to slavery in the south as she because of his color? Would there be friendly riders coming to look for them if they were late arriving at this town Sylvester had mentioned, Vernon?

Then there was Sylvester. What soundless whispers of tenderness had passed between those two most unlikely of partners in their nightlong flight? This boy, in spite of his outward manly appearance, was hardly more than a child and she nearly a full adult. Yet their life experiences had been so diverse that the shock of encountering each other seemed to have drawn them into an immediate unspoken bond. Underneath her dread during the hazardous climb out of the gorge and the long ride on horseback, she'd *wanted* to hold this young man, not just for balance, warmth or out of fear; she had been somehow drawn to his youthful strength, his skill, his understanding ways with her. But it was more, even, than that, something Ivy couldn't have begun to verbalize. She had felt some connection of souls there, some primeval bridge between two dissimilar human beings that transcended logic. And hadn't he felt it, too? What was it he said at breakfast about his feelings toward her being *more* than just those of a good friend?

Ivy suddenly came fully alert, eyes wide open in astonishment. Her sense of attachment to Sylvester, her strange relationship with Marse Tate; had they both risen from the same shadow place in her heart?

Her mind in turmoil, Ivy lay awake. She found herself confronted again and again by these tenacious doubts and her troubling visions. When Sarah woke her at sundown with a gentle hand on her shoulder she was amazed she had slept at all.

After she'd washed and put on the clean men's clothing she found on a chair near the door of her room, Sarah brought her out to the kitchen. "The men have already eaten, Ivy. I thought it would be good to let you sleep a little longer. Did you get some rest?"

Ivy stopped spooning the bean soup Sarah gave her. "I thanks you Missus Tibbets. I got a little sleep, I did. Mistuh Vess still be around?"

226

Sarah chuckled. "He asked if he could hang around out in the barn with the horses so he could see you off tonight. We told him he was welcome to stay in the house with the rest of us. He's a shy boy, isn't he?"

Ivy's face showed her concern. "He still here?"

"He's out helping David and Leonidas do the chores right now. Reverend Cravens has gone home with Lyman Hoyt. He had just arrived at Lancaster for a visit last night when the men invited him to go with them to meet you and Sylvester. I think the boys have been cleaning and oiling the saddles and bridles they took from the outlaws this morning. They couldn't get over that western saddle, first one they'd seen."

Darkness had crept around the windows by the time Ivy looked out to see Sylvester and the other boys' lanterns coming from the barn. They came in talking excitedly to the Tibbetses about the new horse and tack they'd taken from the slave-catchers. Sylvester came straight to Ivy, who had hung back, not wishing to intrude on the conversation.

"Did you get some sleep, Ivy? Feelin' like moving on north tonight?"

She smiled, comforted by his presence in these strange surroundings. "I's feelin' right well. Is that black man gone be here soon?"

"He's already here, drove up with his team and wagon when we was comin' from the barn. He's feeding and watering his team right now, be in directly."

"I's scared and worried, but I's never gone forget what you done for me las' night. If I don't get to say fare-thee-well later, God bless you, Vess." Their faces came close together as she spoke. Sylvester raised his hand as if to touch her cheek, but he hesitated and the hand came to rest on her upper arm.

Before the boy could answer there was a knock at the door and Sarah opened it for James Hackney, a short muscular black man with alert eyes who doffed his hat as he came through the door and greeted the Tibbetses. "Who've you got with you, there, Jim?" Reverend Tibbets said.

"Why, Reverend, this here's my boy, James William Hackney, Junior. He was bound and determined to come with me, so I hope

227

y'all won't mind if he curl up on the floor here behin' the cookstove till I come back in the mornin'."

"That'll be just fine, Jim," Mrs. Tibbets said. "We'll give him a pallet and a blanket. Hand me your rucksack and I'll pack the food I made up for you and Ivy, here." After she made short introductions of the fugitive girl to her conductor, James handed Sarah his sack as Reverend Tibbets sat down and spoke kindly to the younger James Hackney.

"I'm pleased to meet you, son. How old are you?"

"Twelve, suh."

"You like to go out and about with your daddy at night?"

The boy smiled and said, "Yessuh. I be axin' all the time an' finally he say, 'Come on, then.' He say I got to be quiet, though."

"You think you were quiet enough to get to go again sometime?"

Little James answered proudly. "Yessuh! I done jus' like he say."

Amid chuckles and conversation among the older folk, Sylvester brought Ivy over to meet the young boy, thinking it would divert her attention from the imminent departure. "James, this here's Ivy. She's goin' with your daddy tonight. She come from Kentucky, across the river. Your daddy's gonna take her to Vernon, then come back to get you."

"I know. He say he be back 'fore daylight. When I grow up he say I can go with him some night. Pleased to meet ya, Miss Ivy. You sho is a purty gal."

Ivy grinned in spite of herself. "And you sho is a charmer, young James, Jr. I bet you be drivin' them young girls crazy with that big smile and them snappin' eyes."

"I does have me a girlfrien' down at Greenbrier, but she say it's a secret, so I cain't be tellin' her name."

"I know that be right," Ivy said. "If a girl say don't talk, then you bes' not say a word! She raise a knot on your young head."

The three of them laughed and the twelve-year-old said, "Maybe we see each other again one day, Miss Ivy. Leas'ways I hope so."

"That be a good idea, Jim Junior. How 'bout we shakes on it." They shook hands, grinned, and then Ivy, James, Sr. and the others were swept up in preparations for departure.

A few minutes later the elder James Hackney came and laid his hand on his son's shoulder. "Don't be no trouble, now Jimmy, you hear? Do what the reverend and the missus say."

"I will. Bye, Miss Ivy."

James picked up his rucksack. "We thanks you, Missus Tibbets. This be mighty kind of you. Ivy, time we hit the road now. We make them sixteen mile an' be in Vernon town 'fore you know it."

The conductor with the sack slung over his shoulder carrying a lantern went out the door with Ivy following in man's clothing, sturdy shoes and wide-brimmed hat. The Tibbetses and Sylvester came to the door, the reverend holding his own lantern high. "Oh, wait, Jim," John said, stepping back to the kitchen table. "Take this to fight off the chill. A little whiskey and honey for your long ride." He reached to Hackney and handed him a small flask.

The two travelers had turned back to face the house, still close to the door. In the light of the two lanterns Ivy's large amber eyes met Sylvester's in a long look of understanding and gratitude. She was crying softly, tears streaming unchecked, but her eyes were steady, as if to savor the last sight of him.

The boy felt his stomach clench. He wanted to rush to her and . . . and do what? There was nothing else he could do. She was setting off for freedom in Canada. God grant she would stay the course. He marveled at her bravery, knowing she yet struggled with her decision. They nodded to each other in what would be their final goodbye, then he managed what he hoped would be a warm smile for her. He did his best but he was smiling through his own tears.

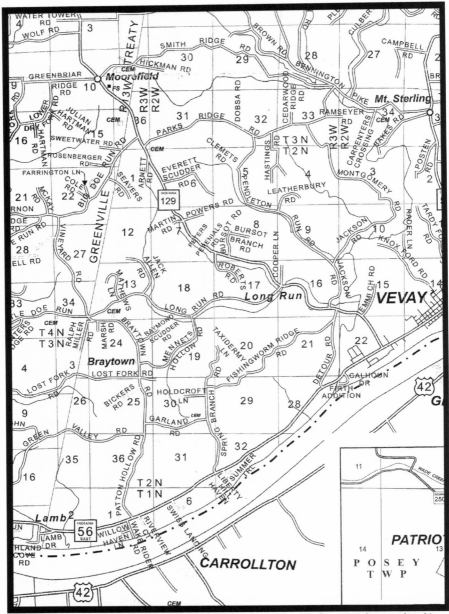

The map above is copyrighted by Universal Advertising Associates, Inc. It may not be reproduced in any form without the written permission of the publisher. Copyright Number VA 970-717.

# PART III

---

# LIZ

The map opposite is a segment of a 2006 Switzerland County, Indiana, road map used by written permission of Universal Advertising Associates, Inc. The area between Lamb and Moorefield on this map was not markedly different in 1860.

# CHAPTER FORTY-FOUR

At midday on February 12th, 1853, twelve-year-old Elizabeth Cunningham heard a faint call from her mother's bedroom. She took her hand off the long stirring spoon in the pot of chili on the fireplace crane, wiped her hands on her apron, stood up straight and said, "Prudence, come stir this chili while I see about Mother!" The older sister left the kitchen for the bedroom so quickly she failed to see Prudence, a little over a year her junior, watching her go with a scowling countenance. She slowly returned to settling four-year-old William into his highchair without even a glance at the chili.

Elizabeth rushed in to find her mother lying in bed with a small towel at her mouth, coughing and choking, trying to catch her breath. The girl rushed to Rachel, placed her left arm under her frail shoulders and lifted her to a sitting position. With her right hand she mopped the sputum and blood from her mother's face with the towel, folded it and continued drying the sweat and mucous, speaking soothing words to her. Rachel's hands and arms dropped wearily to the mattress. Sunken eyes closed, her complexion glowing cadaverous-white in the reflected sunlight from outside, gasping for air, the older woman showed clearly the ravages of consumption that had been wearing her down for the past several months. Elizabeth held her upright for a long moment. "Mother, as soon as I get dinner over with I'll give you a bath and get you into a dry gown."

When she'd recovered enough strength to speak, but without opening her eyes Rachel whispered, "You go on, honey. Make sure the children get fed."

Re-entering the kitchen Liz noticed the chili pot smoking and the spoon in the same position where she'd left it. "Prudence! You let the chili burn!" She hurried to remove the pot from the crane, stirring the contents but being careful not to raise the scorched layer from the bottom.

Her younger sister came from the other side of the kitchen carrying a pitcher of water from the sideboard, wearing the same stubborn expression as before. "You did it! Grandma and Grandpa and everybody else around here thinks you're the only one of us helping Pop and Mother. They're always bragging on you like you're some kind of angel. You just go ahead and be the boss, do it all; you get the credit for it anyway."

"Oh, Prudence, why can't you get over being jealous of me? Now look what you've done. This chili is ruined. Pop will be mad at me."

"So be it. Maybe he and the others will finally see you ain't as perfect as they think, miss goody-goody."

"Listen, you can just get over your snit. Get bowls and spoons on the table before I tell Pop you deliberately let the chili burn while I was taking care of Mother."

Prudence grudgingly went to the cupboard, but only after directing a withering look over her shoulder at her sister.

In the eight years since Sylvester and Rachel collaborated in thwarting Sam's slavecatching attempt and helping to save Ivy Mays, they and their siblings had matured.

Mariah, the eldest, and her husband, Aaron Cochran, already had four children by 1853: Marietta, Lucy, John and Sarah. Rachel and Sam Cunningham had become parents to seven children. In addition to Elizabeth, 12, and Prudence, 11, the children stairstepped down through Mary, Rachel, John, and the twins William and Marietta. The female twin died shortly after birth.

James had married Lovina Reno in 1845, and they had two children, Newell and Roseanna. Philander wed Sarah Hatch in 1850, and by 1853 they already had three children, Clara, Mary and Charles.

Sylvester and Lee Hannah Vandever were married in 1852, and the newlyweds were expecting their first child. John W., Jr. married Matilda Reno in 1849. They had a daughter, Aramitta, and a son, Bartlett, by 1853.

Emerson, the youngest of the siblings, would not marry Mary Ann Campbell until the following year.

Life had been especially hard for Rachel. Babies arrived with exhausting regularity, one every fourteen months, on average, from the time of her marriage to Sam in 1840 until 1848.

Rachel's child-bearing had ceased with the birth of the twins in August of 1848. Marietta, who died in her first day of life, was the only one of Rachel's babies not to survive childhood. Between caring for children and the drudgery of housework, Rachel felt her strength slipping away in spite of her determination to meet the demands of domesticity. She never fully recovered from the birth of the twins, and now, five years later, tuberculosis, that stealthy assassin, was taking its deadly toll. Before the family's eyes, life was seeping from Rachel as visibly and inexorably as sap from a girdled oak.

Voicing her alarm at her mother's failing condition, Liz summoned Sylvester, James and Mariah, who was not well herself, to Rachel's bedside the following day. Sam was away from home following his usual Sunday routine of hunting, fishing or plotting secretive slavechasing schemes with his wastrel sidekicks Homer and Dewey.

The group spoke gently with Rachel, doing what they could to encourage and comfort her, assuring her they would redouble their efforts to support Liz in caring for the house and the other children. Rachel thanked them and smiled weakly, responding to the extent her waning strength would allow, then slipped into a troubled sleep. The worried group reconvened around the kitchen table.

James broke the heavy silence. "You think it's time we asked folks to come if they want to pay their respects while she's still . . . here?"

"We oughtn't to wait. She's failing fast," Mariah said.

Sylvester fidgeted with the wick screw on the oil lamp. "They's many people that appreciates her doin' what she could to warn runaways when Sam and other bounty hunters was out and about."

"We'd need to let the Quakers know," Liz said.

"And the free blacks that works with 'em," Sylvester added.

Mariah coughed into her handkerchief and cleared her throat, then spoke in a hoarse voice. "Don't forget the Indians. Em needs to tell Mary Ann and her family down on Laughery Creek. They'll get the word to the Hackneys at Hanover."

Their youngest sibling, Emerson, nineteen, had been acquainted with the Campbells for some time and was courting their daughter Mary Ann. Her father, Thomas "Squire" Campbell, had married an Indian woman of the Piankashaw tribe, and they were friends with the Hackneys because of the Indian connection.

"They's somebody else would want to know," James said, "if we could ever find him. You remember Adam Coulter, Vess? He gave us a ride in his stagecoach on the way to New York, and him and Rachel had feelin's for each other, though she would never let on about it. I guess you hear'd us talkin' about that, eh Liz?"

The girl smiled shyly and nodded. "Yes, and don't forget, I was there when it happened."

James was caught slack-jawed, then he blushed and grinned. "Why, durned if you wadn't, gal."

Sylvester looked at James and nodded. "I'll tell you somethin' you might not know. Adam helped us save that black girl Ivy Mays. Remember when I was gone so long back in '45? You had to go lookin' for me at the Quaker's house in Madison? Turned out I was workin' with them a few days to scout the area and take her from the river out to Lancaster. We wrote to Adam for help back then, knowin' he worked with them Friends. He put us onto the Quaker Judd Calloway in Madison. I've still got Adam's address but lord that's been eight year ago now."

"Wouldn't hurt to try. I b'lieve he'd appreciate knowin'," James said.

Sylvester volunteered to write immediately to Adam Coulter's old address. He said, "He was still in St. Clairsville, Ohio, the last time we needed him. Maybe we'll get lucky again."

James said he'd get their younger brothers to help him spread the word about Rachel. Emerson would inform the Indians on Laughery Creek and the Baptists at Lancaster.

Judd Calloway and Sylvester had kept in touch after their combined efforts resulted in the rescue of Ivy Mays at Hanover Landing back in '45. Sylvester often went to see the old Quaker on his "egg and cream" runs to Madison. The young man had continued making these weekly jaunts, especially after their intent became more than just the marketing of farm produce. By thus keeping abreast of Underground Railroad activities around Madison, Sylvester had sometimes found ways to again lend a hand to the effort. He always kept Rachel informed of any new venture that helped save fugitive slaves. She, in turn, kept an eye on Sam's activities and set the underground telegraph in motion when the signs warranted.

In the space of only a few days, Rachel's community of kinfolk and friends had been alerted, and they began arriving singly and in small groups at Sugar Branch to spend a few moments at Rachel's bedside. She had become almost a legendary figure for her help in aiding fugitive slaves, even while tied down with babies and a slavecatcher husband.

Sam stayed off by himself with the children as people rallied round his wife to express their love and respect. He seemed to understand that he needed to allow them to speak in private.

Everyone waited impatiently for word from Adam Coulter. A few days later his letter arrived saying he would be on the trail to Indiana within the week. Sylvester informed Rachel of their good fortune in making contact with the road engineer for only the second time since 1840. With a hint of the old spark in her eye, she let it be known to her younger brother that she and Adam had kept in touch occasionally through the years, and she seemed sure he would still be at the same address. Her condition appeared to improve a little on this recent news, and she asked frequently when he said he'd be there.

One night before bed as Liz was seeing to her mother's needs Rachel roused herself and her eyes shone clearer in the lamplight. She spoke between gulps of air. "Lizzie . . . we need to talk . . . just you and me."

"Oh, Mother, maybe we should wait till morning. I'll come and give you a bath and change your gown. You might feel stronger then."

"No, Liz . . . people will come . . . may not be time."

Liz finished the preparations for sleep, then knelt on the floor beside the bed. Tears were already leaking down her cheeks. She took her mother's hand. "I'm here, Mother."

Rachel closed her eyes and seemed to will her breathing to become regular before whispering, "You've had too much on you, child. Sam's never been a hand to take responsibility. Prudence resents our closeness, and the others are too young and needful. Thank god for my folks. They'll be good to you and the others. You must rely on them after . . . ."

Liz held her mother's hand and said, "We'll be fine. Try to rest now, Mother."

Rachel's words came out haltingly, punctuated by coughing and labored breathing. Liz helped her with the towel, but did not interrupt her again. "Listen, child . . . you must be a good girl. Don't give yourself over to lustful feelings for a man. . . . Never marry a man who won't put you first . . . or that you think you can change. When you find the right one, love him completely. Be his partner, but not his slave.

"The best thing I ever did on this earth was give life to you, even when it seemed impossible. But don't kill yourself birthing babies as I did. There are ways to stop having babies when you want to. Talk to a doctor when the time comes."

Liz's tears were wetting Rachel's fingers. "I can't live without you, Mother. I've begged God to make you well."

"Pray for yourself and the others, Lizzie, not me. I can't stay here, not like this. I've made my peace, and your life must go on, hard as it will be for a while. You must learn to seek beauty in your life, and every time you find it, share it with me, for I will always be with you, my dearest Elizabeth."

With her head resting on their clasped hands on the bed Liz whispered through her tears, "I will Mother, I promise."

# CHAPTER FORTY-FIVE

The next morning Elizabeth began arranging for others in the family to spend a few moments with her mother. Fanny and John Wesley came, then Mariah, Sylvester, James and the other siblings, followed by the younger children and then Sam.

In bidding farewell to her husband she said, "I forgive you, Sam, and I'm sorry for the hurtful things I said to you and your folks. You've shown moments of kindness toward me, even tenderness.

"And you were right when you said years ago that I bore some of the responsibility for what happened in the Gibbs barn. I admit I was not entirely innocent in the matter. In spite of all that has happened between us, and though I vowed otherwise in the beginning, I have come to feel a kind of love for you, Sam. I wanted you to know that."

Neighbors came from all around, and Julia Dumont soon appeared in a wagon driven by old Wiley from the livery stable, accompanied by the three women who as girls had studied with Rachel at Julia's school back in 1839-40.

They all expressed sorrow at losing such a heroic young woman, whose life was now being snuffed out years before her time, barely thirty years old, and leaving all those little ones. They held Liz and Fanny's hands and shook their heads.

Liz organized the visits as best she could, trying not to exhaust Rachel. But so many came and so often that sometimes she had to say she was sorry, but her mother needed to rest now.

Rachel kept enquiring when Adam was expected, and Sylvester gave his best guess of his starting date, mode of conveyance and time required for the trip from St. Clairsville. The family nervously awaited him, seeing that Rachel was apparently marshaling her strength in anticipation of his arrival.

He arrived on a spent horse in late evening on March 5th, having started at first light and ridden hard all the way from Cincinnati that day. He swung off his horse, shook hands with James and Sylvester, then hurried with James into the cabin while Sylvester led the lathered horse to the barn. "James, is she . . .?"

"She's anxious to see you, but we're afraid it won't be long, now."

"Thank God, I was afraid I'd be too late. I hadn't heard from her for several months, but we didn't write often, in any case. I didn't even know she was sick."

"She'll . . . she looks different, now, Adam. Lost a lot of weight. Just so's you'll know."

Even after James's warning, Adam gasped at his first sight of Rachel. She turned her head toward him and a weak smile brightened her pallid face. She held out her hand. "Hello, old friend." Then, after pausing to breathe, "Thank you for coming."

James said, "I'll be around close. Just call me if you need anything, sis. Want me to have Mother bring you some tea?"

"Yes, James . . . a cup for Adam. None for me, thanks," his sister whispered.

Adam had doffed his hat and now knelt by her bed. She said, "There's a chair over in the corner, Adam." He rose and retrieved it.

"Oh, Rachel, I'm sorry I didn't keep in touch, write more often. I could have come earlier."

Pausing to breathe and cough, Rachel said, "No matter, you're here now. So good to see you, Adam . . . handsome as ever, haven't aged a bit."

He chuckled. "I surely don't feel as young as when we met. It was somewhere on the National Road east of . . . Zanesville, wasn't it? I had old Luke stop the coach, and after we talked a few moments, you three 'brothers' climbed aboard."

Fanny brought in the tea, and Rachel briefly introduced her to Adam. She propped Rachel up on pillows, then handed Adam a cup.

240

She smiled sadly at him, shook her head, and departed, bringing a napkin to her mouth just before the tears came.

Rachel picked up the conversation. "Yes, I briefly dressed as a boy during those days. You kindly carried us eastward for several days. Riding in your coach was wonderful. We hadn't realized how tired we were from tramping along the road."

"It was around midday, as I recall. Luke and I were eating dinner at an inn. I looked out the window and saw you all snooping around the coach like three young rabbits in a spring garden."

Rachel coughed and then grinned weakly at his humor. "We were trying to imagine what it would be like to ride in such luxury, and thanks to you we were able to do it."

"You know I had more than hospitality on my mind," he said. "I'd seen this third 'boy' from the window of the inn and was determined to act on my suspicion that you were a girl, a beautiful, spritely girl."

"Oh, pshaw, Adam. You wrote those flattering words in a letter some time ago. I never responded then, but now I'll admit to a strong pull on my heart the day we parted company at that town in Ohio, or was it Pennsylvania. My brothers noticed a change in me that day, and wouldn't let me forget it for a while. We had to head north from there toward Pittsburgh and you returned to St. Clairsville, I believe."

They paused while Adam sipped his tea and they spent a few moments in reverie remembering their feelings from so long ago. Then Adam continued. "Yes. That was at Washington, Pennsylvania. Those were memorable days for me, as well, my dear."

"So tell me, how is your family?" she said. "Are your children all grown up, now? Is your wife in good health?"

She was surprised to see Adam's head drop and his shoulders sag. "Rachel . . . ." He could not continue, and only sat with his head bowed, moving his trembling fingers slowly over his hatband.

Rachel turned her head and looked closely at her friend. "Adam, are you all right? Is someone in your family not well?"

Without meeting her eyes, he slid off the chair, dropped his hat and knelt by her bed. He took her hand in his before he raised his eyes. She saw tears starting down his face, and his voice trembled, as if he were a little boy telling a long-kept secret. "Rachel, I've never

241

married. Through all those years nobody ever matched the image I carried in my heart, your image dear Rachel."

"Oh, Adam." He bowed his head again and kissed her hand that lay on the bed. Her other hand came to caress his hair as she lay back on the pillow, closed her eyes and tried to calm her breathing. Tears came to her, as well, and ran unchecked.

Moments later he clasped both her hands in his, then took out his handkerchief and blotted tears for both of them. "I grieved for you when you told me the fate of your Robert Sandlin. I couldn't help thinking that had the time and place of our meeting been more fortuitous I might have had the great gift of our falling in love with each other before you ever met Robert on the steamboat. But it seemed when we met on the National Road you were still shocked and preoccupied by the fresh awareness of your pregnancy and at the rough treatment you'd recently endured at the Cincinnati riverfront. Thus I never had a chance to gain your attention in that way, though I felt love for you from the moment my suspicion was confirmed by your hat falling off as you slept, revealing your long shining auburn hair.

"I felt as though a part of me died as you passed out of my life on that street corner in front of the Mansion Hotel in Washington, Pennsylvania. I'll never forget looking back from the coach and seeing you peering after us until we were out of sight."

The room became quiet as the two friends reflected on what had just been said. Each of their minds wandered for a few moments into the fantasy of *What if things had been different during those bright youthful days in the stagecoach on the National Road.*

# CHAPTER FORTY-SIX

Three days later, on Tuesday at sunset, with Liz, Fanny and Mariah at her bedside, Rachel drew her last weak and rattling breath. The women tenderly laid the sheet over her and went out with drawn and mournful faces to inform the menfolk. Sylvester rode off to tell Arthur Pavy, the undertaker, that his services were needed.

The weather itself seemed to be in mourning. Rain and sleet fell during the morning of the funeral, forming an ice glaze on the dead grass and bare tree limbs. By noon the sleet had stopped, the sky cleared and a raw north wind moaned in the leafless forests and flapped the side curtains of the buggies arriving at the church.

In spite of the weather the village of Sugar Branch had rarely seen a larger funeral. The service was held at the Methodist Church on Saturday, the cold weather having given the family time to inform those awaiting the news. Reverend Allen Wiley, thirteen years older now, silver-haired and stooped, who had married Rachel and Sam, conducted the service. Burial would be at the Melville Cemetery, a quarter-mile to the east, overlooking the small creek that had given the community its name.

The pall bearers, the five brothers of the deceased and Adam, for whom the family had made room during Rachel's final days, carried the casket out to Arthur Pavy's hearse wagon. The minister stood watch at the church door in his wind-whipped black robe, holding his Bible. The pall bearers, the minister, Rachel's immediate

243

family and other mourners would normally follow in buggies and carriages over the frozen ruts of the road to the burial ground.

During the momentary lull while Arthur and his assistant secured the casket, closed the tailgate and checked the horses, Adam gathered Rachel's brothers and whispered something that elicited nods in response. He then spoke briefly to Arthur, who looked at the others, then began unhitching the horses and driving them off to the side.

Adam stepped forward and took hold of one end of a singletree, James taking the other. Across the wagon tongue Sylvester and Emerson followed suit, with other brothers and neighbors forming two columns along the wagon tongue. Slowly the hearse began to move out of the church yard onto the road. A murmur passed among the crowd as other men came forward, neighbors in clean work clothes, black-clad Quakers, a few negroes, even three blanketed and derby-hatted Indians. Each found a place to pull or push the vehicle, moving it along toward Rachel's final resting place, honoring her life. Tears flowed unabashedly down the faces of several of the men.

The pall bearers positioned the casket above the grave and the minister read from the flapping pages of his Bible, his voice sometimes obliterated by the wind. People huddled around the grave, grasping their loose collars and scarves, holding onto their hats, eyes watering and cheeks blanched by the cold. Finally the last amen was uttered and people began dispersing, Liz and a few other family members remaining to throw handsful of earth on the lowered casket.

Liz heard someone clearing his throat and turned to see several men, hats in hands, waiting to be recognized. She didn't know any of them, but she clasped her hands and instinctively whispered, "Thank you so much for coming."

The men arranged themselves awkwardly into a single file, and a bearded older man she thought to be a Quaker because of his clothing stepped forward and took her hand. Looking steadily into her eyes he said, "Miss Elizabeth, my name is Judd Calloway. Please accept our condolences. We Friends know of thy mother's facilitation to our dark brethren in these troubled times. Some have been saved due to her and her brother's heroic service. We shall follow her light." He stepped aside as the next man approached.

"Reverend John Tibbets from Lancaster, Miss Cunningham. You mother was an inspiration to us all in the cause of freedom. May God bless and keep you, child." Two black men approached, the gray-haired older of the two held his hat in both hands and said, "Miss 'Lizabeth, Jim Hackney from Hanover. I sometimes work with Mr. Calloway, and Reverend Tibbets and them at Lancaster. I never met your mother, but I hear'd of her good works towards folks of color. God bless you, miss."

The younger negro said, "Jim Hackney, Junior, miss. Sorry for your loss."

As the men made their way toward their conveyances, Liz's eyes were attracted to a movement at the edge of the forest beyond the graveyard. When she blinked the tears away and her vision became clearer she saw the Indians melting into the woods in the direction of Laughery Creek. Just before they disappeared, the tallest of the three men, the last to enter the trail, turned and caught her eye. He brought his right arm from beneath his blanket in an arc that ended with his hand over his heart. Then he raised his hand in a salute to Liz, turned and disappeared into the darkness.

Afterward Liz found herself alone. She turned back to the grave as the laborers went to work with their shovels. The girl felt as if she might faint, so desolate were the feelings that swept over her. How could she continue living without her mother's presence, her sage advice so lovingly given, even as she lay on her deathbed? The looming tasks of making a home for her father and her young siblings, the overwhelming responsibilities, even with the willing help of her mother's family, filled Liz with despair. She wished she could follow her mother into the grave and be swept away from this gray world of hopelessness. She turned and saw her father in the distance leading the younger children away. She hadn't the strength to follow, reluctant to leave the fading earthly presence of her mother.

Just when she feared she might collapse onto the frozen ground she felt a strong arm come round her shoulders. She looked up into the gentle face of Uncle Vess. He looked thinner now under his black hat, his eyes more solemn, but he gave her the same crooked smile she had come to love, the same steady support she'd always felt in his company. In a moment someone on her other side took her hand, and she recognized Leanna, Vess' new wife. Slowly and without a word the three of them made their way toward her uncle's waiting buggy. They bundled Elizabeth in a blanket and Leanna put her arm around her. On their way back past the church Leanna said, "We have supper waiting for you and your family at home, sweetheart. We'll stay as long as you need us."

# CHAPTER FORTY-SEVEN

Though kinfolk and neighbors offered all manner of assistance to the family, Elizabeth was quickly overwhelmed, not only by the daily work of caring for and feeding the children and her father, but by the absence of advice from her mother. Even after she became bedridden, Rachel would answer questions and provide moral comfort for the girl. As dismal as the girl's life had grown, it was to become much worse.

Ten days after the funeral, Elizabeth had just finished the supper dishes long after everyone else was in bed. She had blown out the lamp and walked softly to the pallet that she shared with her two youngest siblings. She had just removed her shoes and dress and slipped into her nightgown when she felt a hand grasp her wrist and another close over her mouth.

Her father whispered in her ear, "Shhh. It's me. Come over here." He pulled her toward his bed, pressed her down and told her to lie on the side next to the wall. "And don't be hollerin' when I turn loose of your mouth." When he released her, Elizabeth turned quickly toward the wall, gasping and crying into the bedclothes, desperate not to frighten the other children. Sam joined her under the covers, then came to her and enfolded her in his arms from behind. She felt his breath on her ear as he whispered, "Just need somebody to keep me warm. I ain't gonna hurt you. Lay still now."

The girl lay in his embrace for what seemed an eternity, afraid to move, even to cry, remembering the story of what Sam had done to her mother. Some time later she heard her father's deep breathing, but she lay awake waiting for morning light, her eyes focused on the dim moonlit window across the room, praying daylight would come soon. Her arms and legs became numb and she felt painful cramps in her back. Still she tried to lie motionless, waiting, praying.

Suddenly he was clutching her, moving against her, forcing himself between her legs from behind. She came fully awake in an instant. Unmindful of the stiffness and pain in her body, she turned and lashed out with her arms and legs, wresting herself free of his grasp, unaware of the wild howl of a cornered animal that escaped from her lungs. Then she was against the wall, his hands grabbing for her arms.

She kicked her legs and flailed her arms, fingernails seeking flesh. His silhouette loomed over her, he on hands and knees, she on her back. The girl reached down and brought both hands upward, knowing she must inflict pain before he pinned her arms. She felt her nails engage sensitive flesh. Having found her target she gouged and scratched, injuring him in the fraction of a second before he could react. When his hands came down to grab her she instantly attacked his face and eyes, swiping, tearing, poking again until she felt his weight jerk back, hands to his bleeding face, bellowing in agony. With a final kick that propelled her from the bed she found herself free on the floor, scrambling to her feet, running for the door, then outside, her gown flapping about her legs, her bare feet not feeling the chill of the porch floor or the rough ground beyond. She heard him yell, "Come back here!" and when she threw a panicked glance over her shoulder she saw him standing in the doorway in his nightshirt, hands still at his face. She raced on, hearing only the wind rushing by her ears, her own rapid breathing and faint crying from the awakening children.

Elizabeth ran straight to her grandparents' cabin, a quarter-mile away. She followed the well-worn path through the woods between the two cabins, down through the shallow valley of Sugar Branch, across the frozen creek, then up through the trees to the cabin, thus avoiding the rough and rutted road. She pounded on the door until John Wesley opened it. He was nearly bowled over by the girl's momentum as she rushed in and clung to him with all her strength. "Help me Grandpa! He's after me."

Finally able to quiet the hysterical child, John Wesley and Fanny wrapped a quilt around her and sat her down at the kitchen table. Her grandfather built up the fire, Fanny hung the teakettle on the crane, and they drew out her story bit by horrific bit. By the time she finished she was crying in her grandmother's arms while John Wesley took down the long rifle from above the mantle and loaded it.

The sun's first rays were making jewels of the frost crystals on Sam's porch roof when John Wesley knocked at the door with his rifle resting in the crook of his arm. When his son-in-law appeared, the old man stepped back to the edge of the porch, lowered the rifle so it pointed at Sam's chest and cocked it. Sam listened in sullen silence as the older man said, "If I ever hear of you botherin' another one of my grandchildren, the last thing you'll ever see is the muzzle of this here rifle. As for Elizabeth, she'll be stayin' at my cabin from now on, and you better never darken my door. Now, get your ass back in there and take care of them squallin' young'uns."

Within four months of Rachel's death Sam married Phoebe O'Brien. Mary, Phoebe's younger sister, came to live with the family as a domestic servant. Less than a year later Mary suddenly disappeared, some said to Cincinnati. The Sugar Branch rumor mill worked overtime on the possible ramifications of that event.

Liz lived with her grandparents throughout her teenage years, growing into a tall handsome girl of reserved nature. Vess and Leanna became her surrogate parents, filling a major gap in her life. She made friends easily among the families of Cotton and Pleasant Townships, as well as at church and school.

Because Vess and Leanna lived several miles to the west of Sugar Branch near the Old Dutch Settlement, they gave Liz a Morgan mare that she named Lily, and thereafter she rode many times, particularly in summer, between her kind old grandparents' place and the home of her beloved aunt and uncle and their family. As the young couple's children came along Liz became a second mother to them, and after two boys they named their first daughter Elizabeth.

By her nineteenth birthday in December, 1859, Liz had become a cheerful, well-balanced young woman. Several of the taller boys in the community showed interest in courting Liz, but it seemed her devotion to family precluded any inclination to pair off with a young suitor. Her grandparents wondered privately if the earlier abuse at the hands of her father had made her averse to such relationships.

Liz was still living with her grandparents taking on more responsibilities in the role of their household servant when an upheaval occurred in 1860 that was to dramatically change her life.

# CHAPTER FORTY-EIGHT

E vents in the greater world beyond the Indiana-Kentucky border country were moving toward a calamity of monstrous proportions. Back in 1856, Senator Charles Sumner of Massachusetts had made an anti-slavery speech to the U.S. Senate bitterly condemning Senators Andrew P. Butler of South Carolina and Stephen A. Douglas of Illinois for their support of slavery. Later, Butler's nephew, Representative Preston Brooks of South Carolina, who had a history of violence, entered the Senate chamber and severely beat Sumner with a cane at his desk, leaving the man with permanent injuries. Sumner's slander and Brooks's brutality illustrated the deep and growing rift between North and South.

The following year, the U. S. Supreme Court, most of whose justices were or had been slaveholders themselves, ruled in the Dred Scott decision that a negro slave's residence in free territory did not make him free, and that no negro, free or slave, could be a citizen of the United States of America. Further, the decision proclaimed the Missouri Compromise, which had kept the slavery issue from exploding for almost thirty years, to be unconstitutional and that Congress had no right to prohibit slavery in the western territories.

Slavery was a slow-burning bomb beneath the nation's foundation. One of the most outspoken proponents of slavery was the same Stephen A. Douglas, the bombastic, powerful senator from Illinois, whose nickname, "Little Giant," derived from this and his five-foot, four-inch frame.

An unknown lawyer from Springfield, Illinois, took exception to the senator's pro-slavery tirades, and began following Douglas about the Illinois countryside, giving speeches denouncing "the monstrous injustice of slavery itself." His goal was to stop its spread. The young lawyer's name was Abraham Lincoln.

Douglas, a pugnacious debater and unapologetic racist, predicted a blending of the races if Lincoln had his way, and stated that government's role was to benefit white men and their posterity forever. These white men, he said, not the federal government, should be allowed to decide whether they wished to own negroes.

The two men's standoffs culminated in seven formal debates staged in 1858 while the two men were running against each other for a seat in the U. S. Senate. Each bout lasted more than eight hours, but they drew crowds in the thousands. Douglas rode to each debate in style in his own special train, while Lincoln traveled in coach class. Lincoln's political colleagues in the new Republican Party hoped he would be the next senator from Illinois.

That was not to be the case, for Douglas returned to the Senate. To a friend after the election, Lincoln remarked that though he would now be forgotten, he believed that he had made some marks which would aid the cause of civil liberty after he was gone. Far from being forgotten, Abraham Lincoln was elected President of the United States in 1860.

The U.S. Census of that year showed four people living in the John Wesley Morrison household in Cotton Township. John was seventy years old at that time. In addition to Fanny, John's sixty-six-year-old wife and Elizabeth Cunningham, nineteen, there was a man listed as an occupant of the house. His name was James William Hackney, twenty-seven. In the census-taker's handwritten note a one-word description followed James's name in parentheses, (black).

# CHAPTER FORTY-NINE

James William Hackney had been known around the Jefferson County towns of Hanover and Madison as a mulatto youngster of negro and Indian blood. His father, James, had come down the Ohio River sometime in the '30s or '40s with his small family from Shenandoah County, Virginia, where he had married an Indian woman. James the elder had managed to buy his freedom before coming to the Indiana frontier, so by the good fortune of having both parents free, James the younger had never known life as a slave.

Prior to 1850, the younger James had been active helping his father in conducting runaway slaves to and from the Baptist community of Lancaster, Indiana, northwest of Madison in Jefferson County. As he grew older he became an active conductor of fugitive slaves in his own right, as well as harboring them at other negro communities in Jefferson County, such as Greenbrier. But the times were changing for all blacks in Border Country.

After enactment of the Fugitive Slave Law of 1850 and the restrictions put upon blacks by the new Indiana Constitution of 1851, negroes began leaving Madison and Jefferson County in ever greater numbers. Black people living unprotected along the Indiana side of the Ohio River, whether free or fugitive slave, had been under attack and in danger of being kidnapped for several years by pro-slavery men from Kentucky and their Hoosier cohorts. In the case of free blacks, they were sold to the deep South to the "land of whips and chains." This turned out to be a lucrative business for some of the kidnappers as the flow of runaways increased during the 1850s and 60s.

Sometime before 1850 the young James Hackney departed Jefferson County for the more remote and less populated Cotton Township in Switzerland County, some twenty straight-line miles across the rugged hills to the east. Enlisting the help of sympathetic Quaker citizens of Jefferson County, Hackney learned that almost half the families at the settlement of Sugar Branch had migrated there from the northeastern states of New York, Pennsylvania and New England, and were thus predominantly of the anti-slavery persuasion. Some of these families, including the Morrisons, let it be known that if a black fugitive were to appear on their doorstep, they would be taken in, fed and protected.

A smaller number of Cotton Township residents had their origins in the South. So, as was the case in northern Kentucky counties, tension grew between different factions over the slavery issue in southern Indiana.

A factor that influenced to which cabin the Madison Quakers applied for protection for James Hackney was the Indian connection. One of the elder Morrisons' boys, Emerson the youngest, had by this time married Mary Ann Campbell, a half-breed girl of the local remnant of the Piankashaw Tribe, a branch of the Miamis. Her father was Thomas "Squire" Campbell, a white man, her mother an Indian woman whose band of Native Americans had occupied the Laughery Creek Valley for years.

Though they had met briefly at Rachel's funeral in 1853, the friendship between Elizabeth Cunningham and James William Hackney, Jr. did not begin until 1860. It was during this year that he arrived to live with the elder Morrisons just before the outbreak of the Civil War. The flow of fugitive slaves through the Indiana border country was at its height during this time. Before appearing at Sugar Branch, Hack had lived with other white families, keeping on the move.

The Quakers sent a rider to speak with John Wesley two days before Hackney's arrival. Reflecting the nature of the times and the speed at which rumors flew in the remote Sugar Branch community,

254

John Wesley kept the anticipated arrival of Hackney between just himself and his wife, Fanny.

James Hackney appeared at the Morrison cabin escorted by Judd Calloway, a Madison Quaker, in the small hours of a night in late April, 1860. Both men were on horseback. Calloway would return to his home in Madison that night. The Morrisons had agreed to make room for James Hackney in their dogtrot cabin and for his gelding, Old Dan, in the log barn.

# CHAPTER FIFTY

The Morrisons' granddaughter, Liz Cunningham, heard strange whisperings as she lay in her bed that night, the voice of her grandfather along with those of at least two other men. She didn't realize what had happened until she walked into the kitchen the next morning before sunrise with a coal oil lamp to begin fixing breakfast for her grandparents. To her surprise and fright she saw a black man feeding the fire with his back to her. She gasped and ran into the other room from where she peered back around the door. Jim Hackney had turned and witnessed her retreat, then stood up and backed toward the outside door with his hands held out in front of him as if to calm the girl. "Didn't want to scare you, miss. Jus' tryin' to earn my keep. I'll go on out now, so's you can make breakfast."

"Wh . . . who are you?" The words came out as if Liz had been holding her breath.

"Why, miss, my name's Jim . . . Jim Hackney, but folks calls me Hack. Mr. Judd Calloway done brought me here last night. I'm s'posed to stay with y'all for a while, but I won't make no bother, and I'll be stayin' out your way."

"But why are you here? Are you . . . a runaway slave?"

"Oh, no, miss. I'm just a free nigra that helps folks sometimes. No, I got my freedom papers, miss."

"You're like . . . like a farm hand?"

"Why, yes'um. If y'all needs help with the crops or the chores, I'll be glad to pitch in. Sometimes I help black folk, too, if any be comin' through."

Her grandparents explained to Liz that Hack would have his bed in the far side of the dogtrot that had been used for storage since all her aunts and uncles had left to start married lives on their own places. By the unspoken custom of the times, even among anti-slavery country folk, the black man would eat his meals with the family, but would take his plate to the porch in good weather, or sit on a bench by the fire to eat, not with the family at the table.

The first conversation between Liz and Hack of more than a word or two of greeting in the mornings came several days later. Under his father's tutelage from the time he could walk, Hack had become a good hand with horses. When Liz's Morgan mare Lily neared her foaling time Hack was drawn by his love of horses and force of habit to check the mare's condition every couple of hours through the night. Liz, too, took up the watch as the foaling time approached. Their meeting at the mare's stall was inevitable.

When she first saw Hack with a lantern in the stall, she recoiled in fear, but he spoke soothingly to her, offering to leave and go back to the cabin, but she finally asked him to stay.

"I thank you Miss Liz. I seen her kicking at her belly this evenin', and knowed she'd drop her foal tonight."

"Kicked at her belly? Why'd she do that?"

"Mares has pain when they're fixin' to drop a foal. Just like a woman when she has a baby. She was kickin' to drive away the pain."

Together they watched and spoke quietly, almost reverently, he relating to her the stories of his years of helping his father raise and train horses, she telling him the tale of her mother Rachel and uncles James and Sylvester going back to the family's former home in New York to bring the first Morgans to Indiana country in 1840.

When the mare lay down and the foal's front hooves appeared Liz stood up. "We'd better get ready to help her," she said.

"Don't look like we need to do nothin' yet," he said. "This her first foal?"

257

"No, you've seen that yearling filly in yonder stall. That's hers, too."

"Then she knows what to do, done it before," he said.

The labor proceeded quickly, the front hooves puncturing the birth sac, then the tiny muzzle and the head were out, the foal's eyes not yet open. Lily grunted with each contraction and the slimy-wet foal inched forward a little each time. "Shoulders sometime get stuck," Hack said. "We'll watch and pull if she needs help."

"We had to pull a little with the first foal," Liz said. "It's going quicker this time."

The mare laid her neck and head out flat on the straw for a moment, resting, gathering strength. With the next contraction she raised her head, turned briefly to look back along her body, then strained and grunted again, longer this time. The foal's body came out rapidly with a discharge of bloody liquid and the afterbirth. The membrane slipped off the foal but remained attached to the mare as she got up and turned to nuzzle her foal. Liz peered at the dark wet creature lying in the straw. "You think it's breathing?"

As if in answer to her question the foal opened its eyes and its head moved reflexively, then flopped back onto the bedding. "You got a old sack, so we can dry him off when he stands up?" Liz left the stall and came back quickly with a burlap feed sack.

"It's here when we need it," she said.

Hack nodded. "Maybe we wait just a little bit, let her get the scent good." The foal raised it's head again, and Lily's muzzle touched it's face. The mare grunted and licked her newborn, nibbling with her lips and tongue at the foal's muzzle. Liz wondered if Lily did this to clear the baby's nostrils or simply to imprint herself on the foal. The mare's action seemed vaguely erotic to Liz, a supremely intimate moment between two of God's creatures.

The foal immediately responded to that stimulation. Its tiny front legs shot out straight, and after an attempt to rise it fell awkwardly back to the straw. The mare moved about her offspring, nudging, licking, nickering softly in her throat. Liz noticed the afterbirth had fallen from the mare and lay in a corner of the stall. "It's a strong baby," Hack said. Liz turned to see a proud smile on the black man's face.

After two more tries the foal stood unsteadily, gangly legs seeming too long for the small body, then stuck it's muzzle under the mare's front legs. Liz said, "No, other end, baby!"

Hack chuckled. "He'll find his breakfast pretty soon. First thing he needs is movin' around some, see what this old world's like."

"I'll dry him a little now, and turn him around," Liz said.

She approached the mare and patted her neck, speaking softly, praising the mother for her beautiful baby. Then she draped the burlap over the foal's withers and rubbed a few brisk strokes, to dry the coat and encourage circulation. Then she turned the foal so it's muzzle approached the mare's udder. Milk now dripped from the two teats, a drop forming on the foal's muzzle. After licking off the nutritious liquid, the newborn seemed to get the idea, for it latched onto a teat and robustly nudged the udder. "It's working." Liz said, and turned to grin at Hack.

"Yeah, that baby knows what he's doin'. He's goin' to be a rascal, he is."

As he spoke, the foal seemed to lose interest in nursing for a moment. Hack approached and, with the burlap still draped over it's back he knelt and took hold of the foal, one arm around the chest, the other around the rump. The foal struggled briefly to free itself, then stood quietly in Hack's embrace. He spoke gently to the foal, then slowly relaxed his grip, and the foal resumed nursing, awkwardly at first, then with gusto.

"What did you do?" Liz asked.

"My old pap always said if you hold 'em when they're first born, and show 'em that gentle control, they'll be easier to train by 'n by."

"Oh! Is it a she or a he?"

Hack showed a white-toothed grin in the lanternlight, and shook his head. "We plumb forgot to check if you got a filly or a horse colt. Go on, see what the old gal brung you."

Liz approached the foal, which was now nursing vigorously, patted the mare's shoulder as if to ask permission, and eased the foal's short twitching tail to the side. Having sat down with his back against the wall, Hack raised the lantern so she could see. "It's a horse colt!" she said, and turned to the mare's head with more soft

259

words and caresses. "He'll make a fine gelding for me to ride when he grows up."

"If Mistuh John don't decide to keep him a stallion. People might want to use him to get more Morgan blood started round here."

"We'll ponder that later," she said.

Taking one last look to make sure the foal was doing well, they grinned shyly at each other and started to leave the stall. "Let's go tell Grandma and Grandpa," Liz said.

# CHAPTER FIFTY-ONE

Just then, John Wesley's lantern approached the barn door. He apparently wanted to check on the pregnant mare, too. Hack's instant reaction, from years of survival, was to blow out their lanterns, grab Liz and shove her into a space between the stalls. There, he stood in front of her facing the advancing intruder and shielding her with his body. He crouched like a cornered wild animal, drawing a knife from his boot.

The old man caught sight of them in the dim light of his lantern and swung round to face them. He tensed when he saw the reflection off Hack's knife blade. "Who's there?"

Hack straightened up and said, "It's just me, Hack, Mistuh John, me an' Miss Liz. We come out to see 'bout the mare. She's got a fine-lookin' bay colt, suh. He's up and suckin' already." He slid his right hand behind him to hide the knife.

John Wesley remained silent a long moment, holding the lantern high, taking in the scene of Liz's pale frightened face peering out from behind the black man, her white fingers visible as they involuntarily clutched Hack's dark-shirted shoulder from behind. "Looks to me like they's more goin' on here than a mare foalin'," he said. "Liz, you got no business out here alone in the dark with this man!"

"But, Grandpa, it's like he said. We just came to check on the mare and got here at the same time. It isn't what you think. You scared us, that's all, so we blew out the lanterns and hid."

"I'm mighty disappointed in you, girl. As for you, Hackney, I want you outta here by sunup, you understand? We try to help your kind, but there ain't no outlaws gonna take advantage of our women. We done had enough of that with her daddy."

Liz moved out from behind Hack to face her grandfather. She was nearly in tears. "Oh, Grandpa, please don't do this. Hack hasn't done anything wrong, neither of us has. He was just anxious for the mare and foal, so he came out to check on her, like I did, and you, too, or you wouldn't be out here."

John Wesley's voice was low and tense. "Now Liz, you go on back to the cabin and wake up your grandma. We'll have a word with you when I get there." Liz left in tears. "Hackney, you stay right where you are till she has time to get inside, and put that knife away before I take a notion to sic the law on you and bust your ass all the way back to Lou'siana."

After Liz left the barn carrying her unlit lantern, Hack broke the long tense silence.

"It was a accident, Mistuh John. We come out to check on the mare, not knowin' the other was comin', too. I'm sorry, suh."

"If you wasn't up to no foolishness, how come you to blow out your lanterns just before I got here? I seen your light between the logs."

"I don't mean to sass you, Mistuh John, but I been snuck up on too many times. I had to fight my way out of barns before, suh. I learnt darkness is my frien' and them as moves slow is dead meat."

The old man stared for a long moment at Hack, his eyes flashing anger in the lanternlight. Then he stepped to the stall door and lifted his lantern high to look inside. The colt lay quietly, head up, eyes blinking in the light. The mare hovered over him, licking and nudging him gently, making soft sounds deep in her throat. Hack slipped the knife back in his boot, then stood up erect as before.

John Wesley told Hack to come with him to the house where they talked about the incident with Liz and her grandmother, who sat on her bed with her arm around the sobbing girl beside her. Fanny asked pertinent questions, and Liz said something about if she and Hack went out there together why would they bring two lanterns, strict at John Wesley was about wasting coal oil. The old man said they could have gone out separately to meet, each needing a lantern, but they could tell his anger was spent.

Afterward the four people found ways to edge back from their fright and anger. Liz and her grandfather finally said they were sorry, John even apologized to Hack, and said, "In times like these, seems like people finds it hard to trust each other. Trouble turns people again' their own family, sometimes. Lizzie, I'm glad you talked this old fool out of makin' a mess tonight."

Fanny offered them coffee and early breakfast. After all, she said, it would soon be first light, and a celebration of the new foal was in order.

Liz told her grandparents about Hack's experiences with his father training horses, and the two men became engaged in the topic of horses until the bacon and eggs were ready. When Fanny dished up the food Hack took his plate to the porch as usual. On his way out the door, he and Liz exchanged a look that spoke of a new kind of friendship.

John Wesley, Fanny and Liz actively supported Hack's conductor activities. The Quakers brought messages and instructions to Hack at Sugar Branch, and he went on several missions of mercy before Liz began to help him prepare for his nocturnal sojourns.

The rift between the Morrisons and the Cunninghams had become palpable. Sam Cunningham was aware of Hack's arrival at the home of John Wesley, Fanny and Liz, and told his friends he suspected the black man of being a conductor on the Underground Railroad. He still smarted from the humiliation and anger he felt at being caught abusing his daughter. The live embers of his hatred toward John Wesley and Liz were fanned into flames every time Sam saw the black man moving about helping with chores and obviously living in the same house with his daughter and in-laws. He and his friends began to keep a close watch on Hack's nocturnal activities.

# CHAPTER FIFTY-TWO

On a Tuesday in late June at midday a Quaker rider rode up to Hack as he walked from the house to the barn at the Morrison place. The man told Hack that a family of runaway slaves with two small children would need to be guided from Lamb to Moorefield on Wednesday night, and asked if he could take on the task. "The father's been hurt and his wife's ready to have another baby," the man said. "He was in a fight with a white overseer, got hit with an axe handle and it broke his arm. The overseer whipped him and his owner was getting ready to sell him South, away from his wife and family. The man's in bad shape, but they had to run."

"Ain't seen no runaway families with small children," Hack said. "How'd they ever make it this far?"

"They didn't have far to come, Hack. From a farm just back of Prestonville, Kentucky, came in a Quaker elder's wagon. His brother had a skiff waiting at the river near Carrollton. Right now they're in Earl McKay's cellar at Lamb. We need to move 'em tomorrow night before the owner finds 'em."

Liz was eavesdropping from just inside the barn. It was immediately obvious to her that Hack would need help on this mission, *her* help. She knew Hack would not ask her, so she simply told him she was going with him. In helping him prepare all those times and the descriptions he shared upon his return, she had a good idea of what would be expected of her. After all, who else was there? He said, "No, Liz, it's gonna be way too dangerous."

"Listen, Hack, we don't have time to argue. I've already got men's work clothes and shoes on, so I don't need to change. I'm going. Let's get ready."

Hack studied the ground at his feet, then said, "I ain't takin' you 'less your folks says so. You go off with me and not ax 'em, I'd be one dead nigger in the mornin'."

Liz hadn't thought of *asking* anyone, being a girl whose independent nature had grown faster than her age. Of course she needed to tell them of the plan and ask for their consent, but would they give it? What if they said no? Liz stared at Hack a moment, her face blank, mind buzzing. Then she was off at a dead run to the cabin.

John Wesley was putting a chunk on the fire and Fanny had just finished the dinner dishes and was drying her hands when Liz burst through the door. Her grandfather turned and held up his hand. The girl stopped in surprise.

"I seen the horseman ride up just now, and his black hat and coat told me the rest. I hear'd and seen enough of you and Hack talkin' to guess what it is you're about to say, so go ahead and say it quick."

"Oh, Grandpa, I have to go. There's a little family of runaways with two small children. The man's hurt and his wife's pregnant."

"Sounds like they got a slim chance of makin' it. I don't b'lieve you know the danger of it, child."

"Hack's told me how it is, but . . . but if I don't help him they might not get to Moorefield at all. The father was about to be sold away from his family, so they had to leave quickly. Hack will have to help him, and the mother can't carry both little ones. We could lose the whole family back South . . . or worse . . . and Hack, too. Please, Grandpa?"

John Wesley's expression didn't change, but he looked at his wife. Fanny came and took the tall girl in her arms. "Child, you go on, help those people. I see you got your heart set on it. We'll be a-prayin' till you come back through that door."

Liz was already out the door, but she shouted back over her shoulder, "Thank you, Grandma, Grandpa!" The two old people stood in the doorway watching her go. John Wesley's arm came around Fanny's shoulders. "Damn these hateful times," he said.

On long chilly evenings gazing into the fire, Fanny and John Wesley would speak to each other slowly, reliving with aching hearts those moments when they watched Liz go off with Hack on her first mission to help runaway slaves. They would never see their beloved granddaughter again.

# CHAPTER FIFTY-THREE

So for the first time Liz went with Hack to conduct a party of runaway slaves from Lamb to Moorefield. They carried Hack's shotgun. Liz had hardly ever heard the term 'Underground Railroad', but she was soon to become more familiar with its name and its workings than she could ever have imagined.

The pair left home on Hack's gelding under cover of darkness that Tuesday night hoping to dodge any curious observers on their way to Lamb. They headed south six or seven miles to Mt. Sterling, then struck southwest on game trails and farm lanes through rugged hills, skirting the clusters of cabins at Long Run, Five Points and Braytown. Altogether they traveled something over twenty miles under a three-quarter moon.

As Old Dan moved along at a ground-eating pace, Liz reflected on the time since Hack had come to live with her grandparents, the surprise of finding him in the kitchen that first morning, getting to know him better the night the mare foaled, learning of, then helping him prepare for, his work with fugitive slaves.

Though she would have been at a loss to explain it, Hack and his work roused her interest in a way no other man had done. She'd wanted to come with him on his previous nighttime sojourns, but knowing her chances for gaining permission were remote, she watched for an opportunity. This time the slave family had given her a reason that made sense to everyone. She was secretly proud, and she allowed herself a private smile.

She'd asked Hack if she should ride her mare, Lily, on their mission but he reminded her that the foal was still too young to separate from his mother. And, though the colt would follow his mother anywhere, "We cain't be bothered with no more babies. Already got two slave babies to worry 'bout."

They made steady progress through the rough country, Hack riding with confidence, guiding the horse with his knees and gentle movements of the reins against Old Dan's neck. Liz sat behind the young man with her arms around his hard thin body. Her excitement about helping the family of slaves was augmented by her nearness to this mysterious man who had so recently appeared in her life. Now, for the first time she was touching him, able to feel his warmth, his strength, and these perceptions gave her pleasure.

Whenever Old Dan changed his pace suddenly to charge up a steep slope or to ease down into a ravine, she clutched Hack even more tightly. Once, she placed her face above his collar without his noticing, wanting to smell him. She'd heard some of her girlfriends say that black people gave off a strange odor, but now she smelled only worn clothing and stale sweat, horses, grain, hay and the smell of guns: powder, metal and oil. Hack smelled like all the other men she knew, her grandpa, her uncles, even her father.

The morning star was fading by the time they holed up at an abandoned landing with a tumbledown shack on the riverbank above Lamb. Hack made a halter out of the bridle by removing the bit from Old Dan's mouth. He brushed the tall gelding, led him to the river to drink just before sunrise, then put oats in his nosebag and tied him to a dead willow in a canebrake. He carried the saddle into the shack. Liz opened their canvas bag and they ate some of their summer sausage, cheese and cornbread, washing it down with a couple of swallows of water.

Hack cut some cedar boughs and spread them over an old rough bed frame they found in the shack, then spread their blanket over it and laid out their gear, the horse brush, flint and steel, knives, an Indian hatchet, canteens, extra loads for the shotgun and a small coil of rope. After checking everything and repacking it they sat on the bed and considered the task before them.

"I wish we could go on to Earl's place right now and see if there's anything we could do for those people," Liz said.

"The McKays is takin' better care of them than we could" Hack said. "'Sides, if we was to go stompin' in there with the hoss an' all, somebody'd see us and the game'd be up right there. We just need to get us some rest so's we can be wide awake lookin' out for them folks tonight. Moorefield ain't too far but the woods is thick and the ground rough."

"Can the parents ride Old Dan? We can each carry a child . . . ."

"We'll see how it turns out. Maybe one of 'em can walk a little ways and the babies can ride. If not, the older folks both ride. I'll carry a chil' and the shotgun and lead Old Dan. Or maybe you can carry a small chil' and the shotgun, too. Two chillen would be too heavy for you, don't you 'magine?"

"I don't know. We'll have to wait and see."

Their minds turned to the prospect of spending the long daylight hours in the old shack of the fish camp. The river made soft lapping sounds on the mud a few yards from the shack. Insects and birds welcomed the brightening morning outside. Hack said, "You go on, lay down, get some rest."

"What are you going to do? You need rest, too."

"I'll just keep watch a while."

Liz rolled from her sitting position across the bed to lie on her back on the far side. "You come on, lie down. We can't have you folding up on us when we need you tonight."

Hack's eyes grew large and he looked down at her in surprise. "You know I cain't do that. I best lay down outside somewheres. Lord, Liz, what'd your folks say, they find out we been layin' together? You forgot my color?"

"For heaven's sake, Hack! We're helping this black family because skin color doesn't matter. And we're not doing anything wrong, for these runways or for ourselves. Now use your common sense. Come and lie down."

Without further objections, Hack took off his boots and gingerly lay down beside Liz. After a few minutes, realizing sleep hadn't come for either of them, Liz spoke softly, looking up at the cobwebs in the bare rafters. "Please forgive me, Hack, for speaking to you that way. I imagine you've seen many troubles in this white man's world. And here I spoke to you as if you'd never had to suffer these indignities, never had to twist your life around to suit some thoughtless person like me."

"It's fine, Miss Liz. I know you ain't like some white folks, you an' your family. Y'all is good people, Christian people."

She felt tears forming at the corners of her eyes. "Thank you for letting me come with you, Hack. I appreciate that, and what you do for these poor fugitives."

Another long silence followed, during which Liz felt the air begin to hum with unspoken words. Finally she rolled onto her side facing him and said, "And I'm glad you're lying here with me." Her hand came gently to touch his, and they lay like that until his breathing told her that Hack had drifted into sleep.

She lay awake a while longer, berating herself. *I am so naïve,* she thought, *preaching to him as I did. He doesn't need my idealistic words; his bravery and dedication speak for themselves. I just need to be quiet, observe how he does his work and help him whenever I can.*

They woke up a couple of hours before dark. Liz asked Hack about his early life, the Indian connection. She learned Hack and his father were mulattos, of Indian and Negro heritage, both of whose names were James William Hackney. She asked how Hack and his father got their freedom. Hack said his father married an Indian woman. The children of a free mother and a slave father were free in the eyes of Virginia law, the condition of the children following the condition of the mother. Also, Hack's father worked for years until he was able to buy his freedom.

"But jus' to be safe, I carry a copy of my pap's Deed of Manumission, in case some white man don't believe I'm a free black. Pap axed a lawyer man that he shod a horse for to write out two copies of his deed and sign 'em as payment, in case he lose the firs' paper, he told the man. I weren't there, so the lawyer man don't know I have the same name as old Pap. So, the paper works for me, too." Hack grinned at Liz. "So now you think I'm a bad nigger? You gonna leave me here on the river bank and go tell your grandpap to send me away?"

She shook her head at his dark humor. "Don't be silly, Hack. You just said you were born free, so the paper isn't necessary, but I

270

can see it's a good idea to have it with you in case somebody challenges you. You *do* have it with you, don't you?"

"Right here." He rolled toward her far enough to reach into his back pocket, then handed Liz a dog-eared piece of foolscap. "You know I cain't read, so go on, read it out loud. Pap says them's the most beautiful words God ever made."

Liz unfolded the paper and read the tattered and sweat-stained document:

*Will Glixner to James William Hackney*
*Deed of Manumission*
*Know all men by these presents that I, Will Glixner of Shenandoah County, Virginia, for and in consideration of the amount of eight hundred dollars, the receipt whereof is hereby acknowledged, have released, manumitted, liberated and set free the said James from any claim I now have or ever had to any property in the said James as slave.*

*And I do also covenant and agree to and with the said James, that I am and was the last legal owner of him, the said James—and the last person to whom the said James owed service as a slave.*

*In Testimony whereof I have hereunto set my hand and seal this Eighteenth Day of April, in the year of our Lord, Eighteen Hundred and Thirty-Three.*

*his*
*Will  X  Glixner  (SEAL)*
*mark*

*Done in presence of*
*William Wittman*
*G. M. Clarkson*
*Kermit Kitchell*

Liz folded the foolscap gently and handed it to Hack. "Oh, Hack, what if you were to lose this paper? And eight hundred dollars! Where would a slave get that kind of money?"

"Old Pap trained horses and did some blacksmithin'. Massa Glix give all his slaves food and shelter, and he let Pap keep half of what he got from hirin' out. So it didn't take too mis'able long to pay for hisself. Mama said soon as he got his paper, we lit out down

271

the river, landed here in Indiana. I don't remember nothin' about it, bein' but a sucklin' child in them days."

The girl frowned. "If you were an infant in 1833," Liz said, "wouldn't anyone reading this paper think it was unusual to manumit a baby?"

Hack laughed. "Even I don't know for sure what year I was born, and most white folks cain't tell the age of a nigger. So if anybody ax, I just say, 'Don't know how old I was then, suh, but plenty old enough to work in the fields.'"

She smiled and nodded. "Does anyone else have a copy of this manumission paper, in case you lose yours?"

"Lawyer man said take one piece to the county courthouse where we land so everybody'd know Pap is free for good. I axed a man to make me a copy and done that soon as I come over here to Switzerland County when I was about your age."

Hack was quiet a moment before he said, "Mistuh Calloway said your family's connected to the Indians, too. Looks to me like y'all is white folks, no Indians here'bouts."

"My mother's brother, Uncle Emerson, married Mary Ann Campbell from down on Laughery Creek five or six years ago." Liz said. "Her mother is an Indian like your mother."

"They told me the Indian kinfolk was why they axed your granddaddy to let me stay with y'all, but I didn't expect to see no girl there. How come you to be livin' with your grandma and grandpa?"

"I had some trouble with my father a few years ago and had to leave home," Liz said. "My grandparents needed help so I moved in with them."

"Reckon it's kinda lonely not bein' with your family."

"Not so much. You know my mother's dead, and I didn't get along with my next-younger sister. Pop's married another woman now, and she won't speak to me, so I'm better off with my grandparents. My Uncle Vess and Aunt Leanna over in Pleasant Township are real good to me, too, so I try to stay busy and think about the good things, like my mother told me before she died."

They lay quietly for a while, facing each other, the light slowly fading. "Hold still," Hack said. He reached over and whisked a mosquito off her face. "These skeeters gettin' so much of our blood they'll be callin' us kinfolk 'fore long."

Liz sniggered, took his hand, kissed his fingers, then moved close and gave him a quick kiss on his cheek. His eyes flew open wide and he started to draw back from her, but she put her hand behind his head and held him there.

He started to touch her, then let his hand drop to the space between them. Breathing deeply Hack said, "Lord . . . Lord knows you're a sweet gal, Liz, an' I think the world of you, but we cain't be doin' this. We got to get up now, go hep them people."

Liz fixed him with mischievous, smiling eyes as she let the backs of her fingers lie gently for a moment on his cheek. "You're one of those good things I was talking about."

# CHAPTER FIFTY-FOUR

On Wednesday night, after making contact in darkness with the fugitive family at the McKay stone house near the riverbank at Lamb, Hack and Liz led their charges from the safety of the cellar.

Earl McKay said, "George and Jenny, Hack here is the best they is at leadin' fugitives safely to the next stop up the line. Ida and me wishes you godspeed."

While the others were talking, Ida McKay whispered to Liz, "You surely ain't goin' with 'em, are you, gal? This ain't no time for a white girl to go traipsin' through the woods with niggers. They's usually only one conductor guides runaways out to Moorefield."

"That may be true, Mrs. McKay, but you can see with the little ones, and all, Hack will need help."

"Well . . . Lord, be careful, honey. I hate to think what patrollers'd do with you if you get caught."

George, the injured black man with his arm in a sling, turned, wincing at the pain of the stripes under the bandage on his back. He said, "Hope someday we can show our proper thanks to y'all for savin' and protectin' us. God bless you, Mistuh 'n Missus McKay." Then he reached for Jenny and they made their tortuous way toward Hack who was holding Old Dan's reins.

"Reckon you both better ride a spell," he said. "Liz and me'll carry your babies and I'll lead the hoss. Just hang on tight, 'specially goin' up and down hills. Old Dan's got a easy way a-goin' but y'all be ducking under branches and fightin' bushes and briars that's pullin' on you in the thickets. Don't cry out, for we have to talk in whispers, an' not much of that, you hear?"

Jenny drew her two children, little girls of two and four years, to her ample form and whispered to them that they must be quiet and not cry, for Hack and Liz were going to carry them, but Papa and Mama would be close by.

" 'Bout how far we got to go?" George asked, rolling his eyes toward the river bluffs. "We be in woods all the way?"

"If we was crows it'd be but a few miles, but we ain't got wings. We're gonna follow the old Indian Treaty Line pretty close," Hack said. "It was laid out away back in old times, straight from Greenville, Ohio, down here to Lamb, across from the mouth of the Kentucky River. It ain't a trail, but some places they's mud roads that runs along the Line, an' we'll be crossin' some little ol' lanes called Green Valley, Lost Fork and Sweetwater. Mostly, we'll be in the woods, scramblin' north through rough country. Ain't gonna be easy, for sure."

Hack led Old Dan to a stump and helped the parents mount up. Jenny had to ride side-saddle due to her delicate condition and the saddle bags hindering her comfort. Liz whispered, "You don't think the horse will wear out too fast with all that weight?"

"He's tall and tough, 'sides, we ain't got no choice."

Hack picked up four-year-old Maybell and Liz hefted Sally, then reached for the shotgun. They could barely see Ida and Earl waving silently as they started off in the dark, making their way across the river flats on a narrow farm lane toward the forbidding hills.

The small slow-moving party finally came up out of the first hollow onto Green Valley Road and paused to rest. Liz sat down on a fallen log by the roadside and comforted little Sally while Hack looked after Old Dan and his passengers, lifting Maybell up for Jenny to quiet her silent sobs. They passed the canteen around and broke off bits of cheese for the children.

Under way again into the steep valleys and ridges toward Lost Fork, they suddenly heard the dreaded sounds of a gang of patrollers on horseback. The pursuers made no attempt at silence in their hunt. Their voices carried easily to the fleeing family and their conductors. "We got 'em now, boys," a gravelly voice declared. "I told you they was headed for Moorefield, and that black bastard Jim Hackney is guidin' 'em. Old man Archer is a damned abolitionist and real proud of runnin' a safehouse for niggers. They're headed for Archers' sure as hell. This'll be the last bunch Hackney'll ever take north. Looks like we'll have us a right good payday, boys."

Hack quickly moved the group off the trail and down a dark slope, but there had been a blowdown of large trees that left fallen logs in their path, allowing a scattering of thorn bushes to find sunlight and a place to take root. He tried to avoid ripping his and Old Dan's flesh on the three-inch thorns, as well as George and Jenny's legs. He finally had no choice but to flee from the patrollers down a creekbed full of rocks and brush.

As she clambered over a log following the others, trying to comfort the frightened Sally, Liz stifled a sob herself. In those desperate moments her fear and anger summoned the image of a bully who had tormented her back in primer class at Sugar Branch School until the teacher intervened and whipped the older boy. She felt the same bitter resentment toward these hoodlums on horseback coming after them. What right had they to harass these innocent fugitives just because they wanted to live in peace and freedom? *Government officials in their plush chambers ought to be forced out here to cope with the unfair laws they so heedlessly passed,* she thought, *such as the Fugitive Slave Law.* Scrambling down this dismal creekbed Liz saw clearly the dichotomy between the laws of God and nature and those of pompous politicians.

The patrollers had been slowed in their pursuit almost as much as the fugitives by the obstacles in the creekbed, but now they were so close that Liz could hear their horses' labored breathing and their hooves clattering on the rocks. Hack, carrying the larger child and leading the horse, stumbled and fell just as their pursuers were almost upon them. Old Dan's lead reins pulled tight, jerking his mouth. He grunted and shied, nearly dislodging his riders.

Liz put the small child down and told her to run ahead to Hack. She struggled with both hands to cock the shotgun in the dark, swung the muzzle around behind her, braced the butt of the stock against the middle of her chest and fired blindly into the blackness.

She had watched the previous evening as Hack primed the weapon with a heavy charge of powder and meticulously counted out sixteen large shot for the load. The blast's recoil knocked her down, but she heard a scream. Frantic with fear, breathing hard, she raced to catch up with Hack and the others. Along the way she scooped up Sally, who had fallen and lay crying in the gravel and debris of the dry creek. Behind her as she ran, Liz heard the loud confused voices of several men calling to each other, but the patrollers and their horses seemed to have stopped their pursuit.

Hack had handed Maybell to Jenny on the horse. When he turned Liz burst into him and he almost fell again. "I heard a man scream after I shot," she blurted. "Oh, Hack, what if I've killed someone."

Hack held her a moment, until her breathing eased a bit, then he said, "We cain't be worryin' about that now. We've got to move. Bring the child and come on." He led Old Dan as fast as he could up out of the creekbed through the woods, dodging large trees, watching for rocks, logs and uneven ground. George and Jenny wailed as they clung to their precarious perch on the horse's back. Jenny clutched her child and her husband as George tried to steady himself by grasping a handful of Dan's mane with his good hand.

The rest of the journey to Moorefield was a dark blur that Liz would not remember later, except that she kept listening for the sounds of their pursuers, which never came. Having heard the scream she understood her random shot in the dark must have hit one of the horsemen. She remembered that by the time she fired the slavecatchers were nearly upon them. But who were those men? Could they have been her father, Sam, and his hoodlum friends Dewey and Homer, or were they some other band of marauding slavecatchers looking for bounty money?

They stopped again to comfort the children and to let the horse rest. Hack came to Liz. "How you doin', gal? You done the right thing by shootin'. No other way to stop 'em. It don't matter who you hit."

"I was so scared, but they must have stopped. Does that mean I've killed someone?"

"We'll be findin' out soon enough. Right now we got to get to the Archer place before they come after us again."

The party finally struggled up out of the last wild hollow to the Archers' two-story log cabin where Liz pounded frantically on the door.

When Andrew Archer's haggard face appeared at the door under the feeble glow of his coal oil lamp, Hack and Liz introduced themselves and their fugitives. After a short discussion Andrew and his wife Wava took them in, though they expressed their surprise at a white girl helping a black conductor.

Ordinarily Hack and Liz would have made their way back to Sugar Branch on Old Dan that night and the next morning. But the circumstances of their narrow escape from the slavecatchers altered that plan.

The two young people had a brief whispered conversation, then told their hosts the whole story of their being chased, firing the shotgun, then escaping from their pursuers and assuming the blast had injured one of the riders. After listening intently to their story, Andrew said, "You two'll have to go with these runaways. Sounds like whoever was chasin' your group will want to catch you now, even more than the others." Andrew looked sternly at Liz. "And they wouldn't be too likely to show mercy to you, young lady, a white gal travelin' with these here blacks."

Liz controlled her impatience. "I'm here because Hack couldn't have handled all four of these people by himself, and there was nobody else to help."

"Well," Andrew said, "after we get you settled, I'll ride over to Bennie Strickland's. He's got a wagon big enough for all six of you, and a good team."

The Archers began busying themselves with pallets and blankets to make places for six extra people to sleep in the loft during the coming daylight hours.

Liz suddenly grabbed Hack and drew him into a corner in the kitchen. Her panic was evident in her voice. "Oh, god, Hack! Did you bring the shotgun? I must have dropped it."

"I seen we didn't have it when we got here," he said. "We cain't be frettin' over it now."

Even before the next night's travel arrangements could be made, everything changed again. Just as the new day was dawning Jenny's water broke, indicating the imminent birth of her third baby. Wava shook her head, then summoned her husband. After she and Andrew spoke in whispers for a moment the Archers told the others that George, Jenny and their children would have to stay hidden at their cabin for several days.

While Wava and Liz tended Jenny's and the children's needs, Andrew, Hack and George moved wash stands, chairs and pallets to make things more commodious for the family until Jenny and the baby were up to traveling again.

Three hours later a neighbor, Hugh Baker, came galloping up, tied his horse at the hitch rail and ran into the cabin, not bothering to knock. Wava came downstairs to meet him, her jaw dropping at the look on his face. "Mercy! What happened, Hugh? Is Josie all right?"

"A slavechaser was shot dead last night, in the woods down toward Lost Fork!"

# CHAPTER FIFTY-FIVE

The black family, increased in size now by the arrival of a baby boy they named Zachary, stayed out of danger for the moment at Archer's large cabin near Moorefield. But Hack and Liz, fearing the consequences of Liz's action that had taken one life while possibly saving several others, now faced the ugly prospect of becoming fugitives themselves.

They made arrangements for Andrew Archer to keep Old Dan, use him if needed, and take care of him in the hope that Liz and Hack could return for the sturdy old warrior later. They rested at the Archer cabin all day while Andrew made preparations for their white neighbor, Bennie Strickland, to take them farther north with a team and wagon. They would travel along country lanes to a place just south of Versailles, near the settlement of Correct.

That night Bennie stayed on the wagon seat as Wava handed Liz a packet of food, then Andrew concealed the pair under a load of corn fodder in Mr. Strickland's false-bottom wagon. Liz would have panicked from claustrophobia in the tight dusty space that smelled of mouse feces if Hack hadn't been there to calm her. She was experiencing first-hand the conditions fugitive slaves had endured for decades, and now she understood that no amount of storytelling about the tribulations faced by negroes could have prepared her for the suffocating fear and discomfort she felt on this night as the wagon bounced over primitive roads.

Liz and Hack were not acquainted with Mr. Strickland, but sometimes the less the parties knew of each other the better the chances of success for both. Their destination near Versailles was a large shed owned by a farmer, Robert Hertzel. When they arrived at the shed just before dawn, Hertzel and Strickland exchanged a few words as Liz and Hack stood on the ground looking up at the conductor's shaded face. Bennie was anxious to turn his team toward home, beat the sun and not be noticed by pro-slavers with too many questions. Now, in the first words the travelers and their conductor shared, Mr. Strickland answered their query about news he'd heard.

The man spoke in a low guttural voice. "They's a slavechaser been kilt. Man name of Sam Cunningham, family man from Sugar Branch." The pair stood frozen in shocked silence. Liz felt a sudden chill, and a surge of nausea welling up as if she might be sick right here in the road. The horror spread through her like venom. She tried to remember the voice she'd heard just before she fired. It had not been her father's voice. Had it?

After a moment Bennie continued, "Thought you might of knowed somethin' about it, comin' up through there last night and all. Anyhow, this'll be my last run for a while till things settle a bit. Won't be safe for no runaways nor conductors through here for a good long time now. The pro-slavers'll be out for blood. You'uns travel fast and safe, now. Gee-up." He snapped the lines, and his rig turned in the road and disappeared into the darkness. The team's trotting hoofbeats and jangling harness faded into the distance as the frightened pair entered the shed under the guidance of old Mr. Hertzel.

Bennie Strickland's words had thrown Liz's mind into blind turmoil. As her reasoning faculties slowly returned, she felt a numbing awareness that all contact with her beloved grandparents and other kinfolk had been severed by her act. Should she and Hack be captured there could be no doubt they would be dealt with summarily. And even if they were to somehow elude the patrollers and lawmen they would never be able to return to their homes and loved ones. To Liz this was an outlook dismal beyond her comprehension.

281

Later she would spend hours mulling the death of her father at her own hands. Was it Divine Providence or an extremely unlikely accident, the deadly effect of that random shot in the dark? Was her action absolutely necessary? Could they have escaped with their fugitives if she had not fired the shotgun?

In the days and weeks to come she would endlessly relive that fatal moment in their flight to Moorefield. She was nearly overcome by guilt and self recrimination at committing such an act, ending a precious human life, *any* human life. But with all the other grave concerns she and Hack now faced, she never once grieved for her father.

Mr. Hertzel closed the shed door and sat them down before showing them to their hiding place behind a pile of lumber in the loft. His kindness was evident through the concern on the old man's face as he spoke. "I already heard about the slavecatcher bein' killed down in Switzerland County. Everybody in southern Indiana will be lookin' for you two, and a tall white woman with a black man'd be easy to spot as two geese in a chicken coop."

Hack nodded solemnly, then asked, "Somebody else gonna move us on up the line tonight?"

"After I get you hid I'll ride over to see my neighbor Joseph Munford. He or his son would usually take you north to Greensburg or Batesville, but that's the very direction the law and bounty hunters will be expectin' you to go, for that's the quickest line to Canada."

Canada! That word struck fear into Liz's heart. She looked at Hack in bewilderment. Was there no alternative other than fleeing to Canada? Even if they could make the journey successfully, would they ever be able to return to their homes and loved ones? What grief that would cause their friends and families, not knowing their fate.

Canada! She had no concept of the distance, the time or the difficulty they would face trying to get to this place about which she knew almost nothing.

Liz realized she was in the same predicament now as George and Jenny, the two fugitives they had guided to Moorefield. It had been so easy to glibly say the runaway slaves were headed to Canada, without having to consider what a forbidding task that was for these poor naïve travelers. Now she and Hack shared the same

282

destination as the thousands who had gone before them fleeing slavery. Liz felt herself brutally confronted by the chilling reality that for the first time in her life she was a fugitive, wanted for conducting runaways . . . and now for murder.

Liz was shocked nearly to silence by their dire situation and the scope of the task before them, but she managed to speak in a tremulous voice. "Can't we stay here for a while, Mr. Hertzel?"

"That won't work, miss, my place bein' right close to the main north road here. They'll be around here lookin' for you within the next couple of days, for sure."

Liz reached for the security of Hack's hand and gazed beseechingly at his dark face in the lantern light. "What'll we do, then?"

Mr. Hertzel answered her question. "I'm sending the two of you east to Cincinnati instead of north. Joseph knows the east line as well as his son is familiar with the one leading to Batesville. It's still mighty chancy, but we've got a branch that goes to Levi Coffin's place, takes two or three days. Joseph'll take you to a place close to Aurora on the river tonight. Another conductor will guide you on to the Coffins' place."

The earliest European explorers had traveled through the American wilderness in boats on waterways. These streams were the most convenient routes for traversing the seemingly infinite expanse of eastern woodlands on the new continent.

Later, land routes in the east were laid out over courses of least resistance. This meant that wagon roads followed paths trodden previously by men on horseback singly or in pack trains. These in turn had followed old Indian trails used by redmen hunting wild game, and in the beginning these game animals had worn the first traces through forests and swamps, over plains and rocky ridges.

The easiest course for horses and wagons from Versailles to Cincinnati would have been the primitive east-west wagon road that had been a major Indian trail in the not-too-distant past. Most freight wagons and pack trains heading east to, or west from, Cincinnati passed along this busy route, so conductors of fugitive slaves often avoided this road in favor of less traveled, and therefore safer, trails. Remote game trails would be chosen by Liz and Hack's conductors

283

who were to guide them from Versailles to Aurora, then on to Cincinnati. Thus they found themselves about to be led by their conductors on a meandering course that lengthened the straight-line distance to Cincinnati.

Mr. Hertzel continued, "Levi Coffin has helped thousands of runaways make it to Canada, both from his place at Newport, Indiana, before 1847, and after that when he moved to Cincinnati. Canada's definitely your best chance. There'll be notices put up all through Indiana and Ohio in no time showin' rewards for your capture. Most people in this border country is pro-slavery, anyway, so a good many of 'em will join the hunt. I don't need to tell you your lives won't be worth a chaw of tobacco if they catch you."

After Mr. Hertzel brought them food, water and blankets he went away. Liz was stifling sobs and trembling so violently she could hardly climb the ladder to the loft. When they had pulled the ladder up, blown out the lantern and drawn the blankets over themselves behind the lumber pile Hack spoke gently to Liz. "I think we're gonna be all right, Liz. Mistuh Hertzel's smart to send us off towards Cincinnati, and these conductors is all good men that knows what they're doin'. They know the trails through the woods and how to dodge the law. They're like shifty old foxes, never take the same trail twice. We just have to trust 'em like George and Jenny trusted us to take 'em to Moorefield."

By this time Liz had pressed close to Hack with her arms around him, clutching him tightly, moaning softly in her anxiety. He felt her wet cheek and her shuddering breath against his neck. He held her tenderly with his chin resting lightly on the top of her head, caressing her arms and back.

Hack hardly knew what to make of this girl. He'd allowed her show of independence and confidence to convince him to let her come along and help with the runaways, and her help had been a godsend. But she was so young, naïve, inexperienced at this work. He knew he should have asked someone else, a man, to help him, but there'd been so little time. At any moment Liz might make a mistake that would betray their hiding place, or she might say the wrong thing when they met strangers.

Above all, she was white. This compounded the danger they faced. What had he been thinking to allow her to come along? How would he explain to her folks if something happened to her? Allowing her to participate in this mission was foolhardy, to say the least, and at worst, it could get them killed.

Still, he'd welcomed the chance to be around this proud, vivacious girl. She turned him to mush when she kissed him, and when she clung to him those several times. She actually seemed to like him, maybe more than a little. But why? She could have any number of white boys trailing after her.

He couldn't let the question go. Was this another case of a white girl taking advantage of a man of the black servant class? Was she using him to show her resentment toward the rules of behavior between white girls and negro men—at his expense? Though he was totally at a loss to understand white women, he found it hard to believe that Liz was leading him on, or showing him anything but her true feelings.

He'd tried not to respond to her gestures of affection, but if she continued he might do something foolish, get himself in big trouble. And if that happened, would she laugh in his face, gloating that she'd conquered him? Would he be merely a feather in her cap, as if to say, "Look at me! I've got this dumb nigger wrapped around my little finger." He'd heard of white women doing such things.

Or would she suddenly tell her grandparents and have him sent away? She had stood up for him that night when her grandpa found them in the barn together. Would she do it again if the need arose? With everything else he had on his mind, he couldn't allow his feelings for this girl to affect his judgement.

After a few moments lying in Hack's protective embrace Liz seemed to begin collecting herself. Her weeping subsided, she dried her tears on her sleeve and took several deep breaths. He noticed her muscles relaxing, the tremors abating. She sniffled, and he heard her voice against his chest. She spoke with quiet resolve. "I need to stop blubbering like a child and start helping you, Hack. After all, that's why I came with you."

"You're doin' fine, gal, already saved us down on Lost Fork. Where you think we'd be if you hadna shot at them pattyrollers?"

"But now we'll be wanted for murder," she said.

285

"We did what we had to do. But bein' chased an' bein' catched is two diff'rent things. We're fixin' to make it, Liz, all the way to the Queen's dominions."

"I'm scared to death, but I'll try to be strong for you, Hack." She turned her face up to him and kissed him. He started to move away, then briefly accepted her kiss and enfolded her in a sheltering embrace, understanding how frightened she was. Tucking the blankets around her he said, "We're partners, Liz. We'll jus' trust each other and them that comes to hep us." He patted her shoulder and turned away from her. Liz, so needful of reassurance, moved close to him and reached out to intertwine her arms and hands with his. Then, as faint morning sounds of birds and distant church bells came to their hiding place from the ominous world outside, they both drifted into uneasy slumber.

An hour after nightfall Joseph Munford appeared with two horses, three slickers and a canteen of water. Liz and Hack were waiting in the dark for him just inside the shed with their packet of food and other meager possessions. If Joseph took exception to the biracial nature of the pair, he kept it to himself, for which Liz was grateful. Maybe Mr. Hertzel had explained it to him.

After short introductions Joseph said, "Looks like we've got us a piece of weather rollin' in tonight. You been hearin' that thunder in the southwest? Could be a good thing, keep patrollers off of us."

"How far we got to go?" Hack said.

"Aurora's where we're bound, maybe twenty, twenty-five mile to the east, but we cain't take the Old Indian Trail, which is the shortest way. They's a rumor of a big reward for you two dead or alive. Everybody says they knowed Sam Cunningham, and they loved him like next-door kin, even if they never hear'd of him. All that excitement has got these yay-hoos round here loadin' their rifles, grabbin' their whiskey flasks and saddlin' up for a night ride. The Old Indian Trail will be busier than the riverfront at Cincinnati tonight."

"So we'll take a different road, then?" Liz said.

"Ain't no proper road, Miss Liz, just a spider's web of paths and game trails through these woods and up creekbeds. Very few settlers' cabins in this country. I've hunted all through here, and I'll

286

venture I know this country better'n any white or colored man livin'. No offense there, Hack, I was referrin' to Indians, doncha know." Hack gave Liz a quick wink, then rubbed his eye as if it itched. She tried hard to keep a straight face. "That's why we'll be ridin' these bangtails, 'stead of a wagon. A wagon where we're goin' would be awkward as a baby buggy in a briar patch."

Joseph said they should put on their slickers, because it was doubtful they could dodge the approaching storm. "You think we should stay here for a little bit and try to wait it out?" Liz said.

"Might be waitin' all night," Joseph said. "Best we get movin', maybe outrun it. Here we go." He handed the reins of one horse to Hack, then mounted and waited for them to mount up before heading out of the shed into the humid and threatening July night.

Robert Hertzel's shed was near the settlement of Correct, along a trace that would lead them north to Versailles. They rode for an hour, passing a few lighted windows at Versailles, then turned east and moved down into the gorge of Laughery Creek. The lightning had been increasing ever since they left Hertzel's place, and the flashes were now so intense they had no trouble seeing glimpses of the trail ahead of them, and Joseph leading the way on the other horse. Thunder claps came quicker now, following the flashes. Liz had even begun to fear that if someone looked out from a cabin they were passing, the cover of nightfall would have been useless to them.

For all the lightning and thunder, the rain and spitting hail pellets did not descend upon them until just after they'd forded Laughery Creek, and then it seemed to come with the fury of angry gods.

Hack rode up beside Joseph, raising a flap of his slicker to deflect the rain so he could see the other rider in the lightning flashes. "Reckon we need to lay by, maybe get up again' one of them cliffs down in here by the creek?"

"Best keep movin'. This here crick could become a river 'fore we know it. Flashfloods is a danger in this hill country."

Hack reined his and Liz's horse back into single file behind Joseph's mount. They resumed their slow pace upward through tall timber, the narrow trail climbing through switchbacks toward the rim of the gorge. Hack halted their horse a moment and used both hands to tighten the drawstring of his slicker hood. Liz reached around his neck to tie it. That brief stop, causing them to fall a few yards farther behind their leader, those few seconds in the crashing storm almost surely saved their lives.

Just as Hack nudged the horse forward with his knees, they were blasted by a lightning strike and simultaneous crash of thunder. The sound was more a tremendous *Zip-Bang!* than a rumble. Their mount shied and they felt fragments of twigs, bark and fine mist striking their faces, coming from their front, the opposite direction from the driving rain. They were blinded and deafened for several seconds, the horse stumbling off the trail, disoriented, nearly falling, but finally regaining his balance.

Liz clung to Hack until both of them stopped shaking. When they could see and hear again they peered into the darkness, calling out to Joseph. Aside from the noise of the downpour and the thunder all was silent in the forest. As their vision cleared their attention was arrested in the next flash by the smoking snag of what had been a tall tree just ahead of them beside the trail. The shattered treetop had fallen away from the trail, taking smaller trees with it as it crashed to the ground. In that brief glimpse with their attention directed upward, they saw no horse and rider ahead of them on the trail.

# CHAPTER FIFTY-SIX

They roused themselves to action. Hack said, "Come on. I'm 'fraid he's been struck." They dismounted and Hack calmed their dazed horse, leading him forward as they clambered back up to the trail, which was now full of water running down into the gorge. They sloshed upward toward the brow of the hill and the smoldering tree.

Just beyond the snag they saw them. Joseph's horse lay motionless on its chest, hooves and legs doubled under its body, head upright, muzzle touching the ground. Hack said, "He's done been dropped like a poleaxed steer." Their horse pulled back, showing the whites of his eyes, as if he sensed death.

Beside the dead animal lay Joseph Munford. He was on his back, arms flung wide, hood of his slicker under his shoulders, hat tilted off, the back of its brim still under his head as if he had hit the ground and not moved.

Liz rushed to the man, dropped to her knees at his side. She laid her ear to his chest, then pressed a hand against his neck under his jaw and waited a moment, concentrating. Pausing only to clear her face of water she then placed her hands on his face and opened his mouth. Her shriek rose above the maelstrom. A small cloud of foul-smelling smoke from scorched flesh had risen from the dead man's mouth.

She buried her face in her hands, retching in reaction to her grisly discovery. Slowly she rose from Joseph's side and turned to

Hack who stood looking down at the corpse in stunned silence. "What'll we do now?" she said. "How can we get him back to his people?"

"We cain't, 'less we want to get caught. We got to leave him and the horse and move on, quick as we can."

"But when they find him won't they think . . . we killed him?"

"We ain't fixin' to hang round, try to explain it to a bunch of pattyrollers. Quicker we get outta here the better. Any fool can read the signs, see what kilt him."

"What about our horse? Do we dare go on with him?"

"Wish we could, move faster that way, but he'd be hard to hide if need be. I'm gonna turn him loose, take off his saddle and bridle, leave 'em here, so he don't get hung up in brush on his way home."

"You think that's where he'll go?"

"Good chance he will. We ain't went that far. He knows the way, prob'ly make it 'fore mornin'. That'll help Joseph's boy find him."

Liz was holding back tears. "Lord, Hack, what'll we do now?"

"Onliest thing we can do, move on east."

"We don't even know what direction that is."

"Well, firs' we'll just follow this trail Joseph set us on. It's 'bout to stop rainin', now, maybe stars come out by 'n by. Then we'll find the Drinkin' Gourd and the Freedom Light."

"But . . . but we're supposed to head east, not north."

"We'll find north, then turn east from there, take any trail we come to in that d'rection."

Hack quickly relieved the horse of his tack, and dropped it on the ground, then patted his neck, slapped him on the rump and waved his arms. "Hyaah!" The big gelding headed back the way they'd come at a trot. "Come on," he said. "We got to make time before daylight."

Hack's hopeful prediction came true. The sky cleared, a cool breeze sprang up freshening the air, and the stars shone brightly. They heard the storm rumbling off toward the northeast. When they came to an intersection of paths in the forest, Hack chose the right fork and they hurried on.

As the sky began to brighten along the eastern horizon, Hack stopped and told Liz to wait while he scouted the area ahead of them and on both sides of the trail. He came back and drew her behind a huge tree while he explained his plan to her. "We've been leavin' tracks in the mud," he whispered. "We're gonna go to the top of this here hill where the path runs across a rocky place. When we get there you follow me, do what I do."

They continued to the outcrop which seemed to stretch a fair distance down the slope on the other side of the summit. Hack took only a few steps out onto the rocky surface, then turned right and carefully avoided leaving tracks as he stepped from rock to rock under the trees for a distance of several rods off the trail to lower ground. He waited for Liz to come even with him, then turned at right angles again and walked carefully in the direction from which they'd come, parallel to the trail. They were now at a distance of a few rods below the path in a grove of tall sturdy juniper trees.

Hack led her to two of the larger junipers in the middle of the grove. "You climb this tree and I'll go up the one right next to it. We'll be close enough to whisper to each other if need be. Climb high as you can, find a place to sit with your arms and legs 'round the trunk, 'cause we need to sleep. It'll be hard climbin', limbs close together. Cain't nobody see us up in there, but we'll be able to see out a little."

They spent the next several minutes climbing upward through the pungent juniper branches, each densely covered with dark green needles. Liz noticed her hands becoming sticky with sap. Just when she decided she'd climbed high enough there was a disturbance above her. A large bird silently took flight and glided downward toward the depths of the ravine below. As it flew she saw a dark object drop from its beak, something about the size of a mouse. *Owl pellet*, she thought. She remembered when her younger sister Prudence brought one of these home from a trek to their grandparents' cabin through the woods. Their mother had laid the pellet on a sheet of newspaper and picked it apart with a pair of small sticks, showing the children its contents of fur and small bones, undigestible parts of the mice and other small animals the owl had recently eaten.

Sitting in this tree in the middle of nowhere, Liz felt homesickness for a moment, cherishing the memory of her mother who used to take every opportunity to teach her babies the wonders

291

of the world around them. Liz even missed the quarrelsome sister she now feared she would never see again.

Then the sickening memory flashed across her mind of that wild shot into the darkness that had taken the life of her father. The news had filled her with fear for their safety, but why had she not felt remorse over his death, over killing another person, much less her own blood kin? It was true that she'd had little time to ponder that horrible turn of events, having to face one difficulty after another just to survive since then, but now it almost seemed as if that moment had never happened. Yes, her father had wantonly abused her, and her mother before her, but what sort of person must she be to so callously slough off the horror and guilt like some animal shedding its skin? She shook her head and winced, as if to put those self-loathing thoughts out of her head. Right now she had to help Hack save their lives. If they ever made it to safety, there would be time to sort out these feelings later.

Liz tried to make herself comfortable, finding a limb to sit on that enabled her to rest her arms and legs in a position to hold onto the trunk and relax, possibly even sleep. When she had settled herself she looked across to find Hack in the other tree. His presence was visible only in the movements of the branches as he stirred to situate himself. When the green boughs stopped moving, he parted them enough that she could see him. Just as he seemed about to speak to her, his face suddenly showed alarm and he pressed a finger to his lips and pointed back up toward the trail. He turned his head in that direction and cupped an ear to listen. She felt her body stiffen. Was someone approaching?

After a few seconds Liz heard it, too, a tiny tonking sound that seemed to be growing louder. For the next several moments she anxiously watched the short section of trail visible to her with such concentration that her eyes began to burn. From which direction was the sound approaching? Was someone or something following their tracks? That sound, was it made by a bell on the collar of a bloodhound? She envisioned a group of patrollers with the dog on a leash as it followed their trail. But why was the dog silent? Didn't dogs bay or howl when they were hot on the trail of their quarry? And why was the sound coming on so slowly?

Then they came into view, first a horned goat with a collar and a small bell, like a miniature cowbell, advancing slowly along the trail, moving in the opposite direction she and Hack had been traveling. If they had stayed on the trail just a few more minutes they would have run right into this odd menagerie. The first goat was followed by several others. They browsed as they went, crossing from one side of the trail to the other, feeding on weeds, grass and low branches along the path. There must have been fifteen or twenty of these animals of mixed colors, mainly brown, black and white, adults and kids, a whole herd moving along the trail. The scene was strangely biblical, the goats being followed by a single drover, a young boy carrying an honest-to-goodness shepherd's crook, dressed in simple clothes, barefoot, gazing up into the trees. He sauntered along, apparently with no purpose beyond following the goats wherever they led him.

Liz's heartbeat pounded in her empty stomach when the small shepherd dog that accompanied the boy suddenly paused and sniffed the ground at the point where Hack had led her off the trail. Then it followed its nose, moving along the exact route they had walked down to the juniper thicket. Just when Liz expected the dog to announce their hiding place the boy whistled. The dog, apparently not much of a hunter, stopped and looked back. The shepherd called and the dog trotted dutifully up to the trail toward its master. The motley entourage moved slowly on down the trail.

It took the procession several minutes to pass out of view. Afterward, Hack whispered from his perch, "The good Lord's smilin' on us today, Liz. Them goats are gonna mess up our tracks so bad not even a Indian'd be able to follow 'em."

The sun blazed its arc across the heavens as the two weary travelers rested in their perches. If other men or beasts used the trail during the day they were unaware of it, for they slept until light began to fade from the forest. They whispered to each other, ate some of the dry food they carried in their pockets and prepared to abandon their hiding places and forge onward toward Cincinnati.

# CHAPTER FIFTY-SEVEN

The first stop was at a stream where they slaked their powerful thirsts. They hadn't drunk since leaving Mr. Hertzel's shed, not thinking to take Joseph's canteen after he died. Thus refreshed they appraised their situation. Hack said, "We got the settin' sun at our backs, so we'll go on this direction till the stars come out. Pray God it'll be clear again tonight."

"You think we'll eventually get to Aurora? Wasn't that the place Joseph and Mr. Hertzel mentioned?"

"I got no idea where we're gonna come out. Maybe Aurora, maybe the river, maybe middle of nowhere. We got to ax somebody for help findin' our way."

"But who can we ask? Won't everyone know to be looking for us?" Liz said.

"Maybe not ever'body. We'll try to find black folks. They may not heard 'bout us. Anyways, they'd be more likely to help us."

"But we've only passed two cabins after Versailles, and we saw them before Joseph and his horse were killed. We might not find anyone, much less negroes."

"Now Liz, we go far enough, we're boun' to find somebody. Next time we see a cabin we'll look, see if they's any black folks there'bouts."

The pair walked all night, but saw no signs of human habitation. What they did see just before sunrise was a small tobacco patch. Hack said, "Somebody's been workin' that patch just yestiddy."

"How do you know that?"

"See them tops, like flowers? Half the patch got tops, other half ain't. Somebody been toppin' that 'baccer, didn't get done. More'n likely they'll be back to finish the job today. 'Baccer toppin' got to be done when it's time."

"So, we're going to wait till someone comes?"

"Zack'ly right. We're gonna climb this hill, hide in them big rocks and brush up there so's we can watch. 'Baccer's hard work, good chance niggers would be workin' this patch. Maybe we'll get lucky again."

Tired, dirty and hungry as she was, Hack's words struck fire in her brain. "Hack, please don't call your people that name. It has a bad meaning."

"Just a habit, Liz. It ain't bad for one negra to call another one nigger, not like a white man sayin' it."

She was following him up the hill toward the rocks, nearly out of breath. "It's a mean word . . . hurts my ears to hear it." He looked down at her for a long moment, but did not answer.

Morning light flattened and the July heat began to reassert itself, driving off the nighttime chill that had Liz and Hack huddling together to keep warm in their hiding place among the rocks and brambles on the hillside. Sunbeams arrowed through the canopy of trees, burning off the mist and drying the dew that had dampened their clothing. They welcomed the warmth on their backs, but it lulled them both toward sleep.

They had waited less than an hour when Liz roused herself and looked down at the small patch. At first she saw nothing, but her heartbeat quickened as she saw a couple of the tobacco plants move. This was followed by a hand and an arm clad in a long-sleeved shirt reaching up and snapping the top off one of the plants. She gently squeezed Hack's shoulder. He jerked, casting a dazed look at her before he came fully awake. She pointed down at the tobacco patch. "Must be a child," she whispered.

Hack watched intently for a moment, rubbing his sleep-drugged eyes, following the movements as they progressed slowly between two rows of plants, the hand reaching up to snap tops off plants in adjacent rows. "Could be a young boy," he said. "Cain't tell if his hand's white or black, can you?"

"Wait till he comes out the end of the row."

The minutes passed slowly as the child worked the length of the patch, snapping off the flowering tops and apparently dropping them on the ground. "Why's he breaking the tops off?" Liz said.

"So the plant'll fill out, make bigger leaves, not seed. It's the leaves that make good chewin' an smokin' 'baccer after they dry."

The small figure in the patch finally came to the end of the row where the tired and begrimed pair could see a child's close-cropped black hair and a shiny black forehead. Then the boy disappeared between two more rows and began working his way toward the near end of the patch.

"I'm goin'," Hack said.

"Shall I come, too?"

"If he sees us together, he'll be sure to make trouble. Just stay up here outta sight, maybe say a prayer."

Looking both ways, Hack left the cover of rocks and brush and scrambled down the hill toward the patch. He crossed the trail, dropped to his hands and knees and crawled between two rows at the end of the patch near where the boy would soon appear.

"Mornin', boy. Workin' hard, ain't you?" Hack stood up, to be in full view when the youngster came out the end of the row, hoping not to frighten him.

When Hack spoke the lad was only a few feet from the end of his row. All movement of the plants stopped and the small sounds of the boy's work: clothing brushing against leaves, tops snapping off, muted footsteps on loose soil, fell silent. The unseen child seemed to freeze, as if deciding whether to run or move forward to show himself to this man with the strange voice. "Ain't meanin' to scare you, son. Just gabble a minute 'fore I move on."

"You need to see my daddy? He up at the cabin."

"Y'all's cabin be near 'bouts?"

The boy emerged slowly from the row, large eyes looking with curiosity and apprehension at this muddy, haggard black stranger. Then he gazed beyond Hack's shoulder. "He comin' yonder."

Hack turned to see a tall black man approaching from around a bend in the trail. He wore a floppy hat, white collarless shirt under an unbuttoned coat. His boots were muddy and he carried a rifle in the crook of his arm. His hands looked as big as shovels. Hack turned to face the boy's father, raising his hand in a casual wave.

"Howdy, suh. Got you a fine boy, here."

"What you want?"

"Well, suh, I need a little help. I been ridin' to Cincinnati from Mr. Hertzel's place back in Versailles."

The man regarded Hack with a suspicious eye. "Don't look to me like you ridin'."

"Yassuh. Storm caught me night a'fore last, lightnin' kilt the horse, 'bout got me, too. Now I'm plumb lost."

"You a runaway slave?"

"Nassuh, I'm free, but I'm still 'fraid of bein' catched by the pattyrollers."

"What you mean, black man runnin' through the woods all by hisself? Some kind of daredevil, out here crossin' hell on a rotten log?"

"White man, Mr. Munford, he was with me, but lightnin' got him, too, suh."

"You be one lyin' nigger!"

Hack's eyes widened and he spoke urgently, showing his fear. "I done told you the truth, suh. My name's Hack, and I sure need to get to Cincinnati."

"Why you so hell-bent for Cincinnati? Who you wantin' to see up there?"

Hack hesitated a moment, then took a deep breath, looked the man in the eye and said, "Mr. Levi Coffin, suh."

The man reflexively looked around as if to see whether anyone else had heard or seen them talking. He said, "C'mon, Jamie, we goin' to the cabin. You, too . . . what's your name . . . Hack. Lucky you ain't been shot 'fore now. They's a bunch of pattyrollers stomped right up in my cabin yestiddy, like to tore up the place."

That stopped Hack in his tracks. "They say who they was lookin' for?"

"All they say is get yo black asses out in the yard. If you hidin' runaways y'all be dead meat."

"Y'all must be free blacks, then?"

"Folks calls me Kopp. Took the name Freeman when my massa give me my papers down in Kaintuck, but I ain't free."

"Don't understand. How'd you keep them pattyrollers off of you?

"Oh, I's a free black, right enough, but I got a woman at home, so I never be free in this life." Hack searched the man's face for a trace of humor, but saw only a tiny glint in his eye before he turned and said, "Step quick, got to get you outta sight 'fore we all end up hangin' off a white oak limb." Kopp Freeman turned on his heel with his hand on Jamie's back, headed for the cabin at a brisk walk.

"Uh . . . wait, suh."

Kopp whirled to look incredulously at Hack. "C'mon! What the hell you waitin' for?"

Hack looked up the hill to where Liz lay in hiding. Then he turned back to the tall man. "If you think I lied 'bout Mr. Munford, you ain't heard nothin' yet."

# CHAPTER FIFTY-EIGHT

ack told Kopp he had a white woman with him, then called Liz down the hill. The two of them spluttered like lunatics trying to clarify their situation in ten seconds to the dour Kopp Freeman. He seemed at a loss for words, but his angry eyes bored into one of them, then the other, apparently unable to comprehend their message other than the obvious, that they were a biracial pair fleeing from trouble. At length he merely shook his head, put his hand on the boy's shoulder and started walking toward the cabin, motioning the others with a jerk of his head. Hack and Liz looked at each other, then followed. On the way Hack whispered to Liz about patrollers harassing the Freemans yesterday. Liz asked Hack if the men chasing them could have passed them while they slept in the juniper trees.

The cabin was a short walk from the tobacco patch, around a bend in the trail. The front door looked as if it had been kicked in, showing splintered wood near the latch. The cabin sat back from the trail under the trees near the forest's edge. Liz saw a shed made of poles, a pigpen, a small log barn, and chickens scratching around the buildings. As they came closer she heard and smelled the hogs. Looking between the cabin and barn, she could see a patch of corn in the distance. The leaves were still green, indicating harvest was still two or three months away. Behind the cabin she spied the corner of a crude fence, probably built to protect a kitchen garden.

Inside, they met Kopp's wife, Daisy. She had two children in the kitchen, younger than Jamie, a girl and another boy. Kopp closed

299

the door, propped it shut with a stick of firewood, then made the briefest of introductions to Daisy. "These two be in big-ass trouble, an' not just 'cause they black and white."

Daisy greeted them, then rearranged some of her sparse furniture and offered the visitors seats. A broken chair lay in the corner. In contrast to the abruptness of her husband, Daisy Freeman made them feel at home, an accomplishment Liz thought remarkable after the apparent rough night the family had endured. "Look like you two been drug through a hog waller," she said. "You mus' be them the pattyrollers was lookin' for. Lucky you didn't show up yestiddy. Look like you might could use a bite of breakfast, you reckon?" Liz saw that Daisy had one of those faces that seemed always to be smiling. The redolence of real food in her kitchen nearly made Liz swoon with hunger.

"Thank you, Daisy. Let me help," Liz said.

The woman turned toward the bedraggled pair with her hands on her ample hips. "You two ain't settin' at *my* table lookin' like that." She winked at Liz. "Firs' thing you need's a bath. The onliest touch of fancy we got 'round here is the bath house. Kopp'll show you. Both y'all go with him. You take yours first, Liz. Then we talk some while Hack scrub down. Kopp look an' talk like he weaned on a pickle, but he got a heart of gold." Liz looked briefly at Hack. He nodded, indicating they should go with Kopp.

Without a word, Kopp led them out to another shed Liz hadn't seen in her first view of the farmstead. Inside she saw a pipe that fed water from a spring on the hillside into a huge iron kettle, a larger version of the ones she'd seen used to cook apple butter in autumn and to scald hogs at butchering time. The flow of spring water could be diverted when it wasn't needed in the cauldron. A firebox under the kettle warmed the water. When they entered the shed the fire had died to a bed of coals but the water steamed. A crude stove pipe and chimney arrangement vented the smoke from the firebox. Steam collected under the roof and condensed, making the air inside the shed warm and humid, a homemade sauna. "My goodness! Do you keep this water hot all the time?" Liz said.

"Nah, I fired it up last night so's Daisy'd have hot water for the clothes washin'. Today be Monday, you know. I reckon if the pattyrollers would of saw this, they'd of wrecked it, too. Some a-them outlaws had enough liquor in 'em to swim a skunk."

Liz looked down at her grimy clothes and said, "I hate to take a bath and then put these dirty rags back on."

"Daisy'll wash y'all's clothes. When we leave take yours off and get in the kettle. Hack'll come get 'em, bring you some of Daisy's duds till she get yours washed and dried. I'll do the same for Hack later. Liz was beginning to see that Daisy was right about Kopp's heart of gold.

In spite of his exhaustion from the trail and lack of sleep, Hack was suddenly full of questions for Kopp about the construction of the bath house, the likes of which he'd never seen. Kopp said, "Look, we ain't got all day. We ain't had breakfast, neither. Wash up and come in the cabin. You can ax them questions while we eat. I got a passel of questions for y'all, too."

"Mr. Kopp," Liz said. "Hack and I have this sticky juniper sap all over our hands and clothes. Do you have anything we could use to get it off?" She held up her hands for him to see the dark areas where the tackiness had collected dirt and debris.

He thought a moment. "Might use the same stuff my brother mixed up to get 'baccer tar off'n our hands. I bring y'all a little bottle of it, but don't let Hack be drinkin' it, you hear?" Liz grinned and looked at Kopp expecting a smile, but as Hack had seen before, Kopp's face did not betray a hint of levity.

Kopp and Hack left while Liz undressed and got into the warm water with a bar of lye soap she found on a bench near the kettle. She basked in the luxury of the bath, soaking until Daisy knocked and brought in the clean clothing and the bottle of solvent. "You taller than me, look funny wearin' my clothes. Them young'uns better not be laughin' at you."

"I don't care about that," she said.

"Y'all needs to wash quick. We needs to eat, got other things to do."

"Give me five minutes, but oh, this water feels sooo good!"

"You's earned a smidgin of comfort with all this craziness you been through."

She took the bottle Daisy offered, waiting until she left before she raised up and poured some of the aromatic liquid over her hands

301

so the excess would drip outside the tub. She found it effective in cleaning the mess off her hands. She corked the bottle and set it down carefully on the bench, then resumed her bath, reveling in her clean hands and body as her heart filled with gratitude toward Providence and the Freemans.

Later, after Hack washed quickly, they wolfed down the best breakfast Liz thought she'd ever tasted. Her shrunken stomach reminded her she couldn't eat as fast or as much as she wanted. Questions and answers tumbled over each other around the table. Hack and Liz described for the Freemans their journey from Lamb to Moorefield to Versailles to the Freemans' tobacco patch. They skirted the issue of the gunshot. Liz explained why she had insisted on helping Hack, but afterward she thought Daisy, and especially Kopp, suspected there was more to it than just helping fugitives. A young white woman and black man doing anything together out in the woods in these times was beyond forbidden. People had been murdered for less.

A half-hour later Kopp rose from the table. "Daisy'll do the washin' while I slip on over to Keever's place. He my brother, and he been known to lead a few runaways on into Cincinnati. You be able to make it in one night easy, 'cause you's already in Ohio."

"Ohio! Lord, we didn't know where we was at," Hack said.

"State line ain't but a few mile back the way you come," Kopp said. "I been layin' off to whitewash a streak through the woods, put up a sign, 'Buckeye State'. Make it easy for greenhorns like y'all."

The visitors grinned, but got the usual lack of response from their host. "We mus' be close to the river, then," Hack said.

" 'Bout three-quarter mile down the holler," Daisy said.

"Your brother know where Levi Coffin lives?" Hack asked.

"Nah, but he take y'all to a white man what knows him."

"I done laid down two pallets, one in the back room, the other in our bedroom," Daisy said. "You go rest, now, so you be ready to travel tonight. Now, you chillen be quiet, you hear."

Daisy woke them before dark. She said Kee had arrived to conduct them to Cincinnati. "We walkin' or ridin'?" Hack said as he sat up and rubbed his eyes.

302

Kopp leaned over Daisy's shoulder, scowled at Hack and said, "Walkin'. Kee a dirt farmer like me, don't have hosses nor wagons he can afford to lose if he get caught heppin' you, so y'all be walkin'. It ain't like you wadn't walkin' when I firs' seen you."

Kee appeared to be a few years younger than Kopp, and his personality seemed more like Daisy's than his brother's. "We get you two to Cincinnati 'fore daylight if'n we don't run into no trouble," he said. Then, unable to control his curiosity any longer, he said, "How come you to be travelin' with this here black man, miss?"

Liz glanced at Daisy, who said, "Hack needed hep to save a black family with two little girls. They done it, too, left that family safe with some white people. Now, don't need to say no more. Just make sure they gets to Cincinnati in good shape."

"I'm fixin' to do that, sister, slick as a whistle," Kee said. He grinned and nodded at Liz and Hack, who stood there ready to leave in their clean and almost-dry clothes.

The party left after Liz and Hack expressed their thank-yous and said their goodbyes. Then Kee led them out onto the woodland trail to Cincinnati. They walked steadily from dark until two hours before daylight. Toward the end of their trek they began to pass more dwellings, and the trail became a road, then a brick-paved street. At one point they topped a hill and looked down to see the lights of a wharfboat at the riverfront. A big sidewheeler was churning water, casting off headed downriver.

Kee led them around to the back entrance of a two-story house on a quiet residential street. A sleepy black maid finally came to the door and let them inside the kitchen to wait until she roused the master of the house, Mr. Thomson. After introductions they expressed their gratitude to Keever, and he disappeared into the gloomy night. Mr. Thomson and the maid took them to a small back room with two narrow beds and an adjacent water closet. "I'm sure you're both exhausted. You can rest here a few hours until we make arrangements with Mr. Coffin. We'll move you over there after he gets home from his store this evening. Tilly will prepare some food for you directly. Let her know if you need anything else." He turned with a benevolent expression to the small somber-eyed black woman. "Tilley's been with us seventeen years. She has her own story of escaping slavery." He nodded to the two fugitives and left.

# CHAPTER FIFTY-NINE

After Tilley gave them a light breakfast and made them comfortable in their room, she returned to her other duties in the house. Nothing was said about separate rooms for the pair. Had Mr. Thomson and Tilley assumed Liz and Hack were married?

While Liz washed up before bed, Hack looked out the window into Mr. Thomson's back yard. There was a back door near their room, and the yard, so shaded, cool and inviting, was enclosed by a tall fence. Still, he dared not venture from the house with Liz for fear the wrong people might be watching.

When Liz came into the bedroom drying her hair, barefoot and dressed in just her trousers and untucked shirt, she said she'd left things in order for Hack. "Why don't you clean up, too?"

He gave her a quizzical look. "Why? We done took baths at the Freemans' place yesterday."

"Well . . . I thought we ought to take advantage now that we've got the chance. We don't know when the opportunity will come again, so to speak." She knew he saw the smirk she couldn't hide.

"You're makin' a city slicker outta me, woman," he said, grinning. He took a towel from his bed and went into the water closet.

When she could tell by the sounds he had finished washing, she tapped on the door. "Just a minute, he said." She pushed the door open anyway, and found him clothed except for buttoning his shirt.

She stepped close and gave him a quick kiss on the lips. "Here, let me do that." He looked at her as she put her hands on his shirt, but she loosened the buttons he'd already fastened. She opened the shirt revealing his muscular torso, then turned her face up to him. "Your skin is so *black*," she whispered, bringing her arm up by his side for comparison, placing her fingers on him, as if in wonder. She felt gooseflesh forming on his abdomen.

"You know what you're gettin' us into?" he said. He put his hands on her hips and she saw a different look come into his dark eyes.

"It's about time, don't you think?"

"I'm crazy 'bout you, gal, and I want to do this as much as you do. You surely seen me lookin' at you that way ever since the night in the foalin' stall. But if we start showin' out, people gonna see how things is between us."

"Would that be any different from what they think they see now?"

"Look, I give in to you, then you get tired of this black fool, what you think's gonna happen to me? It ain't like you jerkin' a white boy 'round. Nobody's gonna lose blood over that. But a white girl and a negro hookin' up, it ain't no kid's game. All you got to do is let on that I done you wrong and I'm on the end of a white man's lynchin' rope. Even in good times, the wrong white man sees you'n me together he'd up and shoot me just for the hell of it.

"Now, I done showed you and told you, what I feel for you is way too strong for you to tease me like this if there ain't no feelin' in your heart behind it. I'm tellin' you if you draw me into this I'm in for the long pull. It'll never be easy, but there ain't gonna be no backin' out, not for me, not for you. Now, if you ain't ready for that, you better say so right now."

Liz locked eyes with him. "I can't express my feelings any better than this." She took his hand in hers and kissed his palm. Then she moved closer, put her arms around his neck, reached up and kissed him on the mouth. He accepted her kiss, but did not take her in his arms.

"Wait, Liz," he whispered. He placed his hands on her shoulders and moved her back. "Not that way. I got to hear you say it first."

She took his face in her hands, looked into his eyes. "I'm in this with you Hack. It's not a joke, it's real what I feel for you. If we get out of this mess I'll happily stay with you for the rest of my life, in Canada or wherever. I love you, Hack." She gave him a long slow kiss then, and he picked her up and gently laid her on the bed.

For a seductive moment they looked into each other's eyes, holding hands, breathing deeply, before their bodies came together, caressing, fondling, kissing, undressing. The last barriers to intimacy between them were swept away. After days and weeks of hesitation, each not knowing the depth of the other's feelings, they slowly unveiled the mysteries, found answers to questions they'd feared to voice. They sensed each other's surrender at last to shared intimacy, commitment to each other.

Blissful moments passed, their passion rising. As they continued to kiss Liz slid her hand over his body, down to his navel and the trail of hair below.

She desired him, needed to touch him with her mouth. She kissed him, then her lips left his and moved downward, kissing his neck, his chest with its short curly hair. His flat torso had been so desirable to her, even before she saw it unclothed, tempting yet untouchable, now a delight no longer forbidden. She roamed with her mouth across his abdomen, his hip, down his muscled thigh. She felt him against her cheek. She paused, looked up at him. "Would you . . . ?"

He groaned. A small movement revealed his answer. Inexperienced in making love to a man, she nibbled at him with lips and tongue, as she had once seen the mare do with her foal. He gasped and lay very still.

Just then they heard quiet footsteps near their door. Another door eased open nearby and there came muffled sounds of someone flapping sheets, patting pillows, making a bed, but trying to do it quietly. They froze. Was Tilley's room next to theirs?

Liz slid upward and whispered into Hack's ear, "She thinks we're asleep."

"Reckon we oughta tell her we ain't," he said, "an' she can make all the noise she wants, won't bother us none?" They worked so hard keeping their laughter quiet that their teeth clicked together before Liz clapped her hands over both their mouths.

It took a moment for them to control their breathing. "Now, what?" Liz whispered. She soundlessly moved to lie on top of him, holding his face in her hands, giving him tiny kisses on his forehead, eyes, nose, lips.

From the maid's room came sounds of the small woman lying down on her bed, then sighs as she seemed to settle in for a nap. She talked quietly to herself, or maybe it was prayer, but the lovers could not make out her words.

They held each other in a warm embrace, their bodies in full contact on the bed. Then Hack quietly rolled her over to lie beside him. He whispered in her ear, "We cain't move but what she'll hear us. You got to stop teasin' me now."

"Who's teasing?" she said. "I'm going to stay right here and sleep with you."

"After all this, you better!" he said. "You leave me layin' here alone, you're gonna hear a grown man's heart break." This time it was Hack who had to stifle Liz's laughter.

"Does that mean your hard heart is softening a bit toward me?"

"You blind and deaf?" His voice was becoming too loud, and she put a forefinger against his lips. "You done turned my innards to mush a long time ago. But it ain't easy bein' with you, knowin' a nig . . . black man's got no bidness slobberin' over a hot little white gal."

"You didn't seem to mind me slobbering over you just now."

He gazed into the distance a moment to control his response before speaking again. "Woman, just you wait," he whispered. "Next time, you're gonna be in big trouble."

# CHAPTER SIXTY

That evening after dark, Mr. Thomson escorted Hack and Liz a few blocks to the home of Levi and Catherine Coffin, the great Quaker abolitionists. After having survived the hazards of overland trails and poor roads for what seemed like days on end, they now glided over brick-paved streets in a well-sprung buggy with drawn side curtains. The street's surface shone under the street lamps in the misting rain. The clip-clop of the gelding's hooves added to Liz's sense of security as she and Hack held hands in the back seat watching lighted windows glide by in the night.

Liz's thoughts returned to her romantic interlude with Hack that morning. For the first time she had told him she loved him. Now she was puzzled, not by what she'd said, for those words had expressed her true feelings for Hack. But she found it mystifying that she could feel such deep emotion for *any* man after what her father had attempted with her when she was thirteen.

For years after she had fled Sam's house to live with her Morrison grandparents she'd felt no romantic interest, much less sexual fantasies, involving the boys and young men who occasionally flirted with her or tried to court her at Sugar Branch.

Hack, of course, was much different from the other men she knew. Did she somehow feel he, a negro man in a predominantly white world, would be less threatening than a white man, easier for her to trust . . . or to manipulate?

She hoped her attraction to him arose strictly from his qualities as a man, regardless of his skin color or social standing. She knew he was probably seven or eight years her senior, and that his experiences in leading many of his black brethren to freedom had matured him, imbued him with bravery and wisdom she'd never known in a young man before.

She'd have to study on this. Her emotional feelings for Hack were strong, but she must understand her commitment to him. She must be sure her heart wasn't just leading her into a flight of fancy that would lose its charm later in the clear light of reason. That would be an injustice to herself and to Hack. She tried to remember her mother's council on the subject of men.

By 1847 the Coffins had moved to Cincinnati from Newport, Indiana. They owned a home that was also widely known as a waystation on the Underground Railroad. Levi became the proprietor of a store that sold only goods made by non-slave labor. Someone had given Levi the name "President of the Underground Railroad." The Coffins assisted thousands of fugitive slaves on their journeys to Canada from both the Indiana and the Ohio locations.

Sensing that full disclosure to this important man was their best hope, Liz and Hack did not hesitate to tell their tale of being pursued through the forest and of Liz's firing the shotgun into the darkness. When they'd finished, Levi reached to his cluttered desk, then turned back to the pair and handed Liz a newspaper clipping from a recent issue of *The Cincinnati Enquirer*. She read the story aloud to Hack. It gave sparse, and sometimes incorrect, details of their confrontation with the bounty hunters in the woods of Switzerland County, some sixty or seventy miles to the southwest of Cincinnati, and the death of Samuel Cunningham. Near the end of the article, Liz lost her voice and her heartbeat surged as she silently read the next line. Hack looked up at her just as she formed words.

"Hack, was your name on that shotgun?"

He looked away for a moment, thinking. Then he spoke slowly, though the look on his black face needed no words. "When my old pap give me that piece he axed his white friend to cut our letters into the stock, on the belly side. Them pattyrollers find the gun?"

"I was so frightened after I shot that I must have dropped it," Liz said, "or it slipped from my hands as I fell. It says here they found the gun and know who the murderer is, though the article doesn't mention names other than my father's. Oh, I'm so sorry, Hack. They'll think it was you who fired at them."

Hack said, "Makes no diff'rence now. If I'd a'been holdin' the gun I'd of did the same thing. They know by now you was with me, seein' you ain't at your grandpa's place no more. They'll be after both of us, anyways."

Levi Coffin broke the tense silence. "Liz, is thee sure these men were intent on capturing the two of you and the fugitive negroes? They were not just out to frighten you, chasing a different group, or for some other purpose?"

"I heard the voice loud and clear, Mr. Coffin," Liz said. "It might have been my father's voice, but I don't think so. The voice seemed distorted . . . and I was so frightened. He shouted Hack's name to the others, where we were probably headed, and that they'd make good money catching us," Liz said.

"Were there witnesses, other than the two of you and the family you were escorting?"

Liz thought a moment. "No, sir. We were in the woods. The only witnesses I know of were our group trying to escape and the others trying to capture us."

"Liz, we all know that negroes are not permitted to testify in a court of law involving white people, so in a trial thee is saying it would be thy word against that of the pursuers?"

"As far as I know, yes, sir."

"And there in the woods, thee said thee *heard* that the pursuers were nearly upon you. Was there enough light from the moon, stars, torches or whatever, for thee to actually *see* the horses or men coming up behind thy party? In other words, could thee see what thee was shooting at, young lady?"

"No, sir, I didn't even try to see. I just swung the gun around behind me and fired. I probably even closed my eyes."

"Please forgive me if I seem impertinent, Miss Liz, but why, then did thee shoot if thee couldn't see in the darkness?"

Liz thought a moment. "I was desperate, Mr. Coffin. The shotgun was the only thing at my disposal to surprise them, frighten them, make them stop. At least that's what I hoped."

Levi leaned back with his elbows on the arms of his oak swivel chair. He stroked his chin and gazed across the room for a long

311

moment. "The killing of this man, then, seems to be a case somewhere between an accident and an act of self-defense. I certainly cannot advise you to surrender to the authorities, for the application of justice in such cases here in this border country can too often be elusive, unpredictable or, at worst, malicious. Thee and Hack would be at the mercy of the prosecutor, the judge and the jurors, all of whom might be more swayed by political beliefs and prejudice than by their interest in obtaining a fair judgement. And it could be worse. If you, a mixed race couple having killed a white man, were to be captured by the wrong people, the case might never reach the judicial system, if thee takes my meaning."

Liz swallowed before she could speak. "Ye . . . yes, sir, but we're not actually a *couple,* Mr. Coffin. We're friends who were working together."

Liz was struck by what she'd just said. *Have I just lied to this man?* she thought. She quickly decided she had not. Thanks to Tilley, she and Hack hadn't actually consummated their relationship, and they weren't married, so she had told Mr. Coffin the truth.

The old Quaker chuckled and shook his head. He looked at her with a sad smile. "I think thee would have trouble convincing almost anyone but me," he said. "I applaud your bravery and your high-mindedness, but you surely knew the danger involved in that when you started."

Levi rose from his chair and paced back and forth across the room, regarding the pair thoughtfully before he spoke. "Miss Cunningham, Mr. Hackney, allow me to provide a bit more information in view of what you might consider my loose regard for the law in your case." Liz and Hack remained quiet, only nodding as they gazed at him expectantly.

"Catherine and I moved to Newport, Indiana, from North Carolina in 1826, shortly after we were married. We soon learned that many fugitive slaves passed through that community on the Underground Railroad, and generally stopped among the free colored people there. We saw that these runaways were often pursued and captured, the free coloreds not being skillful in protecting them or in arranging their continuing journey to Canada.

"I was pained to hear of the capture of these people, and asked some of the white Quakers, or Friends, in our village why they didn't

312

help these unfortunate travelers. I found they were afraid of the penalty of the various federal and state laws.

"When I was a boy, I told them, I read in the Bible that it was right to take in the stranger and administer to those in distress, and that I thought it was always safe to do the right thing. The Bible, in bidding us to feed the hungry and clothe the naked, said nothing about color, and I said I would try to follow out the teachings of that good book.

"Our house soon became known to the colored people in our village and others as a depot where the hunted and harassed fugitive journeying northward on the Underground Railroad could find succor and sympathy. Thus, in the winter of 1826-27, fugitives began to come to our house as a waystation on their journey to Canada. They kept coming, and eventually numbered in the thousands."

"We thank you, Mr. Coffin, for taking us in," Liz said, "but we've put you in harm's way by harboring us after I've killed someone."

"Ah, yes, I'm coming to that, young lady." He paused a moment, as if getting his thoughts in line. "One time an old Quaker came to see me. He said he was as much opposed to slavery as I was, but thought it wrong to harbor fugitive slaves. No one knew, he said, of what crimes they were guilty. They might have killed their masters or committed some other atrocious deed. Then those who sheltered them and aided them in their escape from justice would indirectly be accomplices.

"I heard him patiently, and then asked if he thought the Good Samaritan stopped to inquire whether the man who fell among thieves was guilty of any crime before he attempted to help him? I asked him if he were to see a stranger who had fallen into a ditch would he not help him out until satisfied that he had committed no atrocious deed?"

"I see what you mean, suh," Hack said. "God bless you for takin' us in."

"What else could I do as a Christian? It's not at all clear to me that in those circumstances on the trail you committed a crime. You are not fugitive slaves, but we are even closer because of what you've done in helping that family of runaways. Regardless of the

313

ambiguous legality of the action you took to save yourselves, you succeeded in rescuing a whole family of fugitive slaves. By that deed you and I have become as brothers and sisters. In view of the current state of the local judicial system and considering your selfless act I have resolved to do my best to ensure your success on the northward journey.

"Now, my wife has made a meal ready for us, and afterward we'll see about making preparations for your trip."

# CHAPTER SIXTY-ONE

Their dinner in the kitchen of the Coffins' house was interrupted by a loud banging on the front door. Levi motioned to Catherine, and she lost no time whisking the two fugitives up the back stairs. He waited until the sounds of their hasty departure had quieted, then went to the door and opened it. He found four men facing him. One of them, apparently the oldest, wore a badge. Holstered pistols hung at their belts, and they had the unkempt appearance and odor of men who had spent several days in the woods.

Levi spoke calmly, as if he were greeting friends. "Good evening, neighbors, how may I help you?"

"You Levi Coffin?" the one with the badge said.

"I am, indeed. To whom am I speaking, my friend?"

"I'm Wright Rae, from Madison, Indiana, Sheriff of Jefferson County. These here's Dewey Sexton, Homer Miller and Cyrus Stenigal, friends and kinfolk of Sam Cunningham of Sugar Branch, Indiana. He was kilt five nights ago. We hear'd you're hidin' them that done it, a damned nigger and his white trull. We aim to take 'em back to Indiana on charges of murder and harboring runaway slaves. They're fugitives from the law and we'll thank you to hand 'em over to us right now."

Levi had heard of Robert Wright Rea. The man had built a reputation for himself in southern Indiana as an iron-fisted lawman and notorious slavecatcher. He was constantly at cross purposes with Stephen Stevens, a Madison judge, who defended fugitive slaves and free blacks when their cases came up in court, after they had been kidnapped by their Kentucky owners or bounty hunters, then rescued while still in Indiana.

One of Rea's ruses was to apprehend runaway slaves by telling them he would arrange their safe passage to Canada. After locking the slaves in his jail, he would scan newspapers for a few days. If he saw the fugitives advertised by their owners, he would return them south for the reward.

He fulfilled his duties as sheriff, and also acted as a free-lance enforcer of the Fugitive Slave Law that had been enacted in 1850. He had no qualms about plying his two occupations wherever opportunity led him. Thus, he came pounding on Levi Coffin's door in Cincinnati, far from his lawful jurisdiction in Indiana.

The man had been known by several different names from his birth near Lancaster, Pennsylvania, to his mature age in Madison, Indiana. In his younger years Robert had been "Robin." Wright was sometimes construed as "Right," and Rea occasionally appeared as "Ray." By whatever name, he was a man feared by fugitive slaves and conductors alike in Border Country.

Wright Rea came by his pro-slavery persuasion honestly, having spent his childhood and formative years in Mecklenburg County, North Carolina. He and his wife, Nancy Patton, moved from North Carolina to Ripley County, Indiana, the year his widowed mother died. Later the census listed him as living in Jefferson County, Indiana, employed as a farmer and wheelwright. He was "home educated," literate, and as an adult served as a Presbyterian elder for fifty years. At some point his pro-slavery neighbors thought highly enough of his character and his hard-boiled attitude toward fugitive slaves to elect him sheriff.

Having listened to Sheriff Wright Rea's demand at his front door, Levi Coffin replied, "That will be impossible, Wright. We are not harboring, nor have I seen any such individuals as thee describes. I fear you men are wasting your time."

"Don't give us that, Coffin. We know you make it your business to break the law by helpin' runaway slaves and criminals escape to Canada. Now, you turn them outlaws over to us, or we're comin' in after 'em." Rae hooked the thumb of his right hand in his belt near his pistol.

316

"Then I shall have to summon Uriah Nelson, the constable. He and his men are good friends of mine, and they take a dim view of anyone who goes about disturbing the peace in our neighborhood. Also, several of my neighbors within earshot of where we now stand would spring to our aid should I but sound the alarm, for they view slavery to be an abomination, as I do."

Rea was not dissuaded. "In case you ain't hear'd of it, they's a federal law called the Fugitive Slave Act that says it's again' the law to harbor this nigger, free or slave, not to mention him and his white whore has committed murder."

Levi drew himself up to his full height and addressed the man. "And in case thee did not hear what I said, I have not seen the individuals thee described. Furthermore, the four of you are trespassing on my property, and are therefore in violation of Ohio law. I've just heard my wife going out the back door to bring the constable's deputy to our aid in this matter. He lives but a few steps away; our backyards join. If thee would like, I'll wait here with thee to make the proper introductions."

The vigilantes were clearly flummoxed. Sheriff Rae, who had done all the talking, turned and mumbled to the others. After a moment the leader said, "All right, Coffin, we're leavin' this time, but this ain't over by a damn sight. We know what you're up to and you can bet we'll be watchin' you."

Levi went back inside, locked the front door, then climbed the stairs where his wife soon joined them with their neighbor, Josiah Davis, the deputy constable. On their way back to the Coffin house, Catherine and Josiah had seen the four rough men leaving, but Josiah came upstairs with her to make sure there was no further problem.

After Levi greeted Josiah and introduced him to Liz and Hack, Catherine said, "Levi, has thee borne false witness? I distinctly heard thee tell those men that thee had not seen these two young people."

Levi's face lit up with an impish countenance. "Now, Kate, thee knows I never lie. I merely stated the truth that I have not seen a 'damned nigger' or a 'white trull,' hereabouts, and I daresay thee has not seen any such persons, either."

"Mr. Coffin," Liz said. "I'm sure the voice of the man at the door just now is the one I heard in the woods the night we escaped from the slavecatchers. That sound still makes me shiver."

317

Levi took her hand and patted it. "Try to rest easy, girl. We sympathize with thee over the tragedy of thy father, and thy fear of these men, but ruffians such as Wright Rae have appeared at our door before, and we haven't lost a traveler yet."

For the next several days their presence in the house was known only to Levi, Catherine and Josiah Davis, in addition to their two negro maidservants. The Coffins placed the pair of fugitives in separate garret chambers of their house and allowed little traffic in or out, except for delivery of meals and other necessities to the fugitives. Levi had stern words for the two young people before he left them that first night.

"We support justice and right dealing with all colors of people, but we're not in favor of amalgamation and do not encourage intermarriage or mixing of the races. With that in mind, we shall not condone any sort of romantic situation between the two of you while under our roof. We expect you both to conduct yourselves accordingly." Liz and Hack assured Mr. Coffin that their conduct would be exemplary in that regard.

Finding themselves foiled, the bounty hunters had handbills printed, stating the alleged crimes committed by the fugitives and offering a reward for their delivery to the vigilantes. They apparently assumed that if they captured and turned in the supposed culprits to the Indiana authorities, they would stand to collect a reward large enough to recoup their expenses several times over.

The sheriff and his men distributed the handbills among the police and scattered more copies about the city. Many of the policemen knew the Coffins and were sympathetic to the anti-slavery cause. Thus, one of the bills came into Levi's hands.

The vigilantes' search continued for several days, but the Coffins and Josiah Davis kept a close watch. From small windows in their rooms the two fugitives could see their pursuers passing up and down the street in front of the house. Often one or more of their company passed by late at night, as if reconnoitering, but no further attempt was made to search the premises. Finally the hunt seemed to be over and the Coffins decided it was time to send the pair on to Canada.

The two travelers, when they had embarked on their errand of mercy from Sugar Branch, had not expected this drastic extension of their journey all the way to Canada. They had not brought provisions, clothing or money enough for such an undertaking. Consequently, during the several days that Liz and Hack were secreted in the Coffins' house, the ladies of the Anti-Slavery Sewing Society in Cincinnati provided them with changes of clothing. Aunt Katie Coffin prepared extra food of the kinds that would travel well for their long trip in case conductors or other people sympathetic to their plight could not provide resources at needful times.

Money would be required to hire a carriage to take them away, and for other expenses along the route. Levi appointed himself to collect it. He approached the proprietor of a store where he was slightly acquainted, and asked the man, "Has thee any stock in the Underground Railroad?"

After inquiring if that was the one on which runaway slaves were sent to Canada, he replied, "I believe I have a little stock in it."

Levi then told the proprietor there was an assessment on the stock and that he was authorized to collect it. He said, "Mine is a dollar. I suppose thine will be the same." He received the dollar, then went on to several other merchants in the neighborhood, making "assessments" on the "stock" in the clandestine network.

From some of the men he received a dollar, from others a half-dollar, but all contributed, even one merchant who put up an objection before Levi said, "I want thee to take stock to help us clothe and forward these people. I know thee would feel better to contribute to their relief. Now, if thee is not disposed to do so, it is thy look-out, not mine."

The reluctant proprietor hesitated, then approached Levi a few minutes later, saying, "I will give you a trifle if you want something."

He said, "I want nothing, but if it is thy desire to contribute I will see that it is rightly applied."

The man then handed Levi a silver half-dollar. He took it and said, "Now I know thee will feel better."

A few days later the same man crossed the street to meet Levi, who was coming up on the other side. The man smiled, shook hands and asked in a whisper, "Did they get off safely?"

Mr. Coffin laughed and exclaimed, "I see thee has taken stock in our enterprise. If thee had not taken stock thee would have cared nothing about it. Yes, they got off safely and by this time are well on their way to Canada."

# CHAPTER SIXTY-TWO

Just before the Coffins sent Liz and Hack off in a carriage one night in the late summer of 1860, Levi sat them down in Hack's small room at the top of the house. He spread a crude map on the table. "You now have enough clothing and provisions for at least the early part of your journey," he said. "I'm also giving you a small sum of money, though your conductors will not ask for anything. This is a contribution toward any charges for fare on coaches, trains, or for the boat that will carry you across the river at Detroit or across Lake Erie. Depending on which boat captain takes you, they may not ask for money."

"So, we don't have to make it to the lake on our own?" Hack said.

"No, no, son," Levi said. "Thousands of fugitives do undertake the long arduous trip on their own, not trusting *any* white person to help them, even fearing betrayal by their own race for the reward money, but the situation in which you two find yourselves is far from typical."

"We'd be too easy to identify if we were out there by ourselves, is that it?" Liz asked.

"Exactly. A white woman and black man sometimes try to escape north by assuming the roles of mistress and slave, but by your descriptions being posted all over the city and countryside, your chances of escaping capture on your own would be almost nil."

"So them conductors know which way to take us?" Hack said.

Levi spread his map on the table. "You'll have conductors who know the stations along the Railroad. I'm sending you up the Sandusky Line through these towns like Blue Ash, Xenia, Delaware, New Haven, Milan and a number of other stations in between." As he named each town he pointed to it on the map. "Sandusky is this town on Lake Erie where you'll be put on a boat, perhaps bound for Detroit. Just before arriving at the destination, you'll be dropped on the Canadian side of the river at Malden, also called Amherstburg. Or possibly you'll board a ferry boat for Pelee Island in the middle of the lake, then go by another ferry to the mainland at Leamington. These decisions will be made by the people you shall meet on the waterfront at Sandusky."

Liz frowned and pointed to the island. "This Pelee Island, is it still in Ohio?"

"It's the southernmost point in Canada, Liz. For many runaway slaves it's where they first set foot in what they call the 'Queen's dominion'. As thee might imagine, Pelee Island has been the scene of much jubilation among arriving negroes."

"So we don't got to worry no more once we gets to the island?" Hack said.

"Thee must be watchful at all times, Hack. Slavecatchers are liable to be lurking anywhere along the line. Still, it is true that the danger there isn't nearly as great as here in Cincinnati. We hope the reward posters for your capture and the newspaper stories haven't been circulated very far north of Cincinnati, but we can't know for sure. There are occasional kidnappings of fugitives even on the mainland of Canada, so you both must always be vigilant."

Liz voiced another question. "Mr. Coffin, these conductors who will guide us northward, do they work for you? Are they trained for this work, or do they just know the roads and conditions in their own neighborhoods and volunteer to lead people like us?"

"There is nothing set in stone about the Underground Railroad. It is a clandestine system, and there are as many different techniques and routes from one station to the next as there are conductors. Even these are constantly changing to fit existing circumstances. The Railroad didn't originate with me, but I am sometimes given credit for organizing the lines that run through eastern Indiana and western Ohio. Our conductors make their living elsewhere, so their

322

conducting is done on their own time, completely voluntary in most cases. These men act on their own higher principles of freedom. When commercial transportation is required, we do try to provide money for that.

"As you have seen, the work entails considerable risk to the men, their families and their passengers. They have to be a dedicated lot. There is even a rather informal organization among these men called the Underground Railroad Society.

"Some of them have composed a sort of pledge. When they sign this document, they feel more strongly bound to the effort than by word-of-mouth agreements. Of course, any such document with signatures makes their work even more perilous. Here, I brought a rough copy of it. Thee will find the handwriting difficult to decipher, and that the word choice, spelling, grammar and punctuation leave much to be desired. This may be the only written evidence thee will ever see that there is a thing called the Underground Railroad. We are not in the habit of leaving documents behind us."

Levi reached into his pocket and handed Liz a folded half-sheet of foolscap. She saw several signatures on the back. Though the writing was smudged, she read it to Hack with but few pauses.

*"I do hereby solemnly and sincerely promise that I will aid the escape of all persons who are making and effort to escape from oppressive and making application to me for aid so far as I can without material injury to myself or family that I will give them aid them with food clothing & money as there necessity may require and that I will if necessary convey them away that I will not give there pursers any information concerning them and whether any connection contrarie with the society or so I promise not to reveal the private affairs of the society."*

# CHAPTER SIXTY-THREE

For the next two nights Liz and Hack were spirited through the darkness by white men who lived in the local areas. They traveled in a cart with high wheels the first night from the Coffin home to Blue Ash. The driver, who gave his name as Abner, told them to stay hidden under a pile of bedclothes in the back. They took shelter the next day in an elderly couple's stone house in Blue Ash. The wife, Mrs. Blanchard, gave them bean soup and cornbread, and her husband showed them to a sleeping room off the kitchen.

A small well-sprung buggy carried them all the way to Mount Holly the second night. Wrapped in blankets, Liz and Hack sat beside the driver on the single seat. The tall sorrel gelding maintained a ground-covering trot for hours over good roads. The fugitives were thankful that they were not stopped by night riders on the way, though their driver kept a constant lookout for horsemen concealed in the woods by the roadside, and he carefully scrutinized all wagons and buggies that passed them in the dark. Shortly before daylight, they stopped at a station in Mount Holly. Elmer Jones, their conductor, dropped them at the house of an Austrian immigrant of the anti-slavery persuasion, Mr. Hauersparger. While the travelers were shown to pallets in a cellar amid barrels of wine, their host sent a rider ahead to Springfield to report that fugitives were on the way.

Liz and Hack had found their conductors' work similar to what they'd done in leading George and Jenny from Lamb to Moorefield, except that they covered many more miles in wheeled vehicles over roads instead of hiking and riding Old Dan along rough trails. When they reached each station, someone at that place immediately rode to the next station up the line to give word that passengers would arrive there the next night.

Wright Rea and Sam Cunningham's friends finally picked up Liz and Hack's trail at Lebanon and followed them to Mount Holly on horseback. They'd received deliberately erroneous information from some of the Coffins' neighbors in Cincinnati concerning which route the escaping party had taken. Rea and his men took the road to Milford, and thus traveled miles out of their way the first night. But by inquiring of local people who were known to be of pro-slavery sentiments, they learned of the more heavily-traveled Underground Railroad route through Blue Ash, Lebanon and Mount Holly.

After a hard day's ride, and learning of suspicious late-night travelers that had passed that way, the pursuing party laid up in a barn just north of Mount Holly, taking turns keeping watch, planning to intercept the fugitives as they passed by during the early hours of the next night.

Meanwhile, Mr. Hauersparger turned the travelers over to his friend, a Mr. Ault, who spoke almost no English. He was to escort them northward to the larger town of Springfield, a distance of approximately thirty miles. They rode in his enclosed surrey drawn by a matched team of gray geldings. Mr. Ault wore his Sunday suit. Liz was given a long coat, hat and veil and sat beside the driver presenting, they hoped, the appearance of man and wife. Hack huddled in a corner of the back seat, wrapped in a dark blanket. They prayed his presence in the carriage would not be noticed in the darkness.

Liz attempted to converse with Mr. Ault, but his responses were limited to "Gut" and "Ya," or "Nein." They tried a few sentences, but the conversation partners showed no comprehension of her questions in English nor his answers in German, so their verbal communication died.

The fugitives' luck finally ran out on this, their third night moving north from Cincinnati. Visibility was foremost among Mr. Ault's problems. Clouds had obliterated the stars and moon and, to make progress even slower, the section of road they traveled submerged itself in mud and ruts. The driver had no choice but to rely on the horses' more acute senses to keep them on the road.

They had gone more than halfway to their night's destination when they heard horses overtaking them from the rear, sloshing through the mud. Liz felt an upwelling of nausea as she looked back, straining to see in the inky blackness, instantly reminded of the attack in the woods below Moorefield. Suddenly the dark shapes of two mounts and riders converged in front of the team, forcing the horses to throw up their heads in confusion and slow almost to a stop. One of the riders shouted, "Now, by god, we got you damned renegades dead to rights!" Liz felt the words cut to her heart. She'd heard that voice the night of the confrontation on Lost Fork and at Levi Coffin's front door, the voice of Wright Rea.

A loud grating sound came from the back of the surrey. The vehicle shook as someone drove a rail through the spokes of the two rear wheels, causing them to drag and further slow the team's progress.

Mr. Ault yelled at his horses and reached for the whip, but a heavy blow from a club silenced him. Someone dragged him off his seat onto the ground where they cursed and pounded him. The other two outriders grabbed the bridles of the team, causing the carriage to come to a complete halt. The last word the fugitives heard from the driver was, "Weglaufen!" followed by a curse and a scream as another heavy blow landed.

Liz sat trembling, helpless in her fear, until something large and solid hit her from behind and swept her off the front seat, then fell on top of her as she hit the ground, causing her to cry out in pain.

"Get up, Liz! We got to run." They ran blindly, stumbling over the ruts in the road, holding onto each other in the stygian night.

"They're gettin' away, Wright!" a voice bawled from the roadside.

"Shoot 'em goddamnit!"

They ran full speed into a rail fence at the roadside, and Hack helped Liz over the obstacle. There followed two shots accompanied by fiery muzzle blasts, and then one more, after which Liz heard Hack utter a loud grunt. She felt him go down, just beyond the fence. She found his hand again and, stifling a sob, she pulled with all her strength. She said a silent prayer of gratitude when he got to his feet and moved forward again.

The hand she held became slippery. She assumed it was blood. How seriously had Hack been wounded? "Grab my right arm, come on," he said, as if speaking through gritted teeth. They fled through what they discovered was a cornfield, following the space between two rows, willing to run wherever it led, the large sharp-edged leaves cutting their arms and hands as they held them up in front of their faces. When they sensed they were at the end of the field, they blindly crossed a brushy drainage ditch or stream, then forged ahead without stopping. They entered another cornfield where the rows seemed to lead at right angles to those in the first field. Once deep inside the second field, they paused to listen. They found they'd succeeded in putting distance between themselves and their pursuers, for they could hear shouts and cursing, still coming from the first field.

While they stood still, catching their breath, a light drizzle began to fall, pattering the corn leaves all around them and above them. The wholesome smell of gentle rain, moist earth and growing vegetation might have been pleasant to their senses had the pair not been so desperately focused on saving their lives.

They moved on to the edge of the field, then encountered another rail fence, which they climbed over, and headed off across what seemed to be a meadow with heavy, wet grass. The meadow sloped downward in their direction of travel.

Hack stopped abruptly. "You go on down to the far edge of this here field. I'm goin' back to get us some ears of corn. This time of year field corn is good to eat, even raw. If we have to lay up tomorrow, we're gonna need food."

"I'll go back with you, Hack. Or, let me go while you wait here and rest. You're hurt."

"No, I'm gonna stay between you an' them. Go on, now. Ain't no time to fuss. I'll give you a sign when I come back, like a old whippoorwill callin'."

Liz went down to the edge of the field as Hack had directed. Presently she heard shouting, then three gunshots. Her heart raced, and for a moment she considered running back to help Hack. Then, controlling her panic, she decided to do as he had told her. She would wait for him until . . . . She didn't let herself consider his not returning to her.

Feeling exposed here in the meadow, she climbed yet another rail fence and went a short distance beyond the edge of the field. She found herself in a dense thicket full of rocks and rough ground. The land fell away steeply toward what she assumed to be a creek. She soon found a place to sit still and rest . . . and wait.

The passing minutes wore heavily on the frightened girl's nerves. She became further confused when she heard several whippoorwill calls over the next few minutes, each coming from a different direction. It turned out that all the whippoorwills in the neighborhood were performing their avian ritual as they'd done for ages, breaking into their plaintive song every morning just before dawn. Any other time the bird calls and the gentle rain would have had a soothing effect on Liz, but all she felt now was mounting fear and desperation.

Straining so hard to hear that her head began to ache, she finally discerned that one of the calls sounded nearer than the others and appeared to be moving toward her. She finally mustered her courage and crept upward through the damp thicket toward the sound. A great weight lifted from her when she saw Hack's silhouette sitting in the dawn light at the base of her side of the fence making the night birds' call. "Whip-poor-will, whip-poor-will." In her great feeling of relief, she thought his mimicking sounded as authentic as the calls of the birds themselves. *Another of his survival skills*, she thought. She rushed forward, fell to her knees, leaned over and kissed him. "Oh, Hack, I thought they'd killed you, the gunshots and all."

He raised his right arm and cradled her cheek in his large hand, looked into her eyes, then kissed her on both cheeks and her mouth. "You're a sight for sore eyes, gal. Ain't hurt, are you? They come close to catchin' me, but we're safe now for a little while."

# CHAPTER SIXTY-FOUR

She threw her arms around him. "Oh, I was so scared, Hack." They tumbled over in the wet grass, unmindful of their soggy clothing, hugging, kissing each other. Then she remembered, "Your arm! I'm so sorry, Hack, did I hurt you?"

He sat up, then spoke earnestly to her. She saw he was grinning. "You ain't gonna b'lieve this, but they was shootin' at a old 'coon that clumb up a corn stalk to get his breakfast. It beat all the way he made that stalk shake and shimmy. I was hid a few rows over, seen and heard the whole thing. If I hadna been so 'fraid and sore I'd a'busted out laughin'. Sheriff Rae and his outlaws was sure they had me cornered. They was so close I could hear what they said.

"They commenced a'cussin' when they saw what they shot. They got 'em one heavy 'coon 'cause he's plumb full a'lead. Then one of the men said, 'Wright, we oughta go back and git the hosses. That nigger might double back, knock old Cyrus in the head an' run 'em off.' I don't think Wright Rea's sidekicks knows much about chasin' niggers . . . I mean negras.

"Now, we got to keep movin', Liz, get on through this thicket. No tellin' how long it'll take 'em to pick up our trail with the hosses. After we hit this creek down yonder we'll cross over, keep headin' north till we find somebody to help us. We're gonna be fine, Liz. I've done some of this bidness before. Thank god they ain't got no dogs."

Gray daylight arrived soon after they reunited. Hack showed Liz the six ears of corn he'd brought from the field. She hardly looked at the corn, but sat on her knees before him and took his left hand in hers, the one still covered with blood. His sleeve showed a hole at a point near his shoulder on the upper side of his arm. "Here, let me unbutton your sleeve." She had to use his knife to slit the sleeve to reach the injury on his upper arm. The wound was ugly, but apparently the bone wasn't broken and the bleeding had almost stopped. Liz tore a strip from her own shirt and bound up the wound, then secured his rolled-up sleeve around it.

As soon as she finished, he said, "C'mon, got to get movin'." He stood up and stuffed the ears of corn into his shirt, then plunged off into the brush on a downhill course.

When they reached the "creek" they found it was larger than they expected, more like a small river. "We'll move on up along the bank, find a shallow place to cross," Hack said. Before long, making their way through tangled vines and brush, they saw a smaller creek entering the other side of the river. "Looks like they's a town up yonder, on the left side of the creek. We'll go on a-past the mouth of that little run before we cross. Don't need to be traipsin' into no town."

Just then they heard a church bell ringing in the distance, coming from somewhere on higher ground across the river. "You think that's the alarm for people to be looking for us?" Liz said.

Hack peered between bushes toward the source of the sound. He had grasped the thin trunk of a sapling with his left hand at a place higher than his head. Liz knew his wound must be hurting terribly.

"Don't think so, Liz. Sheriff Rae and them ain't had time to get ahead of us. It must be Sunday. Preacher's callin' his congregation to services, don't you 'magine?"

They moved on upstream, finding that the riverbanks became wider apart the farther they went. The river, flowing through a wide flat floodplain at this point, seemed more shallow here, flowing over a riffle, but the mud and sand flats on both sides were wider and, though weeds and bushes grew on the floodplain, Liz and Hack wouldn't have much cover as they ran across the flatland and splashed through the shallow water.

Hack stopped and listened for a moment. "They cain't be lookin' for us yet, goin' back for the hosses. It'll take 'em a while to come 'round to where they lost us. We're gonna head straight for the water, and on through it to the high ground on the other side. Don't stop runnin' till we're hid in one of them brushy hollers over there. You hear shootin', don't stop, just stoop down and run like an old snake weavin' through the bushes. We got to go now. Follow me."

Hack broke from cover and raced across the river flats, holding his injured arm close to his chest, dodging rocks and scrubby vegetation, moving so fast that Liz could not keep up. When the distance between them grew long, he looked back and sank down in a muddy depression until she caught up. "So far, so good. Ain't far to the river, now," he said. "You plumb out of breath, gal?"

Her heavy breathing gave him his answer. When her gasping eased a bit, he rose and started off, saying only, "Got to hurry." He cast a wary glance behind them at the wooded slope, then turned and ran again.

The cold water made Liz gasp. She felt pain in her side and saw spots before her eyes from exhaustion and shock, but she kept going out of fear. Though she thought her lungs would burst, she was thankful the water was not much more than knee deep in most places. Occasionally she stumbled into a deeper hole that soaked her clothes up to her neck. The current beat hard against her, but she managed to keep her eyes on the far riverbank and did not lose her balance. In the deep places it was difficult to maintain her motion across the current. Still, she kept her legs pumping, desperately afraid she would lose sight of Hack.

She finally caught up with him and fell on top of him where he lay behind a boulder in the first hollow they came to on the right bank of the small tributary. He held her until she caught her breath and could speak. "I didn't hear any shots, did you?" she said.

"Nah, if anybody seen us they didn't shoot. I think we're safe now. We need to climb up outta this holler, look around, see where we're at."

After a short climb through brushy woodland, they emerged from the hollow and cautiously peered out onto flatlands where they saw several cabins among the trees and small fields, a road and a log church. The church bell had been silent since they'd first heard it from across the river. Judging by the number of buggies and wagons with horses tied under shade trees nearby, it was evident that a service was still in progress.

331

"Believe I'll rake me up a bunch of these leaves and bed down for a little while under this bush," Hack said. "You keep watch, I'll get up directly, let you lay down a few minutes."

Liz helped Hack make his rough bed, searching for the driest leaves from under the bush, and he lay down. She checked his wound and found the bleeding had begun again, so she re-wrapped it as best she could. She could tell his injury was sapping his strength. "How're you feeling, Hack?"

"Not too bad, but I could stand to rest a few minutes, for sure. Then we'll cipher out what our sorry selves needs to do next." He grinned weakly at her, then propped his left arm above his head and closed his eyes.

She stood up and looked around, watching for anyone approaching, listening for sounds of danger. When she had convinced herself that all was quiet for the moment, she sat down and again rested her gaze on the church out there by the road. Something told her this was important, the church, this group of people, the timing of their arrival here. She didn't understand her premonition, but she remained focused on her vigil.

Liz sat concealed among trees and brush at the lip of the bluff, her growling stomach a relentless chronometer as time crawled. She thought of the corn Hack had brought, but he must have dropped it in their run across the river flats. The sky cleared, the day warmed and Hack slept as she waited and watched the church.

The sounds of hymn singing brought back sweet memories of Sundays at the Sugar Branch Methodist Church. For a moment she was enfolded in warm girlhood images of being with friends at Sabbath school, afterward hearing the minister drone on while she dreamed of adventures in far-off lands, perhaps with a handsome young man by her side. How long ago that seemed, and how innocent she had been before the incident with her father that had banished romantic thoughts of men and boys from her mind, made her less trusting of the world.

Now here she was, listening to hymn-singing voices in the not-so-far-off land of Ohio. Yes, and with a handsome young black man nearby. Somehow the present reality did not fit her girlish dreams.

The question struck her over-tired mind and body like a thunderclap. How on earth had it all come to this? She'd have to sort it out sometime, but not now.

She guessed it was after midday by the time people began to leave. They shook hands and spoke with the minister just inside the church door, then gathered in small groups for conversation in the sunshine that now flooded the church yard. The day was turning steamy after the rain. Biting insects began to bother Liz, and she saw a long blacksnake weaving its way between the weeds, moving down toward the creek.

The churchgoers casually passed the time of day with each other before moving to their conveyances. Men led horses to the water trough and helped wives and children climb aboard their buggies and carriages to leave. The hungry girl watching from the woods imagined each group of worshippers returning to their home to enjoy a delicious Sunday dinner. Such basic treasures: church, family, home and dinner. Would her own life ever return to its former simplicity?

A morose mood had descended on Liz. Exhaustion, hunger and homesickness were taking their toll. But now, seeing the people depart, she felt her body tensing, collecting energy like a lion before the chase. There was one horse and buggy left in the tree-shaded lot by the church. She knew this was the moment for action, and she understood exactly what she must do.

# CHAPTER SIXTY-FIVE

$\mathcal{L}$iz stood up, straightened her wet, muddy and tattered clothing, having long since removed her coat and lost her hat and veil, and prepared to go to the church. When she told Hack her plan, he said, "Be careful, Liz. Was the people you saw comin' out the church black or white?"

"Far as I could see they were all white."

"What story you gonna tell 'em? If they're pro-slavers you'll be in deep trouble."

"I hope I won't have to talk about that at first," she said. "I'll say . . . I don't know what I'll say. Have to see what they're like, and then maybe I'll think of something."

"You reckon I better go with you?"

She knelt and kissed him, placing her hand on his cheek. "Stay here and rest, sweetheart. I'll be fine, but we need help and you need a doctor. If they see your bloody arm things might go bad for us." Then she turned to look out from their hiding place again to make sure there were no people about before she headed for the church. "I'll come back as soon as I can."

She combed her hair with her fingers, but realized she must still look like an escapee from prison. Fatigued as she was, to the point that she might make mistakes of judgement, she must move forward. This was their only hope as far as she could see.

She decided it would be best to walk, not run, as if there were no emergency, no hurry, as if she were just a normal woman who happened to be walking toward a church on a Sunday afternoon, dressed in wet grubby men's clothing. With one last look both ways she stepped out into the sunlight, forcing herself to breathe normally, her gaze locked on the church door.

For some reason she silently counted her steps, one-hundred-twenty-eight in all. She moved across the open space, past the horse drowsing between the buggy shafts, up the two steps to the closed door of the small building with its steeple, wooden cross and peaked windows.

Suddenly she found herself in front of the door. Maybe counting the steps had kept her mind from spinning out of control. She considered knocking on the door, but decided to just let herself in and deal with the consequences as they happened.

The place was dark compared to the glare outdoors. Light shafted through the stained-glass windows. Even with her eyes closed, the odor and the echoing silence would have told her she was in a church. She hesitated a moment letting her eyes adjust, then peered about in search of whoever belonged to the horse and buggy outside.

A feminine voice came from the front of the church. "Ansel?"

Then a man's voice, "Hello? May I help you?"

She strained to see the source of the voice. "Why, yes . . . yessir. My friend and I are in a bit of a hard spot out yonder." Why had she said that? Was she giving away too much information too early? She needed to know these people before divulging anything else. "Are you a minister, sir?"

A tall, black-bearded man appeared out of the gloom, his long pale face looking down at her. Apparently not much older than she and Hack, the man wore dark trousers, and a vest over a white shirt and collar with a black cravat. He carried a suit coat in his left hand. "I'm the pastor here at Yellow Springs Unitarian Church, miss. We were just putting things in order before leaving. My name is Ansel Hawkins and this is my wife, Annabell. What's your name? Do you live hereabouts?"

"Not too far, sir. We have . . . we were . . . ." Suddenly she was weeping, quietly at first, but she found it impossible to say more. Her own emotion took Liz by surprise, and she covered her face as the tears became a torrent. All the tension and fear of their harrowing escape from the sheriff and his cohorts came out of her in a rush.

335

Reverend Hawkins guided her onto one of the benches. Annabell came to sit beside her, put her arm around her shoulders and offered a handkerchief. The minister sat on her other side, looking kindly upon this girl who seemed in such great turmoil.

For several moments, Liz could do nothing but cry, her body shaking with sobs. Annabell drew the girl close and held her as she wept, helping her dry her tears. She shook her head, smiled sympathetically and gave her husband a look full of tenderness for the girl in her arms.

When she was able to speak, Liz responded to their gentle questions, identifying herself and haltingly telling the minister and his wife of their flight from the slavecatchers. She made it clear that Hack, the injured black man with her, had never been a slave and that they were being pursued because they had helped a family of slaves reach a place of safety in southern Indiana. She watched the minister's face with the eyes of a frightened child as she spoke, searching for a sign as to his convictions on the slavery issue.

"Where is this man, your companion?" Ansel asked.

Liz would not betray Hack's hiding place until she had some indication whether she was speaking to friends or enemies. "What will you do if I tell you?"

"Why, try to help him, of course. You say he's injured?"

"You won't turn him over to the slavecatchers or the law?"

Annabell answered in a soothing voice that allowed Liz to breathe easy again. "You're in Yellow Springs, now, Liz. There are many abolitionists in our community, including almost all of our congregation, and the others oppose the owning of slaves. Our town is one of the most active stops on the Underground Railroad. Whoever is pursuing you won't find much sympathy or help around here."

Ansel and Annabell closed the church and took Liz in the buggy across the field to where Hack lay in the thicket. On the way she briefly explained to them the events of the past several hours that had brought her and Hack to this place. When she described crossing the river, Ansel said, "That's the Little Miami River, Liz, and this creek down in the hollow below the church is Yellow Springs Creek. What was your destination last night when you were attacked?"

"I believe they said we were to lay over at Springfield today. We started last evening at Mount Holly."

"That's a long drive. You've made it about three-quarters of the way there, but the good Lord has blessed you today, child. You couldn't have come to a better place in search of help than our church."

They found Hack sleeping under the bush where Liz had left him. When he heard them approaching he quickly got to his feet and stepped behind a tree, drawing his knife from his boot. Liz called to him that it was all right, they were safe now. She jumped down from the buggy and ran to him, speaking in a rush, telling him of the two kind people she'd met.

Hack said, "You sure?" After reassurances from Liz, he sat down and reached up with his left hand to take hold of the low branch of a sapling. Liz could see he was tired and in pain.

The minister and his wife came into the thicket, looking intently at Hack, seeming to be concerned by his condition. After quick introductions, Annabell knelt beside Hack, spoke kindly to him and inspected his bloody arm. She unwrapped the tattered bandage. "Oh, Ansel, he's been shot! There's a hole in his sleeve and a wound in his arm near the shoulder."

"Both of you get into the back seat." Ansel said. "Hack, we're taking you to a doctor." He took hold of Hack's right arm and helped him to his feet.

Hack smiled weakly at the minister and shook his head. "I'm much obliged to y'all, Reverend. Didn't reckon no little old rifle ball could bite so hard." Everyone laughed.

After they were settled in the back seat and Ansel had the buggy moving out toward the road, Liz squeezed Hack's right hand and looked lovingly into his eyes. "We'll get you fixed up good as new, honey," she whispered.

On their way to the Hawkins place they stopped at Doctor Brown's office, which occupied three small rooms at the back of his home. While the doctor, a member of Ansel's Unitarian flock, attended Hack, Liz and Annabell sat in the doctor's tiny waiting room by the back door. Liz was concerned that her wet and filthy clothes would soil the chair she sat on, but Annabell comforted her. "After the doctor gets through with Hack I know you'll both want a

337

bath, fresh clothes and something to eat," she said. "We live in a little parsonage not far from here, and you're welcome to stay with us as long as need be."

In his office, after a quick assessment of Hack's bullet wound, Doc Brown walked over and quietly asked Ansel Hawkins to chunk up the fire in the grate, hang a teakettle on the crane, take the short pointed poker in the firestand and lay it across the andirons with its end in the fire. Then he directed the minister to make a solution of warm soapy water in a wash basin on the side table. Finally he told his tall helper to bring the large flat pan that leaned against the wall in the corner and place it in front of Hack on the floor. While Ansel was performing these tasks the doctor went to a cabinet on the wall and removed a tall unmarked bottle of dark liquid. He poured a water glass half full, then corked the bottle and replaced it in the cabinet. He told Hack, "Here, drink this down as quick as you can. It'll taste bad, but will help with the pain."

Then he cut the sleeve off Hack's shirt and examined the wound carefully. "The ball went clean through the flesh of your shoulder, young man. You're lucky it only nicked the bone. With a ball that size a direct hit on the bone would have shattered it, requiring me to amputate." Hack, already sweating profusely, paled visibly at that news. The doctor placed a folded towel on the table in front of Hack's chair and told him to rest his head on it whenever he felt the need.

"Now I'm going to clean out the debris as best I can. The ball carried some of your shirt cloth into the wound. Then I'll cauterize it." He set about picking fragments out with forceps. Hack flinched at the first touch of the instrument, then sat motionless as the doctor finished the task. Doc Brown laid the forceps down and washed the arm and wound.

Hack tried to remain stoic, but his head pounded and his empty stomach churned after he drank the strong liquid. "You had anything to eat this morning?" the doctor said.

"Nahsuh, ain't et since last night 'bout dark."

"Good. The pain medication will act quicker that way."

338

The doctor silently motioned for Ansel to bring the poker. The tool had a steel spring wrapped around the handle to dissipate the heat on that end so it could be touched.

Hack heard Ansel's approaching footsteps, and he smelled the red-hot iron, felt the radiating heat. He heard the quiet words, "Stand behind and brace him so he won't jerk back."

Doc Brown stood in front of his patient and said, "This'll hurt, son, but I'll do it as quick as I can." Without waiting for an answer, he plunged the red-hot end of the poker into the wound, running it all the way through and back, once, then again. Hack heard a ghastly sizzling sound, and a fierce blaze of pain flashed in an instant from his shoulder to his stomach to his genitals, then all over his body.

"Aaaahhh!" Hack involuntarily reared back against the minister's body, dark liquid gushing from the black man's mouth. His right hand reflexively reached for his wounded left arm, but the doctor dropped the hot iron and grabbed the hand before it could touch the wound. The fume of charred flesh filled Hack's nostrils and mouth, making him retch again.

The women in the other room bolted from their chairs at the scream, faces drawn taut as they jerked around toward the sound.

Doctor Brown held Hack's right hand and supported the young man's head with his other hand as he vomited into the pan on the floor. Ansel patted Hack's wet face with the folded towel. "Sorry to hurt you, son, but no other treatment could reach the inaccessible places inside that wound. You may curse me now, but I hope you'll thank me when you've recovered. Hack's only reply as he rested his drooping head in the doctor's hand was audible breathing, a final unproductive gag and a great shudder of his whole body. When he could breathe again, Hack said, "Ooohh, man, I thought gettin' shot was bad, but I didn't know nothin'."

The minister looked at Doc and shook his head at what Hack had just endured. The doctor said, "You're a brave man, Hack." Then he dressed and bandaged the charred wound. "I suggest you keep your left arm in this sling for a couple of days so it won't move too much and cause more pain."

Later that evening at the Hawkins house, Liz and Hack bathed separately at the washstand in the Hawkins's vest-pocket bedroom off the living room. Before their baths Annabell had laid out towels, wash cloths and spare sets of her and Ansel's clothing on the bed. When they were ready the minister's young wife served up chicken and dumplings, spinach, sliced tomatoes and boiled turnips for supper. Liz thanked her and told Annabell it felt so good to dress as a woman again.

After supper, when she and Annabell were alone, Liz said, "We're so grateful to you and the reverend. We didn't realize how tired and run-down we'd gotten over the past few hours and days. I'm ashamed of the way I must have looked when you first saw me." After a moment she added quietly, "What would have become of us if . . . ?"

"You mustn't think about that now; you're safe here," Annabell said. "Liz, why don't you tell me the whole story of your journey. All this seems to be weighing heavily on you, so it might ease your mind to share things with me."

Liz felt an immediate bonding with the minister's young wife, who seemed so perceptive and sensitive to her feelings. The women talked as they washed and dried the supper dishes. A burden slowly lifted from Liz's shoulders for the next few minutes as she poured out their story to the gentle Annabell.

She explained how she and Hack had gotten to know each other at her grandparents' place and the reason for her accompanying him to help with the black family. She described the awful confrontation in the woods near Lost Fork, including the shot in the dark that killed her father.

Annabell gasped and brought her hand to her mouth when she heard this, causing Liz to pause for a moment. "Oh, Liz, I've never heard of such a thing. No wonder you were at the point of collapse when you found us."

"I knew my father and his cronies sometimes hunted runaway slaves," Liz said. "But Hack and I didn't know who was pursuing us that night in the dark. I heard some voices, but didn't identify any of them as my father's."

Liz gazed down at her hands clasped in her lap and continued. "He tried to . . . he accosted me after Mother died a few years ago, and we were not on speaking terms, but I swear my shooting him was a total accident. As I've told Mr. Coffin in Cincinnati, I fired the

340

gun only to frighten them, to keep them from catching us and the family we were leading. Oh, Annabell, I would never have killed my father or anyone else, no matter what trouble we'd had, but now I'm living with the guilt, all the same."

Annabell hugged the distraught girl, then put an arm around her and led her to chairs at the kitchen table. When they were seated, Annabell said, "Oh, Liz, I can't imagine how terrible all that must have been for you, your father abusing you. I don't believe in a vindictive God, and we know so little about divine intervention, but . . . it may not be a Christian thought, but it's tempting to believe that justice was done in the woods that night, dear Liz."

# CHAPTER SIXTY-SIX

Annabell said, "In any event, thank heavens you've arrived here where we can help you and restore your strength. Were you and Hack planning to make Springfield your final destination? Do you have friends or kinfolk there?"

"No, we were told our best chance was to escape north to Canada. Mr. Coffin and the conductors helped us get this far before we were waylaid."

The young wife remained silent and thoughtful a moment. "Yes," she said, "the laws here in the States are against you, both for conducting fugitive slaves and, of course, for the shooting. There are a couple of lawyers among our congregation who could counsel you on these problems, if you wish.

"Many fugitives are fleeing to the safe haven of Canada. On the other hand, if this sheriff and his patrollers can be sent packing, you and Hack would be much safer here in west-central Ohio than where you came from. Please know that should you and Hack decide to stay here in Yellow Springs you would be more than welcome among our people, and we would gladly help you through your legal difficulties."

"Thank you, Mrs. Hawkins. It looks as if we'll have many decisions to make before this is over. Whatever happens, I can't thank you enough for what you've already done for us."

Just as she was leaving Annabell's kitchen to go help Hack, Liz turned and said, "Mrs. Hawkins . . . Annabell . . . I'm aware that I've just incriminated Hack and myself, and you as well, in telling you our full story. I've admitted that we have not only aided the negro family in their escape from slavery, but that I fired a weapon that inadvertently killed my father.

"I understand that you have the right, some would say the obligation, to turn us over to law enforcement officials. So far, knowing only that we helped the slaves, you've treated us with kindness and hospitality.

"You and Ansel have quite possibly saved our lives, but now with this new knowledge of my having killed a man, you may be torn as to whether to help us further. If you and Ansel were to decide to do as the law requires and turn us in, I ask only that you wait until after we've departed Yellow Springs, in order to give us a fair chance to escape to Canada. Even at that, if law officers learn of what we've discussed, they may charge you as accomplices to our crimes.

"We would have no choice but to understand your actions if you should decide to call in the local sheriff. Whatever your decision, please know that for what you've already done for us we are deeply grateful."

Annabell came to Liz then, and took the tired girl in her arms. "Liz, you must believe you are safe here with us," she whispered, looking into the girl's eyes. "Yes, you've just divulged new information to me concerning the death of your father, but who says I have to share that with my husband, much less anyone else? So you see, if we both keep quiet nothing has changed from last Sunday. For the record we know only what you told us then, that you and Hack were being pursued for helping runaway slaves, that's all. In view of public sentiment here in our town I wouldn't expect you to be prosecuted for that. What has just passed between us will be our secret. The rest of your story will go to the grave with me, dear Liz. You have my word on it."

After the bath and supper with the Hawkinses, Hack felt better, though his injury was still painful. Even on this first evening of their stay with the Hawkinses, Ansel's congregation members began coming round with food, clothing, money and encouraging words for the traveling pair. They heard several inquiries about their travel plans, and invitations to make Yellow Springs their home.

343

By the next morning, the doctor's treatment of Hack's wound and the medication for pain were beginning to prove effective. After their much-needed rest, Liz and Hack stepped out into the Hawkins's back yard to discuss their situation privately.

Liz did not tell Hack as much, but her talk with Annabell the night before had made her realize that for them to remain anywhere in their own country would be foolhardy. She shuddered, remembering the fear she'd felt during their flight from Wright Rae and his patrollers. Even in Canada, they might be apprehended and brought back to the U.S. to face a murder charge. She voted for putting more distance between themselves and the Indiana/Kentucky borderland.

Hack agreed. "Even if Wright Rae and them goes back to Madison, there could be another bunch of vigilantes after us tomorrow.

"Remember," he said, "old Mr. Hertzel told us it ain't like the two of us can hide in a crowd. What was it he said, we'd be like two geese in a chicken coop? I'll allow he had it 'bout right." Then, after a pause he winked and said, "How come me to get mixed up with this tall white gal, anyhow?" She shoved him and gave him a mock scolding look.

"These Yellow Springs folks has been mighty good to us," he said, "but since we're already runnin', we better get farther north before we quit."

Seeing that the Hawkinses weren't close by, Liz hugged him, being careful not to bump his shoulder. "You're right, we can't settle for comfort, not until we get farther north. Sad as I am to think of never going back home, and how bad this must be for my family at Sugar Branch, we'll have to accept our new circumstances as we find them and make the best of it." After a thoughtful pause she continued. "You know, with all this talk about the Queen's dominion," she said, "I'm getting a bit curious to see that north country."

He looked down at her and grinned. "You're a wonder for a white gal." Then he kissed her.

She pretended to slap him. Then, eyes wide feigning surprise, she looked both ways and moved back a step. "You'll get me in trouble yet, you black rascal."

They took the Hawkins's suggestion that they stay a few days to rest and allow Hack's wound to start healing under the doctor's care before continuing their journey northward.

As for sleeping arrangements, Liz remembered she'd mentioned to Annabell when they first met at the church that she and Hack were just friends, thus implying they were neither married nor lovers. The travelers secretly discussed the issue on their first evening at the Hawkinses. Liz had longingly eyed the comfortable daybed their hosts had assigned to Hack in their living room. She thought it looked large enough for the two of them, but instead she asked if she could sleep on the bench in the enclosed back porch.

Liz and Hack agreed to resist their carnal urges and conduct themselves with false decorum. However, the appetites of the young people being what they were, Hack managed to catch Liz alone before bed that first night for a brief, but impassioned hug and kiss. Their feelings were mounting, and it would not be easy to suppress their desires.

Thus, on Friday, the visitors' fifth morning with the Hawkinses, Annabell was awakened by a small sound. She lay listening for a moment. Ansel was gently snoring and predawn light had just begun to brighten their bedroom window. She rose quietly and tiptoed across the rug to peek through the doorway into the living room.

Drapes had been drawn across the window beyond Hack's low daybed. The light from outside was thus blocked, except for a space at the bottom of the window where the heavy drape had been caught on the top of a wicker waste basket. This allowed a small opening that dimly illuminated the space under the bed.

The minister's wife could see two shadows on the floor on the near side of the daybed as the light silhouetted Liz's bare feet. She could make out the girl's shape standing beside Hack's bed with her back to Annabell, leaning over, apparently whispering to him. As Annabell watched, one of Liz's feet moved upward, and she realized the girl's knee was now on the bed. Then the other foot rose to the bed. With nearly inaudible rustling sounds, Liz's form slid onto the bed and under the bedclothes beside Hack, then eased over on top of him. They kissed, and her shape began to move, slowly at first, then rhythmically, accompanied by muted whispers and sighs.

Annabell turned with a puckish grin and made her way quietly back to bed. She settled herself beside her husband and had just pulled up the sheet when he awoke. He yawned and said in a sleepy voice, "Good morning, sweetheart. I'd better get up now and stoke the fire for breakfast."

Alarmed, Annabell's eyes searched the ceiling, her mind buzzing, heart racing. She feared Ansel was about to create an embarrassment for everyone in the house.

In the short time she'd known the two young travelers she had seen the signs. Even last Sunday she had suspected there was more going on romantically between them than a mere friendship. And what she'd seen two minutes ago confirmed it beyond a doubt.

Having grown up in Yellow Springs, whereas Ansel hailed from Indianapolis, Annabell had always been more accepting and forgiving of sexual doings between biracial and unmarried couples than her husband. Now, she was determined not to allow him to interrupt the tender scene going on at this moment in their living room. In another second Ansel would move to get up. She had to act quickly.

She made a show of stretching luxuriously, then moved closer to him, giving him a smile and a good morning kiss. "I was just thinking how lucky I am to be lying here in bed with this handsome man, the father of my future children," she whispered. She touched his face, slid her other hand slowly down his front, discovering his morning arousal, then touching it gently. She moved her face close to his, looked deep into his eyes and murmured in a coquettish voice, "Oh, Pastor Hawkins, may I help you with that?"

Surprised, Ansel hesitated a bashful second before he chuckled and said, "Why, sister Annabell, if you don't have the *best* ideas!"

346

# CHAPTER SIXTY-SEVEN

*L*ater, after the Hawkinses and their guests had traded good mornings, they all gathered at the breakfast table. Annabell gave Liz a brilliant smile across the table just before Ansel asked the blessing. The master of the house started the bacon and toast platter around the table, then asked Hack how his wound was progressing and if he had slept well. In that small moment with the men engaged in conversation, Liz directed a brief questioning glance at her hostess, wondering if she somehow knew of her and Hack's dawn adventure. Then, just as the men completed their bit of talk, Liz thought she saw a sly wink from her hostess. She blushed and dropped her gaze to her plate briefly, then looked up with a shy smile and the slightest of nods to Annabell.

That afternoon, after consulting with Hack, Liz told Annabell they'd decided to head north as soon as possible now that Hack was on the mend. Annabell paused a moment, then said, "Liz, you must know from our little acknowledgements at the breakfast table that I saw you and Hack together this morning before we got up. Please forgive me for snooping, but I heard a noise and went to check. That's when I saw you getting into his bed. It's pretty clear that you and Hack are . . . committed to each other, am I right?"

Liz showed a stricken expression. "Oh, Annabell, I apologize. Hack and I do have feelings for each other, and we've . . . gotten together a time or two before. This morning I let my emotions overcome my better judgement, I'm afraid. I'm so sorry, Annabell. We've abused your and Ansel's hospitality by our rude behavior."

"There's no need to apologize, Liz. You two are allowed to have feelings, like anyone else. Now, can you keep a secret? When I slipped back into bed this morning Ansel woke up and was about to get up and start the day. I was frantic for a second, worrying that he'd find you two and cause a big mess, so I stopped him the surest way a wife could, if you follow my drift."

The two young women looked at each other, impish smiles spreading over their faces. Then they had to cover their mouths to avoid laughing out loud. After a moment Annabell continued, "I mean, you've come all this way together, dodging lawmen and slavechasers, enduring all manner of hardships to get this far, and now you're going on to Canada and its promise of freedom. What I saw this morning showed me you two are not just comrades in your work, or in surviving these hardships, there's an emotional bond there, too."

"Oh, Annabell, it's true that Hack and I think the world of each other, but we have to consider the cause of our devotion. Is it just that we've become so dependent on each other in reaching this point in our journey? Or is it that we love each other in the more traditional way?

"I can't imagine our being bold enough to fall in love if we were still living in Cotton Township at my grandparents' house. Even if feelings had grown between us there we would have been forced to keep them hidden. My family, open as they are to helping fugitive slaves, would have been outraged if they knew we were in love, even fond of each other. My grandfather was already suspicious of Hack and me. He was ready to send Hack away when he found us both in the barn one night simply waiting for a mare to foal. So you see, tolerance of relations between a man and woman of different races is not open for discussion in my family."

"It does seem to be a very real concern for the two of you. I was about to offer for Ansel to marry you and Hack before you leave, but now I see there are things you need to resolve before you're ready to commit to marriage."

"That would be an honor, Annabell, but we'll have to see how our feelings mature after we've reached Canada. Hack and I will always be grateful, not only for putting us up these several days, but also for this offer. You and Ansel are among the kindest people we've met, and we'll never forget your hospitality and understanding."

Liz hesitated before she continued. "Annabell, there is another worry. We . . . especially I, have acted irresponsibly in one other matter. It's maybe even more important than our being disrespectful of your hospitality in our . . . relations with each other."

Annabell's face took on a serious expression, and she seemed about to protest before Liz said, "What if I were to become with child, Annabell? Heaven knows that would be a large enough responsibility by itself, without being fugitives as we now find ourselves. What if we were captured, tried in a pro-slavers' court and Hack sent into bondage at the South, and me to prison? Under those circumstances the fate of any child born to us would be too horrendous to contemplate."

"We've come close to tempting fate once or twice already, and then there was what you saw this morning. No, we must not marry now, for that among the other reasons. Marriage would drastically increase our chances of my becoming pregnant before we reach the safety of Canada. So now, dear Annabell, we share one more secret between us."

At supper the four of them discussed the matter of leaving for Canada. Ansel went that evening to ask Ernest Whitman, one of his parishioners, to make preparations for a journey with passengers to Springfield the next night, Saturday. Ansel also gave them a sealed letter he had penned. He said it was a letter of introduction for them to present to one Reverend Isaac Rice at his King Street School in a town called Malden, or Amherstburg, when they reached the Canadian mainland.

"Isaac and I spent time at university together a few years ago," he said, "and we still correspond. I can't think of a better person to contact when you arrive. He has a little settlement in that town whose mission is to maintain his school for the education and welfare of black refugees and their children. You can see his address is on the envelope. It's easy to find. Anyone acquainted with the town can lead you there."

Liz and Hack said their fond farewells and thank yous to Ansel and Annabell after dark on Saturday evening. Annabell gave Liz an especially warm hug and kissed her cheek before they departed. They stepped up into a carriage driven by Ernest Whitman for their journey north to Springfield and the home of Simon Enberg, who would conduct them safely the next night, Sunday, to the Springfield station on the *Mad River and Lake Erie Railroad.*

"Many of our fugitive people take the cars on the *MR & LE* from Springfield on north to Sandusky," Ernest said. "That's by far the fastest and most efficient way to the lake. Of course the slavecatchers know this, and they often scout the cars looking for runaways.

"Simon's got what you might call an 'understanding' with Ed McPherson, the conductor, and Bert Niekro, a railroad detective on the Sunday night train to Sandusky. Ed will get you safely into the baggage car and Bert will make sure nobody gives you trouble on the way north."

Liz, holding tightly to Hack's hand, said, "We've never even seen a train, except in newspaper engravings. Are you saying we'll make it all the way to Sandusky tomorrow night? How's that possible? And what did you call this railroad? The *MR* something or other?"

Ernest laughed. "It's the *Mad River and Lake Erie Railroad,* miss. It ain't the first railroad in Ohio, only the second. The first was the *Erie and Kalamazoo,* beginning in 1836, the first railroad chartered west of the Alleghenies. This here *MR & LE* reached Springfield from Sandusky around 1849.

"You'll be surprised how fast the cars move. Ed'll slip you onto the *Erie Flyer,* an express train. She'll make but few stops, and you'll be in Sandusky a'fore daylight on Monday. Businessmen like to take the Sunday night express so they can be all set to start their week in Sandusky. It's a sign of these modern times that they're willing to sleep in their seats on the cars so they can be first to the customers on Monday morning. Sounds crazy, don't it?

"The baggage car's the customary accommodation for runaway slaves moving toward Canada on the railroad," Ernest said. "Ansel told me you two was almost caught helpin' runaway slaves, and now you're fugitives like them, in a manner of speakin'.

"You won't find any seats in the baggage car, but there'll be plenty of boxes and trunks to set on. When they open the door at stops along the way, you'll have to scrunch down and hide. Just remember, Ed and Bert'll be watchin' out for you."

Sometime in the hours before daylight, they reached their destination at the Enbergs' house in Springfield. Carrie Enberg greeted them and gave them a meal. Then Simon showed them to a space where they could conceal themselves in the cellar during the day. Liz found it difficult to rest, having become accustomed again to a normal sleep schedule. She noted that their accommodations in the cellar were spartan and moldy-smelling compared to their last few days of comfort as guests in the Hawkins home, and among the citizens of Yellow Springs. The old tiredness and worry descended on Liz again. Would they ever reach a place where they could be truly free from danger?

Simon, a man Liz thought to be in his sixties, brought food to her and Hack in the cellar on Sunday evening. He told them what to expect at the train station later that night. They asked if he'd seen any handbills around town offering a reward for their capture. He replied that he had not seen his two guests specifically identified, but many slave owners and others had tacked up messages in public places seeking help locating slaves that had run away from various places in the South. "Springfield is full of slavechasers and bounty hunters," he said, "and they usually gather at the train station. They know as well as we do that the cars are the favored mode of transportation by fugitives hoping to reach Sandusky."

"What's the chances of us gettin' through?" Hack said. "Seems like we're liable to be rounded up like hogs in a pen."

"Yes, some of the black fugitives do get caught at the station," Mr. Enberg said. "But Ed McPherson, the conductor on the night train, is my nephew, so he'll recognize me when we pull up on the platform, and he'll know why I'm there. Remember, it'll be after dark when passengers board the *Erie Flyer*. When I stop the buggy at the back entrance of the last passenger car, which is always hitched just ahead of the baggage car, he'll know to come help us. We'll give you a cane, Hack, and a big hat with a floppy brim. Liz, you won't be wearin' no hat, so anyone can see you're white. We hope it'll look like we're helpin' your old granddad onto the train."

"Won't any slavecatchers on the train see us when we enter the car?" Liz asked.

"Not likely, because the minute we reach the top of the steps, Ed'll open the door to the baggage car and you'll slip in there. Then he'll close the door and lock it. If there's any baggage to be put on the car, Ed'll load it through the side door, next to the platform, and he's one of only two people that'll have a key to that door, too."

Hack grinned. "Looks like Mr. McPherson's got all the answers, Mr. Enberg. Who's the other man with a key?"

"We've had good luck in the past, Hack. The railroad detective, Bert Niekro, will have the other key, which fits both doors of the baggage car. We don't pull this trick very often, so we hope them we call the 'outlaws' won't be expecting it."

The buggy rolled onto the platform of the Springfield train station a little after nine on Sunday night. A light rain was falling and the train sat waiting beside the platform. Far ahead they could see steam escaping from the engine at the head of a line of two passenger cars and the coal car. The engineer leaned out his window watching for the conductor's signal.

Simon stopped his white mare, stepped down from the buggy and shook hands with Ed McPherson who came hurrying up to meet them. Hack played his role well, moving unsteadily with his cane and walking in a stooped posture under his large hat. Liz came right behind him, with the basket of food that Carrie Enberg had given her. She peered toward the station house so that any observer could see she was white, and also a little foolish for not carrying an umbrella.

They mounted the steps into the car with Ed leading, Hack following and Liz bringing up the rear. Simon remained on the platform a moment, scanning the scene as casually as possible for any suspicious activities. Then he joined the others at the top of the steps. Liz looked up the aisle of the car toward the front and saw several passengers already seated with others standing, stowing their small bags on the overhead racks.

Her wary eyes caught sight of three hard-looking men at the far end of the car. They had heavy mustaches and beards and came swaggering toward them with the gait of men accustomed to sitting horses. They were of medium height, muscular individuals with swarthy skin and deadpan expressions. Two wore leather vests over

352

long-sleeved shirts, jeans and hats while the third wore a black seaman's cap, a leather jacket and a kerchief around his neck. They stared coldly at Liz and her companions as they made their way toward them down the car, roughly shoving other passengers out of the aisle. They were obviously not looking about in search of seats.

Fear struck Liz like a blow to the chest. The men's focused demeanor immediately revealed their mission. They had evidently been watching for Simon Enberg and his charges.

At that moment Ed McPherson was occupied unlocking the baggage car door as Hack and Simon stood behind, watching him. They had their backs to Liz.

She was at the point of shouting a warning to them when a tall broad-shouldered man stood up from the back seat of the car, stepped out into the aisle and blocked the three rough characters.

# CHAPTER SIXTY-EIGHT

By this time, Ed had the door open and Hack and Simon were saying their quick farewells before Simon would leave the train. After a quick glance at her companions by the baggage car door, Liz turned to see and hear the confrontation behind her.

"Where you men think you're goin'? This is the end of the passenger compartment," the big man said.

"You'd best sit back down, mister. We got bidness to discuss with them that's behind you, and you're right in the way. Now move!"

Bert Niekro did move, but in a way the outlaws could not have expected. He swept back the right side of his long duster coat and had the muzzle of his revolver under the leader's chin before the man could reach for his own weapon in his belt. Bert spoke in a calm, barely audible voice. "I'm a railroad detective. You ever hear of a LeMat grapeshot revolver?" For emphasis Bert Niekro cocked the pistol with an eloquent click.

The man raised his hands high in the air, swallowed audibly and said, "Yeh . . . yessir, I have. Please don't shoot. Please!" With his thumb the detective rotated the pivot knob on the hammer, thus arming the 20-guage shotgun barrel, the lower of the two.

"I see you're smarter than you look. I've got a load of grapeshot three inches from your brain. If you want to keep your head your yay-hoos will drop their weapons on the floor and sit down in the seat I just left." The three men stood like statues, fear glinting in their eyes. Bert paused only a second before he said, "Well, are you gonna tell 'em, or do I send you on a quick trip to hell?" He poked the muzzle of his weapon farther into the man's throat.

The leader's face was already drenched with sweat and his voice quavered, but he said to his men, "Do it, goddamnit!" Two pistols clunked on the floor and Bert quickly relieved the captive of his weapon and dropped it with the others.

"You'll sit beside 'em next to the aisle. Then, all three of you will raise your hands and keep 'em raised. Now do it!" The men did as they were told. As the leader took his place by the aisle, Bert kept the revolver's muzzle close to his head.

During the seconds that this scene was taking place Ed, Hack and Liz stood frozen in their tracks, looking on in amazement at the drama playing out before them. Simon Enberg was on the top step of the entryway, not moving in or out of the car.

"Ed," Bert said, his voice still cold and calm, "reach under the seat across the aisle there and pull out the handcuffs, if you please. You'll find four pair under there. Bring three sets and shackle these hooligans for me, behind their backs, of course."

In the next few minutes Ed restrained the three slavecatchers, Bert marched them off the train, signaling the engineer to delay his departure, then took the prisoners into the station where he turned them over to a policeman to be taken into custody. After a few words with the lawman, he returned toward the passenger car, waved to the engineer to depart, boarded the car, conferred briefly with Ed McPherson, then moved forward on the train to the next car. The stunned passengers watched him go with open mouths.

While the detective had been occupied with his prisoners inside the station, Simon left the train. The conductor stashed the outlaws' pistols in the place under the seat where the handcuffs had been. He then ushered Liz and Hack into the baggage car, saying he would return soon to see if they needed anything and to explain as best he could what had just happened. Then he left, locking the door behind him.

The two stowaways found places in the dark car to sit on pieces of baggage. They tried to overcome their fright at the recent confrontation. Presently the whistle tooted and the train began to move. After the car jerked into motion they marveled at how smoothly it rolled over the rails, only the slight joint bumps giving any hint that they were moving at all.

Moments later they heard the engineer blow the whistle for a road crossing, after which the train picked up speed. Liz and Hack involuntarily reached to brace themselves as the train rounded the first curve. "This thing must be movin' faster'n a team at full gallop," Hack said.

"I hope they know what they're doing. Can you imagine running into something at this speed, and at night? We'd surely all be killed!"

Sometime later the train slowed and stopped. From the sounds coming from outside, the two travelers assumed they were at a station. When they heard scratchings at the lock on the side door, Liz and Hack lay down on the floor on the far side of the car behind some boxes. The door slid open and two men lifted a trunk inside and shoved it across the floor. Then they slammed the door shut and the travelers heard Ed locking it.

The cars gained speed again, the engineer blowing the whistle at crossings. Presently they heard a key unlocking the door from the passenger car. Liz and Hack dived into their hiding place. The tall form of Bert Niekro stepped in. "It's just me, Bert. I just came to see about you folks. Ed's busy right now and he asked me to check on you." The two travelers stood up and faced the detective across the pile of baggage.

"How you folks doin' in here?" Bert asked.

"We're so grateful to you for saving us from those three men!" Liz said. "I saw them approaching, but had no idea how to escape. Thank heavens you were there."

"I've seen them before on the cars, snoopin' around, grabbing people, mostly blacks, and trying to collect a reward for turning 'em in. They've been warned before to stay off the cars."

"How did they know who we was?" Hack said.

"When I turned 'em over to the policeman inside the station they said they heard a rumor about a black man travelin' with a tall white girl. They started keepin' an eye on the cars hoping to get lucky. They figured a pair like that would be easy to spot, so they saw you and decided you were the ones."

"Yassuh, we done been told that before, ain't we, Liz."

Liz's heart fluttered. She realized suddenly how fortunate they were that the outlaws hadn't mentioned anything to the detective or the policeman about the two of them being wanted for murder as well as for conducting runaway slaves. If they'd known what happened on Lost Fork, Bert and the policeman would have had no choice but to arrest them. She found herself breathing hard, but trying to conceal the fact from Bert. They'd just had a very close call and she hadn't even been aware of it. If she'd been alert to the danger, Bert Niekro's unscheduled entry into the baggage car would have given her a heart attack! They'd have to pay attention, be more careful.

"Miss," Bert said, "you're both leavin' yourselves open to even more trouble by travelin' together like this. You're drawin' extra attention to yourselves that way. I b'lieve I'd part company with this feller and go on back where you come from . . . unless the two of you are . . . together, so to speak."

Liz's reply was short and to the point. "We are." Bert simply nodded and said no more.

The train jerked, forcing Hack and Liz to sit down quickly on a large trunk. They turned to face the detective. "We sure ain't used to travelin' this fast, takin' these curves like a racin' sulky," Hack said.

Bert laughed. "We've had people get sick on their first train ride. It seems you're goin' faster than you really are, sittin' here in the dark. You'll get used to it, I'm sure."

"We stopped once; how many other stops will we make?" Liz asked.

"That was Urbana, just a few miles north of Springfield. We'll stop at Belle Center, Big Spring and Groton before we reach Sandusky sometime before daylight. We stop at those stations for passengers, and also to take on coal and water for the engine. On a night run like this we pass up the other stations."

Hack asked Bert about his pistol that had so disconcerted the leader of the outlaws. Bert chuckled. "This is a LeMat revolver," the detective said, pulling it from its holster and showing it to Hack in the light from the open door. "There's a man in New Orleans, Alexander LeMat, that designed this pistol. He got a patent on it four or five year ago but he's only had a few made so far. I heard of it through a friend of mine, a detective on a Mississippi River steamboat. I wrote back and asked him to get me one. Took him a while, since they're a scarce article in the gun trade, but he finally sent me one. I got it just a few days ago and I've been practicin' with it."

"You told the man somethin' 'bout grape shot. What'd you mean by that?" Hack said, gingerly running his fingers over the revolver in Bert's hands.

"The piece is a revolver that shoots nine regular round balls, plus that other barrel you see underneath that's a 20-gauge shotgun. It shoots small lead shot, or grape shot. This pistol is thirteen inches long and weighs more than three pounds. It's cumbersome and not very accurate, designed for close range, like a man shooting from horseback on a battlefield. But the important thing is, if you use it right you can stop anything that's in front of you."

"Looks like it'd be a bear to reload," Hack said.

"You got that right," Bert said. "Mr. LeMat recommends a man carry two of 'em for that reason, but I don't have that kind of money. Besides, it'd take a war hoss to carry a man with two of these bruisers strapped on." He laughed at his humor, but Liz and Hack showed cautious smiles.

"Anyhow, that feller earlier this evenin' knew about the LeMat, and that's why he changed his tune real fast once he learned what he was up against."

Hack said, "I can see this bad boy'd be right tiresome to pack 'round all the time." Liz could dimly see Hack hefting the piece, lifting it with his good hand placed under Bert's hand.

"Once people know you're carrying a LeMat, you don't often have to take it out of its holster, except maybe to show somebody, like we're doing now."

Hack laughed and leaned back. "I bet that's right," he said.

Bert holstered the piece as Hack continued. "We're mighty lucky you and this here Mr. LeMat showed up when you did." he said.

The detective chuckled. "Just part of my job, Hack."

Liz asked Bert if he'd like to share the food that Carrie Enberg had given them for the trip. "There's more here than we can eat. Won't you have a sandwich? I think there's ham and roast beef, and some pickles."

"Why thank you, ma'am," Bert said. "If you don't mind I'll wrap it up and take my sandwich and pickle with me 'cause we're about to stop at Belle Center and I'll have to get back to work."

After a short stop they pulled away from the Belle Center station and the *Erie Flyer* rumbled on through the night. Tired from the newness of train travel and the threat of capture at Springfield, the travelers made a crude pallet and covered themselves with some cloth sacks on the floor.

Hack's hands soon began to roam in response to Liz's warm body spooned against him in the darkness. "I'm glad you're wearin' a skirt now ruther than them old pants. Don't even have to take our clothes off now to do what we want."

"What *we* want? Where did you get *we*?" There was a grin in her voice.

"Now, Liz, you forgot how you come creepin' into my bed the other mornin'? Turn over this way so's we can see 'bout this."

"These cars may stop any minute, Hack. Don't! Jim Hackney, I'm going to slap you silly." Laughter and faint scuffling sounds came from their makeshift bed.

"Here."

"Oooh, is that for me?"

"Don't see nobody else in here, do you?"

Sounds of kissing. "Mmm, you'd better put that stallion back in his stall."

"He's done out now."

"I'll have to geld that bad boy. He's getting too hard to handle."

"You're half right, he's hard."

"Oh, you! Wait . . . wait a second . . . now. Come here, you outlaw."


Much later, lying warm and relaxed in Hack's arms, Liz slowly aligned her senses to the sounds of the train, the hypnotic motion, finally surrendering even to the plummeting speed. Now, knowing that Ed and Bert were looking out for them on the train, a feeling of well-being folded over her like a warm blanket.

As she descended into soft drowsiness, she thought again of her concern about becoming pregnant. She and Hack had just acted foolishly again, there on the floor of the baggage car, but it was becoming so easy to join him in gratifying their youthful desires. After this recent fright, the threat of capture and imprisonment began slipping ever farther behind them as the cars swept through the night. She smiled in the darkness and shrugged herself deeper into Hack's embrace, assuring herself that things would turn out well. She slept soundly through the remaining stops all the way to Sandusky.

This rendition of mid-nineteenth century Lake Erie shows Pelee Island, Ontario, and Point Pelee, Ontario, as well as other important locations in the story.

# CHAPTER SIXTY-NINE

They awoke when the train stopped at Sandusky in the predawn hours. The Hoosier travelers heard more strange sounds and people moving about outside on the platform. It was several minutes before Ed McPherson escorted them from their hiding place after transferring baggage for the paying passengers. On the dimly-lighted station platform amid chuffing and release of steam from the engine, and the bustle of passengers and porters milling about, Ed introduced them to their new conductor, Cedric Early. Liz noticed a different scent in the chilly air, an odor reminiscent of fish, mixed with the smoke, oil and metal smells from the train. She remembered that Sandusky was a port on Lake Erie. "Cedric'll take you to a safe place to rest while he contacts people at the waterfront to arrange your passage on to Canada," Ed said. "You're in good hands with Mr. Early here. He's been at this business a long time. I'll say goodbye now, and wish you godspeed

361

on the rest of your trip." They watched the train conductor walk into the station, then turned to their new guide, Mr. Early.

"We got to move quick, slavechasers be watchin' for us here?" Hack said.

Cedric glanced at the black man in alarm, then reflexively scanned the platform before his features relaxed and he shook his head. "You must have had some close calls on your journey from the South, but it won't be near as dangerous for you up here. Still, it pays to keep your eyes peeled."

After he'd helped the two passengers into his carriage, Cedric pulled out his pocket watch. "We got about an hour till daylight," he said. "You'll be layin' up at my house today, and I'll see what I can do about gettin' you on a boat this evening."

"Where the boat gonna take us?" Hack asked.

"That depends on where the captain's bound. There's several small boats here known as 'abolition boats' that runs in to shore in Canada on their way to Detroit and other ports. I'll have to see if one of 'em is casting off tonight." Cedric gave Hack and Liz a broad wink and a grin. "They don't advertise their ferry services for fugitives, you know, so I've got to circulate down on the waterfront and ask around.

"You may be travelin' with other runaways," Cedric said. "Seems like there's more of 'em coming north every day. Could be all the talk of war has put a scare into them that's hopin' to make a break. Might be afraid they won't be able to escape at all if they wait too long.

Cedric's wife, Jewel, greeted them and gave them breakfast. While Liz and Hack stayed out of sight upstairs in the back bedroom, Cedric ambled down toward the harbor as if he were on his regular morning constitutional, not hurrying, yet observant of everything around him.

On Lake Erie the paths of escape were generally shorter than those connecting western areas such as Wisconsin and Illinois with Detroit or Amherstburg. These shorter routes ran up and down or across Lake Erie and into the Detroit River. The more important of these routes joined Toledo, Sandusky and Cleveland to Amherstburg and Detroit near the western end of the lake. But in reality there were as many different destination points on Canadian soil and points of embarkation in the States as there were boats and captains willing to transport fugitives to freedom.

For years thousands of runaway slaves had found crossing places along the Detroit River, especially from the city of Detroit. Numerous routes from Indiana along with several of the chief routes of western Ohio poured their passengers into Detroit. There the slaves would be transported by ferries and rowboats to Windsor in Canada West, later called Ontario, just across the Detroit River. This porous international barrier ran between Michigan and Canada for thirty miles, from Lake Erie to Lake St. Clair.

The movement of slaves to this region was a fact of which southerners early became aware. Their efforts to recover their slaves were occasionally successful, just at the moment the fugitives had their safe haven almost within sight across the river. But the majority of the people of Detroit and the surrounding districts rejoiced to see the slavecatchers outwitted.

There seemed to be plenty of these 'abolition boats' in the Sandusky harbor, and they provided ample accommodations for underground passengers. The *Arrow*, the *United States,* the *Bay City* and the *Mayflower* were but a few of the boats plying between Sandusky and Detroit. Their officers were always willing to help negroes reach Canadian ports. Though their official destination might be Detroit, these boats always touched first at Amherstburg or some other Canadian port where they landed their fugitives. Frequent use was also made of the smaller sloops, scows, sailboats and sharpies, with which fugitives could be "set across" the lake to their land of promise.

The *Harlequin*, a Lake Erie sloop captained by ardent abolitionist Ulysses Meacham, of Put-In-Bay on South Bass Island, Ohio, was such a boat. For years she ferried runaway slaves across Lake Erie to Pelee Island.

Legend had it that one day a lawman boarded the *Harlequin* at Put-In-Bay and informed Meacham that he intended to search for fugitive slaves. Ulysses asked, "By what authority do you board this vessel?"

"By the authority of the United States Government."

Captain Meacham said, "Then by the authority of God I cast you overboard," and threw the man over the side into the chilly waters of Lake Erie.

When Cedric Early returned to his house in late afternoon he went to Liz and Hack's room. "We're in luck," he said. "Captain Maynard Stenborg is set to sail to Detroit tonight in his sharpie, the *Lake Swallow,* with two fugitives that arrived yesterday, and he says he has room for two more. He'll touch at Pelee Island to let you and the others off. He's casting off from the Sandusky waterfront about nine o'clock."

"What's a sharpie?" Liz asked.

"It's a small sailboat used by fishermen, Liz. They're long flat-bottomed boats for sailing in shallow waters, but with a center board that can be lowered for stability in deeper water out on the lake. These boats have one or two masts with triangular sails, and they make better speed than a larger sailboat with a deeper draft."

Hack spoke up with a question. "What's this gonna cost us?"

Cedric smiled. "Nothing, Hack. Men like that Mr. Levi Coffin you mentioned, they raise money for fares on transportation like the cars that brought you here and like Mr. Stenborg's boat. We know that fugitives are likely to have little or no money, so we provide for these expenses. The other conductor and I will give Maynard forty dollars for him and his crewman. This will cover the fare for all four of you refugees."

Just before nine o'clock in the evening, Liz and Hack were escorted to the waterfront by Mr. Early. There they met another man guiding two boys who appeared, like Hack, to be dark Africans. Few words were exchanged as Mr. Stenborg quickly helped the passengers on board. His mate raised the sails, Maynard weighed anchor and they began to move slowly out of the harbor in this small open boat. By the time they sailed beyond the breakwater into the open lake, darkness had fallen. Small lights dotted the horizon, indicating other boats in- or outbound on this mellow September evening.

From his position at the tiller, Mr. Stenborg began to talk in muted tones. The passengers soon discovered he and his crewman had pleasant senses of humor. "Welcome aboard, boys and girls," he said. "We're not often favored with the company of females, now are we, Mike?"

The mate spoke up from his task of adjusting the sails, "No, sir, but it's a good omen by my way o'thinkin', Cap'n. Pardon me miss, but I couldn't help noticin' your lighter coloring, in a manner of speakin'. Is it slavery you're escapin', too then, may I ask?"

Liz hesitated, then decided Mike's question bore no insinuation or threat, so she said, "No, Hack and I got into trouble for helping a family of slaves to escape."

"Ah, 'tis a chancy business conductin' slaves to freedom, that it is."

"Y'all is takin' a chance, too, by sailin' us across this here lake. We 'preciate it," Hack said.

Maynard answered from the stern. "I daresay you've escaped worse dangers gettin' here than we'll face tonight, eh. We've a favorable breeze and calm waters, so we'll have you ashore on Pelee Island before we see the light of day."

Hack turned to the other two quiet passengers, who seemed to be no more than teenagers. "Where y'all from?" he said.

After a long silence, one of them said, "Memphis. What 'bout y'all?"

"Southern Indiana," Hack said.

"That ain't slave country, is it?"

"Long story."

Liz took Hack's hand. "Isn't that light coming closer? Mr. Stenborg, is that another boat?"

"Ya, she's a big boat and she's crossin' our bow, eh." Just then they were shocked by a stentorian horn blast that sounded two low notes, each of a power to vibrate their chests.

Liz fell against Hack and nearly screamed in surprise. "Oh, my goodness! Did they blow that horn just to warn us?"

Maynard laughed. "No, miss. He was just signalin' another big boat somewheres out there that we can't see, low in the water as we are. They let us little fellas look out for ourselves, eh."

Hack said, "I hear water splashin', like a paddle wheel on a steamboat down on the Ohio River. They got the same kind of boats up here?"

365

"I've heard they have both sidewheelers and sternwheelers on the Ohio, but we've got only sidewheelers. Most of 'em have sails, too, eh. Saves fuel when they're out on the lake and there's favorable air. In the harbors they use just the engines."

"Why they ain't got no sternwheelers?" Hack asked.

"Along the shore and in small harbors, a sidewheeler can turn in a smaller space than a sternwheeler. Around the lake, maneuverability is important. Like our little sharpie here, the *Lake Swallow*. She can float on a heavy dew and skitter circles 'round the larger craft, eh. In fact, the captains of them big salties like the one we just heard calls us little guys the 'mosquito fleet'."

"Why you call 'em salties?" Hack said.

"Because they come all the way up the St. Lawrence River from the salt water of the Atlantic to Montreal. Then, thanks to the Welland Canal, which connects Lake Ontario with Lake Erie, and the locks at the Soo, they can avoid Niagara Falls and the rapids at Sault Ste. Marie and sail all the way into Lake Superior. Those boats carry a lot of wheat and lumber to Europe. They also carry cargo to Chicago, such as coal from the east and iron ore from Minnesota for the big steel mills at the lower end of Lake Michigan, don't you know."

The nocturnal adventure filled Liz and Hack's senses with strange sights, sounds and smells of the open lake. The gentle motion of the waves was different from the movements of the cars they'd ridden for the first time less than twenty-four hours ago.

To the sailors on board, the soft swells made for as calm a voyage as they'd ever expect to see on Lake Erie, but to one of the two slave boys, even this gentle rocking gave him motion sickness. After each episode with his head over the side, vomiting, groaning, then resting a moment, he would repeat the sequence. Finally Hack went to his side and spoke quietly to him, then, bracing his elbow on the gunwale, held the lad's head as he strained to purge his already-empty stomach.

When he'd been at this work for some minutes, and the boy seemed to have quieted and stopped "hoisting his colors," as Mike said, Hack peered up at the thin rafts of clouds overhead and asked, as if to himself, "That old moon up yet?"

366

The boy stirred from his misery long enough to answer, "It is if ever I et it." This brought sympathetic chuckles from the others on board.

Sound seemed to carry well across the tranquil water. When a light from another small boat came near enough, they could hear unseen men's voices conversing calmly as they went about their routine chores of fishing. Occasionally a louder voice called from one boat to another. Liz tried to reconcile the awful threatening expanse out there in the darkness with the casual confidence conveyed by the fishermen's voices.

Hack moved back to his place beside Liz and she gratefully snuggled close to him in the darkness. He warmed her against the chill of the night air, and a moment later his hand brushed her chest, then loosened the buttons of her bodice. She felt his warm palm cup her bare breast, and she turned her face up to him for a kiss. At the same time she moved her own hand inside his shirt. They remained like this for several moments, each responding to the temptation offered by the other. When their bench seat creaked, it seemed to break the spell. Liz murmured into Hack's ear, "Oh, Hack, we mustn't . . . . Later, all right?" She gave him another kiss, then buttoned her clothing.

A few minutes later Hack, seeming to have his curiosity whetted by this nautical venture, addressed the older man. "Cap'n suh, the weather surely ain't this calm all the time out here on the big water. I hear'd folks say they has bad storms now and again."

"For sure, Hack. Many a sturdy sailor has met his early demise on these waters. These lakes are the graveyards of hundreds, probably thousands, of boats big and small, especially Lake Erie. Erie's the shallowest of the five sister lakes, eh, and as such she's the quickest and easiest riled into a full-blown howler when the wind kicks up, and it can come suddenly. Worst season for storms is fall, which we're comin' into now. Tonight might be the last cross-lake voyage for the *Lake Swallow* till spring. You can see how she'd be swamped by the lightest of rough seas."

"Oh, my goodness! How do you know we won't be caught by a storm tonight?" Liz said.

"We don't, Liz, if you want the fair and honest truth, but if a skipper's been lucky enough to survive a few years out here, he

367

learns to read the signs of foul weather approachin'. On the other hand, there's many a weather-wise captain that's now doin' his navigatin' from the bottom of the lake, eh." After that grim pronouncement the conversation languished.

Liz again leaned close to Hack, trying in vain to stifle her fears that, having made it through all the threats to their freedom in arriving at this tiny boat, they would now fall victim to an act of a vindictive God after all. She finally succumbed to the warmth of Hack's embrace, the motion of the boat, the creaking of masts and rudder. She soon fell asleep.

As she slept the other passengers and crew watched in silence as they sailed past several small lights announcing wharfs of lesser islands. Not all these dots in the lake appeared on maps, so Maynard Stenborg and his peers had to know the lake as well as their own living rooms to avoid disaster.

Long after moonrise the *Lake Swallow* approached Pelee Island, which Liz and Hack had seen on Levi Coffin's map, with its sharp-pointed headland jutting southward, beckoning fugitive voyagers to safety. Captain Stenborg's voice broke the long silence.

"See that strong light a little to starboard? That's the Pelee Island light. We'll put in there well before daylight. Then Michael and me'll bid you fond adieu, for we'll be off for Detroit, and nobody the wiser that four strokes have been struck for freedom tonight, eh."

# CHAPTER SEVENTY

The *Lake Swallow* put in at the wharf on the west side of Pelee Island and the passengers scrambled onto the dock. Their first few steps on solid ground were unsteady, having become so accustomed to the bobbing motion of the little sailboat. "Welcome to Canada!" Mike said as they walked in the pale light from the single lamp post on the pier.

The sleepy Indiana fugitives thanked him, then turned to each other. They were too befuddled to celebrate their arrival in a free country. "I can't believe this is Canada," Liz said. "From what little we can see it doesn't look any different from our country."

Hack took her hand and said, "We ain't finished yet. We got another boat ride, then somebody better meet us, else we'll be helpless as ducklins in mud." In spite of Hack's self-deprecation, his words drew a chuckle from Liz.

Mike said, "I'll put in a word with the mate of the *Courier*, the boat that'll take you on to the mainland at Leamington. She's riding at her berth right over here." He led them to the ferry boat a few yards away, one of the steamers Maynard described. All four of his passengers followed Mike through the darkness to the larger boat where a group of what appeared to be fugitive slaves had already gathered on the wharf.

Mike grinned and answered his charges' worried expressions by allowing that here on Pelee Island, a slavecatcher would face more danger than his negro quarry. Then the mate told them they'd be allowed to board the vessel just after daylight for the four-hour run to Leamington on the mainland.

After saying their goodbyes and expressing their gratitude to Mike, Liz and Hack found themselves among an excited group of perhaps a dozen negroes that also appeared to be waiting to board the *Courier*. Captain Stenborg's passengers were not introduced to a guide or conductor, apparently being expected to negotiate their own way from here. Liz and Hack sat on the ground against a railing near the landing stage of the boat.

Their two fellow passengers ended their long silence when they came among the larger group. There was a bit of spirited conversation among the negroes, and then they began to stir, as if the arrival of the boys had been a catalyst for the whole group to mount a spontaneous celebration, and to voice prayers of gratitude, shouts, songs and impromptu dancing to proclaim their long-sought freedom. Soon they began to sing. Liz, at first alarmed at the volume of sound suddenly enlivening the quiet night, began to be warmed by the infectious beat and harmony of the singing.

*When Israel was in Egypt's land,*
*Let my people go,*
*Oppressed so hard they could not stand,*
*Let my people go.*
*Go down, Moses,*
*Way down in Egypt's land,*
*Tell old Pharaoh,*
*Let my people go.*

The whole group of singers moved to the beat, and Liz felt her tired heart lifted by the people's celebration.

*When the sun come back,*
*When the first quail call,*
*Then the time is come*
*Foller the drinkin' gourd,*
*Foller the drinkin' gourd.*
*For the ole man say,*
*'Foller the drinkin' gourd.'*

"Hack, I've heard the name, 'Follow the Drinkin' Gourd,' but what do the words mean? Some people say these songs carry messages for runaway slaves, is that true?"

"I don't know much about it, but my old pap used to sing some a'them songs, said he learnt 'em as a child before he got his freedom.

"He said that one called 'Foller the Drinkin' Gourd' says when springtime come it's time to run away and head north. Of course the drinkin' gourd means the Big Dipper, and it points to the North Star. Remember I used the drinkin' gourd to find east when we was in the woods just before we come upon the Freemans? You hear'd 'bout how to find the star that points north, ain't you?"

"Yes, Uncle Vess told me. But what do they mean by 'the old man'?"

"Pap said there used to be a story 'bout a black man way down south that went sneakin' 'round the plantations gatherin' slaves that wanted to run away to freedom. He'd lead 'em north, first upriver along the Tombigbee to its headwaters, then 'cross the divide and down the Tennessee River to the Ohio at Paducah. From there he'd find a boat and take 'em 'cross to the free state of Illinois."

"How dangerous that must have been, for a black man to lead slaves out of the deep South."

"Pap said he was a sailor in his younger days, had a peg leg. They called him Peg Leg Joe. He teached 'em to follow his trail, 'cause it looked diff'rent, an' all, a natural left foot and a peg for a right foot."

"Oh, it brings tears to my eyes thinking what those people had to go through."

Hack took her in his arms. "Don't you think you come through a lot, yourself, woman, all the mis'ry you had to put up with to get here? We coulda been dead a dozen times, but you hepped me an' we got through it together. Any wonder I love you, gal?"

"You're sweet, Hack. Listen, they're singing another one."
*No more auction block for me,*
*No more, no more,*
*No more auction block for me,*
*Many thousand gone.*

*No more driver's lash for me,*
*No more, no more,*
*No more driver's lash for me,*
*Many thousand gone.*

When the singing stopped, Liz and Hack continued to listen to the group's animated conversation and prayers of thanks. Then the two who had come with Liz and Hack stepped away from the group, knelt on the wharf and kissed the free ground of Canada. They jumped up to receive hugs and laughter from the others. The group soon launched into more joyous songs.

# CHAPTER SEVENTY-ONE

On the steam ferry to Leamington Liz was the only white member of the group of fugitives, though some of the others were of light mulatto complexion so that brown-eyed, dark blond Liz was hardly unusual in appearance among them but for her height. She tried to avoid standing in conspicuous places, and thus calling attention to herself.

The Hoosier fugitives still wondered if they'd be met at the ferry landing. Many other questions came to mind, as well. But one uncertainty had already been answered.

It seemed as if their feelings for each other had been tested sufficiently on their long journey.

Hack was providing Liz with an enveloping kindness, the very nature of protectiveness, a warmth that relaxed her, even as it stimulated and made her more aware of living.

Because of her father's abuse, she'd held men and boys at a safe distance, observing their behavior. There were some at Sugar Branch she otherwise might have welcomed to court her. As it was, she'd watched. She saw they worked hard, courted, married, fed themselves and their families and made babies, but they seldom *shone*. Often they had not the time to be kind, kind as she was learning now, a man could be.

Now, knowing Hack, realizing day by day his rich, deep, self-contained nature, feeling his goodness, Liz had grown more humble. Her previous quiet rejection of men had been imposed on her by that one horrid experience, but here with Hack that reaction did not fit at all.

Hack seemed to have no dark emotional fevers in him, but he loved, and his love had awakened love for the first time in her. The feeling was hard to describe for Liz. She could more easily describe what she was discovering about the earlier years of her adolescence.

They would stay together, and not just until they found jobs and secure living accommodations. Trusting their safety, their very lives to each other had worked to this point, and they saw no reason to go off singly into their new lives now that freedom was finally theirs. As they had agreed days ago, they were both in this adventure for the long haul, and could not imagine facing the uncertainties of life in Canada alone. Besides, they had both fallen in love, and that seemed all that truly mattered.

Liz stood with Hack at the rail just aft of the pilot house breathing the mellow air with its scent of open water, hair blowing, feeling sunlight on her shoulders, her body thrilling even to the vibration of the engines coming through her feet. Beside her Hack was speaking hopefully about their new life in a new land. In spite of their recent fears and hardships, the dreadful accident on Lost Fork and the long hard journey that had brought them here, Liz was exhilarated. It was as if she were being reborn into a wholly new world, and more than that, into an altered mind and body.

They were met in early afternoon, as they wandered down the landing stage of the *Courier* looking lost, by a Mr. Thaddeus Graves of Leamington. Graves was one of several men there to meet any fugitive travelers in need of assistance. They made daily rounds of the Leamington harbor scouting any arriving abolition boats.

Liz showed Mr. Graves the envelope with the name of Reverend Isaac Rice printed on it. "This is our letter of introduction, sir, from Reverend Ansel Hawkins at Yellow Springs, Ohio, to Reverend Isaac Rice on King Street at a town called Amherstburg, Ontario. Have you heard of Reverend Rice?"

The stiff Mr. Graves seemed a bit mollified at the sight of the letter. "Why yes, young lady, I certainly am acquainted with that gentleman. He's well known in Upper Canada as the founder of a school for children of fugitives in Amherstburg. Um . . . am I to assume, young lady, that the two of you are traveling together?"

"Yes, sir. We've come all the way from the Ohio River in southern Indiana, trying to keep a step ahead of lawmen and slavecatchers after falling into trouble conducting a slave family to safety."

"Well . . . I was about to say it's very dangerous for a young white lady to be traveling with a negro man anywhere, and under any circumstances. I can well imagine that you did indeed face all sorts of difficulties in your journey here. I must say I'm surprised you made it at all."

"We succeeded only because of good fortune and the help of some wonderful people, sir."

Mr. Graves finally seemed to focus on the task at hand then, and he continued with a more cheerful attitude. The envelope containing the letter of introduction seemed to have relieved Graves of the responsibility of getting the new arrivals in contact with a supportive family or group in Leamington. He said, "Well, then, since you're in need of only one night's lodging here in Leamington, you're welcome to stay overnight with my wife and me. I'm sure you'll find her a pleasant hostess.

They were shortly settled at the Graves house in Leamington, after meeting Mr. Graves's charming wife, Marilee, who immediately made them feel welcome without a word or a suspicious glance in regard to their different races or their circumstances. Then Thaddeus was off to quickly arrange for another man, a Mr. Snowden, to convey them in his surrey early the next morning straightway to the home of Rev. Isaac Rice in Amherstburg, a distance of some thirty-five miles. This decision, handled with such expediency, indicated to Liz that Reverend Rice must be a prominent personage in Amherstburg and Upper Canada.

After lodging overnight in the home of Thaddeus and the gracious Marilee they were anxious to begin the long journey to Amherstburg the next day with Mr. Snowdon. Along the way they passed through attractive towns with the names Kingsville and Harrow. Even the smaller villages seemed thrifty and clean. The travelers observed that the harvest season was in full swing in these

375

townships of southern Ontario, and they found the agricultural bounty of the region impressive. Everywhere they saw vast flat fields where people were at work harvesting hay, corn, wheat and numerous varieties of fruits and vegetables, from grapes to turnips. Mr. Snowden told them this peninsula was the southernmost point in Canada and the soil was fertile. "Why wouldn't she be one of the bread baskets of our fair country, eh?" he said. Still, Liz had a sobering thought that winter here must surely stand in sharp contrast to the mellow harvest weather they were having today.

# CHAPTER SEVENTY-TWO

Toward evening Mr. Snowden delivered Liz and Hack in front of a two-story house in Amherstburg, the home of Rev. Isaac Rice. He escorted them to the front door.

A negro maid met them. "This is Callie," Snowden said. "Callie, meet Liz and Hack. They've escaped all the way from Indiana."

Though her eyes were watchful, Callie's smile was warm with understanding for the well-traveled pair before her. She said, "Pleased to meet y'all." The woman stepped back and Mr. Snowden indicated they should enter.

"Is the reverend about, Callie? Thought I'd say hello to him before heading over to my friend's house for the night."

"I's sorry, Mr. Snowden, but Rev. Rice ain't here right now," Callie said, "He been up toward Chatham at church meetin's, axin' for money for his school, but he be home tomorrow. These folks know 'bout the school?"

Liz said, "Yes, we've heard of the reverend's work for fugitives' children here at the King Street School. Mr. Levi Coffin down in Indiana spoke of visiting Rev. Rice and being quite impressed with his work."

"The school is out there in the back yard. Students and the teacher done gone home for the day now. Come on, y'all, I'll show you where to sleep. You must be tired." They expressed their gratitude to Mr. Snowden, then went upstairs with Callie.

As Callie led them through the second-floor, low-ceilinged hallway, Liz asked her, "Were you a slave . . . before?"

"Yessum, I made it up here all the way from Vine Grove, Kentucky a little over two year ago, I did. The good Lord, he bless me with freedom."

"Is Reverend Rice a Canadian?"

"No, Miss Liz; he had a big church down in Ohio before he come up here to do missionary work."

Hack looked around as if wondering where they would sleep. Callie noticed, but before she made the decision she asked, "S'cuse me, ma'am, we don't get many white folks comin' in with the blacks. I mean . . . is y'all married?"

Liz saw the woman's shyness on this sensitive subject and tried to ease her discomfort. "We were helping a slave family when we got into some trouble and had to run away ourselves. We're not married, just . . . friends."

"Yessum. Reason I axed, you the only folks here right now. Since you ain't married I'll put you over here in what we call the women's room, miss, and him in the men's bedroom."

"That'll be fine. We thank you, Callie," Hack said.

"I see you ain't totin' much. You rest a few minutes, then come down to the kitchen. Look like you could use somethin' to eat. You'll find the beds clean, and they's water, soap and towels on the washstands in your rooms."

Hack chuckled. "We 'preciate these here fine fixin's," he said. He and Liz grinned at each other, sharing their relief and gratitude. Callie went back downstairs to start cooking while Liz and Hack washed their hands and faces, then looked around the upstairs rooms. They still marveled at these luxurious accommodations compared to some of the places they'd slept on their northward journey. The two second-floor rooms were tucked under the eaves, one room on each side of the hallway.

When they came downstairs, Callie told them to sit down at the kitchen table. "We won't use the dinin' room this time. That's for Sunday comp'ny. For this evenin' that be too much shefflin' of the dishes for the fewness of the vittles." The travelers simply nodded. The smells of frying pork chops, green beans and boiled potatoes had them swallowing their saliva in anticipation of hot food.

"The way we been eatin' lately, we couldn't name one meal from another, nohow," Hack said. "We 'preciate the food, Callie."

378

Liz added her compliment. "Callie, I don't think I've ever had coffee this good."

As they tucked into the substantial meal, Liz again found that she filled up quickly. Callie said, "Y'all stay 'round here a few days, Callie have you fattened up like them shoats out back. Pack you and the hogs up together, send y'all off to market." The laughter that followed nearly brought tears to Liz's eyes. If felt so good to laugh out loud.

After supper, Callie said, "Reverend Rice done give me this evenin' off, seein's how he comin' back tomorrow evenin'. I'll leave y'all on your own. Nobody gonna bother you and you know your way 'round now." She giggled. "I'm goin' out to see my sugarman for a little while, be back 'fore too late. Callie be here to fix you breakfast in the mornin'."

The setting sun was sending shafts of orange light through the kitchen windows as they thanked Callie again and made their way upstairs. "Reverend Rice be glad to see y'all when he come back," she said.

Callie had told them to take what clean used clothes they needed from a chest in the upstairs hallway and leave theirs at the head of the stairs for her to wash. Relieved that for several days now she'd been free to dress as a woman, Liz chose several pieces of clothing from the trunk.

Hack picked up an extra shirt and pants and a pair of used boots that looked as if they'd fit well enough. "My old boots is plumb wore out, but these here don't have no place to carry my knife," Hack mused, almost to himself.

"Maybe you won't need the knife now that we're here," Liz said.

"We'll ponder that after a while," he said. He took his clothes and boots into the men's bedroom.

Each of the two upstairs rooms contained a wash stand, a dresser, chairs and two beds. Extra pallets lay neatly folded in the corner, for times when the house was crowded, Liz surmised. Sheer curtains framed the single large window at the end of each room. Liz's window faced west, opposite the one in Hack's room with an eastern exposure.

379

The travelers spent a long time enjoying the luxury of sponge baths in their separate rooms. Liz discovered some soft soap with which she washed her hair. She donned her gown and walked around the room drying her hair, fluffing it with one of the soft towels.

She opened her window and stood before it enjoying the cool evening breeze and the fading shades of sunset above the trees and rooftops of the neighborhood. She exulted in the feeling of being clean and relaxed, looking forward to wearing her change of feminine clothes, and most of all, finally being in a place of safety. When her hair was dry she sat on the bed not far from the window, rubbing her rough hands with scented lanolin from a small dish she found on her washstand.

Faint sounds came from Hack moving about in his room, washing, trying on the clothes, springs squeaking when he sat on the bed to try on his boots. When he became quiet, Liz stepped out of her room, leaving the door open, and moved across the hall to tap on his door.

At first she heard only silence. Then a sleepy voice said, "Come in." She opened the door and saw Hack lying on his bed. He lay on his back with only the sheet covering him. She could tell he was nude. He blinked, trying to wake up. She paused a moment taking in the sight of him, this healthy young man in the prime of his life, smelling of soap, the only blemish a white bandage on his left shoulder.

She sat on the side of his bed, found his hand and kissed it, then couldn't resist moving her own hand over his chest under the sheet. "Hack, you're sleeping your life away," she said. She grinned. "You know, we'll have to get our days and nights straightened out. This is so strange. We can begin to act like normal people again."

"We'll work that out tomorrow, lady. Right now I'm plumb tuckered out," he said. "My body's stiff as a rusty gate, now that we ain't got to be lookin' over our shoulders all the time."

"You're not getting sick, are you?" She caressed his arm and shoulder. "Your arm hurting?"

"Not much, just tired. Ain't you sleepy, too?"

"Sure, I'm tired, but I just thought we might spend a few minutes together before sleep."

He chuckled and drew her face down for another kiss. "Listen, little mama, you're gonna be the first thing on my mind in the mornin', so you better rest up, gal."

"We'll see about that, you bad boy. I just heard Callie leaving. We've got the whole place to ourselves. Why don't we go outside for some air? There'll be plenty of time for sleep later."

He sat up. "You're a lot of trouble, woman. I might could do it for another kiss." After she kissed him he patted her backside. "It'll take me a minute to get dressed."

"I noticed there's a high fence around the yard, and it'll soon be dark," she said. "I think I'll wear just my gown."

"I'll slip on my pants and shirt. You care if I go barefoot?"

"Suit yourself, you old Indian. Maybe I'll do the same."

They peered out the kitchen window at the back yard. The weather was cool and dry, and a couple of street lamps from behind the reverend's property cast a sallow light over the yard. By the gate in the back fence at the end of the lot the small schoolhouse and its toy-like belfry gleamed white. The building was empty at this time of day, and to the weary travelers the scene looked inviting. They decided to explore. They found the yard was covered with easy-on-the-feet green grass near the house, but as they neared the schoolhouse the ground had been worn down to gravelly bare earth by the children's play.

At the top of the schoolhouse steps they creaked the door open. Liz was immediately struck by the familiar smell of old books, stale porridge from the children's lunch, and lye soap from a recent floor scrubbing. "This reminds me of the Sugar Branch schoolhouse," she said.

The room's furnishings were spartan. Aside from the worn student benches, a stove, a waste basket, the teacher's chair, and a chalkboard the only other furnishing was a long low table in front of the chair with a small box for a lectern. This apparently sufficed as the teacher's desk. In the gloomy light near the door they discerned a rope twisted around a bracket on the wall, then extending upward through a hole in the ceiling. This evidently connected to a bell.

Liz approached the chalkboard, found a stub of chalk, and printed:

E. C.

T. ✝ L.

J. H.

She started to explain her message to Hack, but he grinned and told her he understood.

Hack yawned and went to sit on the end of the table. Liz walked around the room, nostalgic for her own school days, feeling sad at the separation from her home and family. She stood for a moment looking out one of the tall windows that extended almost to the floor. When she turned she saw Hack looking at her silhouetted form underneath her long gown. Aware that she wore nothing next to her skin, she knew her body was outlined by the lamplight from outside. She felt her mood changing, and she smiled to herself. For a moment she allowed him to continue enjoying the view.

She made a little show of looking downward self-consciously, then changed her expression from modest to coquettish, and spoke with a capricious smile, locking eyes with him. "Looks like someone is getting an eyeful." He grinned, his eyes continuing to explore the contours of her body.

"We may be safe, now, Hack," she said, as she walked toward him. "But Mr. Coffin said we must always be watchful." Then she affected the old Quaker's dialect as she whispered with a teasing smirk, coming close, brushing her cheek against his, speaking softly into his ear. "I see thee has been watchful just now. Has thee seen what thee is looking for?"

Hack said nothing, but she could tell her teasing had the desired effect. The room became quiet; time seemed to stop. Only a cricket's chirp and a passing carriage in the street beyond the fence rippled the total calm of the peaceful evening. Hack finally exhaled. She caressed his face and felt his heartbeat thrumming in his neck. He stood and she moved into his arms.

As they kissed he reached to touch her long gown, collecting folds of it in his hands, lifting the soft material over her head. He let it drift to the floor. His hands came to rest on her bare hips. She lifted her hands to his face and kissed him, then slowly unbuttoned his shirt and pushed it off his shoulders. He let his pants drop, stepped out of them, then pulled her close. They kissed for a long moment before he turned her toward the table. "Lean on your elbows," he said. They soon became oblivious to the squeaking of the table joints, the sounds from the street, even their own groans and heavy breathing. Time slipped by as they indulged their playful and amorous yearnings.

They did not hear Callie come to the open door of the schoolhouse. She had returned home to find the back door of the house standing open, and came out to investigate. She saw the shadow-forms at the table, heard its stressed joints rocking, the muffled voices. She put her hand over her mouth to keep from laughing out loud.

When the lovers returned to the house they slept in Hack's bed with their bodies intertwined, waking occasionally to kiss and caress each other again before returning to dreamless sleep.

They woke early in the morning refreshed, and made love again. Afterward they lay in bed more at ease than they'd ever been with each other, as lethargic as two puppies, licking, kissing, pretending to bite each other, laughing. They had nothing to do but wait for the reverend's return that evening, when they could begin acquainting themselves with their host and their new homeland. They looked forward to beginning their search for permanent quarters, jobs and other arrangements in Amherstburg.

When they came downstairs they found Callie had kept breakfast warm in the oven for them. Afterward, the maid took Liz aside, giggled and whispered, "I's sorry, but I couldn't hep findin' y'all out in the schoolhouse las' night when I come home an' seen the back door open." Liz started to apologize, but Callie stopped her.

"Y'all go on an' squeak that bed in the men's bedroom all day if you want to while I's the only one here. But Reverend Rice come back tonight, an' knowin' y'all ain't married, he be sure to take 'ception to the sounds when you two makin' sugartime. Somebody give the reverend two of them new-fangled beds with iron springs an' he put 'em in the men's sleepin' room. Then he foun' out they make noise to high heaven, and they right above the reverend's bedroom.

"Don't never say who told you this, but you an' your man needs to try one of them beds in the women's room. They be old rope beds what don't make noise. Them be softer, too, with big goose down ticks on 'em." Callie bashfully dropped her gaze a moment before confiding to Liz, "Leastways, that's what some other body tole me. Me an' my sugarman wouldn't know nothin' 'bout it." Callie gave Liz a sly wink, and Hack came into the kitchen to see what their laughter was all about.

After breakfast Hack said, "Here we are, the whole day ahead of us and nothin' to do till the reverend comes back."

"Oh, I'm sure we can think of something," Liz said. She smirked at him. "Come up to my room. We'll try out my rope bed and see if we can't get into a little more mischief." Hack laughed, grabbed her around the waist and pulled her close. When Callie wasn't looking he led her upstairs to the women's chamber. They found the rope bed quiet and delightfully well-adapted to their needs.

# CHAPTER SEVENTY-THREE

That evening shortly before sunset, Reverend Isaac Rice arrived home in a buggy driven by a white-haired negro man. The bay mare stopped before the house and the driver, following the reverend, brought his bags inside.

Callie waited on the step to greet her boss, saying, "Welcome home, Reverend. I hopes you traveled safe. Meetin's go well, suh?"

"Ah yes, Callie, but turnip-squeezing isn't easy. It's good to be home again. Seems as the years fly by travel takes a greater toll. Any important-looking mail, or any visitors of note in my absence?"

Callie and the heavily-loaded driver hurried to follow Rev. Rice as he strode through the house. "You got two fugitives, Reverend. Come in from Leamington yestiddy. They ain't the usual run of fugitives, suh, one's a white lady, the other a black man. They ain't slaves, but had to run off 'cause they got into trouble heppin' a slave family escape from the South."

"Did you get them settled? Are they sick or injured?"

"They be fine, suh, 'cep the nigger man been shot, but he healin' up right good now. I give 'em fresh clothes from the trunk upstairs. They says they got a letter to you from a preacher down in Ohio."

"Where are they now?"

"Upstairs, suh. Shall I fix you some supper, reverend? Them two ain't et yet, neither."

Yes, go ahead and fix supper. Call them down to the kitchen. I'll see what needs to be done."

When Reverend Rice, Liz and Hack had gathered at the kitchen table, Callie briefly introduced them. Rev. Rice enquired about their experiences on the way to Amherstburg. They related the whole story to the preacher, save for the shooting on Lost Fork, while they ate supper.

"I see the two of you have seen your share of danger on your journey," he said. "As soon as you've rested, we shall try to get you situated in our community. Most refugees find work within a week of their arrival, jobs being plentiful these days. We'll also find living quarters for you. Ah . . . what is, may I ask, the nature of your connection with each other? Are you married?"

Hack answered the reverend's question. "Nahsuh, we ain't married. But we're best friends, and we'd like to live close by each other, suh. The days we spent travelin' an' the troubles we seen has drawed us together, you might say."

The minister was silent for several moments as he remained intent on his food. Finally he looked up at Hack. "As you will see, young man, individuals of mixed race are common here, and there are couples who differ widely in skin color and racial heritage. However, it seems that your case is more extreme than most.

"Miss, you must be aware that a white woman and a black man traveling alone together, especially in the States, is seldom done in these times. It's a wonder you've survived at all. Does your family know of and approve your association with this man?"

Liz looked squarely at the preacher and nodded slightly. "Reverend Rice, were some in my family to know how we feel toward each other they would be skeptical, and might never accept us as a couple. But truly, sir, looking back, Hack . . . James and I had become more than just friends, even by the time we left my grandparents' place in Indiana. On the perilous journey here we've found our commitment has deepened, sir, to the point where now we truly love each other."

"Yet you are not married."

"Yes, sir," Liz answered. "We have been offered to be married by a minister with whom I think you are acquainted in Yellow Springs, Ohio, but we declined in order to first reach this land of freedom before we subject ourselves to such an additional responsibility, for ourselves and our future children, sir."

"I see. Yellow Springs, you say? Could you be speaking of my good friend Reverend Ansel Hawkins?"

Liz nodded and brought forth the envelope containing Rev. Hawkins's letter. With tears in her eyes she said, "Yes, sir. He and his wife, Annabell, came to our rescue at that town when it seemed our hope of escape was nearly gone, and he has been gracious enough to send a letter of introduction for us."

She handed Rev. Rice the envelope with his name printed on it. He broke the seal and unfolded the letter.

*September 10, 1860, Yellow Springs, Oh.*
*My dear friend and colleague, Rev. Isaac Rice:*

*I trust that in God's good providence this letter will be handed to you in safety by our good friends, James Hackney and Elizabeth Cunningham. They have lived with us for several days, and have proved themselves worthy, in all respects, of our confidence and regard. The laws of this republican and Christian land, in particular the Fugitive Slave Bill, to which President Fillmore affixed his signature some ten years ago, (tell it not in Moscow, nor in Constantinople) regard them only as desperate felons - he by the color of his skin and she by helping him conduct a family of runaway slaves to freedom. But they have nobly vindicated their right to freedom these previous weeks by winning their tortuous way to it.*

*This letter is written to introduce them to you. I know you will extend your hand to welcome these poor hunted fellow-creatures. Henceforth, Canada is their nation and their home. May God ever smile upon Canada and upon her good, much-loved, and deservedly-honored Queen Victoria, for the generous protection that is given to refugees of every rank, and of every color and clime. It is with real regret for our personal loss in their departure, as well as burning shame for the land that is not worthy of them, that we send them away, or rather allow them to go. But, with all the courage they have shown in their trying hour, they see it is foolhardy to attempt to stay here longer.*

*I shall close with many renewed thanks for all your kind deeds toward us.*
*Respectfully yours, Rev. Ansel Leonidas Hawkins*

# CHAPTER SEVENTY-FOUR

The travelers watched anxiously as Rev. Rice read the letter twice. Then he looked up and regarded the couple a long moment before he spoke. "Hmm, it's good to hear from the Hawkinses, and you need no more than Ansel's letter for us to accept you with no further questions. I see you and your circumstances are even more unusual than I first thought. We'll see what we can do to facilitate your entry into this country, this town and our fugitive community." He paused and gazed out the window, rubbed his chin, then turned back to them.

"I'm going to send Callie over to an associate's house in the morning to ask if he can escort you around to meet various friends and colleagues here in Amherstburg. They will begin looking for living quarters and employment for the two of you. I would take you myself, except I must prepare for a rather challenging meeting at the schoolhouse this evening, and Callie will be occupied assisting me."

Hardly an hour after breakfast the next day Callie returned with Mr. Arvil Zeebart, a white man, in his black buggy with yellow hubs and spokes and a sprightly pair of small black mares in harness. Mr. Zeebart wore a derby hat, coat and dark trousers. His trimmed jet black beard completed his well-kempt image.

Mr. Zeebart stepped down from his rig and enthusiastically greeted Liz and Hack. "Pleased to meet you, Miss Elizabeth, James. Callie tells me you've seen some hard times on your journey to Amherstburg. Just be assured that we and our friends will try to make you welcome. We have no other recent arrivals to aid at the moment, so we can devote the day to just you two." Liz was secretly amused at Mr. Zeebart's fussiness. He seemed a nervous, fastidious little man.

"Thank you, Mr. Zeebart," Liz said. "Taking in all these new sights and sounds is a bit overwhelming, but we feel fortunate to be here, and to have your help."

"After we get settled maybe we can help others like us later on," Hack said.

Mr. Zeebart grinned and nodded. "Come then, let's go meet some people."

For the rest of the day their escort introduced them to ministers, merchants, lawyers, homeowners, farmers and the women at the resettlement office. The helpful people they met seemed about evenly divided racially between blacks, whites and mulattos. The two recent arrivals found much encouragement in the people's offers of assistance.

Late in the morning, after introducing them to a Mr. Langston, a local grocer, Mr. Zeebart took Liz and Hack across the street to a cafe and ordered lunch for the three of them. While they ate, their host said, "Hack, depending on your line of work, there are jobs available here. For instance, Mr. Langston just now told me as we were leaving that he could use your help stocking shelves and making deliveries once you get settled. I'm sure you'll both be able to find suitable work after you get your bearings."

"Sounds good, Mr. Zeebart," Hack said. "I'm ready to start makin' my own way, as the feller says."

Liz added, "He's quite good with horses, Mr. Zeebart. He's done livery and farrier work, training, even some doctoring."

"Good. We'll see about that soon, Hack. Now, Liz," the older man said, "I've noticed you're quite well spoken. May I ask if you read and write, also?"

"Yes, sir. I've completed eighth grade at our Sugar Branch school where my family lived in Indiana. And my mother, bless her heart, was known among our neighbors for her unusual intellect. My earliest memory is of her reading to me, and she started me reading borrowed primer books as soon as I was big enough to hold them."

"Excellent! Should you be interested later our community is always in need of teachers, particularly at Reverend Rice's school and others like it, for children of fugitive slaves. But there are many other opportunities for literate men and women here. The fact that you are white will be useful, as well, but please don't take that as an arrogant or biased statement. I have an idea you'll see the logic in that very soon.

"By the way, I'd like for you both to accompany me to the meeting at Rev. Rice's school tonight. The discussion will deal with educational topics, though this may be confusing to you at this early juncture. There will be several educators there, and the discussion may help determine the direction of fugitive children's education in our communities. The fact that you two represent both sides of the racial equation might be appropriate to our discussion."

"Oh, my goodness, Mr. Zeebart, you're speaking of things that go right over our heads. We're unprepared to join any discussion at this point. And I may be unqualified for *any* job here, much less *teaching*! You must understand that at home I was living with my grandparents simply helping them with their everyday chores."

"Of course, Miss Liz, please excuse me. I've been moving too fast, babbling on way beyond reason. I just see you young people as possessing talents that might later be put to use in our communities. You have no idea of how needy most of our arriving fugitives are, in both the physical and intellectual areas. There are never enough teachers and others available to help.

"By observing our discussion tonight, the educational concerns of our community may become clearer to you, then later you both may find ways to contribute, be it teaching, working with horses, or something else." He smiled across the table at Liz. "Don't let it become a care for you. We'll give you both time to get acquainted here, of course."

By the end of the day, Mr. Zeebart had worn them out. Liz and Hack retired for an hour to their rooms. They could hear bits of conversation between Mr. Zeebart and Reverend Rice drifting up from downstairs. At six-forty-five the five of them made their way to the schoolhouse, the maid bringing a large pot of hot cider and Liz walking beside her with a basket of Callie's cookies.

As they walked along side by side, Callie quietly told Liz that Rev. Rice said they could stay at his house for a while, seeing as how it wasn't crowded, and perhaps after they'd gotten settled their help would be useful to any new arrivals in adapting to life in

Canada. Liz and Callie exchanged elfish smiles, like two school girls with grown-up secrets.

Four chairs had been set up at the front between the long table and the chalkboard, with students' benches arranged in rows for the audience. A little before seven o'clock people began to file in. Liz noticed that Reverend Rice welcomed everyone at the door, directing two women to the row of chairs at the front, along with a distinguished-looking older gentleman.

Waiting for the meeting to begin, Liz found herself standing beside the long table at which she and Hack had enjoyed their pleasures of the flesh less than twenty-four hours before. In mock surprise she whispered, "Oh, Hack! It looks as if we left a drop of our love right here on the table.". She pretended to look both ways, then mischievously wet a finger and wiped an imaginary spot off the wooden surface. She gave Hack a prankish grin, her eyes sparkling.

He merely shook his head as a slow smirk played about the corners of his mouth. His dipped chin and one raised eyebrow said, "I'll deal with you later."

By the time Reverend Rice rose to address the meeting, the audience numbered perhaps twenty or more. Callie had placed several coal oil lamps around the room on window sills and shelves. To last night's nostalgic smells in the room, Liz now noted the additional odor of coal oil and the fustiness of adults' clothing.

Reverend Rice's welcoming remarks were quite brief, and Liz thought he seemed ill at ease. He first introduced the older gentleman as Reverend William King, founder of the Elgin Settlement at Buxton, Canada West. Rev. Rice indicated that Rev. King's school at that location had been visited by dignitaries who gave the Elgin school high marks. The audience applauded politely as the old minister came to the front.

Liz could not follow most of Rev. King's references to the nature of education for fugitives and their children in Canada, but she got the impression that he urged leaders of other such schools in the area to keep standards high, and to actively apply to government officials for regulations that would treat all segments of the population equally and fairly. He complimented the three speakers here tonight, the two ladies, and Rev. Rice for hosting the meeting.

391

After a few minutes Rev. King retired and Mrs. Mary Bibb stepped to the lectern. She and her late husband, Henry Bibb, had operated an abolitionist newspaper at Windsor, Canada West, and she also taught black students in a school she founded.

The next speaker was introduced as Mary Shadd Cary, of near Chatham, Canada West. This well-educated lady, too, had founded a newspaper with family members and opened a school for both black and white students in her town.

It seemed to Liz that after each of the ladies had their say, the meeting took on the flavor of a debate, with Rev. King moderating, taking questions from the audience. Mrs. Bibb argued that the black children and their parents should be educated with self-sufficiency as the goal, while Mrs. Cary suggested that approach would foster segregation, and that both blacks and whites should be invited to their schools in order that racial integration would eventually be realized.

The subject soon turned to the ladies' comments on the methods Rev. Rice employed, particularly in fundraising and in managing the funds he received. Mrs. Bibb and Mrs. Cary were very direct in their criticism of the management of Rice's King Street School. Fundraising had become so frenetic, they alleged, that the institution had been given the name "The Begging Society."

Mrs. Bibb mentioned a fire that had damaged Rice's school a few years ago. Firefighters found an old man living on the premises in very poor condition. Further investigation, she said, showed that Rev. Rice had received a particular grant of more than seven-hundred dollars, but used only ten dollars of it for the benefit of his students. Mrs. Cary complained that Rev. Rice's dramatic descriptions of the blacks' poor physical and intellectual condition to aid his fundraising efforts further encouraged separation of the races in Amherstburg.

Rev. Rice rose to protest that no less a selfless volunteer for the fugitives' cause than Levi Coffin had visited his school and given it glowing commendations in his writings.

Eventually the meeting was brought to an amicable close by the diplomatic Rev. King. He invited the group to enjoy Callie's refreshments and said the speakers would be available to answer questions individually.

Liz, sitting next to the eager Mr. Zeebart and having struggled to comprehend his whispered commentary during the meeting, found herself looking forward to helping Callie clean up and then going to bed. This was not to happen soon, for Mr. Zeebart insisted on introducing Liz and Hack to Mrs. Cary.

The dignified and accomplished negro lady listened with interest as Mr. Zeebart quickly described Liz and Hack's circumstances, and the possibility of their contributing to the educational efforts in Amherstburg. Mrs. Cary said, "Perhaps you young people working as a team could eventually help us demonstrate the high principles we espouse — of integrating people of all colors into our communities.

"Here's my card. After you become settled and adjusted to Canadian life, please write to me. We may be able to work together on a project I have in mind. However, if these persistent rumors of civil war become a reality in my original home south of the border, my work here may be indefinitely postponed. I shall do whatever I can to support the Union Cause, and this may require my returning to the States."

With that, Mrs. Cary smiled warmly, shook their hands and went on to speak with another person who had a question.

Liz asked Hack to put the card in his pocket, then said, "Oh, Hack, I hope you didn't feel left out. Mr. Zeebart was whispering a blue streak explaining what the speakers were saying, but I still don't understand most of it. I'm going to help Callie clean up and then we can go back to the house."

Hack shook his head and smiled, but his eyes were looking off across the room. "Nah, I don't feel bad. I think the old guy got a kick out of talkin' you up. I'd of just went to sleep if it hadn't been for a person I seen 'cross the room over there. I knowed I seen her somewheres before, but couldn't place her till just a minute ago. C'mon, we need to talk to her."

393

# CHAPTER SEVENTY-FIVE

A mong the former slaves in the audience Hack had seen a beautiful mulatto woman he was sure he'd met before, but where? Who was she? Then he remembered; this was Ivy Mays, the fugitive slave girl who Sylvester Morrison guided from the Ohio River to Lancaster back when Hack was a kid. Then Hack's father, James Hackney, Sr., took her on the sixteen-mile nocturnal journey to Vernon. The young Hack and Ivy met and talked briefly that evening at the home of Reverend and Mrs. Tibbets at Lancaster before she and his father left.

When Hack and Liz approached the woman, and Hack spoke her name, she stared at them both a long moment before her attention settled on the black man before her. "Where . . . how do you know my name?" she said, still showing a surprised smile, eyes searching his face.

"Way off down in Lancaster, Indiana," Hack said, smiling. "Remember the night back in . . . when was it . . . maybe '45? My pap took you from Rev. Tibbets's house on out to Vernon? I was just a skinny little kid then, but I told you I thought you was a purty gal, remember?"

"Oh! Oh, mercy," Ivy said, her hand coming to her mouth, eyes wide. She continued as if out of breath. "Your daddy's name was Hackley, wasn't it? Didn't . . . don't you and he have the same first name?"

"Our name is *Hackney*, Miss Ivy, he's James, Sr. and I'm James, Jr. Nowdays people call me Hack."

"Oh, yes! Two James Hackneys. And I remember you talked right up. Didn't you say somethin' about a little girlfriend, but you wouldn't tell us her name?"

They both laughed as Ivy took his hand and shook it.

"Oh my, Hack. Your father and all those people at the Tibbetses were so kind to me," she said, "and the man who brought me to Lancaster on that rugged trail from the river, his name was Sylvester. He said to call him Vess . . . . Don't remember his last name, do you know him?"

"I sure do know him, name's Sylvester Morrison, and this here's Elizabeth Cunningham. She's Sylvester's niece."

"Really! Oh, I'm so happy to meet you both. Sylvester saved my life that night in more ways than one, and I'll be forever grateful to him. Tell me, is he still living there, and is he doin' all right?"

Liz spoke for the first time. "Yes, Ivy, Sylvester was doing well the last time I saw him. He's a farmer, married, and they have three children, two boys and a girl. Uncle Vess and Leanna have been a second father and mother to me."

Ivy looked around at the rapidly emptying room. "Oh, I've got so many questions to ask you both. My husband's sister, Irene, is stayin' with the kids tonight, so I have to hurry home now, but we must meet again when we have more time. Do y'all live here in Amherstburg?"

"For the time bein' we're stayin' right here with Reverend Rice," Hack said. "We have a hundred questions for you, too. Do you live here'bouts?"

"This is a miracle!" Ivy said. "I live just a few streets over. Mrs. Cary and some of us are tryin' to get the trustees to let white and black children go to the same public schools. That's why I came tonight."

"We could meet you tomorrow, or most any time you're free, couldn't we, Liz?"

The three new friends agreed to meet the next evening. Ivy invited them to choir practice at her church just a few blocks away, and said they could visit afterward at her house. "Irene'll have the kids in bed and my husband, Ross, will let her go home by the time we get there. You'll meet Ross and we can talk as long as we want. I still can't believe this. Here we are livin' less than a mile from each other, after all these years!"

Outside the schoolhouse they said their brief goodbyes after Ivy gave them directions to her church. "I just got to hug you both," she said. "I'm so excited to meet you. This is bringin' together two parts of my life!"

On their way back to the house Hack talked excitedly, telling Liz about meeting Ivy all those years ago. Liz complimented him on being able to recognize her, but then she said Ivy would be hard to forget, beautiful as she is, and with those striking amber eyes.

Choir practice at the Amherstburg AME Church reminded Liz of the songs of celebration she and Hack had heard at the Pelee Island dock. She was thrilled at the exuberance of the negro singers, most of whom, Ivy told them later, were either fugitive slaves or their descendants. Freedom still seemed fresh for them, and they celebrated it in song.

Afterward, Ivy talked excitedly as she led them the few blocks along board sidewalks above the muddy streets to her modest home. Ivy explained that her husband, Ross Franklin, worked at the hospital down the street. Before their children arrived she had been a supervisor of cooks at the Malden Lunatic Asylum, she said, not far from their house in Amherstburg.

Noting Liz and Hack's surprised looks, Ivy grinned and said, "Most of the kitchen help there was inmates who wasn't paid for their work, but they hired a few supervisors, and I got the job because I had experience as a cook at the hospital where Ross works. Matter of fact, that's where we met."

In a few minutes they arrived at Ivy's house. Ross, a tall fit black man with a ready smile, met them at the door and Ivy introduced them. "I hear y'all had an unexpected reunion last night," he said. "Ivy couldn't stop talkin' about all the memories it brought to mind. I know you'll all enjoy reminiscing tonight and then I hope we can get together now and then, seein's how we're livin' in the same neighborhood."

Ivy poured her guests hot tea, then took them to the small front room. Ross said next time he'd want to share their company, but this evening he would stay out of the way and let the three of them catch up on each other's news. After bidding Liz and Hack good night he took a lamp and headed for the bedroom with the newspaper.

Liz spied a few toys scattered about the room. "How old are your children, Ivy?"

Ivy shook her head and replied with a loving smile. "Ross isn't as careful as me about picking up after them. We have two little boys, three and five. We give . . . gave them middle names after two men I used to know who made a big impression on me. We named 'em Ross Jacob Franklin and Ely Sylvester Franklin."

Liz gasped, "Oh, Ivy, that is such an honor. You'll have to tell me who Jacob is, but my goodness, Uncle Vess would be thrilled to know that."

In response to gentle questions from Liz and Hack, the main points of Ivy's story began to unfold. She did not dodge the issue of Tate's sexual abuse, but she spared them the graphic details. "I explained some of it to Sylvester," she said. "He was only about seventeen year old then, and I was nineteen or twenty. He told me his sister was abused by a man who made her pregnant."

Hack's eyes turned to Liz, as if she were about to interject that the woman Ivy had just mentioned was Liz's mother, and that she, Liz, was the product of that pregnancy. Liz felt her eyes fly wide open, but at the last instant she checked herself and decided to remain silent. There would be time later to tell Ivy the rest of that story. Right now Ivy needed to let her own feelings out. Liz sensed that Ivy had been holding it in for a long time. Now she needed to let some of it go.

Ivy went on to relate Bessie's intervention with the seeds, the mutual protection that developed between herself and Master Tate, and the eventual betrayal by Clay. She described her friendship with Jacob, the escape and his death on the steamboat on the Kentucky River. She told how Sylvester had guided her through the dangers from the riverbank at Hanover Landing to Lancaster, how he had listened to her anguished feelings and gave her good advice. Then she summarized for Liz and Hack the long journey with other fugitives and many different conductors, all the way from Lancaster to Detroit, followed by a dangerous river crossing to Amherstburg.

Ivy paused for a thoughtful moment. Then she said, "Yes, I'd like for you to share my story with Sylvester, Liz. Through all these years you two are the only people other than Ross who's heard the whole story. Now I'd like for Sylvester to know it, too.

And tell him, if you would, that his guiding me on that long tramp through the woods up to Lancaster and his advice not to go back to the plantation has made a powerful difference in my life."

"We'll let him know, Ivy," Liz said. "I promise."

"I have to tell you, Liz, that your uncle was exactly the man I needed to meet at that moment in my life. He kept talkin' to me, making me see even if I did go back I couldn't have changed things. Clay and Tate, even the slaves, he said, would have to work out their own problems, and I'd have to strike the blow for my own freedom."

Ivy blotted the tears that rolled down her face. "Oh, Ivy," Liz said, "I can't imagine the torment you've been through. It took a heroic effort to get yourself out of that situation, and on to Canada. And now you've made such a successful life here.

"You certainly don't sound like a slave when you talk. And you've evidently learned to read and write, being able to hold the job you mentioned."

Ivy smiled through her tears. "Yes, I've gained my literacy, but my speech slips back south now and then. I'm sure you noticed. I've had all kinds of help from some wonderful people, Liz, and a world of support from Ross."

Hack said, "I hope I can follow your good example, Ivy, and learn my readin' and writin'. I was just a little squirt when we met at Lancaster, but you was kind and took time to talk to me. It sure is good to see you doin' so good after all you been through."

Hack leaned forward. "Ivy, have you ever heard from any of them folks back on the plantation? Maybe Tate or some of the others? Any idea how things turned out back there?"

"Not a word, Hack. And I'm afraid to write to anyone back there. Nobody would give my letter to any slave on the plantation, and they couldn't read it, anyhow, or send me an answer. Tate or Clay might be dead, and even if they ain't . . . aren't they might send somebody after me if they knew where I was. I guess I'll never know. I'll have to live with it, but I try not to think about it."

A smile blossomed, then, on her tear-stained face. "Ross and the kids are wonderful to keep me too busy to think most of the time." Her two new friends chuckled and nodded at her words.

398

Suddenly Ivy sat up straight. "Oh, my goodness! "I've been so obsessed in telling my own story that I haven't even asked you how you two met and why on earth you've arrived here in Amherstburg together. Please forgive my rudeness. Last night I told Ross I was so excited to meet you, and I had so many questions to ask you, but you'd never know it from the way I've chattered on and on about myself. Let me get us more tea, and then you must tell me about yourselves."

Liz and Hack summarized their adventures for Ivy, helping the slave family and escaping the patrollers near Moorefield, except for the part about Sam's death. They described their narrow escapes from the law and slavecatchers in Ohio, their various modes of travel, and the help of dedicated conductors all the way to Amherstburg. It was past midnight when Hack said, "So Ivy, that's how come us to show up here in the Queen's dominion."

"What an adventure! I see we all been lucky to get here in one piece." Ivy said. But here she couldn't hide her quizzical smile, and she eyed them playfully. "But I'm guessin' there's more to it than that. Y'all must have had tender feelings for each other or you'd have split up way back when you started runnin'. I know everybody you met wondered what was up between you two. I mean it ain't . . . isn't every day you see a mixed race couple travelin' together, 'specially a white gal with a black man.

"So, you two had a thing goin', am I right? Come on, now, you can tell Ivy." Her smile turned into a gleeful laugh, as if she'd just struck the truth about her two guests. "This whole time we've been openin' our souls to each other so, come on, now." Her eyes sparkled as she leaned forward in her chair to hear the juicy details.

Liz and Hack regarded each other as if to ask permission, then they both laughed, blushed and cast bashful glances at their hostess. "You tell it, Liz," Hack said. "You women got the words and the understandin' for it. Ivy, I'll stop her when she starts makin' up fairy tales." They all giggled, and after another twenty minutes of questions, coy hesitations and grinning confessions, the details of Liz and Hack's romance had been revealed to the former slave girl.

# CHAPTER SEVENTY-SIX

*I*n their upstairs rooms the next morning Liz took the pen and paper Callie had given her and sat down to write to Sylvester.

*October, 1860, Amherstburg, Canada West*

*Dear Uncle Vess,*

*Forgive me, Dear Uncle, for it is long past time I took pen in hand to let you know that James Hackney and I are safe now. We have traveled through to Canada, as I shall try to explain briefly.*

*You must know by now that I went with Hack on Old Dan to Lamb on a Tuesday night last spring. The next night we conducted a family of runaway slaves, a man, wife and two small children to Moorefield. We were pursued by a gang of patrollers, and when they were nearly upon us we fired a shotgun blindly into the darkness behind us hoping to delay or stop them. The next day we learned that the shot killed my father. I shall live the rest of my life with the horror and guilt weighing on me from that event.*

*We were told the best course was to flee to Canada by way of the Underground Railroad, which we found a daunting thought. We know one of our conductors died and at least one more was severely injured. Hack was shot but has almost completely recovered. We met helpful and self-sacrificing people along our way. We traveled on foot, on horseback, in various horsedrawn vehicles, in the cars, and on boats across Lake Erie. We were given a letter of introduction to one Rev. Isaac Rice here in Amherstburg, and it is at his home where we are now living. He is a well-known missionary in these parts.*

*We have had the great good fortune to meet Ivy Mays, the fugitive slave girl you led from the river to Lancaster back in the spring of '45, she says. Hack recognized her at a meeting we attended. She and Hack met at Lancaster the morning you brought her there, before she was conducted to Vernon by his father. Ivy spoke glowingly of you, Uncle Vess, and asked us to send you her sincere gratitude and to let you know she credits you with helping her decide to continue her flight to Canada in spite of troubling circumstances.*

*Please give your precious Leanna and the children my love, and to other kinfolk, especially Grandma Fanny and Grandpa John Morrison. And give Hack's best to his family if opportunity presents. Our plans are uncertain as to employment and permanent residence, but we may be reached c/o Rev. Isaac Rice, Amherstburg Post Office, Canada West. We will be seeing Ivy, her husband and two small children again, so if you've a mind to write to her we will see she gets it. Please be careful with whom you share our location. You must understand we are now fugitives.*

*Hack and I will continue our lives together, and we hope to see a time when we may once more live as free citizens in our native country.*

*With love and gratitude,*
*Liz*

For months now, unbeknownst to Liz's kinfolk, the Sugar Branch postmaster was being paid to watch for any letter with a Morrison name on the address and a Canadian postmark.

When Liz and Hack passed the letter through the window to the clerk at the Amherstburg Post Office, they had no idea it would be intercepted and compromised at its destination. It would fall into the hands of an unauthorized person, be opened, read, resealed and placed in Sylvester's cubbyhole.

Suspecting foul play from the appearance of the seal on Liz's letter, Sylvester, in his future correspondence with her, would advise her to send any mail to family via his Pleasant Post Office address at the Old Dutch Settlement, Leanna's people's community. But the damage, of course, had been done.

The one whose eyes unlawfully perused Liz's letter swore a vile oath, then looked off into the distance, already formulating a vengeful plan.

# CHAPTER SEVENTY-SEVEN

On a Sunday in early November Amherstburg had its first significant snowfall of the winter. In the evening Hack and Liz strolled along the Detroit River with a group of friends, some of them recent arrivals from the South. Most of the group were unaware that Abraham Lincoln had just been elected the first Republican president of the land of their birth to the south. They could not have known that on December 20, 1860, South Carolina would initiate an ominous drumbeat when it became the first state to secede from the union. Six other states would follow by February 1, 1861, and the flame of secession would eventually spread to Virginia, Tennessee, North Carolina and Arkansas.

Oblivious to these impending developments in their homeland, Liz and Hack fell a few steps behind the others in their group. Liz held tightly to Hack's arm, then stopped and turned to face him. She kissed him and said, "Don't you think it's time we asked Reverend Rice to marry us?"

"What's the hurry, hon? We barely got ourselves landed up here, no place of our own yet. I'm thinkin' we might best wait a while, get our ducks in a row."

Liz laughed and beamed into Hack's face, her cheeks rosy from the cold. "It won't do to wait too long, because that first little duckling is already lined up . . . daddy."

Hack gave her a long, wide-eyed look, a huge grin spreading across his face, then he expelled a cloud of pent-up steam as the air rushed out of him. He whooped and lifted the grinning Liz off her feet. Their companions up ahead stopped, looked back at the happy embrace, then came running.

# THE END

# AUTHOR'S NOTE

There are many accounts of negroes enduring slavery in northern Kentucky and southern Indiana, and of fleeing that vile institution by way of the Underground Railroad. Some of their narratives were recorded long after the fact, but there can be no doubt that under the yoke of bondage and in their efforts to escape to freedom, negroes suffered horrible cruelty and hardships. This stands as one of the darkest chapters of American history.

There were individuals such as Levi Coffin and Reverend John Tibbets whose heroic efforts on behalf of the fugitives are substantiated by accounts from multiple sources. Likewise, certain communities such as Newport (Fountain City) and Lancaster in Indiana, Yellow Springs and Sandusky in Ohio and Pelee Island and Amherstburg in Canada benefit from ample evidence that they served as havens for fugitives escaping from slavery to the north in the nineteenth century. But there were untold numbers of heroic people, negroes and whites, men and women, whose stories have never seen the light of day. Many were slaves like Ivy Mays and Jacob Brown, others free men and women such as James Hackney and Elizabeth Cunningham. These individuals constantly faced capture, torture, rape, mutilation, death and being sold South as consequences of their actions.

Almost any settlement that existed in Border Country during the early-to-mid nineteenth century has its UGRR proponents. They are ready to lead the interested visitor to an old house, barn, remnant foundation, or to a natural feature such as a cave, ravine or overlook that they believe was central to UGRR activity in their area. I have visited places where *The Dark Line* scenes occur, such as the Border Country of northern Kentucky/southern Indiana, southern Illinois, western Ohio, and Ontario, Canada.

Some writers believe the flow of fugitive slaves from south to north slowed at the approach of the Civil War, while others claim more refugees came north then than at any other time. I found this to vary widely from one escape route to another. Authors are divided on whether the majority of UGRR conductors were black or white. My reading indicated the percentages seemed to favor black conductors in the South, whites in the North. The UGRR was secretly organized, and messages between activists seldom documented. One exception is the handwritten and signed pledge that Levi Coffin shows to Liz and Hack.

It became evident in my study of sexual abuse of female slaves by their white owners that sometimes the victim of the abuse grew to empathize with, even to feel a kind of affection for, her abuser. The Stockholm Syndrome was invented by human nature long before it was given a name.

This story is fiction, but real characters and situations were used where they were known. The Morrisons were real people, as were the Cunninghams and the Hackneys, though I found no evidence that the two James Hackneys were related.

As for the younger James Hackney, the Census record of 1860 shows four people residing in the John W. Morrison household at Sugar Branch, Indiana. In addition to John, Fanny and their granddaughter Elizabeth, there was a James Hackney. A single word in parentheses after Hackney's name on the original record, (black), is the genesis of this book.

Further research uncovered a listing called "The 1853 Registry of Indiana Negroes." Free negroes already living in Indiana found they had to leave the state, hide out or submit to being listed on the Negro Register. This listing was not uniformly enforced, and the lists for many Indiana counties were either never compiled or have disappeared, but the 1853 Negro Registers for Switzerland and Jefferson counties along the Ohio River have survived. The younger James's name was entered on the Switzerland County list, along with the names of sixteen other black people in family units with the names Andrews, Blanton and Nivey. The elder James Hackney's name does not appear on the Jefferson County listing, though he is known to have been a negro and to have lived in Jefferson County at Hanover for many years during this time.

The Register included a physical description of James Hackney the younger, probably to aid in identification in the event he was ever suspected of a crime and/or became a fugitive. In 1853 James was described in the Register of Negroes in Switzerland County as: "5'8" high, 165pounds, jet black, two scars on left hand, one across thumb & another across forefinger."

Young James Hackney had lived with at least one other white family after arriving in Switzerland County sometime before the summer of 1850.

Official Listings for James Hackney

| Year | Head of Hsehld, (Race) | Hackney's Age & Race | |
|------|------------------------|------|------|
| 1850 | Isaac Danner (W) U.S. Census | 21 | Black |
| 1853 | (Negro Register, Switzerland Co., IN) | 24 | Black |
| **1860** | **John Morrison (W) U.S.Census** | **28** | **Black** |

Hackney's listed ages on various documents, including those above, show that he probably did not know his true birth date. Communication may not have flowed easily between the black youth and the white authority figure recording his information. Thus, discrepancies in the records are not surprising. These and other records show that James the younger had not married before reaching Sugar Branch, and that he was illiterate.

Rachel's grave may be found close to the road (Hwy 250) in the Melville (Cunningham) Cemetery at Fairview (Sugar Branch). Her sister, Mariah, is buried nearby. They died the same year, 1853, at ages thirty and thirty-two. John Wesley and Fannie, as well as several other Morrisons, are buried in the Lee Cemetery, off Fairview road south of the village of Fairview. Though Elizabeth Cunningham and the younger James Hackney both lived for a short time in 1860 in the John Wesley Morrison household at Sugar Branch, any working or romantic relationship between Elizabeth and James is fictional, as is their flight to Canada.

The original antique map, "Die Staaten von Missouri, Illinois, Indiana, Ohio, Kentucky & Tennessee 1850," which is reproduced on the front cover and again inside the book, is from *Meijers Zeitungs Atlas* published by the Bibliographischen Institute in Hildburghausen, Germany. The map is distinguished by its age and fine degree of detail. It is almost as if the map were engraved with the point of a pin, packing a staggering amount of information into a small area. The original 7.9 x 10.6 inch map is in the author's private collection.

The image "The Runaway," which is superimposed on the map on the cover, has been used many times on southern slaveowners' handbills and in various publications over the years. One of the first recorded uses was in *The Anti-Slavery Record*, published by the American Anti-Slavery Society in July, 1837. The image was collected by Ohio State University Professor Wilbur H. Siebert, and was used on the cover of the Dover edition of his book, *The Underground Railroad From Slavery to Freedom: A Comprehensive History*, published in 2006. This book by Siebert was originally published in 1898.

Many sources were consulted in writing *The Dark Line*, a few of which are listed at the back. Liberties were taken with certain dates, ages and landforms to fit the story line. Any crimes committed by characters in this story are fictional.

*Maryville, Tennessee, March 2014*

# ABOUT THE AUTHOR

Don Morrison is a retired teacher and corporate instructor. He has taught in Indiana schools and in American schools in Korea and Germany. Since retiring he has volunteered locally for the Switzerland County, Indiana, Historical Society, and internationally at Dharmsala, India, and Moshi, Tanzania.

Morrison has written memoir books, short stories, historical articles, and three novels. The inspiration for the historical novels *Sugar Branch* and *The Dark Line* arose from his family's history. He was born and raised near the places where his ancestors lived in antebellum Border Country. Don now lives near Knoxville, Tennessee, with his wife, Suzanne.

For questions or comments about the novels *Sugar Branch* or *The Dark Line,* readers may communicate with the author at:

donmopub38@gmail.com

# SELECTED SOURCES

## BOOKS

Baker, Ronald L., editor. *Homeless, Friendless and Penniless: The WPA Interviews with Former Slaves Living in Indiana,* 2000

Bibb, Henry. *Narrative of the Life and Adventures of Henry Bibb, an American Slave, Written by Himself,* 1849

Buchanan, Thomas. *Black Life on the Mississippi,* 2004

Craft, William & Ellen. *Running a Thousand Miles for Freedom, or: The Escape of William and Ellen Craft from Slavery,* 1860

Cummings, Samuel. *The Ohio River Collection: The Western Pilot 1847,* 1847

Deagan, Virginia. *Descendants of John Morrison* ~ 2000

Dohan, Mary Helen. *Mr. Roosevelt's Steamboat: The First Steamboat to Travel the Mississippi,* 1981

Erbsen, Wayne. *Log Cabin Pioneers: Stories, Songs & Sayings,* 2001

Grayson, Frank. *Thrills of the Historic Ohio River,* 1929

Grose, Francis. *1811 Dictionary of the Vulgar Tongue,* 1811

Henson, Josiah. *The Life of Josiah Henson,* (Edited autobiography) 1849

Horigan, Michael. *Elmira: Death Camp of the North,* 2002

Hudson, J. Blaine. *Fugitive Slaves and the Underground Railroad in the Kentucky Borderland,* 2002

Hurmance, Belinda, editor. *My Folks Don't Want Me To Talk About Slavery,* 1984

Hurmance, Belinda, editor. *We Lived in a Little Cabin in the Yard,* 1994

Jacobs, Harriet. *Incidents in the Life of a Slave Girl (Autobiography),* 1861

Laskas, Gretchen Moran. *The Midwife's Tale,* 2003

Luhan, Mabel Dodge. *Edge of Taos Desert*, 1993

Northup, Solomon. *Twelve Years a Slave,* 1853

Palmer, Gail. DVD: *When Mama Was the Doctor,* (Midwifery) ~2012

Parks, Helen, Kappes, Judy, et al. *The Bicentennial Edition of Cotton Twp. History,* 1976

Prince, Bryan. *I Came as a Stranger,* 2004; *A Shadow on the Household,* 2009; *One More River to Cross,* 2012

Richmond, Ben, editor. *Reminiscences of Levi Coffin,* 1991

Siebert, William H. *The Underground Railroad: From Slavery to Freedom: A Comprehensive History,* 1898 (Map, P 112–113 & footnote #3, P 148)

Snively, W. D., Jr. and Furbee, Louanna. *Satan's Ferryman,* 1968

Staff, Natchez National Historical Park, editors. *Between Two Worlds: The Life of Free Black Diarist William T. Johnson,* 2007

Still, William. *The Underground Railroad: Authentic Narratives and First-Hand Accounts,* 2007

Urdang, Laurence, editor. *The Timetables of American History,* 1981

Walls, Bryan E. *The Road that Led to Somewhere,* 1980

Yanessa, Mary Ann. *Levi Coffin, Quaker: Breaking the Bonds of Slavery in Ohio and Indiana,* 2001

Yetman, Norman R., editor. *When I Was A Slave: Memoirs from the Slave Narrative Collection,* 2002


## ARTICLES

Marsh Collection, 235 A Dalhousie, Amherstburg, Ont. N9V 1W4, (Articles on Rev. Isaac Rice)

Brown, Maxine F. "The Role of Free Blacks in Indiana's UGRR," 2001 (Switzerland County Public Library)

Historic Eleutherian College. "History of Eleutherian College, Lancaster, Indiana," (Originally published in *Indiana Magazine of History,* Vol. XIX, June, 1923, No. 2, Reprinted 2001 by Historic Eleutherian College, Inc.


## WEBSITES AND EMAIL

http://archiver.rootsweb.ancestry.com/th/read/REA/2000/02 /0950229266 (Wright Rea, slavecatching sheriff of Jefferson County, Indiana)

www.encyclopedia.com/doc/1G2-3449600011.html (Bibb, Mary and Henry) www.HeritageBooks.com, xvi. Robbins, Coy D., Bloomington, IN, Compiler, *Indiana Negro Registers, 1852–1865,* from the CD, *Indiana African Heritage,* Copyright 2003 by Heritage Books, Inc.

www.livestrong.com/herbs-for-natural-birth control (Queen Anne's lace seeds)

www.lkwdpl.org/wihohio/cary-mar.htm (Mary Ann Shadd Cary)

www.mental-health-matters.com/...&view=article&id=167 (Article by Carver, Joseph M., PhD.) "Love and Stockholm Syndrome: The Mystery of Loving an Abuser," 2011

www.ohiohistorycentral.org (image "The Fugitive")

Powers, Kevin and Dan, et al. Information by email on their ancestor, Ulysses Meacham of Put-In-Bay, Ohio, abolitionist and captain of the *Harlequin,* an "abolition boat" used to transport fugitive slaves to Canada.

37286872R00255

Made in the USA
Charleston, SC
03 January 2015